International p...

Puntí is a sprightly writer, delighting in taking us down byways and through backwaters as the novel circles Gabriel's disappearance. But the big, bold self-consciously picaresque storytelling never completely loses sight of the book's central theme, the ways in which family, and its lack, can shape a life."

—*Financial Times*

"This is a remarkable work, full of invention and consistently gripping."

—*Times Literary Supplement*

"A book as extraordinary as it is memorable. Jordi Puntí already belongs to the noble tradition of the great storytellers."

—*Rock de Lux*

"A conjuring trick. Incomparable literature."

—*El País*

"*Lost Luggage* is an astonishing literary artefact. Marvellous."

—*El Mundo*

"The best contemporary prose available."

—*El Periódico*

"Pure life, intense and passionate. A thorough and precise creation, very near perfection . . . one can only surrender to the utter force of the story."

—*Qué Leer*

# LOST LUGGAGE

## A NOVEL

## Jordi Puntí

English translation by Julie Wark

MARBLE ARCH
PRESS

Marble Arch Press
1230 Avenue of the Americas
New York, NY 10020

First Marble Arch Press trade paperback edition October 2013

Marble Arch Press is a publishing collaboration between Short Books, UK,
and Atria Books, US.

Marble Arch Press and colophon are trademarks of Short Books.

For information about special discounts for bulk purchases,
please contact Simon & Schuster Special Sales at 1-866-506-1949
or business@simonandschuster.com.

Designed by Dana Sloan

Manufactured in the United States of America

10  9  8  7  6  5  4  3  2  1

Library of Congress Cataloging-in-Publication Data has been applied for.

ISBN 978-1-4767-3031-8
ISBN 978-1-4767-3032-5 (ebook)

*For Steffi*

# Contents

*Part I*
DEPARTURES

1. Photographs                                          3
2. These Things Happen                                15
3. Imperfect Orphans                                  26
4. Age Without a Name                                 52
5. A Home on the Ronda de Sant Antoni                65
6. Women and Petroli                                  80
7. Carolina, or Muriel                               96
8. The Fifth Brother                                119
9. An Adventure on the Channel, or Toxicosmos       137
10. The World's Badly Divided Up                     173
11. The Last Move                                    200

*Part II*
ARRIVALS

1. At the Airport                                    239
2. In the Cage                                       268
3. Mysteries and Swoonings                           298
4. Reclusion                                         327
5. Waverings                                         353
6. The Fifth Mother                                  380
7. We Have the Same Memory                           416

*Acknowledgments*                                    439

*Part I*

# DEPARTURES

# 1

## Photographs

We have the same memory.

It's very early. The sun has just come up. The three of us—father, mother, and son—are yawning sleepily. Mom's made some tea or coffee, and we duly drink it. We're in the living room, or the kitchen, as still and quiet as statues. Our eyes keep closing. Soon we hear a truck pull up outside the house and then the deep blast of the horn. Although we've been expecting it, we're startled by the din and suddenly wide awake. The windows rattle. The racket must have woken up the neighbors. We go out to the street to see our father off. He climbs into the truck, sticks his arm out of the window, and attempts a smile as he waves good-bye. It's clear he feels bad about leaving. Or not. He's only been with us a couple of days, three at the most. His two friends call out to us from the cab and wave good-bye too. Time passes in slow motion. The Pegaso sets off, lumbering into the distance as if it doesn't want to leave either. Mom's in her dressing gown, and a tear rolls down her cheek, or maybe not. We, the sons, are in pajamas and slippers. Our feet are freezing. We go inside and get into our beds, which are still slightly warm, but we can't go back to sleep because of all the thoughts buzzing around in our heads. We're three, four, five, and seven years old and we've been through the same scene several times before. We don't know it then, but we've just seen our father for the last time.

We have the same memory.

~

The scene we've just described took place about thirty years ago, and the story could begin at three different points on the map. No, four. The moving truck might have been disappearing into the morning mist that enveloped the Quai de la Marne in the north of Paris, leaving behind a row of houses on Rue de Crimée across from a canal that, in the dawn light, seemed to have been lifted from the pages of a Simenon novel. Or perhaps the truck's engine shattered the clammy silence of Martello Street, next to London Fields in the East End, as it headed under the railway bridge to find a main road leading out of the metropolis to the motorway, where driving on the left doesn't present the same headache for a continental trucker. Or maybe it was Frankfurt, the eastern part, at one of those blocks of apartments they put up in Jacobystrasse after the war. Here, the Pegaso lurched toward the motorway, faltering at times as if dreading having to cross a landscape of factories and woods and join the convoy of trucks that were likewise plowing through the arteries of Germany.

Paris, London, Frankfurt. Three distant places linked by our father driving a truck that moved furniture from one side of Europe to the other. There was one more city, the fourth, which was Barcelona. Point of departure and arrival. In this case, the scene takes place without the truck and without the other two truckers. One of us—Cristòfol—with his father and mother. Three people in the poorly lit kitchen of an apartment on Carrer del Tigre. But here, too, the farewell takes place with the same calm he has counted on—to the point that it almost seems rehearsed—with the same vague concern that has always worked for him before, in other houses and with other families. That expression on his face, striving for composure but brimming over with sadness that seeped into all of us. Hours later, the next day, or the next week, we'd look in the mirror while brushing our teeth, and see it in our own eyes. A wistfulness we all recognized. That's why we now have the feeling that our emotions were scattered far and wide and why, now, all these years later, our childhood sense of betrayal is multiplied by four. We also like to think of our mothers, the four mothers, as if they were one. Pain not shared but multiplied. Nobody was spared. Certainly not we four sons.

What? You don't get it? It's too complicated?

Well, this is going to take some explaining. We are four brothers—or, more accurately, half-brothers—sons of one father and four very different mothers. Until about a year ago we didn't know each other. We didn't even know the others existed, scattered around God's dominions. Our father wanted us to be called Christof, Christophe, Christopher, and Cristòfol (who was known by the Spanish version of Cristóbal until the dictator Franco died). If you say them out loud, one after another, the four names sound like an irregular Latin declension. Christof, German nominative, was born in October 1965, the impossible heir of a European lineage. Christopher, Saxon genitive, came almost two years later, his birth suddenly enlarging and adding color to the definition of a Londoner's life. The accusative, Christophe, took a little less time—nineteen months—and, in February 1969, became the direct object of a French single mother. Cristòfol was the last to appear. a case of circumstance, completely defined by place, space and time, an ablative in a language that doesn't decline.

Why did our father give us the same name? Why was he so single-minded about calling us that, so obstinate that in the end he managed to persuade our mothers to go along with it? Was it, perhaps, that he didn't want to feel we were one-offs? After all, none of us has brothers or sisters. Once we talked about it with Petroli, who, like Bundó, was a fellow trucker, friend, and confidant, and he said, no, when he talked about us he never got us mixed up and knew perfectly well who was who. We tell ourselves it might be some sort of superstition: Saint Christopher is the patron saint of drivers, and we four sons were like small offerings he left behind in each country, candles lit to protect him as he traveled around in his truck. Petroli, who knew him very well, disagrees, saying he didn't believe in any hereafter and suggesting a more fantastic but equally credible possibility: Maybe he just wanted four of a kind, a winning poker hand in sons. "Four aces," he says, "one for each suit." "And what about Dad?" we ask. He was the wild card, the joker needed to make five of a kind.

"Life is very short, and there's no time..." Christopher sud-

denly starts singing. We let him go on because the words are relevant and it's a Beatles song. All four of us are fans but, right now,
we're not going to play at deciding who's going to be George, or
Paul, or Ringo, or John. We'll keep this kind of exercise to ourselves and, as for this business of interrupting a conversation by
breaking into song, this is the first and last time we're going to
let anyone chime in—do a solo—without the prior consent of the
other three. We're not in a karaoke bar and we need a few rules if
we're going to get along. If all four brothers talk at once it will be
pandemonium. Then again, Chris is right: Life is very short, and
there's no time.

What else? Until recently, we'd been getting along with our
lives, without knowing that the other three brothers existed, but
is it true that our father—or rather his absence—has shaped our
lives in the same way? No, of course not, though we're sorely
tempted to make up stories about his underlying influence. Take
our professions, for example. Christof's in show business, and the
actor's craft, to be or not to be, reminds us of our father's faking
skills. Christophe's a lecturer in quantum physics at the University
of Paris, where he observes the world, questions reality, and studies parallel universes (in which our father would never abandon
us). Christopher has a stall in Camden Town and earns his living
buying and selling second-hand records: His acquisition of collectors' gems and other relics, often by not strictly legal means,
is the legacy of our father's picaresque lifestyle (read on, please).
Cristòfol's a translator, novels mainly, from French, so when he
renders them from one language into another it's like a tribute to
our father's linguistic efforts.

What else, what else? Are we four brothers physically alike?
Yes, we do look alike. We might say that the four of us are from the
same genetic map and that our mothers—Sigrun, Mireille, Sarah,
Rita—are the evolutionary elements that make us different, the
barbarian grammar that has removed us from the Latin. In some
part of Central Europe, at a crossroads where their destinies come
together—or right in the middle of a roundabout, if we're going to
be irritatingly symbolic—we'll have to put up a monument to them

because of what they had to bear. They haven't met yet. It's only a few weeks since they found out that the others exist, that we have half-brothers and that they, therefore, have stepsons. The boundaries, however, stay where they've always been. With a touch of irony, shared by the other three, Sarah says that we sons are like ambassadors meeting up to negotiate an armistice. Later on, we might decide to get them together for a weekend in some hotel on neutral ground. In Andorra, for example, or Switzerland. But that will have to come later.

What else, what else, what else? Are our mothers physically alike? I don't think so. *Diria que no. Je crois pas. Ich glaube nicht.* Do they all fit together to make up some pattern of shared beauty or are they, rather, pieces of some perfection-seeking jigsaw created by a twisted mind, our father's mind? Neither. In any case, it has to be said that when we tell them about our plan for getting them together in the future, all four mothers show the same lack of enthusiasm. Mireille pulls a face, saying it would be like a meeting of Abandoned Anonymous. Sigrun wants European Union funding for the summit. Rita compares it to a club of aging groupies— "Elvis lives, Elvis lives!" Sarah has a suggestion: "If we must meet, why don't we do a production of *The Six Wives of Henry VIII?* There are only four of us? No problem, if we keep looking we're bound to find a couple more!"

This caustic response from the four potential widows must be some kind of defense mechanism. Many years have gone by, but their amorous experiences are too similar, and they don't want to start talking about them now. From the outside, it's tempting to imagine four women getting together to reminisce about a man who left them in the lurch one fine day, without any warning and each with a kid to raise. They drink and talk. Little by little, they start sharing a list of grievances. Their memories bring them together. The distress has been left so far behind that time's removed the poisonous fangs, and it's now as harmless as a stuffed animal. The gathering becomes more of an exorcism than therapy. They drink and laugh. Yet each of them starts thinking privately that the others didn't really understand him, and, calling on their memories, they all start polishing up their love. Mine was the real love, the true love. A slip of the tongue, a joke that suddenly isn't funny, and the alliance of suffering collapses. Any minute now they'll start pulling each other's hair out.

The thing is, there's one detail that complicates everything. Right now, we can't claim that our father's dead. Only that he disappeared, more than a year ago.

In fact, "disappeared" isn't the correct verb, and if we've decided to find him, it's to make sense of the word. Give it a body. Only somebody who's previously appeared can disappear, and that's not the case with our father. We haven't seen him for more than thirty years, and the sum of our memories presents us with only a blurry image of him. It's not as if he was a timid man, or naturally reserved, but he always seemed to have an escape route. He wasn't edgy, anxious, or mistrustful either. Sigrun says she fell in love with both his presence and his absence. Mireille recalls that as soon as he arrived it was as if he was leaving again. The brevity of his visits helped, of course. This provisional air became increasingly evident and we're inclined to believe that, rather than vanishing from one day to the next—Abracadabra!—like a magic trick or some extraterrestrial abduction, our father gradually dissolved. That even now, right now, when all four of us are thinking about him for the first time, he's still slowly dissolving.

This vanishing act can even be seen in the letters he used to send us. He wrote them from all over Europe, wherever he was moving furniture, telling us stories about the trip. Sometimes they were postcards, scribbled by the roadside. In the foreground were equestrian statues, castles, gardens, churches—horrible provincial monuments that all four of us recall with depressing clarity. These postcards were written and dated somewhere in France or Germany, yet they bore a stamp with Franco's marmoreal face because they must have languished for days in the truck's glove compartment, and he only remembered to mail them when he was back in Barcelona. In the letters he wrote us he sometimes enclosed photos of himself, alone or posing with his trucker friends. The words accompanying these images revealed real tenderness and longing, which made our mothers cry if they were feeling fragile, but they never went beyond the two sides of a single sheet of paper. Just when it seemed he was getting into his stride, the writing would abruptly end. See you soon, kisses, and so on and so forth, his name, and that was that. As if he was afraid to give all of himself.

"The only thing he didn't do was write them with that funny ink that makes the words disappear a few days after you read them," Christof remarked.

What else needs telling? Ah yes, how the four of us make ourselves understood. English has been our lingua franca ever since the day we first met, after Cristòfol decided to go looking for the other brothers. We use English because it's the language in which we best understand each other, because we need some kind of standard, but, in the end, our conversations produce a more complex language, a sort of familial Esperanto. Christof has no problems with this because English is a first cousin of German and he studied it from a tender age. Christophe speaks it with that slightly smug accent typical of the French, plus a technical vocabulary he picks up from the conferences and lectures in quantum physics he often goes to. Cristòfol learned it when he was older, taking private classes, because he studied French at school and university. Sometimes when he can't get the words out in English he turns to his second language, which is comforting for Christophe. You can see it in his face. Then Chris and Christof start laughing at their Latin origins, mocking them in their own patter, full of guttural sounds, fragments of the "La Marseillaise," and names of French soccer players.

Chris, however, speaks a bit of Spanish thanks to being pushed by his mother, Sarah. In the mid-seventies, when it seemed clear that Gabriel wouldn't be visiting them any more, she enrolled her son in a summer course to learn the language. Dammit, Chris might never see his father again but at least he'd have the legacy of speaking Spanish. His teacher was a university student called Rosi. She'd gone to London to get experience, and her first discovery was that teaching wasn't her thing. Her method consisted of making them listen to a cassette of songs that were all the rage that summer. That's why Chris sounds like a native speaker when he says things like *"Es una lata el trabajar," "No me gusta que a los toros te pongas la minifalda,"* or *"Achilipú, apú, apú,"* although he hasn't got a clue that they mean "having to work's a pain," "I don't like you wearing your miniskirt to the bullfight," and something sounding like "chili-poo" in a red-hot rumba.

We've discovered that songs in Catalan are another childhood experience we share. At our first meeting in Barcelona we had lunch in a restaurant and tried to pool all the information we had about our father. All at once, some children playing and singing at a nearby table had us reliving the songs he taught us when we were small. Songs like "En Joan Petit quan Balla" and "El Gegant del Pi," in which little Johnny danced and a giant strode around carrying a pine tree.

"I remember a bedtime story Dad used to tell me," Christof said. "The kid was called Pàtiufet or something like that, and he ended up in the belly of a bull, where it never snows or rains, *und scheint keine Sonne hinein.* I'd be shitting myself with fright. Sometimes I tell it to my friends' kids in German, mostly because I like the idea of Pàtiufet competing with the Brothers Grimm."

"Well, I was obsessed with 'Plou i Fa Sol,' that song about rain and sun . . . and witches combing their hair," Chris recalled, singing his own weird Catalan version. "In London that happens a lot, I mean rain and sun at the same time. Almost every day when I went to school or to play with my friends in the park across the road, I used to look anxiously up at the sky and there would always be a ray of sunshine in that constant drizzle. 'Here we go again,' I'd think. 'In some old mansion, here in this city, right now, the witches are combing their hair again, getting ready to go out.' When I told my friends about it, convinced I was revealing a secret, they started teasing me and then I'd sing them the song to make them shut up. But it didn't help."

This linguistic synergy that the four of us are fast perfecting brings us even closer to our father. It's an inheritance of sorts since it seems that he spoke all our languages yet none of them. Over the years, according to our mothers, the words he learned across Europe started overlapping, setting up shortcuts and false friends, simplified verb conjugations and etymologies that only superficially made sense. He took the view that you can't have long silences in the middle of a conversation, so he slipped from one language to another in his head, and then uttered the first thing that occurred to him.

"My brain's like a storeroom packed to the ceiling," they reported him as saying. "Luckily, when I need something, I always end up finding it."

Even if it was only his conviction, his resources worked and the result was a very practical idiolect. Sigrun complains that a conversation with him always turned comic even when it was meant to be serious. Rita remembers, for example, that his Catalan *vi negre* had gone linguistically from black to red with *vi vermell* because that was the color that ruled in France (*vin rouge*), Germany (*Rotwein*), and Great Britain. And, yet Mireille assures us that once, in a brasserie on Avenue Jean Jaurès, he ordered black wine or, as he put it, "*vin noir*" and even "*vin tinté de la maison*," with the inky-black Spanish red, *tinto*, in mind.

Although the reason is an absent father, when the four of us start pooling our memories, the experience never ceases to amaze us. At our first meeting we made the commitment to meet up one weekend in five, more or less. With each new get-together we fill in some gap or untangle one or other of our father's many deceits. Our mothers are helping us to reclaim those years, and, though the details aren't always pleasant, we're often struck by how rewarding it feels. It's as if we can rewrite our lonely upbringings, as if those childhoods without brothers or sisters, which sometimes weighed heavily on us in a strange adult way—making us feel so helpless—can be partially rectified because now we know some of our father's secrets. No one can rid us of the uncertainty of those days, that's for sure, but we want to believe that the four of us unknowingly kept each other company, and that our father's life did have meaning because, if he shrouded himself in secrecy, we were the very essence of that.

Since this solitary fraternity might seem too abstract, we'll give a practical example to make things clearer. When we four Christophers decided to meet up for the first time, communicating with each other in a cold, distant way that was so ridiculous it makes us laugh now, we agreed that we'd bring along the photos we have of our father. The idea was that we'd choose one, a clear image, one that was not too old, and then place an ad seeking information in our national newspapers. We'd publish his picture across half the continent, asking anyone who might have seen him, or who had any idea of where he might be hiding, to get in touch. In the end, however, after a lot of discussion, we gave up on the idea because it seemed futile. If, as we agree, his disappearance was gradual and voluntary with nothing sudden about it, then nobody would recognize him. Nobody would have seen him yesterday, or the day before yesterday, or last week. His absence would appear perfectly normal to everyone.

Although we decided we wouldn't take any steps in that direction, we kept poring over the photos we'd brought, just for fun. We were in Barcelona and we spread out all the photos on a table. Then we stared at them as if they were a graphic novel of an unfinished life. They were images from the sixties and seventies, in black and white, or the kind of colors that, faded by time, lent the scene a heightened air of unreality. There were some he had sent with his letters and others taken during one of his visits. When they were placed side by side, we could see that his pose was always the same, that way he had of smiling at the camera—*Lluiiiiís, cheeeese, hatschiiiii . . .* —as if he was making a big effort, or the recurring gesture of caressing our hair when we appeared in the picture, or embracing whichever mother it happened to be, with his hand placed on exactly the same part of her waist . . .

This sensation of seeing the four of us being reproduced according to a formula, standing equally still before the camera, as if there were no substantial differences between us, was uncomfortable and disturbing. The backgrounds changed slightly and we did too, of course, but sometimes Dad was wearing the same denim jacket and the same shoes in all the photos from any one season. As we were discussing these coincidences we became aware of a detail that infuriated us at first but which was consoling once we'd digested it. Often the photos we received in a letter, pictures of him alone, had been taken during a visit to one of our homes. Dad would say something about the image but was careful not to write anything that might make our mothers suspicious. At most, he'd situate it on the map of his travels in the truck. "The photo I'm sending you was taken by Bundó last September when we stopped for lunch in some tucked-away corner of France," he wrote in a letter to Christopher and Sarah at the end of 1970, and the "tucked-away corner" you can make out in the background was actually the white façade of the house where Christophe and Mireille lived in Quai de la Marne. "A stop for gasoline in Germany, just outside Munich," he wrote on another photo sent to Christophe and Mireille, but Christof spotted in the background, just behind the image of our father, his neighborhood gas station in Frankfurt. Moreover, the photo was from 1968, two years earlier, because we all had some from the same roll of film (and now this coexistence inside the camera also comforts and amuses us).

Given all this evidence, the easiest thing would be to recognize that Dad was a compulsive liar, and we certainly wouldn't be wrong about that, but that explanation seems too simple. For the moment, we're not interested in condemning him but just finding out where he is. Who he is. If we succeed some day, then we'll ask for explanations. At present, we prefer to venture free of prejudice into the shadows of his life because, after all, if the four of us have met it's thanks to him—and his absence. It may not be easy to understand, but we prefer our totally subjective or, if you like, deluded enthusiasm to indignation. The same photos that perpetuated his deceit now serve to bring us together as brothers. We prize them as a sign that, all those years ago, our father foresaw our meeting up as brothers. Yet another dream for us to cling to. Sure, our method of deduction isn't very scientific, but at least it allows us to breathe a little life into these photos.

We must confess: Starting from a certainty helped us forge a bond. The first day we got together in Barcelona and laid out the photos of our father, in order on the table, in our attempt to construct a plausible story, we understood that he'd never revealed anything about himself to us. Not a glimmer. Hardly a hint of emotion. Suddenly, those photos all lined up, mute and faded, reminded us of a series of images from a film, like those stills they used to hang in the entrances of cinemas to show what was coming next. You could study them for ages, staring at the motionless actors and actresses, imagining the scenes in which they'd been shot, and, if you didn't know anything about the story beforehand, it was impossible to work out whether it was a comedy, a drama, or a mystery. Whether they were about to burst out laughing or crying.

That's pretty much how it is. Gabriel, our father, is an actor in a photo, and the more you look at him the more you fall under his spell.

## 2

# These Things Happen

Our father's name is—or was—Gabriel Delacruz Expósito. We'll start there.

It's anybody's guess whether the mother who bore him gave him the name in memory of the man who got her pregnant, or in the belief that if she made this offering to the archangel her child would be looked after for the rest of his days, or simply because somebody in the street that night rained curses on some good-for-nothing named Gabriel, and she was inspired by that. Such suppositions can never be confirmed. Whatever happened, the woman must have had her own good reasons if she went to the trouble of giving her kid a name.

A married couple with a salt cod stall next to the El Born market found the child at six in the morning. They were the first to arrive that day. They noticed a bundle of rags next to the main entrance in Carrer Comerç but, in the dim early morning light, they took it for a rotten cauliflower overlooked by the garbage collectors (who, sometimes, when they were having a midnight break in the vicinity of the market, would get one that was still fairly intact and play a bit of soccer). All of a sudden, the cauliflower started to squall in broken wails that echoed under the market roof. The nightwatchman who was chatting with the couple went over and shone his lantern on the bundle. The cod seller's wife picked it up cautiously and discovered inside it a naked, still-bloody baby boy with bluish skin, moving his hands and lips desperately trying to find a nipple. He was so defenseless, so needy that the woman

15

lost no time in unbuttoning her smock and pulling up her woollen pullover. Right then and there, in front of her husband, the nightwatchman, and several onlookers who'd by now turned up at the market, she released a breast the size of a pumpkin, her left one, which she guided to the baby's mouth. The group watched in silence, captivated by the spectacle of the proud and abundant mamma. The nightwatchman was trying to look dignified, as required by his public office. The baby stretched out his neck as if drawn by a magnet and sucked at the nipple for quite a long time. Miraculously, some tiny bubbles of milk dribbled from the corners of his mouth. When he calmed down, the woman, in some pain but satisfied, disengaged him from her breast—it had been a while since she'd been called on as a wet nurse—and handed him over to the figure of authority. The nightwatchman took the bundle in his arms, his heart melting at the warmth of the tiny thing. He'd take the baby straight to the hospital, and, if he survived, he'd be sent to some charitable institution. Then, as they contemplated the child, they noticed, stuck to his stomach with dry blood and covering the stump of the umbilical cord, a scrap of white paper, not unlike a factory label. It said "Gabriel."

The whole thing—the birth, abandonment, and first suckling of Gabriel—took place early one morning in October 1941. Our father was convinced that he developed a sybarite's passion for salt cod because of that first taste of milk that nourished him. He ate it whenever he could, however it came: baked in white wine with paprika (*a la llauna*), in an olive oil emulsion (*al pil-pil*), shredded (*esqueixat*), in batter (*arrebossat*), or cooked in the oven with potatoes. Oddly enough, he found cow's milk too salty and could only drink it sweetened with three good-sized spoons of sugar.

Our mothers say that he embellished the story of his first hours in the world, as if to somehow gloss over his lack of a mother and all the hardships he had to endure in the orphanage in the following years. In addition, as if needing to provide proof of the legend, he always carried a newspaper cutting in his wallet so he could show it to people. The news item appeared in *La Vanguardia Española*. Unsurprisingly, the author of the piece reveled in the more sensational details, while also highlighting the efficiency of the forces of law and order and the decisive intervention of the stall holder's wife.

In any case, Gabriel didn't know about all this until years later—seventeen to be precise—and thanks to the most extraordinary fluke. These things happen. Not long before, he'd started shifting furniture for a moving company. One day, they had to go to the Sant Gervasi neighborhood and empty an apartment for a family that was moving. His job was to dismantle a solid oak wardrobe that was too large and heavy to be moved by one person. First, he took off the doors and then decided to remove the drawers so the wardrobe would weigh a bit less. He opened the first drawer, pulling it off the runners with a crunch of woodworm-riddled timber. Then he took out the second one and, once he was holding it in his hands, he noticed the sheet of newspaper with which the owners had lined it. It was a folded, yellowing page from *La Vanguardia*. Gabriel removed it with great care and opened it. The corners crumbled between his fingers. He found an article about breaking the Stalin Line, signed by the news agency EFE from "the Führer's headquarters." He understood it was talking about the Second World War and immediately took note of the date on the newspaper. Wednesday, October 22, 1941. He was born the day before, on October 21, the same year! As he was taking this in, he turned the page over to look at the news on the other side. His eye was caught by a Gasogen ad with a prophetic drawing of a truck. Then he noticed the piece above it. It was headed BARCELONA LIFE and, in no time at all, he discovered the news of his abandonment. These things happen.

The piece was titled NEWBORN BABY FOUND AT BORN MARKET ENTRANCE and went on to describe in ten lines the details of Gabriel's first dawn, stressing the goodness of the woman from the salt cod stall and ending with the following words: "Our correspondent can attest that at the time of going to press the little angel was sleeping placidly in the Provincial Maternity and Foundling Home, saved from death and inevitable purgatory, and blissfully unaware of the commotion caused by his first hours on this earth."

Gabriel learned the article by heart, reading it over and over again and reciting it with all due ceremony. This piece of paper represented his only link to his mother. A few days after his discovery, one Monday when he had the day off, he went to El Born market and searched for the salt cod stall. As he lined up to buy his three bits of salt cod—it was Lent and the nuns at Llars Mundet, the children's home where he still lived, would be pleased by his thoughtfulness—he watched the buxom woman whose breast had given him his first nourishment seventeen years earlier, uneasily admiring her. She had peroxide-blond hair. Although the years had taken their toll, she was still a splendid full-bodied woman. Pale with the cold, the flesh of her arms looked as solid as marble. The planetary roundness of her breasts thrust against her white smock. How easy it would have been for Gabriel to regress, to latch on again, there and then, and with the same voracity as on the first day of his life.

Our father never told the salt cod vendor that he was the baby she'd put to her breast that February morning. From time to time, however, every three or four months, he went to the stall to have a look at her.

"Tomorrow, I'm going to escape for an hour or two to visit my adoptive mother," he'd announce when he was returning to Barcelona with Bundó and Petroli, apparently thinking out loud as he drove.

Since Gabriel, the name given by the unknown mother, was appropriately Catholic, the nuns at the Provincial Maternity and Foundling Home were happy for the baby to be called that and limited themselves to providing the two requisite surnames. They decided on "Delacruz Expósito," a typical choice for abandoned children, which literally meant "Foundling of the Cross." In those early years of the Franco regime these names provided a kind of safe-conduct and opened more than one door. People responded to them with compassion, imagining that behind the face of the little waif was a father killed at the front, or a mother who had to break up a large family in order to survive. More than one God-fearing woman made the sign of the cross when she heard the two surnames.

His sons didn't inherit them. Our mothers never married our father, so we got their surnames, and that was that. Sometimes, though, we like to address each other with the surname we would have had—translated—if it had come from our dad. Chris could be called Christopher Cross, like the American singer, or Chris of the Cross, a stage name chosen for its more universal ring, perhaps, by some magician performing in a Las Vegas casino. Christof would be von Kreuz, a name evoking a Kaiser's colonel, and Christophe would have the same surname as the painter in the Louvre: Christophe Delacroix. Cristòfol would be the most faithful and would keep Delacruz, like the Spanish mystic San Juan de la Cruz, or it could even be rendered into Catalan, to become Delacreu.

Most of the parentless children who, like our father, grew up in the Provincial Maternity and Foundling Home and, subsequently, the House of Charity, had been given similar surnames. They were like brothers and sisters without really being so. When our father reminisced about his childhood, Bundó was the only person he regarded as something close to a blood brother. Gabriel was just a few weeks older, and they grew up together. Their friendship was for life, from the tyranny of charity to the tyranny of moving furniture, and only tragedy would separate them. Of course, the time will come in these pages when we're going to have to talk about the tragedy, which was disastrous, or providential, for a number of people.

Now, borne along by these recollections, we too can revisit the labyrinthine passageways of the House of Charity, the tiles disinfected with Zotal, and the little boy who walks along holding the hand of a nun who smells like candles. We too can recall the nighttime comings and goings of the orphans, their adventures and their punishments, the coarse poorhouse clothes, the children's shrewdness in learning to fend for themselves. First, however, in order to make more sense of the whole thing and give it some perspective, we're going to jump ahead about half a century. Hence, as if all our father's journeys were merely a tangle of lines on a map of Europe, we shan't move from Barcelona and we'll enter the apartment in which he took refuge for more than ten years.

Cristòfol has the floor.

"Hang on," Christof protests, "I think we need to give this a title. Let's make it nice and solemn."

Over to you, Cristòfol.

## CARRER NÀPOLS

Very well. I'm thirty now, and it's more than twenty-five years since I last saw my father. This sentence could sound tragic if I said it like one of those idiots you see flaunting their family dramas on television, but, in my case, it's simply a fact expressed in terms of years. Precisely because we were so used to his absence, as we said before, I'm doing the calculations in order to stress the surprise—or rather the shock—of receiving the first news of him after so long. I refer to something so simple but so ambiguous as being able to trace his steps on a map of Barcelona. The call from the police came one morning just like any other. A policeman identified himself and then went on to ask me if I knew Senyor Gabriel Delacruz Expósito. It took me a few seconds to dredge up the name from the depths of my memory as I repeated it aloud.

"Yes, he's my father," I replied, "but we haven't seen or heard from him in many years. We'd forgotten he existed."

"Yes, I see. However, it is our duty to inform you that we have registered him as missing. Not dead, for the record, but missing. There have been no reported sightings of your father for a year. He hasn't paid his rent or utility bills. The gas, water, and electricity were cut off some time ago. The landlord got in touch with us because he's upset about not being paid. His complaint coincided with another one from the neighbors who'd been bothered for several days by a bad smell, like something dead. We took it seriously, entered the apartment, and found nobody there. Everything was in order. The neighbors, as you might imagine, are a hysterical lot. The point now is that you, as next of kin, will have to decide what you want to do: whether you want to pay the back rent and bills while you're looking for him, or whether you think it's better to remove his things and give up the apartment."

*While you're looking for him.*

"How did you find me?" It was the only question I managed to come up with.

"We didn't have to look too hard. We found your name written on a piece of paper. He'd left it on the bedside table, like a kind of suicide note. He seems to have done it deliberately. Only it wasn't a suicide note. There were three other names as well, but yours is the only one that appears in the registry office."

A couple of days later, early in the morning so as to make the most of the daylight, I went to the police station to pick up the keys to the apartment. The policeman showed me the piece of paper torn from a notebook. The other names were, of course, those of the other three Christophers although, at that point, I didn't know who they were or even if they were real names. It looked more like some sort of linguistic game. My father made no mention of the four mothers, not on that piece of paper anyway. The previous day, I'd explained the situation to my mother and asked her to come with me to the apartment, but she persuaded me to go alone.

"Aren't you curious?"

"No. You can tell me about it."

Her way of coping with sudden shock or disappointment was to feign indifference, which is what she always did when we started talking about my father.

The apartment Gabriel had abandoned was on a mezzanine in Carrer Nàpols, very near Carrer Almogàvers and Ciutadella Park. It was an ugly building, erected in the fifties, with a car repair workshop at street level. The policeman told me that they'd confirmed that my father had lived at that address for more than ten years. His choice wasn't surprising if the idea was to become invisible. In the mid-eighties that part of the city was a run-down area with a listless, desolate air, not unlike an industrial estate. It had become a no-man's-land. The Barcelona North bus station, which was not yet renovated, was falling apart in the middle of a large vacant lot where rats scratched around among used condoms. The court building, which was swarming with people in the morning, closed in the middle of the afternoon and slumbered in its own weighty shadow. In that part of Carrer Almogàvers there were only workshops and garages used by transport companies, and the trucks made everything stink of diesel. (Now I wonder whether Gabriel settled there because he liked the smell.) Whatever life there was in the area appeared after dark, in the form of transvestites who plied their trade on the street corners. With their painted faces, four-inch heels and skintight clothes, they drifted like zombies under the yellow glow of the streetlamps, trying to attract curb-crawling customers who, if they weren't interested, were ordered in blood-curdling screeches to fuck off.

At precisely that time, I'd spent two academic years going to English classes at an academy in Passeig de Sant Joan, very close to the Arc de Triomf. Looking back, I've speculated more than once that, one of those winter evenings while I was killing time in the Bar Lleida before my class, I might have come across my father. Two pairs of roaming eyes meet for an instant and move on as each stranger returns to his own world. It could have happened, but I don't find anything very comforting in this thought.

With a lawyer's detachment, I opened the door of the apartment. I admit that my intentions were very hazy: have a look at the place, try to find some clue as to Gabriel's whereabouts—it was years since I'd stopped calling him "Dad"—and forget about the whole thing, the sooner the better. I had no interest in looking for him and still less in paying his rent, which is what happened in the end, but now I'm jumping ahead. Although the apartment was cold and stuffy, I was struck by an odd sense of recognition. I now believe that it was intuition, almost part of my DNA, that I unconsciously projected onto those four walls.

As I started to move through the apartment, I felt reassured. As if I'd been doing it all my life, I raised one of the roller blinds in the dining room, and a little more light came in, a slanting brightness. A meter from the window, directly opposite, was the wall of a parking garage that had been constructed in the middle of the block. Gabriel's absence could be felt in every corner of the apartment since dust lay thick on the furniture, giving it a ghostly air, but, for the record, it was neither depressing nor pathetic. There was no sense of that paralyzed—rather than peaceful—atmosphere that settles over the objects in a house when there's been a sudden death. Rather the whole effect was that of a still life, a perfectly arranged composition. On the table in the living room, a dozen walnuts awaited sentence in a little raffia basket with the nutcracker executioner keeping them company. Next to them was a box of French matches and a half-burned candle stuck in the neck of a Coca-Cola bottle, ready for the nights when there were power cuts. A stainless-steel shoehorn had been suffering for an eternity as it teetered on the armrest of a black leatherette chair. A wall clock, stopped at three minutes past one, was fed up with getting the time right only twice a day and silently begged to be wound up.

I'm making an inventory of these superficial details—and I could offer a lot more—to give an idea of the lethargy that gripped the apartment. As I went from room to room, not touching a thing, I thought it expressed my father's way of being in the world, as Mom and I had known him. Nothing important or revealing surfaced. Another idea came into my head, over the top for sure, but I still want to write it down: "Buried alive." Feeling quite despondent, I was on the point of leaving, closing the door and forgetting the whole thing. Then, all of a sudden, I remembered the piece of paper the policeman had found on the bedside table, which I interpreted as licence, an invitation even, to snoop. Why had he made a list of four names that were the same but different? Cristòfol, Christophe, Christopher, Christof, and their respective surnames. Why was I the first?

In his bedroom, I opened the drawers of the bedside table and didn't find anything interesting. Next to the bed was a wardrobe with three doors and a full-length mirror. The first concealed a series of shelves piled with sheets, towels, and blankets. I felt around in them in case he'd hidden anything there (as people tend to do) but only pulled out two lavender sachets that had lost their fragrance. Behind the second door were my father's clothes. A collection of shirts, pullovers, jackets, and trousers, most of them very old, were hanging there, devoid of all hope. On the floor, looking ill at ease, were several pairs of shoes. A few bare coat hangers, like fleshless collarbones, gave the impression that he'd only taken a couple of changes of clothes. I ran my hand over his clothes as if trying to express solidarity, and, just then, a jacket caught my eye. It was suede, old, with worn elbows. I remembered that Dad often wore it when he visited us. I took it off the hanger to look at it again and smell it, as I used to do when I was a kid but, when I brought it to my nose, something fell to the floor—a bit of paper. I bent over to pick it up and was very surprised to find a poker card, an ace of clubs. I put it in one of the pockets and went to hang the jacket up again. As I was returning it to its place, another card fell out of a different jacket. This time it was the king of hearts. I grabbed five or six items of clothing and gave them a good shake. More cards fell out. I picked them up. They were all aces, kings, queens, and jacks. Some were repeated. Then I had a thought. I took out another jacket and carefully examined the sleeves. The end of the left sleeve had been painstakingly unstitched, and there inside, between cloth and lining, a proud but biddable king of diamonds was exiled.

I was so fascinated by the discovery that I decided, then and there, that I wanted to find my father come what may. I began to rummage systematically through every cupboard, every shelf, and every drawer. (In my place, you'd have done the same, wouldn't you, Christophers?) I pried into every corner of the kitchen, dining room, and bathroom. Tucked away in a dark corner of the apartment, I found a sort of junk room, some six meters square and full of shelves. A forty-watt lightbulb hung from the ceiling. I tried the switch, but it didn't work, of course, as the power supply had been cut off. I went to get a candle. In the flickering light, the room looked like an air-raid shelter. I felt like a detective. My father had stored his memories in that space, which was as minuscule and crammed full of things as the cab of a truck. It's not that he was a meticulous man, or especially nostalgic. It would make more sense to explain this hoard as the result of a nomadic life. You wouldn't have to be a genius to figure out that the belongings that Gabriel had kept after spending half his life on the move constituted an essential part of his biography.

Making the most of the daylight, I took a number of cardboard boxes into the dining room and opened them one by one. I was so engrossed by what I discovered that the hours slipped by until it got dark. Every time I stumbled across some relevant document, or memory-laden object, I left it out on the table to study in more detail later. Thus, clues slowly emerged with mounting intrigue that seemed calculated on my father's part. A black folder bearing the emblem of the Spanish consulate in Frankfurt kept all his expired driving licenses, for example, and passports with pages stamped by customs officials of a good many countries in Europe. In one brass box, advertising Cola Cao with little drawings of African children, he'd tucked away about twenty letters that he'd exchanged with Petroli after they both left trucking and no longer saw each other. Underneath them, yellow with age, was a pile of scraps of paper from another sort of correspondence: the erotic tales that he and Bundó had written for each other in the House of Charity when they were kids.

Another folder—this is it, this is it, this is it!—held a pile of documents concerning the four of us. Names, addresses, copies of birth certificates, photos of our mothers and of us, drawings we did when we were small, which he had taken with him as mementos...It must be said that this folder was the one most battered by use (and I mention this without any filial vanity). Amazed, I set about leafing through its contents and couldn't stop. It wasn't long before the other three names on the policeman's list appeared before my eyes. Christof, Christophe, Christopher...It seemed to be some kind of joke. I went to look for a blank sheet of paper and a pen and jotted down all the details that might make the revelations more plausible. The more I learned, the more the enigma of Gabriel grew.

That evening, as I was going over to my mother's place by the club Metro, stunned and disturbed because, among other things, I'd discovered that I had three half-brothers scattered across Europe, a memory from my childhood came—or burst—into my head. It was the image of a man—my father—who sometimes, for all his apparent composure, couldn't stop touching the edge of his left sleeve with his right hand. A swift, mechanical gesture, not natural, a sort of tic.

# 3

## Imperfect Orphans

S o are we orphans then?"

"All four of us are the only sons of an only son. And an only daughter. You could say that the whole time we were unaware of each others' existence—we were orphaned of brothers, if such a thing is possible."

"Imperfect orphans."

"After Cristòfol's phone call, when I discovered I had three half-brothers, I imagined we'd be united by some sort of birthmark. A secret sign that Dad had tattooed on us in the cradle so we could identify each other, like those abandoned princes in stories. I've got one of those marks, a sort of scar on my right shoulder. It looks like the silhouette of a running greyhound with very thin legs. Do you have that by any chance?"

"No."

"No."

"Well, I do, but it's on my left buttock and it's not a scar but a mark on my skin, a proper birthmark, and it's not in the shape of a dog. When I was a little kid and Mom was bathing me she said it looked like sails on a boat and the freckles were splashes of water, but I see a bat with outstretched wings."

"Ah, if we're talking about marks, I've got one but it's on my chest, like the tail of a comet in orbit around my right nipple."

"By the way, what presents did he bring you when he came to visit? Once he gave me a toy ukulele."

"I got a plastic drum kit. The snare was missing so I used an empty detergent box."

"Lucky you! I was desperate to have a drum kit. But he only brought me one of those really basic pianos with eight notes. I got bored with it right away."

"I got what I'd call the leftovers. By the time I came into the world, Dad was settled in Barcelona and he wasn't visiting you all any more. Sometimes, when he came to see Mom and me, he'd look through his things and bring me a present. He gave me a microphone that didn't work. The batteries had corroded and were stuck inside the casing, but I played with it anyway. When my friends wouldn't let me play soccer with them because they said I wasn't good enough, I used to broadcast the matches live, using the mike."

"Don't feel too badly done by, Cristòfol. After all, you were with Dad when the rest of us were missing him. Anyway, now that I think about it, those four musical presents must have been from the same move. From four rich brothers."

"Ah, and another thing: All the kids at school used to brag about their dads. If I had a fight with anyone, his dad was going to come and cut off my head with his saw (carpenter), ram his hoe into my chest (farmer), or rip off my ear with a wrench (mechanic). When they asked me what mine did, first of all I told them I wasn't allowed to say and then, lowering my voice, I'd tell them the secret: My dad was a spy. He traveled all around Europe in a furniture truck, but that was his cover. The lie gave me kudos."

"Well, I used to say that my dad pissed off one fine day and Scotland Yard was looking for him, that he was one of the Great Train Robbers, and that one day he'd be back, loaded with jewels. That made me popular too, but Mum used to get mad when I said it because the other parents complained afterward."

Et cetera, et cetera, et cetera.

So are we orphans, then? No, we're not orphans. Not yet. Anyway, if we claimed we were, we'd be carrying on like spoiled brats, as if we were somehow trying to relive the hardships suffered by our father as a kid while sparing ourselves the feeling of defense-lessness he must have endured all those years. Sometimes when the four of us are talking about it, we come to the conclusion that everything that came later—his life on the truck, being continu-ally on the move, and his pathological secrecy when he left the motorways and hid away from the world—is simply a result of his unfortunate childhood. But when he used to recall his youth, Dad wasn't self-pitying or bitter or holier-than-thou. He accepted it as his lot, and that was that.

Let's imagine, for example, that fearful, withdrawn little boy who went into the House of Charity in 1945. Just before his fourth birthday. Though he didn't know it, he still bore the stigma of being a "child of war." Heaven knows where all those abandoned children have come from, people said. Harlots, single mothers, naive or shameless maids who'd got pregnant ... Or, worst of all, they might be the spawn of those red separatists who died on the front. The devil's blood ran in their veins. In the light of which the orphanage wouldn't have been such a terrible fate.

The nuns managed everyday life in the orphanage, and a cou-ple of lay teachers were employed for the older kids. The little ones like our father grew up in an atmosphere of Catholic piety. It seems that mealtimes, for example, turned into religious instruc-tion classes in which the nuns thickened the gruel with the lives of the saints.

"This one's for Saint Pelagius, martyred in the name of chas-tity ... This is for the first Christian martyr, Saint Stephen, who was stoned to death ... This is for Saint Cosmas and Saint Da-mian, the twin brothers who died decapitated ... This is for Saint Engratia, the patron saint of Zaragoza, who was dragged around the city by a horse ..."

Dad never forgot the singsong litany, or the strange relationship that was established between the food they made him eat and the horrible, gory deaths of the saints.

In the afternoons, one sister read the children extracts from the catechism, and they had to learn them by heart. Although the nuns felt maternal affection for their charges, especially if they'd come to the orphanage at a very young age, discipline kept them on the straight and narrow. They were spared no punishments, threats, or moral-bearing lessons, but the children always found ways to let off steam. Years later, Gabriel remembered it as a kind of purgatory. A lenient purgatory because hell for those kids was called the Duran Home for Children. When the nuns caught them misbehaving they could put a stop to it with the mere mention of this reformatory in the north of the city. They told all sorts of stories about it. In the hellhole that was the Duran Home, they said, the children slept tied to their beds so they couldn't escape, and their heads were always shaved as a precaution against plagues of lice. One of the gardeners who worked in the vegetable patch of the House of Charity took it upon himself to spread the worst tales. If any children playing hide-and-seek trod on his vegetables, he'd take them aside and strike the fear of God into them by telling them that in the Duran Home, which was where they'd end up if they didn't behave, children who destroyed a vegetable garden were punished by being made to eat rats and beetles, which they had to catch themselves, in the building's cellars and sewers.

The passage of time always distorts reality. In his capacity as a lecturer in quantum physics, Christophe insists that we jot down that sentence. The passage of time always distorts reality. For Gabriel, those eight years he spent in the House of Charity remained half buried in the depths of his memory, as if obeying an order to lie dormant while not quite being erased. The moments or images he recalled with any clarity became fewer and fewer: the thrill of the day he turned ten and the older children abducted him and took him at midnight for his first visit to the institution's miniature museum, to see the fluorescent bones of a human skeleton ("Of course it moved: If you look hard you can see it's laughing . . ."); the contrived warmth at Christmas when some figure of authority came bearing gifts, and it was as if the nuns, together with the teachers and even the gardener, were doing their best to hide something terrible from them and holding back their tears in public.

He'd gradually learned not to be tormented by these memories, which visited him without warning and against his will when he was still young. Only a few episodes survived intact. These were stories that Gabriel and Bundó reminisced about together—and that must have been the important factor—when they were driving around in the truck. They told each other these tales every so often, when something spotted or heard along the way (a song on the radio, the name of a town, a roadside ad) jolted their memories, and they'd learned to take turns at narrating. First one, then the other, they filled in the gaps with convincing new details, small variations on the same story. This patient reconstruction drove Petroli crazy. Since his memory was better than theirs, he had perfect recall of the facts from the last time they'd told the story, but when he joined in the conversation and tried to correct them, they'd cut him off saying how would he know when he'd never even been to the House of Charity. Petroli, who was a decent fellow, let them rattle on. Of all those stories, which they can no longer get nostalgic about together, the most regularly recounted, the most famous of them all, was the one about the lame nun and her secret.

Dad used to tell us this one as a sort of bedtime story. We were too small to understand it properly but, on those occasions, his voice changed and we were riveted. Even now, we fancy we can remember how slowly and mysteriously he pronounced each and every word, and how the spell would often be broken by an incorrect translation or unintelligible pronunciation. As children hungry for affection we took on the task of mentally tying up the loose ends. Sister Elisa, Dad used to say, was very tall and always wore a shiny black habit. She was lame and swayed from side to side as she walked, lurching like a wounded crow. When they saw her for the first time, just after arriving at the orphanage, the smallest children tended to respond by bursting into tears. In fact she never did anything to scare them, but nor did she smile at anybody. Her round face was framed by the white wimple of her order and it rose above her head like the horns of some fantastic animal. At night or when the light was dim, her face glimmered like a pale moon suspended in the air. The torment of her disability permanently twisted her mouth in a grimace of pain. She hardly ever spoke and seemed to sow silence around her wherever she went. Conversations abruptly stopped and everyone went quiet. Oddly enough, the lame nun had a wooden leg. The rhythmic *clip-clop* of her steps made the silence that sprang up around her even more threatening. (At this point, Dad used to stop talking and would suddenly close his fist and thump the wood of the bedside table, the wardrobe, the chair, or whatever was closest to hand four or five times. Our hearts shrank and slowed down, keeping time with those blows. Sometimes they almost stopped beating.)

The lame nun's secret was that nobody had ever seen her wooden leg. Hidden beneath the folds of her habit, the leg fueled the fantasies of all the children who lived in the House of Charity. They grew up obsessed by the mystery of the wooden leg and eventually came to see it as an object with a life of its own. When Sister Elisa was hobbling along a passageway, or when she came into a classroom to give a message to the teacher, or when she escorted the children to the parish church, they couldn't stop staring at her habit, at the place where the leg should have been. Sometimes, if the nun took a long stride, or if she stopped for a moment to rest, a strange angular shape was outlined by the black cloth, like a broken bone sticking out from a badly fractured leg. If it was her turn to keep watch in the dormitories the measured *clip-clop* of that leg on the tiles made the night darker, and the children froze between their sheets. Blood curdled. Nightmares were common.

The stories passed down from the bigger children to the smaller ones ensured the myth was never lost. Some of the tales told about the origins of the false leg were quite elaborate. One of the more successful had it that, one stormy evening when Sister Elisa was walking alone in the garden and deeply engrossed in her thoughts, a lightning bolt struck her feet and charred her leg all the way up to the thigh. It smoked like scorched firewood. The same lightning bolt lopped off the thickest branch of the oak tree under which she was sheltering and dropped it right beside her. Hearing the tremendous claps of thunder, the gardener ran out to see if anything had happened to his favorite tree and thus saved the nun's life. He made a promise at the foot of the tree: Since, by the grace of God, the nun and the tree had survived, he'd fashion a wooden leg out of the branch so she could walk. According to this story, the gardener was the only other person who knew what the leg looked like, but he never talked about it. The legend was further embellished, and one of the more fanciful versions had it that a bud had started to sprout on the oak branch, and the nun's leg would soon have leaves. Some people said that the leg came from an old mannequin in the Can Jorba department store, that it was hollow, and that was why it made that sinister *clip-clop*. A gang of inquisitive kids who'd read *Treasure Island* imagined that, under the habit, they'd find a pirate's peg leg, like Long John Silver's, as thin as a broomstick with a small bowl at the top fitted to the stump of an amputee's knee. If they were anywhere in the vicinity of the nun and wanted to refer to it, but in code because that gave them a certain superiority in the eyes of the others, they'd start chanting, "Yo-ho-ho, and a bottle of rum . . ."

We four, we Christophers, each in his own home and on different nights, listened to the nun's trials and tribulations without really understanding them. Dad, who was never very good at gauging how far he could go in scaring us, used to tell us her story when he put us to bed. We were probably too young. As we were dropping off to sleep, our shivers of fear transported us to the dormitories of the House of Charity. We tossed and turned in our beds, getting tangled in our sheets, sweating in our distress and, when we woke up disoriented, halfway between dream and reality, we were reassured by the certainty that our dad was also sleeping in that dormitory, and if the lame nun came over to our beds, he'd protect us.

Since Dad disappeared from our lives, that wooden leg has remained lodged in our imaginations to this very day with all the symbolism of a votive offering, less threatening now but still impressive. We all agree on that. Some years ago, at one of those huge mass ceremonies they hold in the Vatican, Pope John Paul II beatified several martyr nuns. On the list was Sister Elisa, the one from the House of Charity, and part of the mystery was unexpectedly revealed. The nun lost her leg during the Civil War when a bunch of anarchists had set fire to the Hieronymite Convent in Barcelona, and she tried to stop them from profaning a crucifix. As the smoke and flames spread through the church, a wooden beam fell from the roof, landed on top of her, and smashed one of her legs. The anarchists left her for dead, but she regained consciousness, and some divine power gave her the strength to drag herself a few meters and call for help, for somebody to come and save her.

We don't know if our father had news of the beatification, but doubtless, reading about it or seeing it on TV, hundreds of former wards of the House of Charity immediately remembered—with the odd twinge of conscience—the fears and wild fantasies that this poor, lame, silent woman had inspired in them all those years ago. We're also sure that, wherever he might be, our father still has the tic that harks back to his childhood. Often, in the middle of a conversation, if he wanted to ward off some intimation of bad luck, he'd say "touch wood," like everybody does, but then he'd automatically tap his right leg two or three times.

On his more expansive days, Dad would let himself go and regale our mothers with some of his other memories of the House of Charity. Most were stories of the rebel child, orphanage escapades that tended to end up with a couple of smacks on the bottom or a spoonful of castor oil. Our mothers listened with some compassion, and, if any shadow of doubt crossed their faces, he'd say, "So you don't believe me, eh? Just ask Bundó. He was there too."

When Bundó and Petroli came by to collect Dad on their way out of town again (sometimes, depending on their timetables, they stayed for breakfast or dinner), our mothers made the most of the occasion to question Dad's comrade-in-arms. They asked him whether he'd ever managed to see the nun's wooden leg, or to give them his version of their adventures when they escaped from the orphanage by getting out through an empty cistern in the school grounds, after which they spent hours and hours moving around the sewers of Barcelona until they ended up at the air-raid shelter in Carrer Fraternitat. Could anyone really believe, our mothers asked, that dozens of people were still living underground, in hiding since the war, and that they'd turned blind like moles because they never saw the light of day? As he listened to them, Bundó used to smile, glancing at Dad out of the corner of his eye, perhaps because he didn't fully understand the language, but later he'd vouch for the veracity of these stories with an almost scientific air, like a Doctor Watson verifying the exploits of his Sherlock.

It might have been because he arrived at the House of Charity some months after Gabriel that Bundó always saw our father as a sort of big brother. His full name was Serafí Bundó Ventosa. He came from a village in the Penedès region, and you could say he was an imperfect orphan. The Franco regime executed his father the day he was born. One of life's not so coincidental coincidences. Accused of high treason against the fatherland and attempting to cross the border and therefore condemned to death, he had been awaiting execution in Modelo Prison for seven months, and it happened on that very day at dawn. (In his darker moods, Bundó used to say that his first howl in the world coincided precisely with his father's last, before the firing squad.) The nuns at the El Vendrell maternity hospital hid the news from his mother for a week so that her milk wouldn't dry up but, obliged by the authorities, they had to tell her in the end. With her son in her arms, the girl learned of the death of her husband and didn't cry at all. She just rocked the child, nonstop, showing great composure. Some months earlier, during a visit to the prison, she and her husband had tried to console one another by choosing a name for the baby. It was a way of planning some kind of future together, however unlikely that was. In the hospital she thought again and decided to call him Serafí, after his father.

Then she went mad.

After a few days, now back at home, she started to talk to the baby as she would to an adult. Her unhinged brain convinced her that the baby was the reincarnation of her murdered husband, as if life moved in cycles. "Come on, Serafí, eat up, because you've got to leave at sunrise to work in the vineyard," she told him as she put him to her breast at midnight. Then she'd tuck him up in his cot and leave everything all laid out next to it: his clothes for the next day, tools, rope-soled sandals, the hoe, and the fertilizer sprayer.

Her parents had died young and, since there was no family to look after her, the doctors didn't think twice about locking her up in the Pere Mata lunatic asylum in Reus, where she wasted away and died ten years later. Meanwhile, Bundó set out on the path followed by all orphans from poor families, from the infirmary to the House of Charity. The memory of his mother was a speck on his subconscious, an out-of-focus face that appeared and hit him like a bolt of lightning in moments of extreme sadness (but this could have been a false memory).

As we've said, we four look upon Bundó as our father's brother. In those years, life in the orphanages helped to forge unbreakable bonds and irrational phobias. The children arrived helpless and, in order to survive, they invented clandestine societies and swore secret pacts. The factors favoring childish friendships were instinctive and arbitrary. I like you, I don't like you. Out of some random attachment, then, which not even Gabriel and Bundó were able to explain, they were as good as brothers from Bundó's very first day in the House of Charity. *Carn i úngla. Commé les doigts de la main. Wie Pech und Schwefel.* From the photos we still have, and thanks to our mothers' memories—and Petroli's too—we know that Bundó was solidly built and a salt-of-the-earth type. He wasn't fat, because he got enough exercise with all the loading and unloading of furniture, but he enjoyed his food and his pants were always too tight. For him, the siesta was sacred, whether it was on a bed in some hostel or in the Pegaso. From early childhood, he'd developed a less taciturn and more lackadaisical character than Gabriel's, more given to adventure and less calculating, and, in that, they certainly complemented one another.

As they grew and matured, though they found it hard, the two friends learned to respect each other's space when necessary. They'd been living together almost all their lives, first within the same four walls, and then over the four wheels of the truck. They were now starting to understand that a person's private life takes place in other rooms that aren't shared. Moreover, in amorous matters, they turned out to have almost opposite tastes. Over the years, our father came to have four wives in four countries, a family crescendo that was suddenly interrupted (as we shall explain). Bundó, however, preferred fleeting relations and, during those years, he frequented thirty, forty, fifty women, always in different roadside brothels in France, Germany, and Spain, until one day when he put an end to this frenetic activity and focused on one girl he couldn't get out of his head (yes, we'll be filling you in on that too).

Then again, it shouldn't be surprising that this dabbler's spirit (sorry, mothers) developed in both of them as adolescents. The bond between Gabriel and Bundó throughout their orphanage childhood—each one helping the other to win the respect of the older children, for example, or covering for one another when the nuns accused them of some misdemeanor—bore succulent fruit when they were about thirteen, with the onset of puberty.

"It's your turn this week," Bundó would say.

"Yes, I know. I'll give it to you tomorrow night. I'll write it during math review. Who do you want to be with this time?"

"I don't mind. I think it's better not to know. Or, okay, let's say Sophia Loren."

"Who?"

"Sophia Loren, or whatever her name is, the one we saw in those stills from the film that's on at the Tívoli. That Italian with tits like watermelons. Don't tell me you don't remember her . . . Okay, if you don't . . . you know what . . . you can do Carmen Sevilla. Or the two of them together. That'd be a good laugh. Yes, do that. But don't get carried away because when you get carried away your handwriting's terrible and then I can't understand anything."

Gabriel was one of those people who wrote slowly, making sure the lines came out straight, but he didn't protest at this slur because he knew from his own experience that good penmanship was essential. One badly written word, one bit of scribble, and you fatally lost the thrust of the story. On the rock-solid basis of their friendship they'd come to an arrangement that helped to stimulate their imaginations—and a little bit more than that. Each week they exchanged an erotic story in which they were the stars. Two sides of a page torn out of a notebook sufficed. Gabriel had his feet on the ground and wanted the stories that Bundó wrote for him to feature the girls in the House of Charity. Since the boys and girls weren't allowed to mix, they were in separate parts of the building and they rarely caught a glimpse of each other, but this enforced segregation proved very exciting. He asked for names that were easy to remember so he could feel closer to them. Bundó, in contrast, was more of a dreamer and preferred film stars and exotic backdrops. Over time, each boy refined the preferences of his one and only reader.

In the beginning Gabriel complained that Bundó's stories were too descriptive and not very exciting. He didn't give a damn whether the blond, blue-eyed, very white-skinned girl had a missal, a hankie with her initials embroidered on it, and a framed picture of her dead parents all set out on a crocheted doily on her bedside table. He was dying to know what was going on under the sheets of that bed. When it was Gabriel's turn, the first story he wrote for Bundó was very long, jumbled, overloaded in detail but short on flesh, and the hero was a guy called Serafín. Bundó read it locked in the bathroom, trembling with an unfamiliar kind of excitement. The sexual powers rather crudely attributed to him in the text turned him on immediately, but, even so, Bundó didn't recognize himself. It might have been because one of the teachers at the House of Charity was also called Serafín, which made it hard for him to identify with the character. The next morning he asked his scribe to call the hero Bundó in the future, just the surname would do. Gabriel complied, and Bundó felt he was so well portrayed and so well shielded by that surname that he eliminated Serafí from his life thereafter (although the nuns, of course, called him Serafín and, in the odd case of misplaced maternal instinct, the diminutive Serafinín).

After four or five attempts, the stories began to make progress. They really got into it. Though they always spoke Catalan together, they wrote in Spanish because they thought it was a more grown-up, more perverse language. They exchanged them furtively, and the risk of being discovered, even by the other kids in the orphan-

age, invested the whole thing with a forbidden air of mortal sin—as
the priest who taught them religion called it—which made them
feel more depraved, more like men. Thus transformed, in the isolation of the bathrooms or in bed, inside a tent improvised with a
sheet, it was easier for them to get inside the hero's character.

*A few minutes later, after drinking the amazing potion he'd
concocted all by himself in the chemistry class, pulling a fast
one on the teacher Don Marcelino, Bundó looked in the bathroom mirror and confirmed that his reflection wasn't there.
He'd done it! He was invisible, and his plan was going to work!
He couldn't see it, but he could feel that his dick was getting
hard just at the thought of the pleasures in store for him. [ . . . ]
Passing through the revolving door and now inside the Hotel
Ritz, it was very easy for him to follow the beautiful girl from
Siam, the daughter of a very rich Rajah, to her room. He was
very impatient, so he tried touching her up in the elevator, feeling her big round boobs through her clothes, and she was smiling because he was tickling her and, thinking she was alone
because Bundó was invisible, as you know, she stuck her finger up under her skirt. [ . . . ] Everything was looking good for
Bundó, but when he went into the room with her, sticking close
to her body so as not to arouse suspicion, he discovered that the
Rajah's daughter's mother and sister, who was even more beautiful and pervy than she was, were inside waiting for her, both
of them naked after having a bath together and good and ready
for the fun and games they say Orientals like so much. Bundó,
still invisible to human eyes, moved over to the cute and randy
little bum of the mother and lovingly groped it . . .*

Well, that's just a taste of it. At the end of the story, Bundó's
potion wears off and the three Asian beauties discover him, but
they're so enraptured that they choose not to betray him and to
keep him as their private stud for ever and ever. For Bundó, this
was one of Gabriel's more successful stories.

Sometimes, catching him in class with a dreamy expression, the teacher would yell, "Bundó, you've got your head in the clouds," trying to shake him from his reverie.

"Sorry, sir," he'd answer at once, trying to look awake but thinking to himself, "No, I'm not in the clouds, sir. I'm in a palace in Siam and I'm never going to leave it."

Gabriel was shyer and more prone to feelings of guilt than Bundó. Sometimes, when he was well into it, jerking off, holding a wad of paper in his left hand as his right hand labored up and down, the phantom of Sister Mercedes appeared. She was the youngest nun and she berated him with a pained expression on her face, serious but not angry. He tried to close his eyes to make her go away but, when he finally came, those precious seconds of pleasure were cut short by a wave of guilt. One particularly difficult day, Gabriel confided in Bundó, who promised to sort out the problem. The next day, at review time, sitting in the House of Charity library, he wrote a special story. The climax is as follows:

*Sister Mercedes, dressed in her black habit, heard some telltale moans coming from the bathroom. She went inside and opened all the cubicle doors with her master key, one by one, and, there, behind the last door, was Gabriel jerking off. He had his eyes closed and, all of a sudden, almost at the greatest moment of pleasure, he opened them and saw Sister Mercedes standing there in front of him. He got a terrible shock, but then she went "Sssshh," to indicate they shouldn't make any noise. Gabriel's only response was to hold out his arms and carefully lift up her black habit. Underneath it he discovered a suspender belt and some little pink panties like the Paralelo cabaret artists wear and, a bit higher up, some bare titties that were the most incredible ones he'd ever seen in his whole life. Sister Mercedes took him by the hand and led him to her room, where she revealed to him her best-kept secret: She led a double life, and at night-time she was on the game in Calle Conde del Asalto . . .*

An astounded Gabriel read the story that night and, as the sequence of lewd acts unfolded before his eyes, he got more and more excited and more and more terrified about what might happen if the nuns discovered him. The next day at lunchtime he went up behind Bundó and grabbed him by the neck.

"Have you gone mad, or what?" he whispered in his ear. His friend smiled smugly. "I'm going to burn your story. I'm going to do it this afternoon, as soon as I can."

But night fell and Gabriel, still tormented and very jittery, locked himself in the bathroom again and reread the story. He didn't burn it after all. Proof of that is the fact that we can still read it. How many times, consumed by feelings of criminality and guilt, would the adolescent have given a last-minute reprieve to those two pages, the match already burning in his hand? One puff. The flame goes out. Relief.

In the end, Gabriel kept the story throughout his years at the House of Charity. It was his special treasure, the crown jewel of his collection. Since she was still young, Sister Mercedes was fortunately assigned to different tasks for the congregation and didn't mix much with the orphanage children. Fortunately, we say, because every time he had to talk to her, Gabriel started gabbling and went as red as a tomato. She noticed and tried to help the terribly timid boy, showing affection with gentle caresses, but the cure was worse than the disease. There was a time when Gabriel turned to the story so often that he was convinced that the nun was his partner in crime and that the two of them had secretly fallen in love. When he learned about the effects these quixotic fantasies were having upon his friend, Bundó brought him down to earth by writing new stories that were set in places a long way from the orphanage, in much less salubrious surroundings: in the shantytown of Somorrostro, in the Sant Sebastià public baths, or in a Gypsy shack at the foot of Montjuïc.

We calculate that the pornographic chapter of their friendship lasted almost a year and a half. Each one wrote about forty stories, although, by the end, many of the characters cropped up again, and plots were rehashed. The pages were showing the wear and tear of use and abuse. However crazy it may seem, both Gabriel and Bundó had decided that the best way to camouflage their stories was to tuck them into their Religious Instruction notebooks. Accordingly, the erotic tales always bore titles that wouldn't arouse the suspicions of any nun who might discover them, for example "Flowers of the Virgin of May," "The Calvary of Father Salustio," or "The Mystery of the Nails of Christ."

When they began to work with the moving company, life in the outside world slowly replaced words and fantasy with the much more prosaic reality of ravenous sex. Nonetheless, we Christophers are convinced that their erotic library colored their relations with flesh-and-blood women. In any case, as they were rattling around Europe in the truck years later, the tricks of memory made them relive more than once that intimate bond between religion and sex, a mutual transaction, as if they were two sides of the same coin. Like most truckers, Gabriel, Bundó, and Petroli had decorated the inside of the cabs with calendars of naked pinups. They were calendars from 1967, 1968, and 1969, a New Year gift from service stations in Germany and France, with a gallery of fecund Valkyries and coy sex-kittens posing on Pirelli tires or draped over the shining hood of a car that was always red. The three friends had seen them so often that they were at home with the presence of their paper harem. Homeward bound and approaching the border post at La Jonquera, however, they had to turn the calendars around and display the pictures they'd stuck on the back to disguise them. Devout scenes featuring His Holiness Paul VI or the Virgin of Montserrat then guided them along the straight-and-narrow of the badly cambered roads of Franco's Spain.

If we're going to make progress, we Christophers now need to return to Carrer Nàpols. The first time we four brothers met in Barcelona, incredulous, suspicious, and still dumbfounded by the revelations, Cristòfol showed us our father's mezzanine apartment.

It was one Saturday in May, a sunny spring day, and the three of us from the other side of the Pyrenees thought it was a gift from the gods. We'd arranged to meet in a hotel restaurant in the center of town where Cristòfol had reserved rooms for us. We did the introductions and had lunch together. The first few hours were cordial, a sort of testing of the waters, but all four of us were too stiff and wary, and then there was the awkwardness about language, so we didn't quite manage to break the ice over lunch. The only meeting point was our father, but we talked about him as if he were a stranger to us (and he was), a capricious host who'd engineered a surprise get-together, and now we had to find out why. Midafternoon we walked through the Ribera neighborhood, stopped at the El Born market—the building now under lock and key—in honor of our father's first cries and, crossing Ciutadella Park, made our way to Carrer Nàpols.

We were silent and solemn as we went up the dark stairway leading to the mezzanine floor—as if someone had died and we had to go to the wake—and as soon as we entered Gabriel Delacruz Expósito's apartment (as the mailbox in the entrance failed to say) we began to recover our shared past. There was nothing mystical about this. It's just that the objects that he'd kept, set out by Cristòfol on the table, triggered memories, and the distances that separated us were whittled away. Four boys reliving anecdotes, obsessions, words, disappointments, and emotions. After three hours it was as if we'd known each other all our lives. Each one of us seized upon coincidences in the happy certainty that any mention was enough for the other three to endorse them unanimously. The game got us laughing. Since there was no light in the apartment, when it got dark we went off to find a café so that we could get on with our forensic examination. One thing led to another. At three in the morning a sleepy waiter kicked us out of the hotel bar.

After that first joint visit to the apartment in Carrer Nàpols, we agreed that the four of us would pay our father's overdue rent. A first step. This is how the apartment became a sort of social hub, the headquarters for our inquiries. Rita, who still refuses to set foot in the place, mocks us, saying that soon we're going to turn it into the Christophers Club, "a museum with a guard, dusty display cases, and red ropes blocking entry to the conjugal bedrooms."

This is slightly over the top. We're not father worshippers, not us. You could even say that if we've ganged up to find him it's got more to do with satisfying our curiosity than concern for him. Right now, if we set our minds to it, we could reel off a whole catalogue of shared grudges just as effortlessly as we're weaving together our childhood memories. And, needless to say, all of us, each one of his own accord and without discussing it, have more than once been tempted to throw in the towel. It would be very easy right now to pretend that Gabriel no longer exists. We've had many years of training for that.

"He's a real nowhere man, sitting in his nowhere land . . ." Chris intones as if capturing our thoughts.

What is it that impels us to look for him, then? We might say it's the urge to complete an impossible family portrait of our father. During that first visit when we all went together to the apartment, we were entranced by the clues that our meticulous examination of Gabriel's belongings threw up; they proved impossible to ignore. One parcel contained ten brand-new packs of cards, all wrapped up in cellophane. Three carefully piled boxes held a jumble of improbable objects, painstakingly stowed away so as to make the best use of the space: a tortoiseshell comb, a ceramic figure representing Actaeon and his hounds, a teakwood paperweight, the shell of a tortoise, a radio-cassette player, a tape of María Dolores Pradera and another one of Xavier Cugat's orchestra, a foldout postcard book with pictures of London, a toy camera, some Swiss nail clippers, a collection of casino chips from Monte Carlo for playing poker . . .

The only link that could be established between all these knickknacks was, of course, our father's peripatetic existence. For some years—and we're jumping ahead now—Bundó, Gabriel, and Petroli retained some souvenir from every move they did. A box, a bag, a suitcase went astray by accident, and they shared it out like good brothers. They knew it was an offence but had made the excuse that it was social justice, portraying it as a well-deserved tip after so many hours of nonstop toil in conditions close to slavery. Anyway, who hasn't lost a box during a move? It's a fact of life.

Gabriel had confessed these thefts to our mothers, with the nonchalance of a Robin Hood, and even made us beneficiaries. Thanks to one of Cristòfol's finds, we were better able to follow the course of those years. In a shoebox, nestling among restaurant cards, city maps, and road atlases, was a black oilcloth notebook. It had a clandestine look about it and was somewhat battered by use. In it Gabriel had noted down the contents of each of the cases, boxes, and trunks they'd taken as booty from their moving jobs. Since he was a diligent person, there was nothing missing in the notebook: the route, date, and an itemization of everything that had been plundered, which they divvied up like proper pirates.

This highway robbers' existence, if you'll permit us the expression, afforded something close to an idyllic lifestyle for Gabriel and Bundó. It was idyllic because it compensated both of them for the instability of their early adolescence, while establishing them in a sort of itinerant paradise. Before talking about that, however, we have to get through a period of apprenticeship of hellish proportions.

It was the beginning of 1958, and Bundó and Gabriel were sixteen. The orphanage had moved to an establishment known as Llars Mundet, as had been planned for some time, and the change was very unsettling. The new institution, located high up in Vall d'Hebrón, was a mammoth construction, built a long way from everything, a whole city in itself that obliged them to turn their backs on Barcelona. Within four weeks of the opening of the new building, they were longing for the labyrinthine passageways of the House of Charity. Now, from a distance, they were tormented by the conviction they were missing out on a world contained in the noisy vice-ridden maze of streets beyond the orphanage. So, what on earth were they doing up there, in that mountainous semiwilderness? A few pensioners from a nearby old people's home wandered around filling their lungs with fresh air, and the younger kids had more space for playing outside, but what about these two? "This is the Wild West," they said and frittered away their time trapping lizards, improving their aim by throwing stones at an old tin, or plotting heroic escapes. Their indolence horrified the nuns, who wasted no time in finding a remedy. Since the boys were not especially brilliant students and, more importantly, because there was no family to take them in, the Mother Superior decided that they were old enough to leave their studies and get a job.

Gabriel wrote Spanish without too many spelling errors so he went off to be apprenticed to a typesetter in the House of Charity printing press. It didn't take him long to realize he didn't like the job. His main task was removing the residue of dry ink from the pieces of lead type that had gone through the printer. Sometimes they told him to stow the wooden pieces they used for titles in their correct boxes. At first he found it entertaining enough, not unlike doing a jigsaw puzzle—*F* with the *F*s, *B* with the *B*s . . . but it wasn't very exciting, and the supervisor often shouted at him to hurry up. "Move it, boy!" Only occasionally, as a consolation prize, did they let him compose half a column of news or a few ads paid for by the word, but, since the dingy place was airless and he was weak and malnourished, the upside-down letters made his head spin and brought on attacks of queasiness. He was locked up in the printers twelve hours a day, from seven to seven and, in addition, he had to work Saturdays and Sundays twice a month because the Monday newspaper *Hoja del Lunes* was printed in the House of Charity. After work he would have liked to amuse himself for a while in his old neighborhood and, now that they gave him a bit more freedom, to venture on to the Rambla, or beyond Plaça de la Universitat into Carrer Aribau. But he had to run to get the tram and bus, crossing the whole of Barcelona to get to Llars Mundet. The nuns were very strict about punctuality and, if he got back late, they wouldn't give him dinner. To add insult to injury, he got a good reprimand as well.

One evening, as the tram climbed Carrer Dos de Maig and the sooty façades were lit up by the flashes of electrical sparks, he noticed that two young girls were pointing at him and laughing. He instinctively looked at his reflection in the window and didn't recognize himself in the face staring back at him. There was an inky moustache under the nose, and in the masked features he saw a dejected, shabby man. All of a sudden he saw himself twenty years later, doing the same commute, and this made him unhappier still. "This must be what it's like to grow up," he resignedly told himself. A series of flashes from the overhead wires shook him from his reverie, and the reflection vanished from the window.

Bundó was more fortunate. It must be said that his sturdy build and resolute air in the face of life's surprises were a help. The Mother Superior, Sister Elvira, came from a well-heeled family of the Bonanova neighborhood. While she harbored a few pangs of conscience, her parents and siblings had repositioned themselves with surprising ease after all the upheaval of war and, ever since their kind of people had been in charge, had set about reestablishing the old order of things, which had worked so well in their favor. Needless to say, in January 1939, after two long years of eking out an existence in a property on the outskirts of Barcelona, in hiding and shitting themselves with fright, without any maids and grudgingly rationing their breakfast coffee, they'd been the first to hang a white sheet from the balcony of their apartment and to go down to Avinguda Diagonal, all of them together, to cheer on Franco's troops as they marched by in their victory parade. Robert Casellas, Sister Elvira's older brother, had inherited the family business and had to get it going again from scratch. Every July 18, on the anniversary of the start of the Civil War, he celebrated the godsend by making a generous donation to the House of Charity. By this we mean big money. He saw it as the best way of earning himself a privileged place in heaven. In return for the favor, he sometimes asked his sister to send him the odd boy to lug stuff for his moving company. He wanted them brawny, without any bad habits, and orphans because then they wouldn't bother him with family celebrations. This was the fate of the young Bundó.

The company was called La Ibérica Transport and Moving. The offices and garage were in Carrer Almogàvers, very close to Rambla del Poblenou. Three DKV vans and three Pegaso trucks, all boxy and gleaming, slept on the premises. The DKVs were used for the simpler jobs and rarely ventured outside the province, while the trucks were assigned the big moves and, when necessary, traveled from Barcelona all over Spain. The collectivizations of 1937 had

stripped the company of men and machines, but Robert Casellas
had got them back after some slick wheeling and dealing with the
Ministry of Transport. His pride and joy, all six vehicles looked
practically new, and he could spend hours and hours gazing at the
shiny beasts with paternal love. When they came back to roost
after a move, he'd have them washed and buffed by the latest arrivals among his workers until they looked as if they'd just rolled
off the assembly line.

Even though he was getting a miserly wage as an apprentice—
and, moreover, part of the money went directly from Casellas's
pocket to the nuns' account—Bundó enjoyed remembering those
days. It makes us suspect he conveniently forgot the suffering for
the sake of anecdote: minimizing it without recounting the true
measure of its pain because, that way, it was worth recalling.

"I remember the first days after I went to work at La Ibérica,"
he told Petroli in one of those nostalgia sessions he shared with
our father, "and I'd get back to Llars Mundet after dark. My back
would be totally done in. My arms and legs wouldn't do what I
wanted. I was so worn out I'd go straight to bed. In a morning
and an afternoon, for example, we'd dismantled and packed up
a second-floor apartment in Carrer d'Aragó and set it up again in
Avinguda del General Mola. The whole thing without an elevator,
hauling up the bulkiest pieces with a pulley and lugging the rest
up a narrow, twisting service stairway, as dark as the catacombs,
with the hysterical lady of the house following us everywhere to
make sure we didn't break anything and screeching at us, 'If anything is missing, you oafs, you'll be paying for it out of your own
pocket.' Even so, I liked it. I slowly got used to it and learned to see
the funny side. It's also true that going into other people's houses,
diving into Barcelona streets I never knew existed, and then riding around the city in the DKV or the truck (with a windshield
like a panoramic lookout) was something new for me, and it made
up for the effort, the hard sweats, the bruises, the scratches, the
complaints of the uniformed concierges, and the yelling of Senyor
Casellas."

Although he was shattered, Bundó's face was a picture of contentment when he slept after the day's labors. In their shared bedroom Gabriel watched him enviously and couldn't resist waking him up to moan about his troubles. Day after day, the House of Charity press took on the dimensions of a huge foreboding cave, as black as the forge of hell. It sounded as if he was describing being tortured by the Cheka. With heavy eyelids and emerging from the sponginess of sleep, Bundó listened, trying to cheer him up by making him see that his job as a furniture mover wasn't a piece of cake either. To make his case and impress his friend, he displayed the rope-burn slashes gouged into the palms of his hands from all the lifting and lowering of pieces of furniture. Secretly, however, he poured balm on his wounds by recalling the day he'd been given a two-peseta tip. Then, he'd drift back to sleep with a sucker's smile on his face once again as his placid little snores marked the rhythms of his dreams.

After he'd been working for La Ibérica for four months, during a moving job that the boss deemed to be of "the utmost importance," Bundó witnessed at close quarters an accident that would turn out to be providential. Providential for him, for our father, and, when all's said and done, for all of us. A new provincial secretary of the interior had been appointed by Franco and was moving to Barcelona from Segovia. Among the objects he'd decided to bring from his home was a massive, medieval-looking wood and cast-iron desk, which was to take pride of place in his office.

"This is an heirloom that has been in my family for centuries. Although it is cumbersome to move, it would pain me to leave it behind at this crucial point in my political career. Take great care with it, please," the government representative had solemnly announced to the three movers from Barcelona and two lads from the property who'd been told to help.

Carried by ten arms, the desk made its exit through the monumental doorway of the Segovia mansion, and docilely submitted to being eased into the truck, but, once in Barcelona, as four men unloaded it, it started bucking like a wild animal and, with a twist and a flip, shot out of their hands. The result of the disaster was—

in this order of importance, according to Senyor Casellas—one split desk leg, a crack that would be very difficult to repair, and the broken—in fact, smashed—right foot of one of the La Ibérica workmen.

The bones of Bundó's injured workmate, who was on the point of retiring, had seen too much wear and tear, and the insurance company doctors advised him not to carry any more weight and to get on with claiming his invalidity pension. Senyor Casellas spent a whole week, until the crack in the desk was fixed, bemoaning his bad luck in a lachrymose singsong dirge, so gratingly shrill that it set the workers' teeth on edge. When the storm had passed, Bundó went to see him and in a barely audible voice asked whether he'd thought about a replacement for the injured man. A replacement? No, not yet. Then Bundó began singing Gabriel's praises, waxing lyrical about his physical makeup, which was all sinew, and his willingness to work. He was a Hercules. If necessary, he could ask the nuns for references.

"Good heavens, anyone would think he was your girlfriend," Casellas replied with a sneer in his voice. "All right, let him come and see me one of these days."

A week later, making the most of having a Monday off from the press, Gabriel asked Sister Elvira for permission to go and see Senyor Casellas. Bundó had more than once described his employer's grotesque appearance, sparing no details or snide observations, but at that first face-to-face interview at which he was very nervous, Gabriel had the impression that he was looking at a dummy from some sideshow at a fair. Senyor Casellas was short and fat. His pendulous jowls met in a double chin, which divided like two rolls of fat on a baby's belly, and the skin of his fleshy cheeks shone as if he'd just demolished a very oily roast dinner. His voice, too high-pitched, didn't match the bloated body. Now that he could actually see the man, Gabriel realized that Bundó could imitate him with comic brilliance. When he spoke, he smirked without being aware of it, and waved his hands around, pointing and gesturing with fingers as short and thick as sausages.

When he was silent, listening to somebody, he had a strange tic
that involved moving his top lip up and down, then clenching it in
his teeth as if about to start munching on it. Trying to hide this,
perhaps, he'd cultivated a pencil moustache of the kind favored by
the regime. Since his status as a businessman required some mark
of authority—and somebody must have pointed this out because
it wouldn't have come naturally to him—he'd taken two further
steps toward establishing himself as a tyrannical boss and, at the
same time, appearing utterly ridiculous: One was his choice of
suit, made to measure by the Santaclara tailoring establishment,
with which he always wore a bluish shirt—not the official blue,
but hinting at it—and secondly, although he was from a Catalan
family, he addressed everyone at work in Spanish.

Gabriel knocked at the door of Senyor Casellas's office and
heard the jarring voice telling him to come in. He entered.

"Hello, I'm Gabriel Delacruz. I've come from Llars Mundet.
Bundó . . ."

"Hello, hello . . ." Casellas cut him short, looked him up and
down. "You're a bit on the runty side, aren't you? How much do
you weigh?"

"Seventy kilos, Señor Casellas."

"That's not true, you're skinnier than that. I'm telling you. Go
back and weigh yourself. Don't the sisters feed you? Tell them to
give you more to eat if you want to work here. Especially spinach.
It's got a lot of iron. And lentils. And meat. You've got to eat more
meat. You've got to eat the same as Bundó, who's built like a bull."

Gabriel nodded. He was all too aware that neither he nor
Bundó had tasted a veal steak or stew, let alone a beefsteak, for
months, probably since the day when a rake-thin woman with the
face of a scavenger bird, Doña Carmen Polo de Franco, had come
to visit the House of Charity. All of the children had been made
to put on their best clothes and parade in the courtyard before the
local authorities, and the choir of the Female Section had sung
the "Salve Regina."

"Do you really want to work as a furniture mover? It's a very
hard, demanding life . . ."

"Yes, Señor Casellas." Bundó had recommended that Gabriel should call him Señor Casellas because he liked the formal address and it made him more amenable.

Casellas looked him up and down again and was just about to say something when the phone rang. At the first ring, the company owner squared his shoulders like a soldier and sat up straight backed in his office chair. Then he picked up the handset and started talking with an important client, some big fish. He listened with great attention and said "yes, yes, of course, of course, yes, naturally, *sí, sí, claro, claro, sí, cómo no,*" to everything, oozing sycophancy with every word. A good two minutes went by until he remembered that Gabriel was still standing there. Then he covered up the earpiece for a moment and said, "Go on, off you go, off you go now. Tell Sister Elvira you'll be starting next Monday. You won't be paid for the first two weeks. You'll be on trial. You'll go with Bundó in the van. He'll be responsible for you. Ah, and as I was saying before, eat more spinach, lad. You've got to be a Popeye, or whatever his name is."

# 4

## Age Without a Name

The change of job was a tonic for our father. From the front of the van, wonderful views of the city replaced the dismal sight of printing presses. The narcotic smell of ink faded away into some cranny of his memory, only to resurface when it was completely inoffensive, for example when it occasionally drifted out of the open pages of a newspaper at breakfast time, or when a leaking pen decorated his chest with a navy-blue medal. In Gabriel's first weeks with La Ibérica, when he and Bundó were arriving or leaving in the DKV, Senyor Casellas watched them from a distance, smug in the confirmation of his own good judgment when he took on the new orphan mover. It seemed that, rather than leaving him tired out, lugging furniture and boxes was doing him good, making him a little hardier every day.

About to turn seventeen, Gabriel and Bundó had bodies that obeyed them. With muscles as pliant as rubber they could carry any weight. Besides being in good physical condition, the two friends were both easygoing by nature, which also helped. They'd shed the age of innocence but hadn't fully entered the age of calculation and were breezing through life with just the right amount of baggage, unburdened by any extraneous weight or terrible hardships. They'd reached an age that isn't an age, one that has no name and, in all likelihood, the job of shifting furniture, emptying and filling houses and loading up the trailer with all the useless things that people accumulate protected them against the temptation of growing up, thinking about marrying the first girl to nab them and surrendering to more mundane worries.

This sensation of weightlessness was enhanced both by the excitement of novelty and the contrast with their workmates, who were more accustomed to routine and yoked to everyday affairs. Neither Gabriel nor Bundó had a driver's license, of course, and they had to wait a few years before they could get one, so when they went out it was always as flunkies for some more experienced worker. The owner wanted to toughen up the apprentices and tended to assign them to one of the vans covering the moves within the city of Barcelona. As they were learning the trade they gradually got to know everyone on the La Ibérica payroll. There was Romero from Murcia, who used to spit out of the window not giving a damn about anyone else and who, with the deftness of a one-armed man, could roll cigarettes while he was driving; there were Sebastià and Ricard Nogueró, two mutually ill-disposed brothers from the neighborhood of Sants who were at each other's throats all day long; El Tembleque, "The Wobbler," a once-promising bullfighter from Andalusia who now lived in Sant Adrià; Sirera and Brauli, who were supporters of the Espanyol Soccer Club; Fornido, a hefty chap who did honor to his name; Tartana and Petroli, who were brothers-in-law and friends; Wenceslau, known as Vences, who made the most of any break to set up a game of cards (and who, we suspect, taught Gabriel the cardsharp's arts); Baltanás, brother of an executed militant of the Iberian Anarchist Federation, who'd dishonored his family by becoming a Franco supporter; Deulofeu—"God Made Him"—another foundling, as his name suggested, also raised in the House of Charity where he was despised as a snitch, the nuns' little spy; and then there was Grandpa Cuniller with his unfortunate attacks of lumbago whenever things needed to be carried upstairs . . .

What a bunch of riffraff! The older ones must be dead by now, or about to make the final move, the one where instead of lugging the box they're inside it. Apart from Petroli, who was soon to enter the scene as their companion in notching up thousands of kilometers of European roads, the two friends' favorite comrade-in-arms was El Tembleque. El Tembleque, who had a picture of the Virgin of Rocío on his dashboard altar and the Betis Soccer Club pennant hanging from the rearview mirror, often drove them crazy with his misadventures-of-an-ill-starred-bullfighter stories that he told in a gravelly voice, the product of his partiality for *sol y sombra*, a brandy-and-anise concoction that evoked the "sun and shade" of the bullring. If bad luck decreed that the move that day should take them past the Las Arenas or La Monumental bullring, he'd lean on the horn of the DKV with all the passion of a fanatic, after which he'd resume his monologue about that August afternoon in 1948 when he was about to make his debut as a fully fledged bull-fighter in Linares. The great Manolete had died there barely a year before. Had he ever told them about that? His career, he recalled with shining eyes, lasted exactly eight minutes and twenty sweeps of the cape, followed by a chorus of *¡Olé! ¡Olé!* from an enthusiastic public, but the animal, as treacherous as they get, charged and put an end to his vocation forever.

"D'Artañán, the fucking bull was called..." he'd say at that point in the story, and then he'd continue dreamily. "I was no coward, mind you, but sometimes I think I should have snuffed it then. Could a bullfighter know greater glory than dying in the same ring as the legendary Manolete?"

The only consolation left to him, the only way to offset the tragedy was to fight the odd *vaquilla*, some hot-blooded little heifer, in his neighborhood's annual festivities every June. The Neighborhood Association people looked for a patch of vacant ground somewhere around Besòs, down by the river and, with a few sticks and bags of sand, improvised an enclosure that they could use as a bullring for an afternoon. Alongside the ring, they set up a snack bar, open day and night and lit up by a string of colored light bulbs that were also used for the local Christmas tree. Although more than ten years had gone by, El Tembleque always summoned up that *corrida* in Linares to give himself pride of place on the poster and, lest there should be any doubts, presented himself in the ring dressed in his "suit of lights," the same *traje de luces* he'd worn in Linares. His admirers, the novice bullfighters of his neighborhood, endowed him with a legendary aura. Of scrawny build, El Tembleque slipped easily into his bullfighter's gear with the same courage as on the first day, but the cloth had faded over the years, and the rhinestones and sequins had lost some of their luster, even though his wife put a lot of elbow grease into polishing them. "It just goes to show, there's nothing like the sun of Andalusia!" he'd shout by way of justification. They say the bullfighter displayed his old skills when it came to distracting the heifer, but what most impressed the onlookers, especially the kids, was that the trousers still retained the hole made by the fateful goring. A superstitious man, El Tembleque had never wanted it mended, and when his fans and friends had a close-up look, sometimes even asking if they could stick their finger in (which he was delighted to agree to), they discovered a dreadful scar. The usual reaction was to make a sign of the cross, begging for God's blessing.

His fixation lasted half a lifetime. Years later, when the Sant Adrià Bullfighting Club languished and the neighborhood associations joined up to have a stand at the April Fair in Barberà del Vallès, El Tembleque felt unappreciated and hung up his matador's cape for the last time. Then, burning with Catalan nationalist fever, he became so enamoured with the country's ancient tradition of human castles that he joined a group of *castellers* in the neighborhood, whereupon they promised him that, at the very least, he could have a place among the third-level group.

Thanks to the hours they spent in the DKV, Gabriel and Bundó ended up with doctorates in El Tembleque's doomed biography. The bull D'Artañán had grown in the retelling to take on the dimensions and power of a beast from Hades. And according to El Tembleque, there were plenty of important people in the bullfighting world who—just imagine!—regularly begged him to leave the fucking moving business and get back into the *ruedo* like a real man. The two friends learned that these crocodile tears were only shed after a shot of *sol y sombra*, or two shots when necessary, even if that meant delivering the load an hour late and then having to invent some excuse and put up with Senyor Casellas' wrath and insults.

El Tembleque could be a pain in the neck, sure, but Gabriel and Bundó preferred him to the rest of the workers.

"There were exceptions," Dad explained to our mothers, "like Grandpa Cuniller and Tartana, old-timers who'd seen it all, but most of the workers were full of their own importance because they drove a DKV and we didn't. On the days when Casellas sent us out as roustabouts in their vans, they carried on as if they were the right hand of the big boss. They yelled at us for the slightest mistake and often lectured us like puffed-up generals. Even when the conversation was relaxed and we were talking about women (a subject that, as mere fledglings, Bundó and I gladly joined in with), they'd give us an earful of their tacky Don Juan advice on everything, as heroes of the most amazing sexual exploits. What Tarzans! And if we didn't show enough admiration, or if they caught us exchanging glances trying not to laugh (because we'd been sending them up outside of working hours), they took it badly and then they made our lives impossible when we were loading and unloading. You know what all that was about? They were boiling over with frustration and they didn't have that combination of dreamer and Andalusian appeal that El Tembleque had."

Here's another example of that contrast. When they were driving around in the van, or stopped at the traffic lights, El Tembleque was the supreme master when it came to tooting the horn, leaning out the window, and flirting with girls in the street. He liked them all and had no inhibitions. His repertoire was imaginative, and he knew how to be saucy without causing any harm. At first the girl would act offended, but she always ended up smiling and sneaking a look at them out of the corner of her eye. Then there were drivers like Brauli or Baltanás who, trying to impress the youngsters Bundó and Gabriel, parroted lines they'd learned ages before from El Tembleque, but, lacking conviction, the words were just stale blather that only revealed their innate coarseness. Then the women scoffed at them or wouldn't as much as look at them while the two friends cringed with embarrassment.

"They're all tarts," the driver would then say and, after a contemplative pause, "except for my wife, and she's a saint."

For us, the Christophers, and especially our mothers, El Tembleque is the only La Ibérica employee whose name survives
with its qualities intact. Our mothers all agree when they recall
the affection with which Gabriel, Bundó, and Petroli spoke of
the bullfighter trucker. Our father used to praise his absence of
malice—"a really good guy"—and Petroli said that his greatest virtue, leaving aside the bulls, was that you always knew where you
were with him. Bundó couldn't resist imitating the spectacle of El
Tembleque picking up a box or helping to heft some piece of furniture. Whenever he set about lifting up a load, the gored leg sent
out rhythmic spasms that soon had his whole body jiggling like a
wind-up toy. Shuddering with the weight he bore in his arms, his
face contorted and neck so strained you could see all the muscles
and tendons standing out, he looked as if he was going to fly apart
any moment, like a marionette that's suddenly lost the support-
ive tautness of its strings: one arm here, a leg there, belly on the
ground, bits and pieces everywhere. It seems that, even when he'd
deposited the box inside the truck, these convulsive tremors took
a few more seconds to subside. Years later, as was to be expected,
the same fits of trembling came over him when he was up on level
three of one of the Sant Adrià human castles: a column with Saint
Vitus' Dance, threatening to bring the whole thing tumbling down.

Sometimes, when he turned up to work with his head befogged
by recollections of his bullfighting days, or woozy after a night of
too much *sol y sombra*, El Tembleque used to let Gabriel or Bundó
drive the van while he dozed in the front seat. Since they didn't
yet have a license, the two friends celebrated this as if they'd won
the lottery and divided up the route, half each. These were always
trips within Barcelona and, if El Tembleque was fast asleep (they
could tell by the deep rumble of his snores), they'd take a longer
route or make a detour when they saw they were getting close to
their destination. Sometimes, with the excuse of getting in some
driving practice, they'd venture into one of the neighborhoods with
higgledy-piggledy streets, like Sants or Sant Andreu, so they could
practise maneuvering in tight angles. The only hitch with this was
when they got to the house where the move was happening: Fast

asleep, El Tembleque wouldn't wake up, despite the most brutal tactics. They could torture him by tickling, or shouting in his ear that their cargo was on fire in the back of the truck, or telling him that a procession of naked majorettes was coming down the street, without him showing the slightest sign of emerging from his slumbers. Needless to say, he always woke up when Gabriel and Bundó had already dealt with more than half the load.

And now that we have introduced El Tembleque, we need to go back to the day when, under his patronage, Gabriel and Bundó kept their first box. (We could also say "stole," but that has an accusatory ring that we don't like and that doesn't suit our purposes; or "side-tracked," which was Gabriel's favorite word; or "mislaid," which was how the matter appeared officially in the reports for Senyor Casellas). In any case, the very first, half-involuntary theft never appeared in the notebook in which our father recorded all the loot from the moves, but it did inaugurate a tradition that would bring them moments of great happiness.

As happens with most tribal rituals, the initiation in pillage was supervised by a champion, none other than El Tembleque. Let us locate ourselves. The departure point of that job was Madrid. An out-of-favor bigwig from the Banco Zaragozano had been transferred to the branch office in Barcelona. Although he'd been sent into exile, his destination was an apartment in Via Laietana, high up, ostentatious and boasting more rooms than the Prado Museum. The previous day, the three workers had loaded up the truck in the capital and, at nightfall after a strength-gathering dinner in a Zaragoza roadhouse, they bought some *adoquines*, the large cobblestone-shaped toffees they make in Catalayud, and set off again. El Tembleque drove all night without stopping while Bundó and Gabriel slept beside him. In order to stay awake, he listened to the radio, tried to nibble the toffees, and smoked his Tres Carabelas cigars with the window half open. All at once. By the time they got to the top of the hill at El Bruc, the lines on the road were going blurry on him so he stopped the truck and asked the two friends to take over for a while. He'd have a nap and take the wheel

again before they got to the hill at l'Ordal. They couldn't wake
him up. Gabriel and Bundó took turns at driving, commending
themselves to God and praying that the Guardia Civil wouldn't appear to stop them. They went through l'Ordal, down to Martorell,
entered Barcelona, and stopped the truck in front of the building
in Via Laietana at about ten o'clock in the morning. El Tembleque
hadn't as much as twitched the whole trip (except in Gran Via, as
they passed the Las Arenas bullring, when his slumbers had been
disturbed for about thirty seconds by a few bovine snuffles), and,
if it wasn't for his sunken chest rising and falling as he breathed,
they would have sworn he was dead.

El Tembleque vegetated for a couple more hours and woke
up when most of the work was done. The building had a service
elevator at the foot of the stairs, and Bundó and Gabriel had made
good progress with the more hulking bits of furniture and objects.
In keeping with the reversible order of the move—the last thing
loaded is the first to be unloaded—by the time El Tembleque
joined them they'd already started to remove the cardboard boxes
piled at the back of the trailer, all of them the same. It was clear
that El Tembleque had woken up because, while the two of them
were mechanically picking up the boxes like a couple of somnam-
bulists, the man wouldn't shut up. Each time they passed on a box
in the chain he'd come out with some random comment.

"These boxes smell of money." He sniffed. "Don't you notice it?"

"Lovely apartment, eh? You can see that these folks have got a
lot of dough."

"Come on, boy, shake a leg. The reward's the rest of the day
in bed."

"Want a toffee, Bundó? We've still got some in the cab."

"They're hard but good for strengthening the jaws, these damn
toffees."

"*Soy minero, y me quito las penas...*" Now the singing miner,
he's drowning his sorrows in wine, beer, and rum.

"Well, I'm telling you these boxes smell like money. Get a whiff,
get a whiff."

Gabriel took the last box from El Tembleque's unsteady hands. The trailer now only contained ropes, pulleys, and a few blankets they'd used to wrap up lamps and other fragile objects.

"See you later, alligator . . . In a while, crocodile."

Then they went up to the apartment to get the delivery note signed. One of Senyor Casellas's clerks was in charge of collecting the payment later. They found the banker's wife in one of the rooms counting boxes.

"I count fifty-two boxes," she said.

According to the delivery note, they'd been entrusted with fifty-three boxes in Madrid.

"That's impossible, madam. You must have lost count . . ." El Tembleque replied. The two young men, El Tembleque, and the lady of the house started counting all over again. They checked all the boxes scattered in disorderly piles throughout the residence, each one starting at a different point. The numbers mingled in the air as if at a fish auction.

"I make it fifty-four," said Bundó. "One more than there are supposed to be."

"Come on! I get fifty-three boxes and that's the right number."

"Well, I get fifty-two," Gabriel weighed in. El Tembleque shot him a killer look.

"And . . . fifty-three. You're right. Fifty-three. They're all there," the lady said and duly signed the delivery note.

Down in the street again, before heading back to the La Ibérica warehouse, they finished the job of picking up the ropes and folding the blankets.

"Fucking hell! The missing box," Bundó shouted, after picking up a blanket strategically positioned in one corner.

"I'll take it up . . ." Gabriel offered.

"No, you won't, sweetheart," El Tembleque interrupted him. "Isn't the delivery note nice and signed? Well, there's no missing box here. These people are rolling in dough. They're from the Banco Zaragozano."

The next morning, as soon as he arrived at La Ibérica, El Tembleque called the two friends and presented them with a pair of matching bookends, one each, reproductions in polychrome wood of the famous Egyptian Seated Scribe. He informed them that, as his share of the box, he'd only kept an illustrated dictionary and the three almanacs from 1956, 1957, and 1958.

"Not much there. For my little girl. They'll be useful for her at school and all that."

Gabriel and Bundó gave the bookends to the nuns at the home. For some days a sense of guilt gnawed at their stomachs, a legacy of their upbringing at the orphanage. After a while, though, when they were traveling around Europe and boxes and packets got sidetracked, were left lying in the truck, mislaid, or never loaded, this primordial guilt underwent a decisive shift. Excuses, justifications, and evasiveness had become their manifesto, and it only got better and better. If ever they thought about that original day, Bundó and Gabriel felt an ingenuous, almost cloying tenderness, just like memories of one's first girlfriend.

Though it may seem that the opposite is true, we're making progress with the life of our father. Things are getting complicated. The passage gets dark and narrow, there are doors with stuck hinges or a lock rusty from disuse, and when we try to open them they won't cooperate. If we spy a glimmer of light escaping under the door, a narrative thread too faint to follow up, we're assailed by a mixture of discouragement and doubt. Well, it's not easy to make our memories fit together, we say, trying to encourage each other. Here you have the Christophers—four sons of four sceptical mothers and only one escape-artist father—who are trying to reconstruct a common past. We've been striving to speak in a single voice for some time now, but we've decided that each one of us will eventually have his own chapter to let it all out. His turn for the solo. Meanwhile, we're all wondering: *Are* we getting anywhere? In moments of euphoria, when dates tie up, events dovetail, and witnesses are in agreement, we can discern some secret but we don't know what it is. It could very well be that we're wrong and it doesn't even exist, this secret or whatever it might be.

Things are getting complicated, as we say, because Gabriel and Bundó are finally on the verge of settling into the age without a name, and everyone knows that nothing in life is final.

"We're about to change into third gear," says Christof smugly, but we other three remind him of the promise not to overdo the motorway and driving school metaphors.

Now we're flipping through the pages of the calendar at vertiginous speed, as if they've been caught by a blustery autumn wind, and we come to rest on a day in October 1958. We're at Llars Mundet. Evening. Gabriel and Bundó have been together at La Ibérica for about a year now and have just got back from work after a long day's labors. Today they've done a short but god-awful move, the kind that really does you in, from the Sant Gervasi neighborhood to a dump in the old city center. Narrow streets, obdurate stairways, tiny rooms. A widow and her good-for-nothing son can't make ends meet. Tears. And tomorrow, the same damn thing. The two friends have a quick wash and a liberal squirt of cologne to cover up the acrid stink of sweat. They're sitting on the beds in their shared room waiting for dinnertime. They're summoned to Sister Elvira's office. Off they go. Bundó's stomach is roaring loudly. They knock at the door, and from inside the energetic voice of the Mother Superior tells them to come in.

Another door opens for us.

The nun looked up and observed Gabriel and Bundó's entrance with a pang of tenderness. For more than ten years she'd watched these two boys growing up as if they were her own children. She'd fed them when they were small, seen them take their first communion, scolded them, and punished them for their own good. Now, as she contemplated the two of them, she could glimpse both the sheltered years of the House of Charity and the jungle-like future, full of the temptations they were going to find when they went out into the world. Her eyes glistened—it always happened when she had to deal with this situation—and, to take heart, she reminded herself that the two lads were working at her brother's trucking company. One way or another, everything was still in the family.

"I've asked you to come," she said, "because I have to give you two bits of news. One good and one bad. Which do you want first?"

"The bad!" Bundó declared, but he really wanted to hear the good news first.

"The good," Gabriel answered in chorus with Bundó although he really preferred to have the bad news first.

Before speaking, the nun paused for effect. "You've grown up," she observed, adopting a solemn tone. "Time flies. You're seventeen years old now. Almost men. We've spoken with your teachers at the school and have decided that it's time for you to make your own way. Thanks be to God, you're now working and earning a wage, is that not so? And now you will have to learn how to manage your own money. There are other more needy children who require our attention. Bundó, Gabriel"—and here she paused—"at the end of the month you'll have to leave the home. That's the bad news."

Their faces began to light up but they quickly masked it. So leaving, getting away, getting the hell away from the home—at last, at last!—was the bad news.

In a bid to buy time, Bundó said, "You're right, Sister. My bed's got too short and my feet stick out over the end."

"And the good news?" Gabriel inquired.

We'll spare ourselves the nun's speech, which took the form of a sermon crammed with Mothers of God, prayers, and declarations of gratitude winging heavenward. And, indeed, the good news was very good. Thanks to their being orphans and, in particular, thanks to Senyor Casellas, who had a childhood friend in military headquarters—and this was big-time string-pulling—the two friends would be exempt from military service. At first, the good news impressed them less than the supposedly bad news—because they'd always seen military service as their ticket out of the home—but it took less than a minute for it all to fall into place. The shiny vision beyond the prison walls beckoned them, brighter than they'd ever imagined. They were unable to stifle a shout of freedom and couldn't stop laughing. In the midst of the frenzy, Bundó rushed over to the nun and planted kisses on both her cheeks. The nun gave him a friendly shove—get away with you!—and blushed. Gabriel was tempted to imitate his friend but, at the last minute, merely opted for doing something awkward with his arms and making an affectionate bow in her direction (and one can't discard the possibility that he'd suddenly remembered the titillating tale starring Sister Mercedes).

Making a big deal out of the little kerfuffle because she had a secret penchant for this kind of familiarity, the Mother Superior straightened her coif, smoothed out the non-existent creases in her habit, and immediately set about putting a damper on things.

"You must be eternally grateful to God and to Senyor Casellas, in that order, for what they have done for you," she said, shifting from Catalan to Spanish to give more gravity to her words. "In fact, it's not entirely true that you have been exempted from military service: You're going to enter the ranks, so to say, of La Ibérica moving company and it is my expectation that you will serve Senyor Casellas with the same devotion as our soldiers serve the fatherland and General Franco."

Only a few months earlier, declaring that Spain represented "unity of destiny in the universal," Franco had presented the principles of the National Movement, and the Mother Superior had learned them by heart. The two boys cagily agreed with her pronouncements. As they heard her out, Gabriel mentally drew a fine moustache on the nun's pasty face and realized that she and Senyor Casellas were like two peas in a pod.

And now, if we may, we'll close the doors of the House of Charity and Llars Mundet forever.

# 5

## A Home on the Ronda
## de Sant Antoni

Destiny, playful and mischievous as a puppy, landed Gabriel and Bundó in a boarding house. Whenever a youngster left the orphanage, the nuns made inquiries as to whether there were any relatives, even distant ones, with a view to handing over responsibility to the family. This time, however, they'd known for years that the two friends were alone. They let them leave, then, with the recommendation that they should install themselves in some economical, but above all decent, lodgings. Gabriel and Bundó didn't need to be told twice. Acting on the advice of Grandpa Cuniller at La Ibérica, who'd spent more than half his life in boarding houses, they opted for a room with two beds in an establishment on the Ronda de Sant Antoni. The building was on the corner of Carrer Sant Gil, just a few steps from the local market, although the main reason for choosing that particular place was that it was very close to the House of Charity. They only had to walk along Carrer Ferlandina to get to one of its entrances, the one opening into the Nadal i Dou courtyard. It's not that the two friends were yearning to hang around their old orphanage again—indeed Gabriel had fled from the printers with the guilty conscience of a deserter—but they had a sense of going back to the neighborhood where they'd grown up. They wiped the slate clean of the time they'd spent in exile in Llars Munder and were at last able to satisfy an urge that had been repressed since early adolescence. They almost swooned at the thought of the bittersweet perfume of the streets of the red-light district, the Barri Xino, at nightfall. Now free of the nuns' vigilance, they were longing to roam its most notorious corners, and nothing would deprive them of the thrill of these so-often-imagined attractions.

It was autumn 1958, and the boarding house captured perfectly the frontier spirit of that part of Barcelona: It overlooked the cramped spaces of the Barri Xino at the back, while its front door opened on to the Ronda de Sant Antoni with its ambience of a Parisian boulevard. The establishment occupied the whole of the spacious second floor of a four-story building, and it had a well-lit living room thanks to the glassed-in balcony overlooking the street, but its interior offered much less than what the façade promised. This was a modest boarding house, in the shape of a funnel and organized around a long passageway. There were six dark bedrooms with high ceilings and fake moldings, a bathroom with a translucent door—on the other side of which you could always make out gelatinous shadows—and a separate toilet in a narrow little room. The landlady's kitchen and bedroom were set apart, a kind of secret annex that was off-limits to the lodgers and, immediately after that, the apartment widened out into the luminous living-cum-dining room that looked on to the Ronda.

With no known name beyond the dented sign at the entrance— "Pension. Travelers and Long-term. Second Floor"—the boarding house belonged to a Senyora Rifà, who hailed from the plain near Vic. A petite energetic woman, a human dynamo, Senyora Natàlia Rifà had inherited the business ten years earlier from a first cousin of her mother's. A spinster, well over fifty, suspicious and coquettish by nature, she scurried around her domain as if there was a constant danger of one of the rooms being set on fire. Notwithstanding all the disappointments she had borne, she hadn't renounced the pleasure of a little primping and preening every morning, and she had great faith in a corset that made her backside look misshapen. Her boarders only ever saw her in a dressing gown when she went into the kitchen. She always got dressed up to serve the food at mealtimes. She was clean and required the lodgers to be clean too and, if she saw that they had a future in her house, she educated them in all-around tidiness. She cooked passably well, which is to say not stinting on the salt but without much joy, and that might be why she only accepted men in her pension—because she knew they were easier to please.

The second floor of the building in Ronda de Sant Antoni hadn't been renovated since well before the Civil War. The walls sweated in summer and patches of damp, which took ages to vanish, appeared in some rooms after rain (and an insanely superstitious student from Jaca saw faces in them). The furniture creaked with age and the kitchen utensils were blackened by fire. This rather fusty atmosphere was accentuated by the most outlandish feature of the house: its collection of stuffed animals.

Birds, Canidae, rodents, or members of the feline species: each room exhibited its own variety of embalmed creature. It was a veritable natural history museum. In the vestibule, crouched in semi-ambush above the coat and hat rack, a shiny-pelted fox stood sentry: You can come in; you can't come in. On the floor, beside the umbrella stand, a kindly looking dalmatian kept it company, sitting up on its back legs, apparently soliciting caresses from anyone entering or leaving. A squirrel with its tail all fluffed up like a feather duster and on its way up the bookcase in the hallway propped up the volumes of *Reader's Digest Selections* (the landlady had also inherited the subscription). In the display cabinet in the dining room, a sky-blue parrot and a multihued cockatoo with permanently open beaks chattered incessantly, miming the most frequently used words of the occupants of the house. In a different corner of the same cabinet, a hummingbird with iridescent feathers, its wings whirring in perpetual still motion, imbibed at an exotic plastic flower. On top of an old cocktail cabinet, a genet with its mouth half open sighed over such succulent prey.

This obsession with taxidermy even extended to the landing. Next to her door and with permission from the other residents of the building, who saw it as a touch of class that graced the whole house, Senyora Rifà had mounted the head of a wild goat, the kind that has spiraling, sharp-tipped horns. Once they'd earned their landlady's approval, the most faithful clients were let into the se-

cret of the goat: The semibared teeth of the beast guarded a copy
of the key to the pension for latecomers and the absentminded.

The inhabitants of the pension took a while to get used to the
disquieting presence of all these creatures. As they lingered at
the table over coffee, tall stories were told about the poor quality of the taxidermy in some specimens. Hearing them, newcom-
ers started scratching uneasily and, for some time afterward, their
dreams were filled with bloated-bellied beasts and revolting flies
buzzing around them.

Senyora Rifà also had a cat, a live cat. The animal, which had
become unapproachable after the half-hearted caresses of so many
hands—a sort of pension levy or toll—seemed to revel in startling
people. Without any warning at all, after spending hours and hours
sleeping on the sofa or immobile atop its favorite piece of furniture,
it would let out a screech and leap onto the shoulder of whoever was
nearest. The lodgers hated it, and the sentiment was mutual. Apart
from the cat, which was the original furry occupant of the house, the
invasion of animals, the motionless ones, had occurred in the days
when one of Senyora Rifà's lodgers was a traveling salesman promot-
ing Rioja wines. Gabriel and Bundó just missed out on meeting him,
but some of the residents made it their business to induct them into
the mystery. The gentleman in question, a widower with two daughters of more than marriageable age who were the bane of his existence, lived in the pension for almost four years, from 1954 to 1958.
At first, he was there one week a month, just enough time to do
the rounds of Barcelona's restaurants and businesses, but, after six
months, his stays extended and, claiming a terrific amount of work,
he was now spending twenty days in the boarding house and ten in
Logroño. He and the landlady used the familiar *tu* and they enjoyed
each other's company—on the mattress, every night. The happiest
days in Senyora Rifà's life were those she spent as this man's concu-
bine. She confessed this to Bundó on more than one anisette-soaked
evening, whereupon he gave her his shoulder to cry on. In the end,
the gentleman also endowed her with his stuffed-animal collection.

It seems that, thanks to some childhood memory related to an
old Republican schoolteacher, the gentleman from Logroño was a

great lover of taxidermy. Every Friday afternoon he went off, like an explorer setting out on a hunt, to pay a visit to the taxidermist's that used to be in the Plaça Reial. He gazed and gazed again upon the exhibited items and, from time to time, when one of them stole his heart, spent a few pesetas and brought it home. Senyora Rifà tended to receive the new acquisition with a wrinkling of her nose—"dust and more dust," she said to herself—but immediately set about looking for somewhere to put it. She saw each new adoption as a sign of permanence. As long as the animals were there, she reasoned—and it wasn't as if they were going to be escaping all by themselves some fine day—it would never occur to the gentleman from Logroño to leave her.

She was wrong, of course.

She was wrong because on her return from the market one September morning, that time of day when the house was empty and she listened to the serial on Ràdio Barcelona while she was cooking lunch, she found a folded piece of paper on the dining-room table. The gentleman from Logroño informed her, with immoderate stylistic flourishes, that he'd been obliged to hasten back to his home town. His two daughters, together and in concert, had attempted suicide. He'd write with further news as soon as he could. Lots of kisses, et cetera. Senyora Natàlia Rifà shuddered at the situation and felt sorry for the man. She then noticed the reek of Dandy Male and realized that the paper she was holding in her hands was perfumed. What a strange thing. Who would perfume such a sorrowful note unless he was soliciting forgiveness for something? She rushed to the room that the gentleman from Logroño still rented in order to keep up appearances and flung open his wardrobe. Empty. Fearing she was going to faint, Senyora Rifà flopped onto the bed. Immobile on top of a chest of drawers, a ferret mocked its landlady with a scornful leer.

In the first few weeks, Senyora Natàlia Rifà pinned her hopes on the stuffed zoo, but her longing for a letter postmarked Logroño gradually dwindled away to nothing. One evening at dinnertime, after two months of resisting renting out the man's room, she realized that looks of compassion were being exchanged between her lodgers. She was an expert at deciphering the undercurrents running among them. She asked a few questions and was met by the same deadpan expressions, but, in the end, a young fellow from Berga, a notary's assistant and a blabbermouth by nature, couldn't stand it any longer: That very afternoon as he was returning from the courts he'd seen the gentleman from Logroño walking along carrer Trafalgar. He. Was. Accompanied. By. A. Floozy—if one might put it thus.

Senyora Rifà immediately started putting him down. Just what you'd expect from a good-for-nothing who owes me money. That's the kind of thing that happens in Barcelona. When she was a child her family, God-fearing people, had always taught her to repress any show of feelings. The next day she squeezed another bed into the vacated room and filled it with two new heaven-sent boarders, Gabriel and Bundó. This convinced her that she was starting a new chapter. The very same day she moved some of the animals around and threw one out, but only one. She got rid of a poor raccoon that had traveled halfway around the world only to end up in the garbage, and all because it too painfully reminded her, with the mask around its glassy eyes, of the gentleman from Logroño, whose expression darkened every time he started carping about the problem of his unmarried daughters.

From that day onward, Senyora Rifà got into the habit of naming the rooms according to the animals they housed. The Badger Room. The Woodcock Room. The Lizard Room. Bundó and Gabriel entered the pension occupying the Ferret Room, a modest two-person room but with the small luxury of a window opening into the light well. In the summer one was grateful for the little bit of air that came in. Senyora Rifà rented them the room for a ridiculously low price. She was in a hurry to fill it with life again. Furthermore, since they were so busy with the moving, always traveling about, they came to an agreement that they'd never have lunch in the boarding house.

When our mothers asked about where he lived in Barcelona, our father didn't deceive them and told them about the pension, although he never elaborated on specific details of the neighborhood, the rooms, or what kind of life people led there. He and Bundó were in the boarding house for many years—first sharing a room, then, after a while, each with his own room—and the six rooms of the house were jumbled up in his memory as an indivisible whole. A bed, a wardrobe, a chair, a bedside table, maybe a mirror and a washbasin, and the stuffed animal. Senyora Rifà established a sort of hierarchy, or lineage based on length of stay in the pension, so if a lodger decided to leave or if he died (something that also happened), the next on the list had the right to move into the empty room. Gabriel went through the whole process of these minimoves, from room to room, until coming to occupy the best of the lot, the Falcon Room—although, at this point, we can't confirm whether he got to the one that was really the best, which was the landlady's. When all's said and done, the arrangements imposed by Senyora Rifà were not so different from the way of life in the orphanage and the two youths weren't really bothered by them. If they knuckled under it was because they didn't want to upset her.

Then again, living with the other inhabitants of the house helped them to get settled in the new world. The two friends spent the better part of the day with the workers at La Ibérica. Hours of toil in that particular microcosm dulled their thoughts but conversation with the other lodgers, over dinner or waiting to proceed to the dining room, often had the effect of jolting their brains into action. The cement was still wet and the footsteps thereon were forcibly imprinted. Bits of advice given, anecdotes and overly emphatic statements stirred them up. Faced with some new comment, they'd be immoderately irritated or they'd laugh as they savored the pleasures of a private joke and knowing looks. Although the friendship that had united them since their early childhood always remained staunch, Gabriel and Bundó learned in the boarding house that there was nothing wrong with having differing opinions. Besides, their age without a name still provided a safety net.

It would be impossible to reproduce the list of transient and long-term tenants our father consorted with in the boarding house. If we do the sums, the figure skyrockets. At the end of the sixties, by which time we'd been born and he was visiting us from time to time—in Paris, Frankfurt, and London—Senyora Rifà's establishment had been his fixed address for more than ten years. More

than ten years: mind-boggling. In 1969 Bundó used his nest egg
to make a down payment on a public housing apartment. A year
and a half later he moved into it. Gabriel, however, didn't follow
suit. He was comfortable in the imperfect nomadic existence that
combined truck journeys around Europe and the ever-provisional
hospitality of a pension, and was loath to abandon the status quo.

"It's as if all the to-ing and fro-ing of the boarding house, all those
people coming in and going out, just like him, prolonged the pleasurable sensation of always being on the move," Christof remarked.

"We're Sergeant Pepper's Lonely Hearts Club Band. We hope
you will enjoy the show . . ."

Okay, Chris, we get the drift. In that lonely hearts club, Bundó
and our father met all sorts of people. The place must have been
frequented by friendly types and show-offs, misers and depressives,
timid souls and loudmouths, swindlers and jokers. For some years,
there'd been periods in which the city had started buzzing again, as
it had done before the war, with the agitation of an anthill. There
were weeks—though not many—in which the jittery energy of the
outside world permeated the pension. Tenants came and left. Senyora Rifà got fed up with washing sheets and towels. A grudging
Barcelona woke up in a bad mood, and thick and sore headed from
nightmares, but the frenetic activity didn't ease up for a single moment. In the streets, trams and buses and trucks and cars and people tweaked the nerves of the city and, eventually, the city reacted.

One Sunday morning when we four Christophers were wandering around the Sant Antoni neighborhood looking for signs of
those times, we went to the second-hand book market and bought
a book of photos from those years.

"And what if we stumble across a photo where, in the background,
in a corner or sneaking by, Bundó and Dad appear?" we joked.

It didn't happen. It was unlikely that they would have been captured in those days because they were never still. The photos in
the book were printed in high-contrast black and white. The larger
ones were very grainy. The first image of the book, probably taken
midafternoon from the foot of Mount Tibidabo, shows the whole
city spread out from the port and the mountain of Montjuïc to the

chimneys of Sant Adrià. Veiled by sea mist, it is an incandescent mirage. Then the photographer got down to particulars and captured a thousand and one details of daily life. In those pages, where night fell just as easily as dawn broke, there was a place for everybody. From the society debuts of young ladies from good families to equestrian events at the Polo Club; from the farriers near the old slaughterhouse to the beer guzzlers in the Plaça Reial; from the raffles and fun and games at the festival of Gràcia to the procession on Saint Eulalia's Day with traffic cops all decked out in feathered helmets; from the white squares after the great snowfall of '62 to the skeletons of public housing blocks being constructed in La Verneda and the shanties of Montjuïc. If we are to stay hot on the heels of our father, then, we're obliged to plunge in among the throng and stop the shifting shadows. We tried to get inside each photo, breathing in its odors and listening to its cries. We really did try.

While inner courtyards filled up with the rankness of boiled cabbage, the concierges of the buildings in the Eixample neighborhood listened to the radio and cursed under their breath. The whores in the Barri Xino straightened their bra straps and touched up their cheap makeup. Shopkeepers decorated their windows with castles built of canned foods. Doormen nodded sleepily inside their vestibules. As piss fermented and stained the cobblestones, a small girl ate lupine beans next to a fountain. A soldier on leave bought flowers for a little seamstress at one of the stalls on La Rambla. An old man in pajamas came out on to his balcony and scratched his balls. A kid in an undershirt killed rats with a catapult. Sea air blew up from the port to caress the legs of a girl in a short, not-quite-knee-length skirt. A tiny man dressed in a white work coat with a threadbare jacket on top sidled through an alley, trying to conceal a well-wrapped packet . . .

"Now. Now, yes! Stop here!"

This scraggy little man with permanently floury hair was a baker's assistant called Lluís Salvans, and he lived in Senyora Rifà's boarding house. Although this is only conjecture, we'd say that the packet, wrapped in brown paper and about the size of a thick book, probably contained incendiary leaflets that were about to be distrib-

uted at the entrance to one of the markets, or at the exit door of the
Liceu opera house, or in the middle of Plaça de Catalunya. Salvans
was, for a time, the most enigmatic lodger in the pension (a repu-
tation inherited by Gabriel when he eventually disappeared). He
always seemed to be fleeing from something and was wary of the
other tenants. If he met anyone in the hallway he didn't shun conversation but preferred to conduct it in conspiratorial whispers. The
strange nature of his job only added to the mystery. Since he worked
the night shift in a bakery in Carrer Hospital, he only coincided
with the other residents on his days off, which is to say Saturdays
and religious holidays. On these occasions he often left the table
after dinner, went out the door and let ten seconds go by, waiting in
the hallway—like one of the stuffed animals—after which he made
a surprise, theatrical reentry into the dining room to see if he could
catch anybody criticizing him or conspiring against him. The other
lodgers knew what he was up to and were always on the alert for his
reappearance. When he burst in again they stared at him in silence,
trying hard not to laugh when they saw his face darkening with
rage. The trail of Salvans and his neuroses peters out on the other
side of the French border at the end of the sixties. His surname
appears in the odd history book, interred in the mass grave of footnotes. From what we've been able to ascertain, which isn't much,
he must have kept up some kind of contact with what remained of
the anarcho-syndicalist trade union CNT and sometimes took part
in subversive activities. A couple of times when she was sweeping
his room Senyora Rifà found books that looked as if they ought to
be prohibited stashed under his bed. Bakunin, Kropotkin, Malat-
esta . . . these too-Russian or too-dangerous names made her suspicious and apprehensive. Salvans bought her silence by presenting
her with a kilo loaf of bread every morning, still hot from the oven.

"Take it off my rent, as we agreed," he'd say in front of the
others to put them off the track when anyone caught them red-
handed in the transaction.

When they knew him they were very young and innocent, but
both our father and Bundó spoke affectionately of Lluís Salvans,
whose libertarian ideas—although they were expressed in mysteri-

ous and cryptic words that the two friends barely understood at the time—ended up as part of their ideological education. It must have been a meager introduction, it has to be said, for neither our father nor Bundó ever embraced politics. These pages don't accommodate daring deeds or lofty epic achievements. The train of heroic exploits passed them by, for they were kept busy at the House of Charity. When not being obliged to memorize the "Formation of the National Spirit" under the vigilance of a nun of doughy complexion, they were otherwise distracted, for example by getting dressed up in uniform and tie and having their hair neatly parted for the Eucharistic Congress children's procession. Of course, later on when they became aware of them, they hated the restrictions and austere life that had been foisted on them by the dictator and his henchmen—and even more so when they started to travel around Europe in the Pegaso and understood that people had much better lives outside Spain—but the daily grind of moving furniture kept them on too short a leash. In that, they were victims indeed. And that's why they schemed every single day. Like them, a lot of people got through those years putting up a modicum of resistance that was crushed day after day by such loathsome characters as Senyor Casellas. Petroli told us, for example, that La Ibérica union meetings had always been a farce conducted by Deulofeu, the boss's favorite hireling, the nuns' little squealer in the orphanage, who had subsequently built his career on being Casellas's spy.

To return to the other end of the spectrum, to the influence of Lluís Salvans, we need to go back to the first winter Bundó and Gabriel spent in Senyora Rifà's house. One Saturday night in their nineteenth year, too cold for them to be roaming the streets, they lingered at the table for coffee and a chat and, with the challenge of finishing a bottle of Soberano brandy, they started playing cards. Their adversaries that night in the Catalan game of *botifarra* were Lluís Salvans and the student from Berga (sorry, friend, but we don't know your name). A brazier under the table kept the four of them warm but, as further protection against the cold, the chap from Berga was also wearing the fingerless gloves he used when he was studying. As usual, Bundó and Gabriel began to win easily after three or four hands. They'd been playing together for some time now and had a finely honed repertoire of gestures and face-pulling that were fail-safe and invisible to others (Gabriel's cheating must have helped them too, obviously, but Bundó didn't know about that then). After one especially long hand, Gabriel made the killer move and set out his cards on the table, whereupon the student threw his cards down in a gesture of surrender.

"You've got fucking good luck!" he shouted. "You've been getting the winning cards all night."

"That's not luck, friend," Gabriel defended himself with a brandied whiff to his words. "It's all about knowing how."

"Yeah, yeah, look at the pro! Where did you learn that, at the Monte Carlo casino?"

"No, come off it! We got our degree in the House of Charity, I'll have you know," Bundó mocked, offended by his remark. "The nuns taught us catechism first and then cards—*botifarra, brisca,* and seven and a half. And yeah, always with real money. They nicked it from the church donations."

Brooding and glum, Lluís Salvans dealt out the cards again, and it seemed that the matter was closed. They kept playing and, at the end of another game, he turned to Bundó and blurted out, "So, you were raised near here, in the House of Charity...Are you an orphan, then?"

"Yes, we both are," Bundó answered, tilting his head to include Gabriel. He felt a quiver of pride. That didn't happen often.

"And where were you born, if one might ask?"

"Of course one might ask. My ID card says El Vendrell. Why?"

"Nothing. Curiosity..."

Lluís Salvans was a man of few words, and his curiosity ran out then and there. The game lasted another hour, until the brazier and the Soberano called it quits and the four lodgers went off to bed. A couple of days later, when Bundó was walking along the hallway one evening, a door half opened and someone murmured his name. It was Lluís Salvans. He called him into his room and immediately closed the door. He was in the Woodcock Room.

"I've been making some inquiries among the right people," he announced with secretive flourish. He was bowing slightly as if this were protocol demanded by the weight of his knowledge. The look on Bundó's face was one of total bewilderment.

"Do you know who your dad was?"

"No," Bundó replied. "I never knew him. Once the nuns told me he was a bad man because he abandoned my mom and me, and then my mom died of a broken heart and left me all alone."

"Well, now you'll know the truth, Bundó." Salvans lowered his voice. "Your dad was killed by the fascists. In Camp de la Bota. They had him locked up in Modelo prison, and some bastards, some of the dictator's butchers, took him off and shot him. They killed a lot of other combatants in that place." He looked at a scrap of paper on which he'd jotted down a date. "This says they killed your dad on November 29th. In 1941."

"But that's the day I was born!" Bundó exclaimed.

Lluís Salvans could hardly believe his ears.

"What fucking bastards! What utter fucking bastards!" His face hardened in a way Bundó had never seen. Not even when he was doing his dining-room routine trying to catch the other boarders conspiring against him had he ever shown such rage. "Always remember this, Bundó: Your dad was a hero."

Bundó never forgot Lluís Salvans's words, but it took him some days to digest what they really meant. Until then, his idea of a hero had been shaped by the exploits in the Captain Thunder comic books. He'd been buying them at the Palacio kiosk as his bedtime reading material ever since they'd become popular in the newsstands. A few days after that first encounter, Salvans knocked at the door of their room and, sneaking in with his own particular brand of stealth, he showed Bundó a photo.

"Take it, you can keep it," he told him. "Keep it well hidden away. You'll know right away which one's your dad. You're identical. You only have to look in the mirror. He must have been the same age as you are now."

The photograph, in black and white, showed a bunch of youngsters on the trailer of a truck. They looked like a group of friends, united in their festive spirit. Some were smiling and boldly raising their fists high in the air. The youngest one, aged about fifteen, had wrapped himself in an anarchist flag. Bundó recognized himself in a boy who was clutching another boy, trying to keep his balance and at the same time holding up one end of a banner. They were indeed identical. He gazed for a long time at this figure, waiting for the pain to hit, some sadness, some sign, but nothing happened. When he raised his eyes from the photo, Salvans had disappeared.

Instead of hiding it, Bundó dug out a silver frame filched from one of his first moves, put the photo in it and placed it on his bed-side table. The next few nights, after getting into bed, he picked it up and gazed at the group of youths. They made him feel good. He started with his father—the tension in his arms, the clothes he was wearing, the expression of triumph—and then went on to his comrades-in-arms. He studied their features, trying to imagine what they were thinking just then. Who would have been his father's best friend, his Gabriel? Maybe that skinny lad he was embracing? The ultimate pessimist, Salvans had told him that they must all be dead.

Two weeks later, on one particularly pleasant March afternoon, Bundó completed the imaginary process of reclaiming his father. He, El Tembleque, and Gabriel were coming back in the DKV from a move to Badalona. As they were driving along the Mataró road, just after the Besós bridge, Bundó asked if they could stop for a moment at Camp de la Bota.

"I want to see the place where they did for my dad," he announced.

El Tembleque went white and stopped the van next to some open ground. He made the sign of the cross, a reflex action. Then he told them that, if they didn't mind, he wouldn't go with them. Since they were nearby he'd go and visit some old acquaintances in the Pequín neighborhood. In the forties, before getting married and taking his mother to live in Sant Adrià, he'd grown up in one of those whitewashed shacks without running water or toilet—the ones that used to be there just beyond the Quatre Torres castle in Camp de la Bota. More than once when he was lying in bed early in the morn-ing just as the sun was coming up, he'd heard the sinister volleys of firing-squad bullets borne on the wind and then, still more baleful, the dry crack of the coup de grâce. He counted them and knew how many people they'd shot dead. During the day they played ball on the beach where bullet casings, mixed with the seashells, cut their bare feet. There were kids in the neighborhood who collected them and then went off to sell them at the Els Encants flea market.

Gabriel and Bundó got out of the van near the castle. The salty sea air was disagreeably sticky. The sun, which was slowly starting to set behind the factories and the first blocks of apartments of the La Mina neighborhood, rose-tinted the sky with illusory clarity. The castle with its four towers and clearly outlined battlements loomed before them like a cardboard figure in a diorama. Leaving a huddle of shacks behind them, the two friends walked down to the water's edge and then along the beach for a hundred meters or so. Gabriel continued on from the point indicated by El Tembleque as the start of Camp de la Bota, and Bundó stopped. With his shoe he drew a straight line about ten meters long, plowing through the wet sand and vigorously pushing aside all the pebbles he'd dug up. He didn't know why he was doing it. The sound of the waves that hour of the afternoon, their unrelenting sinuous rhythm, made him start retching, although he didn't vomit.

In the distance, some kids were playing around the shacks and occasionally they all screamed in unison. Their screeching sounded like some strange tribal call. Two dogs started to bark, first one and then the other, round after round until they were hoarse. When they both went quiet, there was a new silence and Bundó felt utterly alone. He closed his eyes and, there in the painful, absolute, hermetic solitude of Camp de la Bota, the whole legacy of his father came to him in a flash. It was the first time in his life—and probably the only time—that he sensed he was close to the truth.

Feeling Gabriel's arm around his shoulders, he opened his eyes again. They didn't speak. They returned to the castle in silence and waited for El Tembleque to come and pick them up in the DKV. But there must have been something in the air, or Bundó must have transmitted some kind of shudder, because the next morning Gabriel left the house early and, before going to La Ibérica, stopped off at the El Born market. From a distance, wordlessly, he said his last good-bye to the salt cod seller who'd put him to her breast.

# 6

## Women and Petroli

*Number 49. Barcelona-Biarritz.*
*February 6, 1965.*

*Two shoeboxes tied up with twine. One is bigger than the other. In the small box is a pair of men's shoes with worn soles. They are size 42 and still look quite good. Gabriel will have them. The bigger one was probably for boots but now it contains a chessboard and a wooden box with alabaster pieces. A white pawn is missing and they have replaced it with a domino tile, a double blank. We don't play but we'll take it to the pension and give it to La Rifà. They've used the space in the box for a leather cigar case with three Havanas inside. Petroli will smoke them, though one of them has a damaged tip from the move. There is also a solid wood paperweight. Then there's a figure of an elephant with its trunk raised and a slot in its back to hold a box of matches. Bundó will have those.*

We've started a close reading of the catalogue of pilfering—or robbery, or permanent loans, or borrowings, or sidetrackings or rescues, or whatever your moral code chooses to call it. Now that we've come to 1963 in this itinerary through Gabriel's life, and the Pegaso engines are warming up to drive across half of Europe, each of the hauls that our father detailed in his notebooks is like a secret passageway that leads us directly back to those times. Going back four decades in a single paragraph. At first, in the early pages, the description was simply factual. It's possible that Gabriel and Bundó still didn't totally trust Petroli since he was older and more experienced than they were so they recorded the division of spoils to make sure it was fair. Slowly, however, the lists became more elaborate. Although he never spoke in first person, we know that Gabriel wrote them and can see that his descriptions became increasingly detailed and persnickety. Sometimes he even permitted himself a reference to the family they'd pillaged. We're not saying they're literary because that's not the case, but what you can see in those pages is deep empathy with their only two readers, Bundó and Petroli. It's as if, after a certain point, the game of writing the list became an important part of the purloining itself. Although Petroli has never wanted to give credence to this interpretation, it's a major source of fascination for us: Since he never expected that anyone else would read his notes, this would have to be the place where our father is most guileless, without subterfuges or masks. Where we can best intuit the essence of his character.

We've just transcribed one of the entries in his catalogue in which the process of elaboration is evident. Now we offer one of the early rudimentary checklists, for your comparison:

*Number 4. Move to Düsseldorf. April 18, 1963.*
One old traveling bag.
Petroli: Two ties. Pair of suspenders. One Dux jersey.
Bundó: One tie. Leather gloves.
Gabriel: One tie. One dark-green jacket.

Only a year later, Gabriel would have described the dark-green item (which we found still hanging in his wardrobe) as a tweed jacket with a shield sewn on the breast pocket, noting that it was probably used for hunting or horse riding. In his more inspired moments he might even have reported that inside one of the pockets was a dry oak leaf, probably overlooked by the owner the previous spring.

As for Petroli, after that first trip to Düsseldorf, he stopped wearing a belt and became a wholehearted member of the suspender-wearing sect. We discovered this a few months ago when we spent a weekend visiting him so he could summon up those times for the four of us. Even at the risk of imitating one of those television programs that dredge up sweaty old anecdotes and bring together old school friends who actually hate each other, we believed that Petroli's memories would help us in our attempts to fix the point when our father took flight. For almost ten years after Senyor Casellas pulled the right strings and La Ibérica got a toehold in the privileged business of international transport, Petroli, Bundó, and Gabriel cohabited—if we can put it like that—in a Pegaso truck. Our father's notebooks record almost two hundred departures heading all over Europe, mainly to France, Germany, and England (Italy and Portugal were excluded as another company had negotiated an exclusive deal with the government). We're talking about an average of two or three journeys a month if you calculate that each one lasted three or four days, what with getting there, unloading and returning. And after a certain point, the three friends almost always worked together as a team with moves inside Spain as well.

Nowadays, Petroli's a very well-preserved eighty-year-old. He lives in a German city by the North Sea where winter evenings smell of log fires and smoked fish. He asked us not to give any more details. Please. That's his only condition. Looking back, retracing the route of his desires, he can now say that he's achieved what he most yearned for during his years as a truck driver: He has a house with a back garden in a quiet neighborhood next to a bay, and has been living there for years with an Oviedo-born woman, Ángeles, who emigrated to Germany at the end of the fifties. Since Petroli is a good-looking chap, slightly bandy-legged, with a vaguely athletic set of muscles—and tormented by back pain, like all truck drivers—Christof reckons he looks like a retired soccer player, a famous center forward of the Bundesliga who occasionally agrees to interviews. Like ours.

Chris, however, goes for the patriotic vein and starts fantasizing, "Imagine what would happen if Madame Tussaud's in London exhibited figures of our father and his friends. I reckon that everyone would want to be photographed standing next to Petroli. With that good-natured, slightly crafty self-assurance of his, you'd only have to dress him up in some dark-green overalls and people would take him for a Lord Mountbatten in aviator's gear. He'd still have that intriguing air about him, a sort of relaxed control, the stamp of years of hard battles." He pauses, mulls over something and then goes on. "And, if you'll indulge me a little more, Bundó would be a replica of Dylan Thomas, moon faced, with tousled hair and a stained pullover . . ."

"And what about Dad?" we other Christophers ask as one.

"Dad? Gabriel? That's easy. Dad would be Houdini, the museum's escape artist. Immobilized for the first time in his life. With a nest of thick chains coiled around him, his face tense, almost asphyxiating, he's still trying to strike a powerful pose, the showmanship of someone who knows that, with one wave of the magic wand and before thirty seconds have elapsed, all those padlocks will click open like toy ones. And then he can make his getaway."

It must be said that this image of Gabriel as an escape artist was suggested to us by none other than Petroli. Ramón Riera Marcial, Petroli to his friends, agreed to meet us after lunch one Saturday in July, at one in the afternoon (the Germans, and even nonnatives, have lunch very early) His workmates at La Ibérica nicknamed him Petroli years ago because of the intense blackness of his dyed hair, which was so shiny and gummy that it took on a bluish sheen in the sunlight. The first thing we discovered when we went to his house was that he'd got over his hang-up about his hair, thanks perhaps to his peaceful life as a pensioner, or maybe Ángeles's insistence. Now, his mop of neatly combed white locks gave him a venerable, good-natured look. He might have been our paternal grandfather.

Petroli and Ángeles ushered us into a living room crammed with objects and ornaments and looking out to the garden. In the next few hours, as the interview lengthened, we couldn't resist trying to identify items on our father's theft list among the vases, pictures, reproductions of old maps, coasters, lights, and the other more or less valuable pieces that surrounded us. They were cer-

tainly conspicuous in their out-of-place opulence in that little living room. While Ángeles was in the kitchen cutting *Apfelstrudel*
and making us coffee, Petroli asked us to sit on the sofa and in two
armchairs he'd lined up in the living room. Standing in front of
us, he subjected us to careful scrutiny, one by one. In an interval
of half a minute three different cuckoo clocks struck quarter past
one. Petroli had got dressed up for our visit in an old-fashioned
suit, shiny with frequent ironing and slightly baggy. His expression was mischievous and he seemed to be wondering whether
or not he should crack a joke. He then guessed our names, one
version of Christopher for each face, and he got us all right. He
hadn't seen us for more than thirty years so it must have been
his way of accepting that there was some kinship between us and
his past. Then, sitting in a leather armchair, our father's friend
made the grueling effort of remembering and remembering and
remembering. We imagine that, for him, the afternoon must have
been both pleasurable and painful. Every question we asked led to
some description by him, which at once opened up new questions
for us. His words wove together even more tightly the combined
existences of Bundó, Gabriel, and Petroli himself. Very discreetly,
so as not to lose the thread, the four of us glanced at each other
when he disclosed some crucial detail. Ángeles noticed this and
joined in the conversation as our ally, asking him some of the more
awkward questions. Meanwhile, she kept serving us coffee, and
we drank it without a second thought, as if accepting that insomnia in a hotel bedroom that night was the price we'd have to pay.

We left off at nightfall. The next day, Sunday, we returned with
the promise that we wouldn't take up too much of their time, but,
once again, it was dark by the time we finished. There was a point
beyond which Petroli began to ramble and repeat himself, but there
was no way we were going to interrupt him. It must have been
years since he'd had a chance to talk about his adventures. On the
Monday we had to be back in our everyday worlds, and at seven
that Sunday evening we said our good-byes to the couple with
sincere hugs and promises to come and visit them again some day.
Christophe watched them disappearing in the rearview mirror of

the rented car, waving at us from their front door, veiled in ghostly shadows. Only two kilometers down the road, as we were discussing the finer points of Petroli and Ángeles's recollections, Cristòfol interrupted the conversation. He wanted to make a confession. On his way to the loo he'd been snooping, had opened a couple of cupboards in the hallway, and couldn't resist nicking a French silk tie. His share of the perks from Move 165. Petroli would never wear it again, he claimed by way of justifying the theft. Then there materialized, amid scandalized giggles, a Cinzano ashtray (Chris), a paperback edition of Quevedo's *El Buscón* (Christof), and a keyless key ring with the Mercedes-Benz star (Christophe). Okay, it's not good manners, but it's in our blood.

Besides our acquisition of pieces for the Christophers' private museum, we'd spent the two days cramming Petroli's stories and emotions into our cassette recorder—which he did consent to—and now they've been tidied up and slightly tweaked in the interests of narrative structure, we offer them in Petroli's own words.

## PETROLI SPEAKS

Where shall I start, boys? Let's see. Sometimes, when I'm trying to get through those especially *trübsinnigen* days, those gray ones that fog up your mind (and, I can assure you, we have a string of them every year here in the north of Germany), I cling to the memory of a certain sensation. Now it's just a vaguely remembered feeling, if you like, but in those times it was alive in all three of us. Something bestial. I'm almost embarrassed to talk about it. The first thing Gabriel, Bundó, and I did whenever we started a new move was, of course, to introduce ourselves at the residence in question. One of us stayed in the street, keeping an eye on the parked truck and getting the ropes and pulleys ready, while the other two went to the house to present ourselves and organize the move. The sense of excitement kicked in as soon as we rang the doorbell. Oh, those seconds of waiting till someone opened the door! We could hear the footsteps coming closer, the click of tentative heels, then the eye looked through the peephole, the key turned in the lock, and, in that heavenly sequence, we forgot we were long-suffering La Ibérica workers. It was like they were opening the gates of paradise. The woman who opened the door, always a woman—a maid or the lady of the house—looked us up and down with a mixture of relief and agitation. We'd done dozens of moves and we had them figured out immediately: the one that would suffer, the one that would ignore us, the one in a hurry, the one that wouldn't say a word, the one that would need to talk to calm down, the one that would be buzzing around us like a blowfly, the one that would give us a tip so she'd feel good. Instinct guided us and we adapted to their moods so we could do the move without hassles, but all of us kept nursing that excited feeling we had at the beginning.

I can tell you now that at that stage of my life, I used to go out of my way to meet older women, especially married, mature ones. Now over forty, I'd got through the physical and mental quarantine and had, let's say, a twenty-year head start on Bundó and Gabriel. I blame it on the war. It made me grow up fast. I went from a schoolroom with a Republican schoolteacher and playing leapfrog in a dusty street of a little village in the Matarraña region to dressing up in soldier's gear with my mom crying over me as if she were already watching over my corpse. I still remember how her weeping and wailing terrified me, how it made me feel even more like a baby. Before I knew how to shave I could mount a rifle, so to speak, and those ten months I spent buried in the trenches by the River Segre nipped my adolescence in the bud. When it was all over, after the humiliation of defeat and the daily nightmare of military service in Teruel, I went home a man, but I was a grotesque man. I tried on my clothes from before and everything was pathetically small. My mom started crying again, for two whole days, as if she'd seen my resurrection. When I look at the photos of those days I don't recognize myself. I'd turned into a sort of big brother to the Petroli who'd marched off to the front, one of those brothers that are so overprotective they destroy you in the end. Inside, too, my real self was all messed up. It was like a constant jabbing that starts in the stomach and goes up to the brain. Once it was there, it nagged at me to walk out on everything. I tried to resist. A few weeks after my discharge and return home, I tried my luck courting a girl from the village. She was a bit younger than me and was dazzled by my half-invented adventures at the front. In the beginning things worked okay but taking it all so slowly, step by step, got on my nerves. I'd done a fast-track course in sex during my military service, thanks to a string of prostitutes from Teruel— wrecked women, poor things, but tender and affectionate—and I was bored to death with that girl. One Saturday night we went off for a bit of slap and tickle and I ran out of patience. You know what I mean, don't you? Her dad's still looking for me. Meanwhile, my older sister had married a fellow called Tartana, from the next village, and they went off to live in Barcelona. He was working at La Ibérica and managed to get them to take me on too. As soon as I got the news, I took the first bus to the city.

So, now you've got me living in Barcelona in the forties, fifties, and sixties, a long way from that piddling little life of the village, I want to go back to what I was saying before: In those days I used to go out of my way to meet older women. Every time one of those doors opened and a proper woman appeared before us, ripe and in her prime, I was as excited as a little kid. I often forgot all about my lust after half a minute of asking questions and getting only monosyllables but, very occasionally, I had a hunch that there was a chink of hope. Then I'd get to work, using all the tricks in the book. In general, housekeepers, governesses, and maids (the ones that weren't young any more) were difficult: They were so full of themselves they hardly spoke to me. They were too set on keeping the castle safe from strangers that stank of sweat and whistled while they were working. On the other hand, the ladies of the house . . . they were almost always rich, bourgeois, right-wing, and they'd had plenty of training in telling the difference between appearance and reality. The husbands, starchy Franco supporters, politicians, and bankers, were at one extreme, and we were at the other. The situation helped too. With all the objects in boxes, with the furniture dismantled and piled up ready to go, there were ladies who suddenly felt that they were at the mercy of the elements, lost and kind of incomplete. Those hours they spent in no-man's-land were like a little gift of freedom, and they had to make the most of it, even more so when they realized that being romanced wasn't something that happened too often at their age. Now, don't go imagining a whole heap of adventures and entanglements, but I—Ángeles, *Schatz*, cover your ears, please—laid more than one high-society lady on a wool mattress or rug that was too old to survive a move. It tended to happen toward the end of the day, when Bundó and Gabriel were in the truck tying down the load. The ladies always went for the empty conjugal bedroom—out of inertia—with the silhouettes of furniture and the crucifix outlined on the walls. Our panting sounded more mournful than anything else, as if it was fated to turn into ghostly voices that would haunt the future inhabitants of the house. Sometimes the attempt ended after a bit of kissing. Other times you could see that the ladies were a little reluctant to cross the line, and that they only wanted that sinful quickie so they could have a very secret secret, all for themselves, which they'd turn to later to relive their daring as a kind of vaccination against the deadly dull life they were going to lead in some other country. Needless to say, our sweaty, sticky working clothes had a basic part to play in all this and, once the adventure with those pedigreed ladies was over, I got all puffed up with an unexpected side effect: what you might call working-class pride.

I don't know what Gabriel and Bundó thought about my getting off with the high-class ladies. In terms of complaining, well no, they never complained about it—maybe because, right from the start, Senyor Casellas had made me their boss—but I don't think they saw me as a model of behavior either. In amorous matters, it was each to his own. Those two also loved the sweet moments just before the door of a new home opened, though their motivations seemed kinkier to me. Once inside the house, Bundó only had eyes for the objects that were going into the truck. He took charge of supervising the packets, appliances, and furniture, checking to make sure the boxes were properly closed and work-

ing out the order in which we'd take it all down to be sure that
the weight was properly distributed in the trailer. He used to get
well and truly carried away when he was organizing things (while I
was doing my bit, wrapping up the lady of the house with my pre-
liminary questions). With the excuse of only having limited space,
he opened up boxes and suitcases to peek inside and redistribute
things. Covetousness and love were the ruin of him. Basically, he
was a harum-scarum (not that we have any right, all these years
later, to criticize him for that, understood, boys?). Gabriel and
I were always breathing down his neck to make sure he didn't
break our rules of thievery: The three of us had agreed to choose
the box, package, or suitcase by chance, right at the end, without
knowing what it contained. That was part of the game, and it was
against the rules to mark it beforehand because it contained some
valuable or especially desirable object. We also had to be discreet.

Bundó's obsession only got worse as the years went by and
caused us more than one headache. The reasons behind it have
a woman's name—Carolina, or Muriel if you like—and we really
shouldn't try to sum up this part of the story in a few words because it was very important for all of us later on. I mean, we could
go into a lot of detail but it'll have to be some other time, if you
don't mind. As for Gabriel, I hope I'm not disappointing you, but
I could never understand what kind of kick he got out of it, what
it was that turned him on when we rang the doorbell of a house.
Well yes, I've got a vague idea based on a few intuitions. Gabriel
never seemed to get worked up over carnal needs like Bundó and
me. I see him more like a vampire. He'd get into people's houses
and suck up the atmosphere, that presence of life you could still
detect in an apartment just before starting the move. Smells, shadows, laughter, chills, silences . . . Maybe that's why he liked to start
the move by getting to know someone who'd lived in the house so
he could construct his theories more exactly. With every object
and every bit of furniture he lugged, he also seemed to be studying the traces they left behind in those empty rooms. He raised
blinds and opened windows, claiming that there wasn't enough
light, and looked out over the street to contemplate the view while

he smoked a cigarette. As if it was part of the job, he used to start chatting with the person who was keeping an eye on us. "The siestas on this couch must have been wonderful, isn't that right, Senyora?" "I'm sure the whole family must have got together for more than one Sunday lunch on such a lovely veranda." That's my version, but I'd say that his fantasies about other people's lives—which he later projected with the same enthusiasm onto the place where we had to unload as if it was a blank canvas waiting to be painted—helped him to breathe better. He absorbed it and stored it like oxygen for when he returned to the boarding house and its fragile comforts. Proof of this compulsion is that, when he got to know your mother—your *mothers*—and you lot were born and he could finally taste family life in small doses, he lost interest in empty houses. All the moves we did after that were simply an excuse to travel closer to where you lived so he could visit you.

In the early seventies, I think it was, when Bundó had just moved to the apartment in Via Favència and three of you already existed—only Cristòfol was still to arrive in Barcelona, if I'm not mistaken—I took Gabriel aside more than once and insisted that he should leave the boarding house and go and live with someone. I asked him to do me a favor and change his way of life and maybe even—and why not?—his country.

"I wouldn't know how," he answered. "In the orphanage they taught me how to survive like this: alone, yet surrounded by people. Anyway, if I decided to change one day and settle down for good, which family would I choose?"

His question gave me goose pimples.

*Number 104. Barcelona-Manchester.*
*September 10, 1967.*

*One old wooden box, still with a lid. Once it held French wine. We know that from the half-torn label (Château whatever it's called) and the smell when we opened it. There were three the same and we picked this one. It's got some bathroom things in it but it all seems to be for a summer vacation place.*

*Petroli will keep the brushes and combs, still with tangles of wavy blond hair from the lady of the house, an almost-used lipstick, and some vampish mascara. Maybe in his spare time he has strange fancies about being a transvestite in the Barri Xino [the last few words are crossed out with red lipstick, probably by Petroli]. We'll also let him have a bottle of English aftershave that smells very masculine. There are two bottles of French lady's perfume, very expensive we suppose. They'll go to Carolina, via Bundó. By the way, no one believes that Bundó hasn't planned this [there's a note in the margin, in red and Bundó's handwriting, that says "Lie!"]. The hairnet and brilliantine that must have belonged to the future consular attaché in Manchester are Bundó's. The talcum powder is for him too. He often complains of chafing on his thighs because he sweats so much. We'll keep the bottle of peroxide, the lotion for mosquito bites, and the flask of Mercurochrome inside the cab, just in case. The portable first-aid kit goes to Gabriel. It contains a plastic syringe, a rubber tourniquet, gauze squares, and adhesive tape. Aspirins. One unopened stick of Termosan local analgesic. Cough lozenges, past sell-by date. A packet of Band-Aids with a smudge of dry blood. Gabriel will also take a real stethoscope: Some village doctor must have forgotten it, and now a little boy can play with it [Christopher confirms that he got it a couple of years later]. There's a calendar from last year, which is for Gabriel: It's got pictures of racing cars on Montjuïc, and, on the page for July, there are ten days marked with a cross and, underneath, the name of some kind of medicine. No one wants the enema bulb.*

## PETROLI SPEAKS AGAIN

The trips abroad marked the beginning of the meteoric rise of the La Ibérica moving company. From one day to the next, without having to fork out too much or take on too many new workers, Senyor Casellas's business started crossing borders, and this made him even richer. The plan—or conspiracy, as we used to say—was hatched in an alliance of offices and churches. Carnations and cigars. One of Senyor Casellas's daughters, the young one, married a boy from an upper-class family that ran the Banco de Madrid, I think it was. (We La Ibérica workers, of course, had to scratch around in our pockets to buy them a gift.) Among the many other stuffed shirts that attended the wedding, there was a certain Ramiro Cuscó Romagosa, a very well-known Franco man in those days and a relative of the new son-in-law. After that, it was like a game of snakes and ladders, but it was ladders all the way. With a good throw of the dice, Senyor Casellas shot up to land in the office of José María de Porcioles, the Lord Mayor of Barcelona. Two plus two equals four. A year later, when they baptized Casellas's first grandchild at the Sant Gregori Taumaturg church, Porcioles was at the party, carrying on like the chummy old uncle you found in all the pro-Franco families. Juan Antonio Samaranch—who people know about nowadays because of the Barcelona Olympics—was also there among the guests. He was shyer and more reserved then and had some job concerning sports at the Town Hall, but he was obviously aiming higher and they had a very good opinion of him in Madrid, right at the very top, in the El Pardo Palace. Casellas knew how to soft soap him. Four plus two equals six. Of all the wheeling and dealing among the Falangists in those golden years, it's quite likely that La Ibérica only got the dregs. It's also a good bet that Casellas, with his piggy voice and pachyderm waddle, often played the part of buffoon, amusing them with his stories of domesticated communists and immigrants from Murcia—after all he had the dubious privilege of dealing with them on a daily basis.

In less than two months Casellas's good connections began to kick in. La Ibérica got the monopoly on all the diplomatic moves to France, Germany, Switzerland, and Great Britain. Six plus two equals eight. The ambassadors, consuls, vice-consuls, and people in other cushy jobs schemed. Franco nominated. The machines of power did the wheeling and dealing. The game of musical chairs got going. At the end of the chain, three flunkies loaded up a truck for the trans-Pyrenean route, and the big boss pocketed wads of cash. It might have been peanuts for some of them but eight plus two equal ten. In those years, the sums always came out right.

In the summer of 1960, when word got around that La Ibérica was going to do international moves, all the workers started to dream, each one of us imagining he'd be chosen. Nobody had ever been out of the country, and it was about that time when the first Swedish tourist charter plane landed in Málaga airport. A picture emerged of a modern, idyllic Europe. We saw the Nordic and Central European countries as having a more advanced civilization. Soon we were all going to be some kind of Alfredo Landa—you know who I mean, don't you?—that film actor drooling over the striped bikini of some uninhibited blond foreigner. We were so green that we thought working with a truck outside Spain meant unloading furniture at the foot of the Eiffel Tower, with three sexed-up Brigitte Bardots waiting for us to finish so they could give us a massage, and the reality—I'm sorry to say, Christophe—is that, in ten years of moves to Paris, we never went up the tower. We could always see it there on the horizon, but that's as far as it went. In the end, Senyor Casellas chose us three for practical reasons, which he dressed up as a matter of family conscience when his workers were informed. For better or worse, Bundó, Gabriel, and I were footloose bachelors. We didn't have a family to feed or kids to educate. No one was going to miss us on weekends.

From the very start you could see that the European moves were a godsend for La Ibérica. In no time at all Senyor Casellas did up the offices, took on a qualified secretary—Rebeca, with the legs and waist of Cyd Charisse and the patience of a saint with that army of blowflies she had to put up with every day—bought the premises next door to expand the garage in Carrer Almogàvers, and had a map of Europe painted on the façade. The painter obeyed the boss's orders and produced a grossly inflated Spain. It looked as if it had elephantiasis and it was shooting out red arrows that disappeared into different parts of the continent. Those arrows were supposed to represent the trail of speed and good service delivered by our trucks. Supposed to, I say. The reality is that the first vehicle lasted a year and half, and it wasn't fast and it wasn't safe. But we had a soft spot for it. It was a second-hand Pegaso Barajas, really uncomfortable when you had to fit three people in the cab and, when it rained, the water came in from ceiling and floor (a rust hole near the brake pedal left the right leg of your trousers good and muddy). Then we wore out a few other models, always second-hand, and, after we'd been driving around for a few years, Senyor Casellas got fed up with our complaints and paying repair bills so he dipped into his pocket and got a brand-new flying horse, the Pegaso Europa 1065. That one, yes, that one went well. It seemed to be tailor-made for us. A two-axle chassis, a 9100 engine, 170 hp, a very wide windshield like cinemascope, and, at the back of the cab, a narrow bunk if you needed to rest. The trailer could handle a maximum cargo of twenty tons, and, sometimes, when we loaded it up chockablock, the engine rumbled away, happy and purring like a cat that had got the cream. "The beast's got a full belly," we used to say.

As you'll understand, it's impossible for me to recall all the words and silences that filled the cab when we were on the road. I'm talking about ten years, and, in ten years, the stories mount up. Your mind goes back, as if it's leafing through old tabloids and, from time to time, it stops at a page that grabs its attention. MURIEL STEALS BUNDÓ'S HEART IN A ROADSIDE BAR, one headline screams. The story titled TWO TRUCK DRIVERS STAKE THE WHOLE LOAD THEY'RE CARRYING IN A GAME OF CARDS AND LUCKILY THEY WIN takes up five columns. SPANISH TRANSPORT ENTREPRENEUR USES DRIVERS TO STASH FUNDS IN SWITZERLAND is news too. Read like that, any old how, these statements take on an air of prophecy that you shouldn't underestimate. In any case, I suppose you'll follow them up yourselves. But there are other kinds of things, too, little anecdotal things that refuse to die. They keep coming back to me, cheekily popping up out of nowhere. Bundó's brusque movement when he was changing gears, as if he was throwing every muscle of his body into it. My habit, which those two hated, of eating sunflower seeds and throwing the husks out the window: If it was windy they stuck to the glass outside, and they thought that was disgusting. The interminable arguments about which were the best service stations, the French or the German ones. The even more interminable sessions when we started telling jokes we already knew, for the simple pleasure of laughing together all over again when we repeated them. Then there were times when we all got hooked on repeating some expression or other over and over again: "Well, fuck me," "What's with you, bugaboo," "Veteranoooooo brandy, a splash would be dandy." Our different musical tastes, as varied, contradictory, and vulgar as those shelves of cassettes you find in service stations. Gabriel's flair for finding the international service of Spanish National Radio on the days when there was soccer, which was only comparable with Bundó's talent for detecting engine problems by putting his ear against the hood. Or the different ways of driving, for example. Bundó, with his fantastic sense of direction and maneuvring skills, was the one who took us in and out of cities. When we were coming up to a border post, Gabriel took the wheel since he got on best with the police: He made good use of his peculiar mastery of languages to deal with them without misunderstandings and thus avoid wasting more time than necessary with the inspection of the load. I asked them to let me do the night shift because the darkness and the monotonous lines on the road relaxed me and let me think. Gabriel, by the way, was the safest driver. Bundó and I were quick-tempered, but he never swore out loud—well, he moved his lips like he did when he was reading, but that's all—and he never tried to get back at reckless drivers by leaning on the horn. His way of driving was calm and contemplative, and, sometimes, trying to wind him up, Bundó used to get cynical and he'd say, "If we have a real accident one day and if we're going to die I want you to be driving, Gabriel. You're so on the ball you'll give us plenty of time to see our lives flash before our eyes before they close for good. Isn't that what they say, that in your last seconds you see it all running before you in images, like in a film? Well, I want those seconds to be very long so there's time for everything."

Then Gabriel looked at him without looking at him, without taking his eyes off the road, and took him to task in his laconic way. "You're such jerk. What a bullshitter."

# 7

## Carolina, or Muriel

*Number 131. Barcelona-Geneva road-Frankfurt.*
*July 3, 1968.*

*With a lot of difficulty, because an employee from the Span-*
*ish consulate in Frankfurt had been told to monitor our*
*movements—and this German spook certainly took the job*
*seriously—we commandeer a dented box that looked half*
*empty. Such a long trip, being forced to stop near Geneva to*
*see Senyor Casellas's friends, and such a lousy reward. Inside*
*the box are only a few dusty toys covered with cobwebs. The*
*two spoiled brats, the boy and girl of about thirteen who were*
*bored to death while we were organizing the move (we had to*
*ask them to get off the sofa so we could take it down to the*
*truck), must have played with them a long time ago. Petroli*
*keeps the set of wooden skittles, for his nephew, he says. He*
*also takes a bag full of cowboys and Indians and a wooden*
*fort. Bundó's kept a tin frog after promising not to make it*
*croak in the cab. He also took a Nancy doll dressed up as a*
*Spanish soldier (heaven knows why he wants that). There's an*
*album of stickers—complete—from the film* The Ten Com-
mandments. *Bundó and Gabriel will give it to Senyora Rifà*
*because she loves Charlton Heston, who plays Moses. Gabriel*
*will take a sheriff costume that looks new and a ventriloquist's*
*doll that's supposed to resemble some variety-hall artist, but,*
*with the wide-brimmed hat it's wearing, it's more like a Chi-*

*cago gangster. The dummy's got a hole in its back and a stick
inside it to make it move its mouth when it's speaking. He'll
give both toys to C.*

～

This enigmatic C, this attack of embarrassment on the part of our
father—as if he was trying to shield us from his murky affairs—
concealed the name of Christof. Thanks to geographical proximity
and age, he was the lucky one who got the sheriff costume and
the ventriloquist's dummy. While the posh brother and sister were
discovering (if they ever did) in one neighborhood of Frankfurt
that their neglected toys had vanished, a small Christof, in very
different circumstances less than ten kilometers from where the
theft occurred, was busy impressing his friends with a sheriff's
star that shone so brightly you could see it a mile away, a Stetson
hat that made his head look small, and a Bakelite Colt 49. The
dummy, however, with its haughty air and big dark eyes, gave him
nightmares and was banished to a corner cupboard. Some years
went by before Christof remembered it and, having liberated it
from exile, stuck his hand into its entrails.

Every time we choose an entry from the inventory and copy
it down, all four brothers wish we could have taken part in one
of those sessions of divvying up the spoils! We now know about
it thanks to Petroli, who told us that, on the way home, with the
truck emptied of furniture, the three friends would stop at the first
roadside bar they found on the city outskirts and, out of the way of
indiscreet eyes, they'd open up the booty and examine it. The ceremony filled them with excitement mingled with stabs of fear, as
if it was always the first time, and, if the treasure was worthwhile,
they felt very pleased with themselves, almost like real bandits
or highwaymen. Afterward, with bloated egos, they'd go into the
bar to celebrate it with a whisky or two and a cigar. At that point,
Petroli used to feel obliged to pronounce a few words of contrition,
after which a chortling Bundó followed suit, while Gabriel calculated an equitable distribution of their trophies. Before getting
back on the road, Petroli would call the office in Barcelona to tell

them that the move had been accomplished without any problems and they were homeward bound.

The three friends presided over this ceremony with little remorse. If any of them was ever in danger of feeling guilty, the other two talked him out of it by reminding him that the goodies were a miserable tip in comparison with the hush-hush (and, they suspected, dangerous) favors they were doing for Senyor Casellas. Now, he was the real robber. It quite often happened that, taking advantage of some trip to Germany or eastern France, their boss would order them to depart from their route and head for the Swiss border. Once they'd reached a certain clearly specified point along the way, always close to a forest, they had to stop, turn off the engine, get out of the truck, and open the trailer doors. A couple of minutes later, some fellow dressed up like an alpine hiker would emerge from the trees and greet them with a nod of his head, after which he'd climb into the trailer. Then, with all the expertise of a professional burglar and clearly knowing where he had to look, he'd poke around in the neatly piled objects and furniture and, from some hiding place or other, would extract a very well-wrapped packet. It didn't weigh much and was about the size of an encyclopedia. Any idiot could see it contained bundles of banknotes. The man would then stow it in his backpack, acknowledge them once more with the ceremonious nod of a Swiss banker, and disappear into the trees again. Casellas's instructions stipulated that "once the small detour is complete and the item handed over," the three friends had to get back into the cab and resume the journey as if nothing had happened.

"Another big shot with his back well covered," Bundó used to say when they were back on the road again.

Petroli would then calculate. "With one of those packets the three of us would have enough to live off for a year, and I'd bet this truck on that if it was mine."

"Or two years. Don't worry, one of these days we'll get to keep the loot," Gabriel tended to add, sending shivers down three spines.

We can't claim that they frequently carried out this operation near the Swiss border but, thanks to its success—when the boss established that he wasn't running any risks—they certainly did it with increasing regularity. We should also explain that when they were carrying "the Czar's mail," as Bundó liked to call it, in honor of a book he'd read, *Michael Strogoff: The Courier of the Czar*, the Spanish border was wide open for them and they breezed through without their cargo being checked. The ad for La Ibérica emblazoned on the door of the Pegaso seemed to eliminate barriers, even when manned by the Guardia Civil. Somebody must have greased the palms of those uniformed Dobermans.

Compared with the funds that Senyor Casellas and company managed to deposit on Swiss soil over the ten years of European moves, the trinkets lifted by the three friends were very meager pickings indeed. Too meager. If they were exhibited together one day, more or less as Petroli had done in his home but multiplied by three, the whole collection would look like the contents of a flea market. Nonetheless, even in its entirety, that hoard of junk wouldn't be sufficient to account for the level of hysteria it induced among the victims of these thefts. Since it usually took them a while to notice the losses, the complaints would come in a few days after the move, when the family concerned was already installed in the new home and the three friends were loading up the Pegaso once again in Barcelona. The secretary, Rebeca, would take the call, coping with the first blast, after which she dutifully put it through to Senyor Casellas. The second blast must have been even more irate because, once it was over, the boss of La Ibérica would rush out of his office in a rage, his voice resounding around the garage.

"Petroli, Gabriel, Bundó! It's happened again! It's happened again! Scoundrels! Get into my office right now. Ipso facto!"

Incensed by the nagging suspicion that someone was making a fool of him, Senyor Casellas overdid the outrage and carried on like some head honcho in a comic book. Often, however, these explosions occurred when they were out with the truck again and then it was the secretary Rebeca who had to calm him down. He couldn't tell them off until some days later, by which time he'd cooled down somewhat and Gabriel, Bundó, and Petroli responded to his bluster by acting like simpletons. The repertoire of evasions, excuses, and alibis with which the three friends made a sucker of Senyor Casellas was wide-ranging and elaborate. Bundó, moreover, could adopt the face of an innocent child that would have disarmed the cruellest of torturers. The boss had a short memory and didn't file away the excuses from one occasion to refer to them on another. "Sorry, but this lost box was never loaded on our truck," they informed him, sounding worried. "This accusation offends us, chief: We would never dream of stealing from the consular corps of Spain." "And what if it was that hiker near the Swiss border? Well, goodness gracious, we should have kept a closer eye on him." The reference to Swiss matters always had the effect of appeasing Senyor Casellas, who would then let them go with the stipulation that such losses must never be repeated.

"We keep these things out of pure self-preservation," Gabriel said when he was telling our mothers about the stolen objects. "Years go by and we don't even look at them but we need to know they're there, inside such-and-such a cupboard or such-and-such a box. If we have an attack of pining or panic one day we can get them out, touch them for half a minute and then stow them away for a few more years. These personal objects conserve the past like a kind of relic that protects us from oblivion, which is the worst evil of all. Nobody wants to be forgotten. At one point there was a man living in Senyora Rifà's pension. He'd lost his house and his whole family in a fire, toward the end of the war. I've never known anyone so vulnerable. Apart from the pain of losing the family that loved him, he was completely helpless because he hadn't been able to save anything associated with his past. All his memories went up in smoke. When he talked about it he sounded crazy. His former life was only alive in his memory and with every day that went by, it faded a little more, like the colors of a painting dropped in a river."

Our father's words suggest that he wasn't aware that his situation was quite similar to that of the man whose whole existence had gone up in flames. The uncertain course his life had taken since the moment of his birth (foundling home, orphanage, boarding house) had left him with very few substantial memories, and yet he never seemed to complain. Who knows whether these appropriated objects didn't act as a sedative, or a balm. At the end of the day, this is the legacy we Christophers have received from our father. Lost suitcases, strayed packets, and boxes accidentally falling off a truck provided him with memories that weren't as unhappy. And now we, half scholars, half scavengers, are shamelessly poking around in the heart of things.

We've been driving around European roads for a while now. This might be a good point to stop and talk about Carolina, or Muriel. Her appearance in this story can be dated November 1965, during move Number 73 (we can date it with certainty), and it marked a turning point in the relationship of the three friends, especially between Bundó and Gabriel. We even believe that it had something to do with the general decline of the friendship, although the word "decline" is excessive perhaps, and Carolina is in no way directly responsible.

"Just to clarify, she was no Yoko Ono," Christopher wishes to add.

When we visited Petroli that weekend in Germany, he made a huge effort to describe Bundó and Carolina-Muriel's relationship. He talked about their codependence, which was exacerbated to the point of physical pain when they weren't together (they had simultaneous migraines, even when they were hundreds of kilometers apart), and he recalled their joint projects, cut short—like almost everything that matters to us—by the tragedy that we're going to have to talk about one of these days. Nonetheless, we left Petroli's house with the sensation that he'd only skimmed over the story. Either his memory failed him that day, or the prudence that comes with age wouldn't allow him to relive certain emotions for fear of betraying them so many years later. This is understandable, but, the thing is, we don't really trust his version. Anyway, we have the leading lady's account now.

Today, Carolina lives in a nondescript town in the center of France. It would appear that she has made peace with her destiny, or whatever you want to call it. Still youthful, in her late fifties, she's married to a moderately wealthy gentleman and bears a French surname that enables her both to shield and forget about her past as Muriel. In some writing-desk drawer, under a bundle of letters and newspaper cuttings, she must have hoarded a few photos of Bundó, or maybe just one, the one that shows him at his best. In her jewel box, too, she must keep the earrings he bought for her, after much deliberation and shelling out a fortune, at the Bagués jeweller's shop in Barcelona, or a bijou ring from one of their purloined boxes. Carolina professes an intimate devotion to these objects and, precisely because of that, she forces herself not to look at the photos or wear the jewellery too often. From time to time, however, she goes back to them, compelled by some desperate need. If she's alone at home, she takes out a photo of Bundó and leaves it on the kitchen table where she can see it all morning, or she'll put on the earrings even though she's not going out. "The past hurts," she says and then feels guilty because she can't help it. Without Bundó, the past turned into forbidden territory.

In our inspection of the boxes that Gabriel had left in the apartment in Carrer Nàpols, we found a recent address book. We checked through it and discovered where Carolina was living in France. We didn't know whether she was still alive, but we wrote to her explaining who we were, the Christophers, and that we were trying to find Gabriel. Then we asked if we could visit her. The answer came two months later when we'd given up hope, and it was brief and disappointing. In wavering handwriting, as if she doubted every word she penned, she said she didn't know where our father was—"where he's hiding," she said in fact, as if that were the only possible verb. She was happy that we four brothers had finally met—yes, she knew there were four of us—but ventured to say she didn't think it was a good idea to see all of us together. (Her lack of curiosity, by the way, reminded us of how our mothers felt about the enigma of Gabriel. With time one forgets these things.) The best she could do, said Carolina at the end of her letter, would be to meet Christophe for an hour and a half when she next went to Paris. Immediately after that, betraying a sense of urgency—and who knows if she would come to regret her words—she suggested a time and a place.

The appointed day arrived. In the end, with considerable difficulty, Christophe managed to stretch the hour and a half into a two-hour conversation (a monologue, rather). It was a Friday, lunchtime, at the beginning of September, at that time of year when the clear blue Parisian sky stretches like a balloon about to burst. Carolina had arranged to meet Christophe in Gastronominus, an old-style brasserie with mirrors, wooden benches, and a display of oysters in Avenue Gambetta, not far from the Père Lachaise cemetery. We'd decided to move one of our nonessential meetings to Paris that weekend. Disguised as tourists, cameras hanging from our necks, and using an open map as a foil, we other Christophers spied on them from behind the greasy windows of a Chinese restaurant across the street. (Carolina, if you read this, will you forgive us? We were full of admiration and got carried away.) It wasn't through lack of desire, but we refrained from showing up at the brasserie and confined ourselves to observing her from a distance. We were carrying on like lovesick adolescents, we admit, and each of us kept to himself the libidinous thoughts that afforded us a false intimacy with a sort of *belle de jour* Carolina (and Bundó would surely have forgiven our playful fantasies). The two hours went by in a flash. When she decided that the conversation had run its course, despite Christophe's best efforts to distract her and keep her talking, Carolina paid for the lunch, gave him a kiss, and disappeared up the avenue in a taxi. We other three Christophers came out of hiding and dashed over to Gastronominus as if we wanted to breathe in the essence of whatever trace she left, or were trying to keep a flame alive before it definitively went out. Seated at the same table, fetishizing the moment, we demanded that Christophe recount every inflection of her voice, every word that had crossed her lips.

Having pooled all the—at times contradictory—information at our disposal, we can now find our way through part of the maze.

Bundó met Muriel first and gradually, like someone peeling a thick-skinned fruit, he discovered the sweet Carolina hidden beneath. That November of 1965, Mademoiselle Muriel was only nineteen and had been working in the brothel for less than two months. She was a tall girl, more than a meter seventy, of firm yet svelte build. She was what the Spanish truck drivers of the time called a *maciza*, a well-built woman. In the salon, dressed only in a negligée, she displayed graceful flesh that seemed to have soaked up the sun, like that of a professional tennis player at Roland Garros during afternoon play. Her long hair, of such bright blondness it looked false, gave her a Nordic appearance that was only belied by the unmistakably Latin features of her face. At some stage in her genetic history there'd been a festival. Her Latin features were especially appealing: She had dark eyes and soft rounded cheeks, while a slightly outsize nose and mouth gave her a Gypsy-like physiognomy. More than beauty, her main attraction was her proportions: Seeing her height, her long legs, terrific breasts, and the bone structure of her body, you might have expected some awkwardness or possibly equine features, but she was perfectly proportioned. (Christophe confirms somewhat cautiously that, more than thirty years later, her elegance is still intact.) Our mothers, who saw photos of her at the time, shown off by a very proud Bundó, agree that she had a film-star aura. Sarah says she looked like an ingenuous, virginal starlet just before she's discovered (and messed up) by a Hollywood director. Mireille, the one who saw most of her, says she could have been a pin-up girl on a fold-out poster from *Lui*. Sigrun recalls her as having a touch of Monica Vitti in Antonioni's *The Eclipse*, as if she'd become bored with life too soon.

This profound disaffection must have acted as a protective carapace, and only Bundó was able to break through it. He did so in the only way possible: by not especially wanting to. At first, the frosty distance Muriel presented to her clients, unaware that this only heightened her charms, was simply the translation of Carolina's shyness into sexual confidence. Something the French are good at. Not long afterward, when the trade of spreading her legs for strangers left her innocence in tatters, Muriel learned to exploit this *froideur*, in order to spend more time with her legs closed and charge for it anyway. Bundó's good fortune—the transition from client to lover, the subconscious desire of most men who enter a brothel—is that he was able to bed Muriel while he was in love with Carolina, seeing them as two different people. We won't go into the intimate details because we don't know them, and too much time has gone by since their expiry date for them to matter much, although it is worth going back to the beginning in order to understand the situation.

In the spring of 1965, Carolina's parents decided to leave the little village in Jaén where they'd lived all their lives and to move to the outskirts of Barcelona. Some relatives, the pioneers, who'd taken a chance on leaving the village six months earlier, had written them a hope-inspiring letter. They talked about a metallurgical factory that needed workers and some cheap, very nice little houses that were being built on the outskirts of the city. It was like an Andalusian village, they said, but relocated close to the sea and shaded by a mountain. When they seriously pondered this uncertain future, Carolina's parents found, incredibly, that it had more appeal than the deadening silence of the street they lived on. Her father, a daydreamer who listened to the radio every night, tried hard to imagine a hectic, noisy city full of cars and people, but the pictures were never clear. Then his stomach knotted up with the familiar, uncomfortable sensation of regretting the fact that he'd never dared to leave. In the end, mainly because he was tired of grappling with these difficult thoughts of a different future, he decided to take his family to the prosperous Catalan region. Responding to a challenge or, if you like, looking to the future.

Carolina cried all the way on the train to Barcelona. Once there, her mother settled easily into the new neighborhood, a microclimate outside of which she rarely ventured until the day she died. Her three brothers, younger than her and all quite callow, accepted the father's plans without too much adolescent angst. Two weeks after the family had moved into a rented shack in Can Tunis, all three boys were working and were allowed to keep some of their weekly wages. Meanwhile, Carolina's tears regularly gushed forth with all the despair of a Juliet. She stayed at home, helping her mother and incessantly complaining that her parents had dragged her away from the village with the sole intention of separating her from an overly wild boyfriend who drank rum and coke and wanted to be a motocross rider when he was old enough. Her sense of injustice put her in a perpetually foul mood. She also wrote daily letters to the boy.

"They were such crazy letters that the poor boy must have been scared to death," Carolina told Christophe in the Paris brasserie, disowning that stage of her life. "I can't even remember his name. Benito? Indalecio? It was one of those names you'd expect a bachelor uncle to have. I wrote to him in pencil, which I do remember, and I imagine him replying to me scared stiff and praying I wouldn't do anything stupid because at the end of all my letters I threatened to cut my veins for love. Cutting your veins, in Jaén, in the sixties, was something done only by women who weren't right in the head or were possessed by the devil."

The boy couldn't have been such a good-for-nothing by the standards of the day because he replied punctually to all her letters once a week and, in his way, said yes to everything. That he'd rescue her from that hell. That they'd escape and travel the world—or Spain at least. That they'd have a big family, like in that film *La Gran Familia*, with Alberto Closas, the one where he's got fifteen kids. One day, in a letter of early June, amid all the tremendous promises that Carolina extracted like manna from him, the boy came up with a proposal. In the summer he'd be joining a group of local seasonal farm workers to go grape-picking in France. They planned to be there almost two months, until the end of September, and the employers promised a good wage. They'd be paid in French currency. What if she did that too and they met up there? He could add her name to the list of grape-pickers and then, once the season was over, they could have a week's holiday. Two months of being together every day, could she imagine that? He'd been told the south of France was very beautiful.

Carolina received the offer with some chagrin. She was delighted with the idea, genuinely moved, but she was also loath to emerge from the state of anguish into which she'd settled over the last few weeks. Happiness doesn't exist; it is only desired. Then again, she found it suspicious that, when her mother heard about it, she didn't hesitate to encourage her to put her name down as a grape picker.

"She would have wanted me out of the house, and the further away the better, of course," Carolina recalled. "I don't blame her. That silly stubborn little girl, a rebel without the slightest cause, probably deserved everything that happened to her shortly afterward in France." A few seconds of meditative silence. "Even now, I don't know if my life's been a punishment or a prize."

Finally, Carolina got on the train that took her to Perpignan. Once there, she had to get the bus the Andalusians were traveling on and go with them to pick grapes somewhere near the Rhone. The last-minute preparations and the telephone conversation with her boyfriend, frequently interrupted by interference and tearful laughter, cleared up any lingering doubts. The Carolina who said good-bye to her parents one Saturday morning at the Estació de França was a soul in expansion. She was nineteen, with kilometers stretching ahead of her and a head full of dreams. Barely four months later, the Muriel who attracted Bundó in a roadside brothel just outside Lyon, near Feyzin, had given up hope and confined herself to surviving in no-man's-land.

"So what happened? Well, my poor little boyfriend couldn't cope with the French air," Carolina said. "We met in Perpignan, and sat in the back seat of the bus holding hands all the way, but when we started picking grapes he went strange on me. To begin with, the men and women slept in separate shelters. The first three or four nights we waited patiently until everybody had gone to bed to sneak off and meet secretly in some hiding place. In the morning at breakfast, when we were eating our slice of bread with olive oil, he was congratulated by the men in the village. I, however, was given dirty looks by the women. Before long, tiredness got the better of us. In our free time, he went looking for out-of-the-way places, but I didn't dare to move away from the women. Then he told me that Barcelona had changed me. I denied it and—without really wanting to, I can assure you—I began to defend my parents and their decision to leave the village. He told me I'd got stuck-up. We had a fight and went to bed early. In our separate shelters. The next morning, in the vineyard, we sought each other out to make up, but it was difficult to exchange even a few words because the overseers were always watching. For them, we were just dirt-poor Spaniards. They yelled at us in French and those storms of guttural sounds hovered over us like a threat. Today, I doubt they'd yell so much. Well anyway, what happened was that our first day off was a Sunday. We'd decided to take some lunch with us and go and swim in the river. My little angel was quite a sluggard. I waited for a while with the sandwiches ready and finally went to wake him up. He'd skipped out. His bed was empty, and there was no sign of his suitcase. One of the people from the village took me aside and, before saying a word, handed me a nicely ironed handkerchief. Then he told me that the boy had gone home, the wimp. He said he was missing his family." Carolina let out a sarcastic laugh. "Poor little chap. I never heard another word from him and I didn't want to either. I got through the two months as best I could. The women in the village must have consoled me, though I don't have good memories of them. I finished the grape picking with a bit of money in my pocket. It wasn't much but, since I'd earned it myself, it gave me a sense of freedom and self-esteem. At home with my family, I never knew that existed. The day the bus went back to Spain, I didn't turn up at the bus stop. Instead, I went into a baker's and asked for a slice of cake. I wanted to feel important. Then I phoned home and told my mother I'd been offered another job working on the land and wouldn't be back till Christmas. I didn't go back to Barcelona at Christmas. One of the overseers in the vineyard had introduced me to a friend of his from Saint-Étienne. He had a bistro in Lyon and needed waitresses."

The so-called bistro or roadside brothel was called Papillon, a

name that in the sixties, through some absurd entomological association of pinning down and captivity, conveyed eroticism. The arrival of the new *cocotte* was seen as a major event in the area. The
only missing touch was coverage in the local newspapers. Made
up *comme une poupée de cire*—as the madame required—and
wearing a flimsy dress that the red lighting conspired to make still
more transparent, she could at once look like a thirteen-year-old
kid and a housewife out for a bit of extramatrimonial fun. In either
case, she had a surfeit of admirers.

"*Muriel, ma belle, sont des mots qui vont très bien ensemble...*"
Chris had to have his say, profanation of lyrics included.

Bundó didn't discover Muriel's real name until their third
meeting. The first time he entered the club was in the course of
Move 73: Barcelona-Strasbourg. The three friends had unloaded
that same day and were dog-tired. It was getting dark as they approached Lyon and, in the interest of health and safety, they decided to stop and sleep somewhere on the outskirts of the city, on
the way to Valence. They were looking for a roadside hostel that
appeared in *The Expert Trucker's Guide to Europe*. Gabriel, who
was driving at that point, tended to put his faith in cities with a
more or less famous soccer team. As they approached the first
houses, and though he was half asleep in his seat, Bundó spotted
in the distance the glittering eye of a neon butterfly and asked Gabriel to stop in front of the establishment. In the darkness of the
cab he smiled smugly, well satisfied with his fine-honed instinct.
He couldn't resist. "It'll cost me about the same as a room with
breakfast and, as you know, I never eat breakfast. I prefer to get
my fill at dinnertime... if you get my meaning," he said by way of
justifying himself. It wasn't true, of course. His partiality for these
places cost him quite a lot more, and, besides, he couldn't put it
down as travel expenses, but the other two always went along with
it. He was a big boy now. They agreed to pick him up, at the front
entrance, at five the next morning.

Bundó went inside. It was winter and the place was practically
deserted. Seated at the bar were half a dozen bored girls and a
couple of loners who preferred boozing. Outside, the red neon-lit

façade sparkled with such intensity that its light seeped through the cracks in the door and boarded-up windows, outlining everything with a sanguinary aura. Later, on subsequent visits, an exhausted Bundó would be mesmerized by this effect while Muriel was upstairs with another client and taking too long to come down. That first night, however, he set about securing Muriel's company because no other alternative was possible. You know these things immediately. There's no need to think about it.

Once upstairs in the room, what sort of conversation would these two have had? We Christophers like playing with this.

BUNDÓ (*taking his shoes and socks off*): Comme tu t'appelles? Tu es très jolie.

MURIEL (*pretending to smooth down her dress*): Muriel, mon cheri. Et tu?

BUNDÓ (*unbuttoning his shirt and yawning*): Je m'appelle Bundó.

MURIEL (*looking in the mirror, pretending to brush her hair*): Bondeau, mon chéri? De dond es-tu?

BUNDÓ (*taking off his pants, seated on the edge of the bed*): Espagnol.

MURIEL (*watching his reflection in the mirror and pretending she's got a problem taking off one of her earrings*): Wow! I'm Spanish too. From Jaén. I'm Andalusian.

BUNDÓ (*climbing into bed*): Well, actually, I'm Catalan. I'm a truck driver. Hey . . . what kind of name . . . is this . . . ? Who . . . called you . . . that?

MURIEL (*sitting with her back to the bed, mumbling and pretending to blush*): It's just a name. And you, what part of Catalonia are you from?

BUNDÓ (*in bed*): Zzzzzz . . .

MURIEL (*pretending that she loves him a little*): Bon soir, mon chéri.

Instinct woke Bundó at quarter to five the next morning. He started moving although it took him a few seconds to work out where he was. This often happened to him. The warmth coming off Muriel sleeping at his side helped him to get his bearings. He gazed at the girl while he got dressed: her body curled up under the sheets, her straight blond hair—*à la France Gall*—such beautiful features, slightly swollen with sleep . . . Bundó remained there for a minute, holding his breath, and in this suspended time he realized that the girl had got to him in a way that had never happened before. Perhaps it was tenderness. The blast of the Pegaso's horn outside snapped him out of his reverie and brought him to his senses. He washed his face in a basin in one corner of the room—in freezing water—put on his anorak and, with a look, he said good-bye. When his hand was on the door handle, however, he stopped, went back and slowly, very carefully so as not to wake her, lifted the bedclothes and contemplated Muriel. She was naked under the sheets and the magnificent body curled up like a seed in a husk emanated an intense, female, nocturnal smell. He sniffed greedily, trying to absorb it, and covered her up again.

Even before reaching the bottom of the stairs, he knew that it wasn't going to be easy to get the girl out of his head.

The second meeting in the brothel took place nine weeks later—Move 77, Barcelona-Paris—and Muriel took a while to recognize Bundó. It was a shorter visit, a quick upstairs-and-downstairs, while Gabriel and Petroli washed the truck, topped up the diesel, and had breakfast at a nearby service station. Bundó spoke to her in Spanish, but Muriel was having a bad day and would only answer him in her shaky French. He thought this must be part of some game—all this *mon chéri* and *mon chouchou* whispered in his ear, so badly pronounced and so exciting—and he followed suit. They got to work, and au revoir. But the girl's reserved character occupied Bundó's thoughts the whole trip.

The third encounter took place only two weeks later, a radiant Saturday in a gray February and, for both of them, it was the confirmation that something was going on. Bundó wasn't working that weekend. Some strange feeling tugged him to the Estació de França very early on the Saturday morning. He took a train to Perpignan and then, after changing platforms, went on to Lyon. He then took a taxi and told the driver to take the Saint-Étienne road.

The train and taxi fares cost him a week's wages, but, far from letting that worry him, his pulse was throbbing with heroic urgency by the time he reached the whorehouse door. Such high spirits. He was the king. The adventure was worth it for this incredibly powerful sensation alone. He got out of the taxi at what must have been around seven in the evening. What with the traveling, pauses, and delays, almost twelve hours had gone by since he'd left Barcelona that morning. He'd told himself the whole thing was a jaunt and, with the same flippancy, dismissed one tricky thought: He hadn't worked out how or when he'd be getting back.

As his eyes adapted to the false darkness of the brothel—there were lots of clients, a scrum of men and women—he looked for Muriel and couldn't see her. He spotted the madame at one end of the bar and asked for her.

Muriel? It was her the day off.

What? He didn't understand . . .

Muriel wasn't working that day. Women's things, you know.

The world caved in. The madame smiled pityingly—she'd seen this kind of doomed addiction before—and pointed at the other girls who might be able to save him. Bundó looked mechanically at the faces of the people around him, trying to react, and only managed to see himself as an imbecile. He'd dressed as if he was going to work, with his anorak on top so it would all look more natural, and now these clothes made him feel even more ridiculous. Without finishing his whisky, he turned tail and went outside. The reddish light fell over him like a rain of shame. Right then, he would have given another week's wages to be back home again unscathed and to wipe out the memory of this farce, including the memory of Muriel. Then he heard the click of high heels, turned around and saw her coming down the outside stairway that led to her room.

We'll only give a brief account of the scene. Muriel had circles under her eyes, wore no makeup, and was so listless she was almost unrecognizable. Bundó worshipped her even more. She saw the attractive, chubby-cheeked, naughty-boy face framed by curly hair. The Barcelona truck driver. Muriel stopped halfway down the stairs. He started to move as if in response and then stopped too. Later, Bundó would describe how he was about to kneel down dramatically and declare his love but desisted because he didn't have the bunch of flowers. It was lucky he didn't. Muriel had experienced several such episodes and had sent the fellows packing without a second thought. For a prostitute, there's nothing more detestable than a client who thinks he can lure her—and redeem her—with the promise of a spick-and-span life in the provinces.

"It's my day off today," she finally said in a wan voice when she got to the bottom of the stairs. "But will you invite me to dinner? I want to ask you something."

It's difficult to imagine that there could have been, in the whole wide world, on that Saturday evening, two people more in need of affection.

Bundó invited Muriel to dinner. Of course he invited her. Since they had neither car nor truck they decided to go to the service station cafeteria, five minutes away, where they did quite a good *croque-monsieur*. As they walked along the roadside, Muriel took Bundó's arm. In heels, she was taller than him. They were silent, the breath steaming from their mouths. Every time a car passed, they stopped for safety's sake and she clung to him a little more. Then, for a few seconds, the headlights lit up a pair of furtive lovers. This particular image summed up the future as Bundó wanted to see it. It monopolized his thoughts and, although the night was very cold, sweat was running off him. Muriel felt the warmth coming off his body, like a stove, and clutched him all the tighter.

In the cafeteria, they played cat and mouse as they ate. Now more focused, Bundó tried to penetrate the girl's inner life and started asking questions. Muriel answered evasively and deftly changed the subject. It was a trick of the trade. They could have been at it half a lifetime. Then she asked him to do her a favor, and the first chink opened up.

If Bundó was going to help her, Muriel had to tell him that her real name was Carolina and that less than a year ago she was living with her parents in the Can Tunis district on the periphery of Barcelona. She then specified what the favor was: She would give him a sum of money, and he was to take it to her parents. Naturally, when they asked for news of her, he had to lie about her work and where she lived. They'd sort out the details together. As he listened and nodded, Bundó mentally repeated her name. Carolina. He liked it more than Muriel, a lot more. Carolina. Maybe it was more normal, more familiar—Carolina—but to him it sounded like the password to a precious secret.

Now that she'd begun to unburden herself, Carolina breathed more easily. She went into the restroom to tidy up and looked in the mirror. Her face had changed. Bundó then paid for their dinner and they returned to the brothel. They went up to her room and, between the two of them, cooked up a story that was sufficiently plausible for Carolina's parents. Her practical imagination combined very well with Bundó's crazier concoctions. It got late, very late. Bundó started yawning and Carolina hastened to say he could sleep there if he wanted to.

"As a friend."

The next morning, before returning to Barcelona, Bundó gave her the first gift: a silver chain bracelet (Lot 66, Barcelona-Cologne).

He showed up late at La Ibérica on Monday. He had a terrible cold.

After work one evening that week, Bundó went to visit Carolina's parents. He introduced himself as an acquaintance of their daughter and handed over the envelope containing the money. Carolina's mother cried when she read the letter inside. The father whistled in astonishment when Bundó calculated the exchange value in pesetas of those francs. They ushered him into the living room, invited him to have a glass of wine with them, and then they both began to badger him with their questions. One of the things that most impressed them was that their daughter, who was now working as a secretary for a fruit exporting company, had learned to speak French in such a short time.

The same scene was repeated on future occasions, depending

on when the La Ibérica destinations took Bundó anywhere near the brothel. The wariness with which her parents had received him on the first visit turned into total trust and, little by little, Bundó became Carolina's official biographer. In accordance with her wishes, he tried to give them only the barest details, in dribs and drabs. The fewer the details the better. After a certain point, however, since the parents kept demanding news and Carolina continued to be the hostage of Muriel, the messenger was obliged to invent a double life for her. Enthusiasms, friends, projects, setbacks. With each visit, Bundó constructed another episode of the story of Carolina in France. As long as he didn't make things awkward for her, anything could be used to give substance to the false life. Eventually not even Carolina was au fait and, when she phoned her parents on special days like birthdays or Christmas Eve, she was taken aback by some of their comments. Then she had to improvise and invent. Immediately afterward, very indignant (and slightly frisky too), she phoned Bundó at the boarding house and gave him an earful. What on earth did he think he was doing? How dare he tell them that her best friend was called Muriel? Or that she might be transferred to Paris? Ah, so she had a French boyfriend, did she? And what did this boyfriend look like? Like him, Bundó?

We know that Bundó enjoyed Carolina's outbursts but suffered in equal measure. It was 1967, more than a year since they'd been seeing each other intermittently, and their relationship had entered a new phase. Bundó stopped frequenting other prostitutes. This abstinence now meant that the La Ibérica trucks stopped more frequently on the road from Lyon to Saint-Étienne. While he went upstairs with Muriel, Gabriel and Petroli waited in the service station cafeteria. They ate *croque-monsieur*, as Bundó had recommended, and worked on the excuses they'd have to offer to Senyor Casellas to explain the delay. Carolina, meanwhile, had begun to incorporate Bundó's fabrications into Muriel's life. When a client got too heavy, she'd blow him away by telling him she was finishing a university degree in Lyon, that she had a brawny, evil-

tempered French boyfriend and that they were going to live in
Paris very soon.

There were days when the to-ing and fro-ing between reality
and fiction caught even Bundó off guard. Sometimes, when he
was lucky enough to spend the whole night with her, he'd get into
bed with Muriel (paying, because the brothel norms and the madame's monitoring required it) and would wake up in the morning
lying next to Carolina. However familiar he was with her double
identity, he wasn't spared a certain degree of anguish because of
it, and, when he was back in the truck again, his two friends had
to try to lift his spirits. Petroli, the most methodical of the three
of them, advised him to take Carolina back to Barcelona, and the
sooner the better. Nevertheless, since the beginning, since the
first Saturday he'd stayed to sleep with her—as a friend—Carolina
had warned Bundó that he should never make plans for the two
of them, or try to convince her to do anything. She, and she alone,
would decide about her future.

Bundó then plotted his own, more gradual strategy. The idea
was to be patient and to swaddle Carolina in a mesh of gallantry
that would make her see the light. He visited her with sexual devotion, brought her news of her parents (sweetened up, when necessary, to disguise the grayness), and presented her with objects he
acquired through the moves. With each step he took, she ceded
him a cubic millimeter of her future. They were vague references,
comments made as if in passing and, for any one of us, would have
been imperceptible in terms of any advance, but Bundó knew how
to interpret them as a stimulus to keep going.

Early in 1969, after three years of dithering that threatened
to go on forever, Bundó made a down payment on an apartment
in a building that was going up in Via Favència in Barcelona. He
put it in both their names. Here we have a sea change. When
he eventually took possession of the keys, he left Senyora Rifà's
boarding house and went to live there alone. Carolina approved
of the change (and maybe even started to make plans), but it was
very difficult for her to decide to return to Barcelona.

Before Christophe met her in the brasserie in Paris, we Christophers had asked ourselves more than once: Did she really love Bundó? We had no right to do so, but we questioned her motives. We must confess that this uncertainty continued for some time after the lunch. Senyora Carolina, in her late fifties, friendly but distant, could only go back to that period of her life sheltered behind a shield of cynicism. This artifice didn't convince us, and, unjustly, we left Paris oppressed by feelings of frustration. Three weeks later, Christophe opened up his mailbox and found the following note. Read it and declare us guilty.

> Mon cher *Christophe,*
> *It is now some weeks since we had lunch together in Paris, and not a single day has gone by when I haven't reproached myself for that meeting. I should never have agreed to it. I talked too much. You shook up my memory as if it was a glass ball, and now the snowstorm won't go back to settling at the bottom. Don't blame yourself, though. In the last few days, thinking hard, I've realized the whole thing was a question of self-defense. It was so hard to get over Bundó's absence! The only way out, eventually and paradoxically, was to leave the brothel in the way I did. After moving to Paris and cutting myself off from the world for a while, I said yes to a man who was convinced that he loved me, and went off to live with him in the provinces, in just another anonymous city. Happiness doesn't exist but is only desired. You can desire it all your life and you'll never have enough. I'm not complaining, but I changed my life just as I would have done if I'd gone with him, with Bundó. It was the only way to survive.*
> *Now, Christophe, I'm going to tell you—tell all of you— something intimate that should release me from this pain, or at least ease it. Many years have gone by, but this is the most alive thing that is left to me of Bundó: He was the only man who was ever able to make me confuse sex and love. I hope you will forgive my frankness. The French say that every orgasm is a little death. Yet each visit from him gave me the gift of experiencing little births: He took me back for a few seconds*

*to that patch of perfect, inviolable darkness when you still
haven't been born and the world expects nothing from you.*

*You see? Things are looking calmer inside the glass ball. I
alarmed myself too much. The snowstorm was just a rain of
confetti.*

*Give my best regards to your mother, please. Oh, Mireille!
Tell her I often think about her.*

*I hope that you and your brothers will understand me
when I make my final farewell now, with a kiss.*

*Your Carolina*

*P.S. They were your brothers, n'est-ce pas, those three Ga-
briels who were spying on me from the other side of the road
when I got into the taxi in front of the restaurant? You are so
alike!*

Oh dear, she found us out. What more can we say?

Perhaps this is a sign. Maybe it's time for each one of us to
speak for himself. Get ready, Christof: In keeping with strict bio-
logical order you have to start.

# 8

## The Fifth Brother

The first thing you have to do, before anything else, is beg my forgiveness. In front of everyone."

"Beg your forgiveness? May I ask why?"

"Because you've known our brothers for months, Christof, and you haven't introduced me yet. You haven't invited me on any of your 'research' trips, as you like to call them with your usual pedantry. As if Gabriel wasn't my father too. I bet you've never even mentioned me to them." He lapses into reproachful silence. "You've never told them about me, have you?"

"There's no time for that now. Get it into your head that this is my turn, I'm the soloist in this concert and I have a lot to say. You should be grateful that I've let you come along this time."

"So you're going to ignore me and hog the limelight... Have it your own way then. But don't complain later if I clam up and refuse to say a word. You're winding me up to the point of insurrection. Anyway, you haven't got a clue how to do a monologue. We always do our gigs together."

"Okay, calm down. Christophers, listen: This is our brother Cristoffini. He was born in Italy—"

"—in a little village in Sicily, in the middle of the island, and don't make me go into any more detail. They haven't made me Favorite Son because they already have one, Don Vito. And don't make me go into details about that either. It all stays in the fam-

119

ily. We might share a father, Christophers, but I'm from a famous lineage on my mother's side, *capito*? I'm also the oldest of us five brothers, and, in case you haven't worked it out yet, that makes me the heir. When you four were born, I'd already spent years with this cardboard carcass"—he taps his head, *toc, toc*—"dragging it around the world, dressed up in my striped diplomat's suit and this hat that never goes out of fashion. If I look younger than you, it's because I'm immortal."

Cristoffini's voice rasps out hoarse and asthmatic sounding, as if his vocal cords were made of esparto grass.

"Okay, perhaps I owe you an explanation. Cristoffini and I do shows at weekends. We go to nightclubs, matinee shows, birthday parties, wherever they ask for us. We have a go at the government and famous folk, and make people laugh. Sometimes Cristoffini gets stuck into the audience, and then I have to gag him to stop him from going too far. It's our pastime and, besides, we make a bit of extra cash."

"Do you know what our publicity says? Christof and Cristoffini. I let him put his name first only because it sounds better like that. He gets to keep the loot (not much), and I get the fame (lots). How many years have we been doing our show, sonny?"

"More than fifteen. We made our debut when I was in high school, one of those Christmas festivals they put on, remember? Mom came every year, and Dad never came once. To tell the truth, we've been very good company for one another over the years. Right, Cristoffini?"

Cristoffini lays his head on Christof's shoulder, making out that he's moved by his words, but his mocking expression betrays him. A lurid pink scar follows the contour of his left cheek.

"I know you're messing with me, as usual." With a well-aimed shove, Christof extricates himself from Christoffini's embrace. "Sometimes I think you don't know how to tell the difference between truth and fiction. It's one thing for you to play the cynic in our show—we've agreed that's your role—but it's quite another for you to do it when you're with the family. I'm sure my brothers—our brothers—know what I mean when I say that we've been very good company for one another. Christophers, I'm referring to that sadness that used to descend on us all of a sudden. We've already talked about it, right? When we were about eleven or twelve. You come home from school in winter. You're all alone because Mom's at work and there's no news of Dad. You look at yourself in the hall mirror while you're taking off your coat and scarf, and, all of a sudden, the face of the boy, numb with cold, is darkening with distress. That loneliness didn't last long, but it was absolutely searing! It came out of you, and it died in the image in the mirror. It was only natural that we wanted to exchange that reflection for a brother who would have helped to fill the silences."

"If you'd woken me up sooner from my slumbers in that box, you might have saved yourself all that."

"I've apologized for that millions of times," Christof says in a stage whisper. "Don't make me repeat it in front of my brothers. Now let me talk about our father, which is why we're here."

"*Va bene,*" Cristoffini says condescendingly. He closes his eyes and nods encouragingly, like a priest about to hear a confession. "Where are you going to start?"

"Well, I could say that when I saw Dad for the first time I was over a year old and he didn't even know I existed. His appearance made a huge impression on me, and maybe that's why it's so prominent among what I like to think are my first memories. We're standing by the front door, and this tall, thin man picks me up with inexpert hands. No one says a word. I look at my mother, wanting her to comfort me, but she's so shocked I don't recognize her and then I start howling."

"Just a moment, just a moment. Wind the tape back, and get inside your mother's belly, please. If necessary go back as far as the *coglioni di tuo padre.* We want to know all the details."

"If you insist . . ." Christof looks gratified. "Then I'll have to go back to January 15, 1965, during a move La Ibérica did to Bonn. In the catalogue of pilferage it would appear as Number 47, I'd say, and the pickings were notable for a collection of zarzuela records. At about two in the afternoon, after unloading in the capital of West Germany, Gabriel, Bundó, and Petroli set out on their homeward journey, but near Koblenz something like a thick white eiderdown wadded the sky. Less than ten kilometers down the road they were slap-bang in the middle of a snowstorm of biblical proportions." Cristoffini makes the sign of the cross. "They'd got through similar difficulties on other occasions, but this time it was a return trip. With an empty trailer and no ballast, the truck slithered on the asphalt like an elephant on an ice rink. They followed the motorway along the Rhine for a few more kilometers to see if the ominous whiteness in the sky was going to clear, but when they got near Mainz and Wiesbaden, they gave up. It was getting dark, and the only landscape they could make out, increasingly enshrouded in snow, filled them with a very Germanic state of anxiety. Bundó, with his talent for finding good roadside hostels, recalled that some German truck drivers had been singing the praises of a place near Mainz. In those days before Bundó met Muriel-Carolina, he enjoyed chatting with other truck drivers in service areas and exchanging recommendations for the best motels and brothels along the European transport routes. Since he was meticulous about these matters, he marked them with a red cross on the map, writing the names alongside them."

"Hang on, Christof," Cristoffini interjected. "A hostel, near Mainz? Don't tell me it was the Herz-As, that Ace of Hearts dive you dragged me into so you could have a beer when we were on our way back from a gig in Frankfurt?" Christof nods resignedly. "I thought so. How decadent! The stench of spilled beer! Those wooden benches and walls must be caked with thirty years of truck drivers' vomit, including our father's and his friends'. And the ladies who were tempting us at the bar (me more than you)— *Madonna!*—they've been at it for three decades . . ." He shuts up for a moment, nodding and pondering in silence. "In other words, to go back to that original night, a mere snowstorm provided the perfect excuse for the three friends to take refuge under the well-warmed eiderdowns of those *meretrici*. And, meanwhile, Gabriel's spermatozoa, poor little things, were preparing for the great race of their lives."

"Don't go jumping to conclusions, Cristoffini. Listen and don't interrupt me, please. Let's not start on that. First of all, if we went into the truck drivers' hostel that night, it was to do some research, even if you object to the word. Petroli had told us, the four flesh-and-blood Christophers, about the episode, and I wanted to check out the scene. I agree with you, it's a dump nowadays. Second, for your information, the only one who stayed in the Herz-As that night was Bundó. He couldn't resist. Sometimes his need to jump in the sack with an easy-going woman was almost a matter of life and death, like eating or sleeping, and it had the side effect of clearing his head. Though the sign of the hostel said Ace of Hearts, which must have called out to Gabriel's gambling instincts, he and Petroli opted for a more conventional alternative . . . and if you imagine for one moment that my mother, Sigrun, worked in the Herz-As, I'm sorry to disappoint you because she didn't."

"It never as much as entered my head, Christof, I swear it. Mothers are sacred."

Cristoffini blows a kiss off his fingertips. Christof's managed to read his mind, and, for a moment, Cristoffini's dummy face seems to be blushing. The scar on his cheek glows like a hot coal.

"So much the better."

"Keep going. Come on, it's getting late. So far we've got Bundó in the Ace of Hearts chatting up a lady who could also be his mother but she isn't. That's clear. She's not his mother or anyone else's mother. Now we need to know what's happened with Gabriel, Petroli, and, more than anything else, the twitchy little critters that are wriggling around inside Gabriel's balls."

Christof lights up. Normally he doesn't smoke but he uses it for effect and to draw out his words. He inhales then blows the smoke in Cristoffini's face. The latter shuts his eyes, coughing violently, about to split his backbone in two.

"People who spend their lives on the road, in a truck and a long way from home, need to be alone," Christof resumes. "I call it a refuge. Most of all it's a mental refuge, though it's often dressed up as physical need. Locked in the cab day and night, running here and running there all over the map, they get fed up with each other in the end and are dying to escape for a while."

"Like us two," Cristoffini chimes in. "Like those times when you bed me down in my cardboard box (because he keeps me in a miserable cardboard box, Christophers!) and go off traveling without me."

"If I remember rightly, the last time we had a Christophers' meeting in Barcelona I brought you along."

"Yes, in your suitcase, keeping your underpants company. And you know very well that I've become claustrophobic with age! And then you're ashamed of me, which is the most horrible thing that can happen between brothers, and you don't let me leave the hotel..."

"Okay, that's enough talking about you. You're vanity personified. And now, if you'll be so good as to let me continue, we have an appointment with Gabriel, Bundó, and Petroli." Cristoffini's ready with his riposte but Christof won't have it. "As I was saying, after six months of traveling together, the three friends had learned to spot those extremely scarce golden opportunities for being alone, and to keep them for themselves. The repertoire included (real or invented) breakdowns of the truck, the breathers after getting rid of a whole truckload of stuff, fortuitous hitches like the customs office being closed at an international checkpoint, a detour because of road works, the ban in some countries against driving on Sundays, or a bad storm. On these occasions we've seen how Bundó rushes off to take refuge in the arms of the first tart he can find on terra firma. Our father Gabriel's refuge is still a mystery: complex, intangible, fleeting, and inaccessible all those years, it might well be that its only manifestation is here in these pages (like footsteps in the snow revealing the passage of an invisible man), and putting the last period in place will be the only way of giving it substance. Right, Christophers? As for Petroli, we know that he tended to prefer older women, but he also thought that paying prostitutes was cheating. He was more partial to the adventure of flirting with housewife-cum-mothers, even if it turned out badly. He admitted that his aspirations tended to be romantic, not to say utterly unrealistic, but the smallest sign of success was so pleasing to him that it gave him the confidence of a Casanova, which lasted for several days."

"Casanova? Petroli a Casanova? *Ma tu sei pazzo!* You really enjoy undermining the legend of my compatriot . . . Not even I"— and an indignant Cristoffini stretches out his neck and closes his eyes—"and take note of what I'm saying, I, who have spent many hours locked up in wardrobes or hiding under the beds of mistresses, trembling with fear that the cuckold's going to discover me (the Italian cuckolds are always little pricks), not even I can compare with the great Giacomo!"

Christof lets him prattle on.

"Listen to the sound of gently falling rain, Christophers. Now you can see why I haven't introduced him to you before now, right? He might say he's our older brother but he's unpresentable!" Christof looks upset for a few moments but then realizes he's losing it and tries to calm down. "Anyway, he doesn't give a damn. He always carries on like this, and I'm not going to let him rattle me. As I was saying, outside of Spain, Petroli turned into a sort of Casanova, yes, and he always took refuge in nostalgia. For some sentimental reason, he could only find peace when surrounded by his fellow Spaniards. Thus, with the same devotion that Bundó put into his highway harems, Petroli sought Spanish emigrant associations scattered across Central Europe. It all began with a childhood friend of his who'd emigrated to the south of Germany to work in a metallurgical plant. For the first few summers after that they continued to meet up whenever they went back to the village to visit their parents, but, after the old people died, Petroli lost sight of him. Years later, one day when they were passing close to where his friend lived, he called in to say hello. While Gabriel and Bundó waited in the cab playing cards, the friend took him to have a glass of wine at the Spanish Workers' Center. He showed Petroli photos of his wife and German-born kids. For want of practice, his Catalan had lost its native accent. That long half hour of conversation, although it teetered on the brink of sorrow, lifted Petroli's spirits for the rest of the trip. Thereafter, without needing the excuse of finding a friend, he turned to anyone who would listen in these receptacles of melancholy. He'd walk in glum, unload his troubles onto the first Spaniard he found, and come out a new man. Very occasionally, when his art of seduction worked, he managed to leave the place with some liberated Iberian lady wanting a bit of fun. As you can imagine, it wasn't long before he could rattle off by heart every club, association, and center where the emigrant workers met. Do you remember, Christophers, what Petroli said when we went to visit him? 'Those people with their ordinary concerns, ambitions, and attacks of homesickness, made me feel I was in good company. I was almost in the same boat. The only difference was that my frustration didn't stay still and my adopted country was everywhere and nowhere.' Petroli's round included associations of Catalans, Galicians, Extremadurans, and Aragonese. They had evocative names like Centro García Lorca, Hogar del Maño, and La Santa Espina, and they always appeared in industrial cities cut from the same pattern. Eindhoven, Mannheim, Reading, Béziers, Kaiserslautern. Neighborhoods with factories and chimneys, cheap housing, and milky skies."

"That's enough. You just want to make us cry, Christof. I hope, for your own good," says Cristoffini, fingering a bump on his jacket at about rib level, "that you're not about to do something daft like singing one of those hymns along the lines of 'Oh, I shall never see again the sunny shores of my land . . . Oh, how I long for you, little birds and my garden's flowers' . . . We agree that going to another country to work must have been a drama for all those people but, fuck it, goddammit, let's not lose sight of Franco's Spain, which wasn't exactly a variety show in the fifties."

"No, I didn't want get folksy or overdo the pathos. On the contrary. What I wanted to tell you was precisely (before this parasite butted in as usual) that today's Petroli, the pensioner in the north of Germany, is convinced that time proved him right and that his fixation with the emigrants' centers sorted out his life, but that's only partly true. The fact is that, after several years of running around in the truck (by February 1972 to be precise), Petroli was well known among the emigrants, to the point of being a caricature. Everywhere he went, they all knew his troubles and complaints and took pains to avoid him. The thousands of kilometers he'd swallowed up had begun to dampen his spirits and age him prematurely. Then, on a visit to the Asturian Center in Hamburg, which we might describe as routine, he met Ángeles. The mutual attraction was so immediate and electric that, first thing next morning, without a second thought, he phoned Senyor Casellas and, amid bursts of demented laughter, announced that he was leaving the job. Gabriel and Bundó were already on their way back to Barcelona. Casellas tried to dissuade him, appealing first to his responsibilities and then tempting him with the prospect of a raise. Petroli, however, wasn't in the least embarrassed about pronouncing the word . . ."

"What word?"

"The word. You know what it is."

"No, I don't. Go on, say it. I want to hear it."

"You just want to mess with me, I know."

"I'm telling you I won't. Promise. What word?"

"Love. Love. He told Casellas he'd found the love of his life."

"*Ooooooh! Che bello! L'amore!*"

"You're disgusting, Cristoffini, and you've got no soul. If the devil appeared one day wanting to buy it, you'd have nothing to sell him. You're empty inside. You're a bottomless pit. A glacier, an abyss that gobbles up everything . . . Shall I go on?"

"Well, do you know what I think?" Cristoffini counterattacks, demonstrating that criticism is water off a duck's back to him. "If I don't have a soul it's because you stole it when you were a kid. Every time you stuck your hand inside me without the slightest qualm, just like you're doing now, you took a pinch of my soul and kept it for yourself. You're a thief. You're worse than a thief!" He pauses to let the venom take effect. "Is that what you want? Shall we get out our dirty laundry and show it to our brothers?"

Christof's been stopped in his tracks. With drooping shoulders and a lost look in his eye, he's turned into a lifeless dummy. Cristoffini raises a haughty head, lie a newly crowned king, savouring his victory. When the silence starts to weigh too heavily, he taps

Christof's shoulder as if trying to snap him out of a daydream. It's a defiant gesture.

"Come on, stop carrying on like a baby, little brother. Don't get cross. We're dying to hear what you've got to say. You were saying that Petroli fell in love with Ángeles..."

"Yes, I was saying that he met her in one of those emigrants' places," Christof says self-consciously, "but what I wanted to remark on is that, apart from that detail, you won't find anything else that matches Petroli's normal erotic ambitions: She wasn't older than him, she didn't carry on every five minutes about being homesick for her motherland, and neither did she want to return to Oviedo."

"Very good. Have you finished, Barbara Cartland? Sorry, sorry..." From Christof's deflated reaction Cristoffini realizes that sarcasm is no longer seemly. "I just want to ask you one thing. What does Petroli's sentimental life have to do with the famous day of the snowstorm, which is what concerns us right now?"

"Everything, Cristoffini, everything. Let's see if you get it. Life's full of surprises and that's what's so great about it. Right, Christophers?" Christof wants supporters. "If there's one thing we've confirmed since we began following the trail left by our father, it's that our lives (everybody's lives) are capriciously entwined and knotted together, sometimes playfully and, more often than not, in an impossible twist. Try to follow a strand from the end, undo all the knots to observe each thread separately, and you'll soon find out that it's totally useless. At the moment of birth we're already tangled like wool. In the end, the paradox is that a life as solitary as Gabriel's could have been braided with so many different people. So, in our father's case, the skein of realities and dreams that is the stuff of intimate life starts to become dangerously snarled up the day of the big snowfall in Mainz."

"Translate that for us, please. All this philosophy's making my head spin..." Christoffini makes his point by twisting his neck in a way that is horrible to watch.

"Well that evening, with the same speed with which Bundó located the Ace of Hearts, Petroli consulted his list of emigrants' centers in Germany. The highly industrialized bank of the Rhine and the environs of Frankfurt were teeming with them and he soon discovered that there was a Spanish workers' center in a place called Rüsselsheim. The town was about ten kilometers away from the motorway. In other words, it was worth taking a chance. Since night was falling and Gabriel had a better sense of direction in the dark, Petroli asked him if he wanted to come along too.

"And poor Gabriel had to choose between the bitch and life's-a-bitch," Christoffini added.

"You and your wordplay. Oh, we think you're so witty . . . My guess is that on those occasions what often happened was that our dad really wanted to be left alone. Any roadside snack bar was fine by him, however inhospitable it was. He'd have something to eat and then, while he was having his coffee and a smoke, he'd get out his cards and play solitaire until it was time to go back to the truck. If the other two still hadn't arrived, he'd tune into some music on the radio, stretch out on the bunk, and try to get some sleep. That was fine by him because he tended to take the wheel after dinner. He said it helped his digestion. Sometimes, however, if he didn't feel like being alone or if it was too cold to wait inside the cab of the Pegaso, he went along with one of his friends' proposals. He tried to be evenhanded, and it wasn't unusual for him to flip a coin. The sexual excursions with Bundó were flavored with a joviality that made him relive his adolescence. Furthermore, by keeping him company he could also keep an eye on his wallet. Carried away by euphoria, his soul mate had an immoderate capacity for gratitude and leaving lavish tips for the ladies (without thinking, of course, of the abyss that separated pesetas from francs, marks, and pounds). Then again, Petroli's visits to partners in melancholy offered Gabriel the chance to play cards . . ."

"Sex or gambling, I get it now. So that was the choice," Cristoffini chips in. "What an edifying life our dear father led! Now I know who I take after."

"No, with those people he didn't play for money. He didn't cheat either. As soon as he arrived Gabriel sat down at a table, took out his Spanish deck, his *baraja*, and shuffled the cards. The majestic presence of the king of swords, or the perfidious presence of a knave (fuck you, Jack), was sufficient to fire up two or three emigrants and get a little game going. They played the time-honored games, *mus*, *remigio*, and *botifarra*. In the background, like a TV turned on in a bar, they could hear Petroli droning on as he bashed the ears of his compatriots. He was so over the top that the other card players didn't take long to start criticizing him, and then Gabriel had to leap to his defense because, well, that's what a little brother does. These visits weren't always so cosy. On some occasions, especially in France, it turned out that the emigrants' center had a more political orientation, marked by exiles and refugees from the Civil War, and then the two friends were welcomed as survivors of another time, heroes of the past still resisting in the inferno that was the workers' struggle in the motherland. Gabriel and Petroli then stuck out their chests, repeating the few basic things they knew about feudal oppression and denouncing the exploiter Casellas to the four winds. If they needed to back up their account, they recounted their long list of grievances about interminable moving jobs, wretched conditions, and subhuman wages. Gabriel also tended to remember the revolutionary sermons with which Lluís Salvans had indoctrinated them in the boarding house, even citing him as a reference in case there was some old anarchist present, some CNT or FAI militant who'd known him or who might know his whereabouts. The emigrants, somewhere between mournful and combative, heard them out and agreed with them. At this point, somebody would get out a guitar and they'd all start singing a few songs together to counter the distress. They'd jump from 'Cucurrucucú Paloma' to 'España Mi Emperaora', from a Republican song to 'Asturias, Patria Querida'. In the end, they always sang a song about émigrés, toasted their new comrades in friendship, and raised their glasses to Franco's speedy death, for once and for fucking all."

Cristoffini raises his left fist and hums the first few bars of the partisan song "Bella Ciao." It's not clear whether it's in jest or not but, in any case, it's a dramatic gesture. Christof covers his mouth with his hand, but you can still hear the humming somewhere in-

side him. When he's had enough of being asphyxiated, Cristoffini
bites him. It looks for a moment as if the palm of Christof's hand
is stained scarlet with drops of blood.

"Sigrun, my mother," Christof resumes, trying to ignore him,
"who was very active politically when she was young, recalls that
Petroli and Gabriel got tired very quickly and would leave as soon
as they could come up with a good excuse. Their long hours of
driving left them too whacked to enjoy a session of libertarian anarchist theory. She knows that firsthand because it happens that
the very day of the snowstorm, the day when Petroli and Gabriel
opened the door of the Rüsselsheim social club, she'd gone with a
friend to the Spanish workers' center."

"Aha! About time! Gabriel's little critters are warming up for
the race. Christof, advancing toward existential doubts about the
future, isn't there yet but he's about to get there. Come on, tell us.
Tell us."

"First, I have to say that age and frustrations have colored my
mother's memory. When she got pregnant, Sigrun was a twenty-
one-year-old student. I won't bother you with her CV now except
to say that she studied sociology at the University of Frankfurt,
went to Habermas's classes, and was a member of the famous
Socialist German Student Union. She'd even been at the odd
students' dinner with Angela Davis and, if she hadn't had to feed
me, she might even have got mixed up with the Baader-Meinhof
Group in the end. After I was born, she started to work in a university library. She was an only child and needed the money. Her
parents hadn't accepted the shameful pregnancy and her student
grants weren't enough. She kept going to classes when she could
but at a different pace, trying all the while to forget about Gabriel.
But every time she managed to get him out of her head, he'd turn
up again to top up her hope tank (*Entschuldigung!*). Sigrun was
living in a vicious circle. When Dad finally stopped his intermittent visits and never came back, her love life turned into a parade
of men. Long live sexual freedom! Names and faces have merged
into an Identikit picture of those allegedly open-minded and critical young German men of the sixties. Yet it's a deceptive portrait:

What emerges is a serious, strange young fellow, politically committed or otherwise, with a big weakness for sexual contact but who unfailingly took to his heels when he discovered that the tender, well-read girl had her own homegrown son."

Christof pauses to take in a deep breath. With a clout to the back of the neck he rouses Cristoffini, who's yawning, pretending to be dozing off.

"It's taken some years, then," he resumes, "for Sigrun to separate the important experiences from those that simply served as distraction. Nowadays, her men, when there are men, don't look remotely like that portrait. Questions don't scare her any more, even coming from her son, and I've finally been able to half satisfy my curiosity. Here's the story. It happens that, in Rüsselsheim that January night of 1965, a bunch of Spaniards had got together in honor of one of their friends who'd just retired. He was from Galicia, had come to Germany more than a decade before, and, like many others at the gathering, worked in a car factory. A Republican through and through and committed to the workers' struggle, the man had exerted himself to learn German so he could be the union representative of his shop-floor compatriots. Everyone recognized him as a pioneer among the emigrants to Germany (an excuse, like many another, to crack open a few bottles of wine). At the time, Sigrun had got her first grant to study sociology and had just applied to become a member of the students' union. One of her classmates, a daughter of Spanish emigrants, invited her to the party. She'd definitely have a great time. If the Galician worker had a drink or two (and he liked a tipple), they'd get him to relive the brief, glorious interval of the Second Republic. The friend would translate the most important bits for her. When, appearing from nowhere, Petroli and Gabriel walked into the center, the older emigrants were singing the last bars of "El Himno de Riego." Immediately afterward the Galician worker, choking with emotion, intoned a "Long Live the Republic!" and everybody applauded. In the silence that followed the two friends said good evening to all the people who were staring at them. Petroli instinctively rubbed his hands and added, "Quite a night, eh? And this is a great place to be!" His comment offered them safe-conduct, and the thirty-odd people in the room welcomed them with open arms. They asked the usual questions, and the two truck drivers said what was expected of them. The night wouldn't have been especially noteworthy if it hadn't been for the fact that, an hour and a half later, having said their good-byes, they discovered that the temperature had plummeted to ten degrees below zero and the roads were buried beneath a layer of ice. Since they weren't going to be able to drive even five meters in the Pegaso, the emigrants rallied to organize accommodation. Two ladies who worked in a handkerchief factory vied over Petroli, one of them a widow from Altafulla and the other a spinster from near Manises (the widow won, of course, since she was the older of the two candidates). Gabriel accepted the offer of a shy, quiet girl. She was wearing a green wool scarf and matching cap and behaved with the unaccented assurance of one whose convictions have not yet been put to the test. She didn't know a word of Spanish but was attractive, and he was flattered by her insistence. Moreover, out of the whole group, she was the one that least intimidated him since she wasn't Spanish.

"Yes!" Cristoffini barges in. "What a great seducer our father was! Long live bad weather! Long live ice storms! Long live dumb love!"

"Sigrun and Gabriel spent those first hours like two strangers on a blind date. From Rüsselsheim to my mother's neighborhood on the outskirts of Frankfurt it was five S-Bahn stops. On the way, they used the little English they knew to ask the obvious questions, the ones that, luckily, need no more than a monosyllable in response. Are you a student? Have you been in Frankfurt before? Once they got to her apartment, small and untidy as befits a sociology student, Sigrun poured two glasses of wine and, while she was fixing the sofa bed, tried to offer some conversation. Gabriel's particular idiom must have given rise to a few funny misunderstandings. They laughed, gesticulated awkwardly and let themselves go, laughing even more. There was a pregnant pause. In Dad's memory of that night there were two candles on the kitchen table giving off just enough light to make the wine glow with a more

intimate red. Today's Sigrun, however, denies the whole thing, saying that's a cliché and she can't stand clichés. Whatever the case,
I've never been able to take it any further than that. She won't play
the game. We can only blow out the candles and leave the German
student and expatriated truck driver in the dark. Let them get their
act together."

"No, no, no, the one who's got to get his act together is you,
Christof. Come on, it's about you! Go ahead, waggle your little tail.
That's what the chosen spermatozoon's supposed to do. Come on!
Are you going to leave it to my imagination?"

"No way!"

"While they're talking about this and that," says Cristoffini, trying to imitate Christof's unhurried way of speaking, "the clock's
moved on to three in the morning. They're both thinking that
body language would be the best way to make themselves understood. Gabriel and Sigrun say goodnight, gazing into one another's
eyes . . ."

"I said no! Stop that. We're now going to take a leap forward to
one year and ten months later."

"What a party pooper! That's cheating."

"November 1966," Christof bellows in order to retake the floor.
"I've been born. I'm already walking. I'm curious. I wreck things.
I'm really cute. Mom works, studies, reads, prepares my bottles,
and changes my nappies, so she's got no time for anything else.
Weekends come around like a blessing for us both because then
we can be together and play. It's Friday afternoon and we're at
home, half an hour after she's picked me up at the day-care center.
She hasn't even taken her coat off when there's a ring at the doorbell. She opens the door and it's Gabriel, my father. She recognizes
him at once but is dumbstruck. They look at each other. "We've
just done another move to Frankfurt," he attempts to explain, "and
we finished early. I had your address written down and thought I'd
come and visit you. It's been such a long time." Mom asked him in
at once—"Komm' rein"—and then there's a sort of déjà vu replay
of their first night: In the narrow entrance they're both taking off
their coats at the same time and getting in each other's way, but

it's a pleasurable obstruction. The main difference is that I enter the scene, toddling in from the kitchen to stand staring at the tall, thin man rooted to the ground before me. Then Mom says, 'Gabriel, this is your son. He was born in October. Last year.' Sigrun explains things in her beginner's Spanish. All those months, in her free time, she's been learning the language using a Berlitz manual and records."

"Hang on, hang on," Cristoffini springs into action again. "How could Gabriel be sure you were his son?"

"That's exactly what he asked her shortly afterward, once he'd got over his stupefaction. You've got to understand, he was only dropping in for a visit. Maybe with some sexual expectation, let's not deceive ourselves, but without any intention of perpetuating things. 'Don't get me wrong,' he said making himself understood, 'but how do you know he's my son?' They'd put me to bed by then. There were a thousand ways of answering his question, from drama to sarcasm, but Sigrun chose the following: 'Because his name is Christof.' That put an end to any doubts. 'Don't worry. No obligations,' she soothed him, seeing how his face had changed. 'But, well, I'm really pleased,' he stammered. According to Mom, he seemed very touched, and they at once set about celebrating his paternity. Now, we have to go back for a moment to that first night, to confirm that the mystery of the Christophers goes back a long way. The candlelight dances in the wine glasses (we accept that, Mom), and the words and gestures come out enhanced by the alcohol. The impossible conversation careens from one subject to another, and Sigrun asks Gabriel if he has children. He pats his pockets, as if his wallet's been nicked, and hastens to say, 'No, no children.' Later, however, he tells her that, if it did happen some day, if he did have a son, he would want to call him Cristòfol or Cristóbal. He picks up a pencil and notepad that Sigrun has on the table and writes the Catalan and Spanish names. She follows suit and writes the name in its German version below: Christof. We were right at the crux of the matter, Christophers, we were so hot on the trail, but my mother didn't ask the right question: Why did he like that name? Instead, she said, 'And what if it's a girl?'

Then he said, 'Sigrun, like you.' Oh, the art of seduction, how it tames us!"

After that final exclamation, Christof and Cristoffini fall silent. Cristoffini has apparently been waylaid by some thought.

"Which is to say that, basically, you're a mistake," he finally remarks. "I always thought so."

Christof lights up another cigarette.

"Or a bull's-eye. Depends on how you look at it. Before meeting the other Christophers, I might have been an error, the arithmetical error of a girl who miscounted when it came to taking the pill. But now that the four of us have met, our life has become a bull's-eye."

"The five of us. I count too, don't I?"

"I'm not sure what to say . . ." Christof sniggers. "Let's see, let me listen to your heart. I want to hear how it beats . . ."

"Don't be cruel, little brother!" Cristoffini looks scared. He starts to tremble. "What's that look in your eye? Don't leave me, Christof. Don't abandon me. You won't abandon me, will you? We're inseparable, we are. We've helped each other so much in difficult times! What would you do without me? Who would protect you? What would I do without you?"

Christof remains in silence. The expression on Cristoffini's face is pure panic. Desperate, puppy-like, he burrows into Christof's neck.

# 9

## An Adventure on the Channel, or Toxicosmos

### CHRISTOPHER'S TURN

Rain. That fine, unrelenting rain that so regularly veils Great Britain in grayness, from one end to the other. And water, fresh water and salt water, everywhere. I warn you: My part of the Christophers' story is going to be damp. To begin with, go and check out a few British pop bands from the eighties—the Smiths, the Pale Fountains, Lloyd Cole, the Cure—all those songs wavering between wintry and self-consciously melancholic. Play them and you'll be listening to the soundtrack of my adolescence. Like the characters immortalized in that music, my solitude only got worse on Saturdays as I settled on the grotty sofas of local pubs or lined up in the rain to get into a club (with nervous fingers fiddling distractedly with a couple of pills in my coat pocket). My mum worked as a nurse at St. Andrews Hospital. When I say that, I don't mean that she got me the speed but that once a month—when she was doing the weekend shift—she granted me two days of total freedom. I hated those weekends off the leash. They were endless. And following the dictates of some kind of unwritten teenage law, my friends wouldn't let me pass up this opportunity to go on an all-day bender. My mum started work at the hospital at eleven on Saturday morning and didn't come home till midnight on Sunday. My Saturdays, you might say, were launched by New Order's "Ceremony" and crashed with Joy Division's "Shadowplay."

Listen to them and you'll get my drift. We often took a free ride on the train to Charing Cross. At the age of fifteen, London meant Oxford Street. We'd get lost in narrow side streets. We'd go into music shops and get them to play records for us until the shop assistants, fed up with our New Wave screams, kicked us out. We nicked books from Charing Cross bookshops just for the thrill of it, and then tried to resell them to the competition a couple of doors down. We sidled up to the hookers in Soho and pinched their bums, and, because they were junkies and sick as hell, they reacted as if we were flaying them alive, hurling insults and spitting at us. "Fuck off, you fucking cunt!" As the hours went by, my clothes began to stink with accumulated layers of smells: fish and chips, tobacco smoke, beer, resoaked sweat, puke. It was a cosmic mystery, how I ended up surfacing from a night out in my bed on Sunday. Rather than waking up, I recovered consciousness, and painfully so. Dazed and hungover, I hid at home until nightfall.

A tic remains from those days: I sniff my fingers.

Why am I telling you all this? Well, Christophers, those hungover Sundays all by myself at home were the times when I was most affected by Dad's absence. That's how it was for me. Ever since we met, we've all been trying to identify the bonds that unite us so that they'll lead us to where he is. Yet, in fact, there are plenty of details that separate us. Agreed? There's nothing wrong with that, and I'm not trying to make problems, either. I see it like this: We're four people pulled together by destiny at a specific moment. It's like being stuck in an elevator. We're talking in order to keep fear at bay and discover a shared past. Our lives are an accident. Our father is an accident. And don't forget that, of the four of us, I'm the one who saw him least. I could probably count the number of times on my fingers: about ten, the last time when I was four. I was so young, I don't even remember it.

The La Ibérica trips to the British Isles didn't happen very often. What diplomat wanted to live and work in Great Britain in the sixties? Fog, hippies ... London, maybe, but Manchester, Liverpool, Southampton! Grubby industrial cities that never appeared on any high-society map. Besides, back then Buckingham Palace and all those lords were still well out of reach. The high-ranking Spanish officials who had to endure the English purgatory preferred to leave their families in Spain, to sublet a mansion in Belgravia and submit to the martial regime of a traditionally disagreeable war-widow housekeeper. I believe that Mr. Casellas wasn't too unhappy about this arrangement. Moves to British destinations meant that the three workers had to put in more hours than made sense, the insurance cost more because of the sea crossing, and profits suffered. But then, at the beginning of 1964, the Norwegian company Thoresen merged with the English company Townsend, and they launched a fleet of ferries that criss-crossed the Channel. The word was that the crossing from Calais to Dover was much faster, cheaper, and safer—good business—and Mr. Casellas stopped turning up his piggy nose at requests for a move to Great Britain. And it wasn't the only way he made himself useful, as you'll soon discover.

First, however, I want to go back to the last time I saw our dad, in November 1971. His visit lasting a whole weekend—from Saturday midday, after they'd unloaded the furniture, to early Monday morning—began with a gift. He walked into the house, picked me up to give me a kiss, and presented me with a globe of the world (Lot 192, Barcelona-London). It had a bulb inside and was supposed to light up, but it didn't work because the Spanish plug was different from the English one. There was a crack in it that turned Italy into a Mediterranean island. It never occurred to him that the best gift was his presence. On the Saturday evening, to amuse me while I was having my dinner, he took the globe and traced the route that he, Bundó, and Petroli had taken in the Pegaso all the way to London Fields. I was fascinated by the journey recreated on the globe by his tobacco-stained finger. Pyrenees, Perpignan, Saint-Étienne, the River Rhone, Lyon, Dijon, the River Seine, Paris, Calais . . . Heard for the first time and in Dad's execrable pronunciation, the French names took on fantastical dimensions. Heaven knows what I imagined. All of a sudden, the finger stopped at the French coast. Dad began to imitate the sounds of the wind and rain, and the surging waves of a storm, then slowly advanced his finger over the blue patch of water.

"If you look carefully," he said, acting scared, "you'll see how we're crossing the Channel on a ferry."

"What's a ferry?"

"A ferry's a great big boat that can carry people, cars, and trucks. This ferry of ours is called *Viking III*. Always remember that name, Chris. When you're missing me, get out the magnifying glass I gave you last time and look for us in that patch of sea. I'm sure we'll be there. Petroli, Bundó, and me."

Can you imagine, Christophers, how many, many times, like a Sherlock Holmes of stolen memories, I scoured that miniature sea with my magnifying glass? And I saw them! I saw the *Viking III* with Dad and his friends on board! Of course I saw them, and they waved at me just like they did when they said good-bye from the Pegaso window!

Months later, when it was clear that Dad wouldn't be coming back—no sign of life, no letter, no phone call—Mum had to hide the globe from me because I became obsessed with it.

She gave it back to me after eight long years, on my thirteenth birthday. At first I thought it was ridiculous. What was I supposed to do with that kid's toy? Automatically, though, or instinctively, my eyes sought out that patch of sea in the Channel. The dark blue had faded. I was seized by years of pent-up rage. Every age cruelly mocks its predecessor and adolescence tends to be tough on child-hood naivery. I grabbed the globe, went out into the street and kicked it as hard and high as I could. I went back inside without looking to see where it had fallen but couldn't avoid hearing the thud of a shattering world.

Inside the house, Mum hugged me for ages until I calmed down. Then she gave me the birthday gift of telling me about the chain of events that led to my birth. Why do we always like to know about these prenatal episodes when they're just the purest expression of vanity—placental vanity?

It all began with an adventure my future father and his friends had on the Channel, on board a ferry creaking ominously, at the mercy of six-meter waves in the middle of a storm that Turner would have loved to have painted. The denouement comes, with the dregs of an especially crazy day and the inevitable product of cause and effect, when Sarah and Gabriel got together.

Am I, then, the result of the calm after the storm? It's hard to believe. On those Sundays of my sixteen lonely years my bed was adrift on high seas and I was dashed again and again upon the rocks of a terrible hangover. If I opened my eyes, I was even more seasick. If I closed them, I could see Dad's silhouette in the darkness.

Now I want to tell you about the adventure on the Channel. Maybe I should add a footnote saying that I owe the peculiar scenes featuring the Barcelona bourgeoisie to Cristòfol, but I'll skip it because I'm not writing an academic paper.

Let's go.

The ferry departed from Calais on time. Ten in the morning. At that time of year—early October—the English Channel was a narrow corridor where the winds came to play, like city kids confined at home. The La Ibérica truck had arrived at the port in good time and was the first to park on the car deck. Now, as the *Viking III* was going through the motions of casting off and the city of Calais was dissolving into sea mist, the passengers were up on deck watching the whole thing. There must have been about fifty of them scattered here and there, not many if you consider that the ferry could take six hundred. It was autumn and the summer tourist madness had abated. Gabriel was grateful for that. Four months earlier, in June, they'd done the same trip—Move 88—and the two long hours to Dover had been torture because there were so many people crammed on the boat. He shuddered at the mere memory of it.

The shipping company and its capitalist instincts were to blame. A few years earlier, in 1964, they'd revamped the ferry fleet, axing the first-class section in the absurd belief that the whole thing was going to look like first class. The "Channel crossing," as people called it, was suddenly fashionable in provincial towns of France and Middle England. They offered several routes: between Calais and Dover, Cherbourg and Southampton, Dieppe and Newhaven. The passion for day-tripping became a spectacle in itself. Arthritic, heavy-smoking, thirsty grannies from Birmingham sipped their whiskies in the bar and then stocked up in the duty-free shop. Butchers from Leeds and their lady wives strolled around the deck with lah-di-dah airs as if they were cruising back from New York on the *Queen Elizabeth II*. On sighting the white cliffs of Dover, lonely beadles from Oxford or Cambridge recited a few lines from Matthew Arnold, which they'd learned from some obtuse don with whom they'd been secretly in love. The French spent the trip trying to avoid the British riffraff. Pensioners from Amiens, heads held high and a Second World War medal pinned to their chests, got lost in the boat's corridors. The prettiest *demoiselles* from Rouen, looking like characters in a Resnais film, sipped crème de menthe and deplored the uncouthness of certain waiters from Brighton. Little children from Chartres, overwhelmed by the sight of English ladies sporting beehives, burst into tears.

Back in June, oppressed by this carnival, Gabriel and Bundó had found respite at a table in the most out-of-the-way corner of the cafeteria, killing time with a game of cards. Now, in contrast, the calm on deck augured a smooth, swift crossing. Seeking confirmation, Gabriel glanced at the people around him. A hiker, reclining on his knapsack, was reading in a well-sheltered corner. A couple took photos of one another with the sea as their backdrop. Five English soldiers stood in a ring, smoking and chatting. A solitary man was declaiming something out loud, but his words were lost midair. Bundó was stretching his legs at the other end of the deck. A first blast of wind, unexpected and chilly, tousled everybody's hair. Gabriel looked at the girl at his side. She was leaning on the rail and lost in thought. For all her apparent calm, he could see one of her eyelids twitching.

"Are you nervous?" he asked. Then he realized that this wasn't the time to be asking that. There were still a few hours to go.

"No. Yes. No, it isn't nerves. It's a gnawing sensation in my stomach, but not nerves. I must be hungry."

"I'm not surprised. You haven't eaten anything since we left

Barcelona. We'll go down to the bar, if you want, and get you something. The sandwiches here are . . . different." He'd been about to say "disgusting." "They're Norwegian, like the ferry company. And Norwegians like butter, smoked salmon, cucumber, raw onion, that kind of thing."

Unable to shake off her nausea, the girl said nothing. Her only response was to try to light a cigarette. After she'd struck three matches, Gabriel came to her aid, cupping his hands against the wind and then, making the most of it, lighting up himself. They smoked in silence. The tips of their cigarettes glowed in the sea air. Gulls circled the boat in erratic swoops.

"Don't think about it," Gabriel said after a while.

Again the girl said nothing. She merely forced a half smile. The whole trip, he and Bundó had had to drag the words out of her. Gabriel felt uncomfortable in the role of escort, or father almost. He hated this vassalage that Senyor Casellas was imposing on him, for the third time now. The girl was called Anna Miralpeix and she, too, had to leave something in London: The La Ibérica truckers were taking her to have a secret abortion. She was seventeen years old and six weeks gone. Small, slender, olive-skinned and of angular features, she affected a tomboy look. Her blond hair was cut in a gamine style and she was dressed as if summer wasn't over (white trousers, blue-and-white horizontal-striped T-shirt, yellow Windbreaker). At first glance, she seemed as fragile as fine porcelain and free of any emotional excess. However, this pose was fashionable among the Costa Brava smart set in the summer of '66 when the offspring of well-to-do families got together at private garden parties or beach bars and night clubs and amused themselves by exhibiting a feigned disregard for life, a contrived emptiness that, moreover, distracted them from the real emptiness that haunted their futures. Sometimes when they were still green, as in the case of Anna Miralpeix, the game sucked them in completely, seducing them with its novel sensations. The rite of passage always included the verses of some trusted poet (a friend of the family and at once an ally), the odd French song, grilled sardines, laughter, intellectual conversations (it was always the same ones, but she didn't give a damn), a longing to drive around in a convertible, reckless love affairs, and the glazed, party's-over languor and vague Marxist pronouncements that marked the climax of every booze-up. Alcohol, of course, protected them from the outside world, like amniotic fluid replenished each evening.

With the end of summer, the fun and games adjourned to Barcelona. A few unlucky ones had to pay the price in September. Thus it was that, just a week before, sin had visited the Miralpeix house in the Sant Gervasi neighborhood. Anna's first classes of her university-entrance course had been punctuated by several attacks of nerves, giddiness, and vomiting. A Galician maid who could read the future in the sheets of an unmade bed apprised the lady of the house. That very same day, the mother took her daughter to the family doctor to see if she was expecting. "She's expecting, yes she's expecting, your little girl's expecting," the doctor confirmed. On their way home in a taxi the mother asked Anna to tell her the name of the baby's father, the wholly guilty party. Would they have to suffer? Juan Marsé's novel *Últimas tardes con Teresa* had recently been published, and its account of the love affair between a social-climbing, working-class Spanish immigrant boy and a blond, upper-class Catalan girl had unleashed a wave of hysteria in the swanky part of town up on the hill. No, Anna conveyed with a shake of head. She wasn't going to give the name. At the very thought of him her mouth filled with the bitter-orange taste of Licor 43. The mother was satisfied with her revulsion. Then the appropriate cogs began to turn in order to sort out the awkward situation. The doctor had written a letter in English (for the third time that autumn). Senyora Miralpeix had calmed her husband. "Our little girl is our little girl." Senyor Miralpeix knew somebody in the Equestrian Circle who, faced with the same plight, had entrusted the matter to a certain Casellas. Phone call. No, no phone call, personal visit. Dark glasses. References. Casellas bowing and scraping. Luck would have it that there was a move to England scheduled for the following week. Was the timing right, or should it be brought forward? Rebeca, the La Ibérica secretary, immediately made a few phone calls to a contact in a London hospital.

Appointment made.

Throughout this entire process, nobody had given as much as five minutes to ask what Anna thought. Neither had she, in fact. The diligence with which everyone rallied around to solve the problem had left her with no alternative. If she'd been four years older she might have protested but, at seventeen, and coming from an upper-crust family, what could you expect? Swaddled in cotton wool, Anna was heading for London without too many worries. Her uneasiness arose from something else, an understanding, perhaps that the scar—physical and mental—of an abortion would give her new status in her circle of friends and, like someone sitting for an end-of-year exam, she was afraid of not being up to it.

What with all this agitation, the incredibly tedious journey by truck (fifteen hours) and the ferry crossing were now assuming epic proportions that would help her to shore up the future. Furthermore, she would eventually learn to take refuge in the adventure, at the heart of which, of course, was the company of Bundó and Gabriel (Petroli had remained in Barcelona so she could travel in the truck). "Saved by the working class!" she thought. Those men wore pullovers ripped by hard work, smoked pungent, dark-tobacco Ducados, drank beer from the bottle! It could be said that she appreciated them and felt an anthropological attraction toward both of them. The feeling was mutual. In a food break they'd seen how tired and pale she was, and Bundó opened the trailer, made a space for one of the mattresses they were carrying and let her have an hour's sleep. These kind gestures, such a small matter for the two drivers, lent a human touch to the lonely journey of Anna Miralpeix.

"Do you do this very often, Manuel, I mean transporting pregnant girls?" she asked, tossing her cigarette butt into the sea. There was no way she was going to learn their names. Gabriel didn't want to correct her. It was the first time she'd initiated a conversation, and, unlike the other girls, she wasn't asking how long before they arrived.

"You're the third," he replied. "You're also the youngest. Don't imagine that we're crazy about this. In theory we're breaking Spanish law, we're delinquents, but our boss is one of those people who do favors and your parents . . ."

"I don't give a fuck about my parents," she cut him off. "I'm doing it for me and that's that. I don't want to have a kid, ever. Children give me the creeps."

Her words were emphatic but devoid of any anger. They weren't far from a plea.

"Don't say that," Gabriel told her. "You're very young and who knows where life will take you. I myself . . ."

"Do you have kids?"

"Not that I know of," Gabriel lied.

"Do you want to have kids?"

"Yes, yes, sure, of course." He didn't have to give it much thought. "One day. If I stop carting furniture all over the place and find a woman who'll put up with me."

"How old are you now?"

"Just turned twenty-six. Why the interrogation?"

Anna thought he looked older. A new, more violent flurry of wind raced across the deck, catching them unawares. The ferry started rolling in the surging sea. The few people still remaining outside hastened inside. Gabriel found it a good excuse to put an end to the conversation and invited Anna to go down to the cafeteria. She waited a few seconds by herself (as fine rain began sprinkling her face) and then followed him. When they'd reached the foot of the narrow stairway, they saw Bundó running up to them along the passageway. He was very agitated.

"Hi, gorgeous, how are you feeling? You're okay, aren't you?" he asked Anna. Without waiting for an answer, he turned to Gabriel. "Guess who's in the bows . . . or is it the stern? I always get it mixed up . . . Never mind. Guess who's at the other end of the ferry." A suspenseful pause. "The French fellow, the one with the horse. With that groom of his."

From that moment on, it was as if Bundó's words, so seemingly straightforward, had cast some sort of spell on the ferry and its occupants. Gabriel's face changed. Anna noted that his expression grew even sharper, making him look like the fox in storybooks.

The muscles and veins in his neck tensed. His lips went dry and he ran his tongue over them to moisten them. The transformation lasted just a few seconds and ended in a strange gesture: Gabriel quickly patted his chest and arms as if looking for his wallet and immediately pulled down his shirtsleeves to check that the cuffs were well buttoned. Then he was his usual calm self again. Bundó rubbed his hands together to fend off the cold.

"Do they want to play?" Gabriel asked.

"They sure do," his friend replied. "They haven't forgotten last time."

"Play what?" Anna interrupted.

"Cards. We play cards. Poker," Bundó explained.

Gabriel disappeared down one of the long upholstered passageways, heading for the cafeteria at the other end. While they followed him, staggering with the rocking of the boat, Bundó explained who the Frenchman was in a burst of nervous chatter.

The Frenchman, a Parisian aged about fifty, was aptly named Monsieur Champion. Churlish and arrogant, a bastard through and through, he was loaded and under the impression that the whole of humanity worked for him. He was a horse breeder with a stud farm in Brittany. The pearl of his stables was a thoroughbred that he took to race on different tracks in the south of England. A glance was sufficient to confirm that this was a glorious horse. He was called Sans Merci. Monsieur Champion always traveled with Ibrahim, a reserved, monosyllabic Algerian youth. According to Bundó, it was a weird, dodgy kind of relationship, if you get what I mean. Sometimes the Frenchman treated Ibrahim as if he were his slave and threatened to strike him. Other times he gazed at him enraptured. The lad seemed very amiable and never complained. His job was to look after the horse, groom him, feed him, and ensure that, once he was in the horsebox for the crossing, he stayed calm and docile. The two men crossed the Channel a few days before each race and took the horse to the racecourse in question, where an English jockey trained him and got him into shape for the Saturday event. He was a winner, great for the betting business. The four men had met for the first time on La

Ibérica's previous ferry trip to London. That was the day when Bundó and Gabriel had been playing cards at a corner table in the cafeteria, seeking relief from the throng. The Frenchman had approached them and challenged them to a game against himself and Ibrahim. For money, French francs. That trip, Gabriel and Bundó had played for more than an hour with Monsieur Champion and the groom. Since it was a short crossing, they didn't have time to clean them out (clean him out, the arrogant dickhead who doled out money to the lad so he could play), but the winnings had been considerable. Now Monsieur Champion wanted revenge. It was his right, he said.

If Petroli had been traveling on the ferry that October day, Gabriel wouldn't have fallen so easily into temptation. The older man was well aware of his weaknesses, remembered some of his earlier gambling episodes, and knew how to rein him in when necessary. Bundó, in contrast, went along with Gabriel because their card-sharp partnership amused and pleased him. Soon it would be his and Carolina-Muriel's first anniversary, and he was dying to give her a classy present. Thus, every move they did, he ferreted around in the boxes in a way that bordered on pathological, and any chance to make a bit of money, by cheating or otherwise, was welcome.

Guided by this gleaner's spirit, Bundó made his entrance into the cafeteria, beaming from ear to ear, with Anna Miralpeix at his side. Gabriel, already seated at the table with Monsieur Champion and the groom, was shuffling the cards.

"Hullo. And this lovely young lady, where has she sprung from?" Monsieur Champion greeted them. It was clear he'd learned some Spanish hobnobbing with people from the Basque coast of France. "Aha, I see, she's your . . . how shall I put it, your lucky charm."

"I'm nobody's lucky charm," Anna replied in the man's language. She'd been a student at the Lycée Français, and her accent impressed Monsieur Champion. He looked her up and down disdainfully and decided that he didn't like the brat.

"*Alors tais-toi, ma petite*," he shot back, instantly enraged. "You have no place here. If you want to stay, keep quiet. Sit down and learn a thing or two."

Anna grew quiet but stayed where she was, holding her ground. She wasn't going to be bossed around by anyone. She'd keep standing there, right by his side, just to piss him off.

"Shall we start? We've agreed that I deal first," Gabriel said, as if nothing had happened. He then quietly informed Bundó of a further condition. "We're going to play with pesetas. The Captain mustn't know that the stakes are higher. He'd shut down the show. Remember, every peseta's worth a franc. It's like playing with chips. We'll work it out in francs at the end of the game. Minimum bet's one peseta; maximum a hundred."

"Jesus!"

"They're good and worried today, Ibrahim. You can see they don't trust the luck that comes with pregnant girls."

Gabriel shot him a reproving look, and the Frenchman winked in response. Still standing at his side and biting her tongue, Anna remained unruffled. Gabriel dealt out the cards. The ferry lurched again, and Anna nearly fell but saved herself just in time by grabbing Monsieur Champion's shoulder. The Frenchman gloated and the groom watched her out of the corner of his eye. Bundó picked up the first cards. After looking at his hand, he took a swig of beer and addressed Anna.

"If I was you, I'd go and sit down at some table and have a bite of breakfast. It's self-service, so you've got to get it yourself and pay at the till. If you want my advice, go for a nice hot coffee and one of those teacakes. The sandwiches are disgusting."

The girl took his advice and sat down by a thick-paned window, staring out, fascinated by the battle between clouds and sea. From time to time, with rhythmic surges, a large wave loomed, a shimmering enamel-gray slick like a whale's belly glinting in the sun, engulfing the view and then collapsing back into the water. Then the whole boat shuddered with an undulating thrust, and Anna felt the spasms of seasickness again. The coffee and teacake remained untouched on the table. She lit another cigarette.

In the distance she could see the four men concentrating hard on their game. They dealt, placed their bets, and the cards slid across the white Formica tabletop. In 1966, a franc was a lot of money for a Spanish truck driver. Gabriel and Bundó had begun by checking out the lay of the land and betting low. Monsieur Champion had immediately adopted the distant, overstuffed look of an aristocrat in Monte Carlo, holding his head high and looking down his nose as he placed his bets. He was smoking a cigar but didn't seem to be enjoying it, as if his real aim was to foul the air. Ibrahim limited himself to following his master's instructions. He was only winning back his bets, but whenever they lost the hand Monsieur Champion went for him.

*"Nom de Dieu! Que tu es simple, mon Ibrahim! Quel gaspillage!"*

A spray of water hit the window, and Anna's view went cobwebby as if the glass had cracked on impact. A few seconds later, a screech on the public address system shattered the players' concentration. First in English and then in French, the Captain announced that the ferry had been caught in an unforeseen storm and they'd have to make a detour south. There'd be an hour's delay in the crossing, perhaps even more. He apologized for any inconvenience this adverse weather might cause—totally contrary to the wishes of the company—and suggested that passengers entertain themselves with the facilities offered on board the *Viking III*. In response to the formal, droning voice, a fast-whirling eddy sucked in the ferry then spat it out. The jolting was terrifying. The lights flickered and there was a collective shriek from the passengers. A din of smashing crockery. Anna's coffee spilt over the table and she stanched the tide with paper napkins. The four players simultaneously performed the same reflex action of holding their cards in one hand and pinning down the coins with the other. Even so, three or four of Bundó's went rolling across the floor. An Englishman, the same one who'd been talking to himself on deck, somehow climbed up on the handrail of the stairs and started reciting Shakespeare.

"Down with the topmast! Yare! Lower, lower!" he shouted, gesturing as if commanding the multitude with the words of the boatswain at the start of *The Tempest*.

"Will we be arriving very late?" Bundó asked, gripping the coins in his hand. "What time are they expecting our young lady?"

"She won't be admitted till tonight. They're doing the job to-morrow morning. There's plenty of time."

The ferry made another giddy movement, not as violent as the last one but more startling as if it were skidding across the water. The actor responded by raising his voice.

"A plague upon this howling!"

Monsieur Champion dealt out the cards, still looking smug. He'd just won a hand, a small fortune, with a bit of bluffing that the truck drivers hadn't spotted. Ibrahim, in contrast, had been twitchy and squirming in his chair for some time. Finally, he dared to stand up.

"I'm just going down for a moment to check on Sans Merci. I'm worried that . . ."

"You're not moving from here, Ibrahim," the Frenchman ordered. "Sit down. Sans Merci's used to this kind of turbulence—more than you and I are. It's in his blood. One of his ancestors pulled the royal coaches in the revolution. And anyway, we're on a lucky streak and we've got to make the most it. These Spaniards owe us."

Bundó opened the betting with a timid peseta. A humiliated Ibrahim mechanically picked up his cards. His mind, however, was down in the hold, picturing the horse, frantic, trying to stay upright in his narrow box, sweating like he did on the racecourse, waiting for the signal in the starting box. Except, this time, there was no course ahead where he could let off steam.

"Lay her a-hold, a-hold! Set her two courses; off to sea again; lay her off."

The English actor was quieter now, though he persisted with his recital. The cafeteria had gradually filled with an unrelenting but oddly harmonious din, like a village social club. The roaring of the sea outside might have been background jazz. If it weren't for all the movement, no one would have known they were in the middle of a storm. In one corner, thick cigar smoke gave the table of the four card players an aquarium-like glow. A new sound rose to join the hubbub: On the far side, two boys were sitting on the floor, one playing the guitar and the other singing unfamiliar songs, by Bob Dylan, Donovan, and Eric Burdon. Anna had never heard them before. She could tell that the boys were French from their accents. After a while she went over to them, greeted them with a nod, and sat on the floor with them. They looked at her without interrupting their music. She offered them a cigarette and both accepted.

"Anna," she introduced herself.

"Ludovic."

"Raymond." He accompanied this with a guitar riff.

Ludovic gave him a shove for showing off. Both had long tousled hair. Unshaven. They'd applied black eyeliner and were wearing a sort of uniform of shabby corduroy trousers, woolen pullovers, silver-threaded scarves, and military jackets. They must have been about twenty, no more, and they were brothers. From Paris. Their grandmother had knitted the pullovers. With a good distance between her and the truck drivers, left to her own devices and speaking French, Anna now felt more secure. She asked where they were going (London). They wanted to know if she was traveling alone (yes), and then they invited her to travel with them (we'll see). They'd been given an address in Brixton where they could stay for a few days. They'd be visiting music shops, putting up ads saying they were looking for a drummer and bassist. They were going to form a band. Didn't have a name yet. They were going to hit the big time.

"Do you know anything by Brassens?" Anna asked when she finished her cigarette. She felt like singing with them.

"Shit no!" Raymond rejoined. "We don't play French stuff. We're fed up with all that poetry. We don't want to save anyone. Each to his own, okay? Life's got a lot of colors. It's not just black-and-white. And we don't like cats."

"Brassens, Brel, Ferré! They're a pain in the arse!"

"Gainsbourg! Serge Gainsbourg! All right, he's okay. And Boris Vian. But we want to make our name in English. So we sing in English."

Raymond couldn't resist strumming the first few bars of Donovan's "Sunshine Superman," and Ludovic shut his eyes. Psychedelia was so powerful, even when reduced to a simple acoustic guitar. Anna felt wounded, as if these two long-haired boys were attacking her summers of singing "La mauvaise réputation" on the beach.

"Oh yeah? And how do you think you're going to make your name?" she challenged them.

The two brothers looked at each other again, smiling as one. They apparently shared some secret.

"I feel free, I feel free, I feel free . . . Dance floor is like the sea; Ceiling is the sky . . ." Ludovic sang.

"What cares these roarers for the name of king? To cabin: silence! Trouble us not." From the other side of the cafeteria, Shakespeare's words answered Cream's.

"We've got a few songs," the more practical Raymond added. "And if they don't work for us because they're too predictable or too strange, we know how to write new ones."

"How?" Anna asked.

The boys exchanged another glance. They were expecting the question. Ludovic put his hand in a pocket of his backpack and pulled out a matchbox. He opened it to reveal a few scraps of blotting paper.

"Tripping. We're the dukes of the stratosphere, we're the liquid flame that nourishes the sun . . ."

"The skin of the chameleon between two shades, black diamond held between a Javanese girl's thighs . . ."

Anna was amazed. She didn't know if they were making fun of her or not.

"They're the words of our songs," Raymond informed her.

That summer, Anna had smoked her first joint. A Belgian painter and his girlfriend had joined her group on the beach one night and passed around a few spliffs. She'd tried them. At first she felt giddy—it was scary—but by the third toke all the muscles of her body were tingling so agreeably that, like everyone else, she started giggling nonstop. Later the same night she heard talk of psychedelic drugs. Someone said there were some English guys in Platja d'Aro, who were at Tiffany's disco every night putting on the Byrds and the Animals and, around daybreak, they would invite their friends to try some amazing new stuff. The lucky ones went down to the beach near Ramis Point and were blown away by an indescribable mystical experience. The word was that, for a few hours, they inhabited parallel dimensions. The initiated said a fount bubbled up in their brains, a wellspring of sensations that transformed the world, turning it into a richer place, a sort of comic strip but with more love in it. Coming down from the trip, everyone described it differently, but everyone wanted to have another go the next day.

"What are those bits of paper? LSD?" Anna asked. The three letters felt thrilling on her tongue. Chance had dropped her right at the heart of this world of privilege. The two boys nodded. A spark of intimacy bonded the three of them. "I want to try it."

"Now? Here?" Though they were playing at being the experts, the brothers had only dropped acid three times, very much behind closed doors, in the place where they rehearsed. "It's too dangerous."

With a new onslaught from the sea, the ferry juddered from bow to stern, a shiver running up Neptune's spine.

"More dangerous than this? This trip's getting to be too much." Anna pronounced the words looking at once desperate and angelic. The brothers couldn't say no. Raymond opened the matchbox again.

"Let's share a small hit, okay? To last a couple of hours. We need to have our wits about us when we get to the English coast."

Raymond took out one of the brownish bits of paper, broke it into three equal shares and handed them out.

"Put it under your tongue and it'll dissolve," Ludovic instructed, showing her what to do. Anna imitated him with trembling fingers.

The next day, or months later, when she tried to remember those first moments, Anna would be incapable of providing any logical sequence to what happened next. The version she offered her friends, like a dream narrated to a shrink, wove between snippets of the two brothers, her own experience, and the astounded looks on the faces of their fellow passengers, Bundó and Gabriel included. She could clearly recall, for example, that it took ages for the acid to take effect, half an hour that seemed to stretch forever in which she and the brothers gazed into each other's eyes, creating a kind of visual circle that contained the three of them, and only the three of them. Shakespeare's lines reached them from the background, very far away—the English actor was indefatigable—coupled with the voice of the Captain, addressing the passengers once again because the storm was getting worse, with thunder and lightning, Saint Mark, Saint Matthew, Saint Barbara don't leave me now, it'd be much better if the *splasssshfff* of the pounding waves wasn't too close, otherwise the booming *barrrrummm* from the bottom of the sea—*sluuurp!*—will show no mercy and will suck everyone down, amen.

"Are we too good-looking, do you think?" the brothers asked. We want to be uglier. Ugly, horrible. Ugly. Horrible. Like Serge Gainsbouuuurg, with great big eeeeears, and great big hooooked Jeeeewish nose. Beauty lies wiiiiithin, or it iiiiiisn't beauuuuuuty, Anna Aneeeette."

Her only response was to kiss their mouths, which had the iodized taste of an oyster and a pearl (not that she really knew what a pearl tasted like).

Her first experience of the LSD appeared in the simple, perfect form of a drop of water. She was the center of that drop. It had fallen from the sky without a sound, and, all around it, concentric circles were expanding and painting the world. Outside, the rain splashing the glass was a bubbly orange, Fanta orange. Anna opened her eyes wider (now that they were enjoying a life without oppressive eyelids), mentally embracing everything the circles contained. First of all, it was the two brothers. Like a Hindu deity, Raymond had sprouted four more arms and an elephant's trunk and was playing the guitar, but instead of music, it radiated golden light, the color of happiness, which he was sniffing at with his trunk. At his side, an ecstatic Ludovic had gone so pale that he was white and two-dimensional. Every part of his body, every piece of clothing had a number written on it. Anna only had to read it to know what color she had to apply with a paintbrush made of eyes. While she was filling in the colors of the jigsaw, Ludovic was weeping with joy, and his tears were watering his trousers. A floral penis was growing in his groin, as succulent and threatening as a carnivorous flower. Anna spotted the English actor in the distance (a fluorescent skeleton trying to hold its skull in place and reciting Hamlet's monologue) and saw that the four card players, who were now five (as a purple-skinned, cigar-smoking baby had joined them), were dressed up in medieval gear and holding hands as they played.

Once the first acid ripple had passed, Anna and the brothers started adapting to the new reality. Inside their heads, the nonstop movements of the ferry and the tempest battering the Channel turned into a thunder-and-lightning Wagnerian soundtrack. The seashell of the world encased them with maternal warmth. In the midst of the airy cavalcade of these sensations Anna's thoughts fixed on a horse with a wild mane. And all of a sudden, with hyper-real, visionary clarity, she understood that she had a mission, and that mission was to liberate the horse that was dying of a broken heart down in the hold of the *Viking III*. She got up, kissed the brothers on the forehead and, tugging at the silver threads that joined all three, explained that they had to go and find a horse called Sans Merci and take him to the English coast. The two young Frenchmen followed her somewhat cagily.

*Exeunt omnes.*


Meanwhile, at the poker table, Gabriel and Bundó were losing. They were being massacred. Monsieur Champion and Ibrahim's winning streak was leaving them stone broke. If they counted in pesetas, it wasn't such a huge sum but when that was turned into francs—as they'd agreed—the total was distressingly large. To make matters worse, every time he won a hand, the Frenchman poked fun at the truck drivers and Ibrahim giggled at his witticisms. Gabriel, who had rare insight into the psychology of the poker player, suspected that behind these outbursts of glee lurked a bent for bluffing, for lying and for winning without holding a good hand, yet he couldn't find the chink in the armor—a repeated gesture, a way of breathing, the underlying tic that devious players can't control. Bundó was doubly on tenterhooks. He wasn't getting the right cards, and was waiting for the moment when Gabriel would ask for a bathroom break. They played four more hands. Gabriel won the first, but the next three went to the Frenchman and his groom, making the initial win look like a lousy tip. Just as he'd done the first time on the ferry, just as he always did, he asked for a break so he could go to the loo. Monsieur Champion looked him up and down, nodding magnanimously as if conceding a last-minute stay of execution.

Gabriel's intention was very clear: He was going to lock himself in the men's room and slip a few cards through the open cuff seams of his shirt. A couple of aces, a king, a queen at the most. The ace of spades hadn't turned up yet, had it? Well, he'd bring that out when it was needed. Cheating was an art too.

It was only after he'd walked a few steps, leaving behind the microcosm of the game of cards, that Gabriel realized that they were in the midst of the most incredible storm. Its movements made his head spin and he nearly fell. Any sense of time and space was gone. Hanging onto a chair, he looked at his watch and saw that they'd been playing for nearly two hours. Passing by his side, the English actor flung a few words by old Prospero in his face: "No more amazement: Tell your piteous heart there's no harm done."

Not understanding a word, Gabriel ignored him and staggered off to the men's room. The last time he'd checked on Anna, although he couldn't say when that was, she was with the two hippies with the guitar. He saw their backpacks stowed under the stairs, but the three kids had disappeared. His eagerness to get back to the game of cards dispelled ominous niggling doubt. Lost in thought, he went into the men's room.

As he emerged with stiffened sleeves (which the other players wouldn't notice because they never noticed), he ran into a girl. I'd venture to say that, right then, that moment in October 1966, the only person in the world who could have distracted him from the game of cards was precisely that girl: Sarah. Sarah, twenty-two years old, red-headed, white-skinned, with bright, fearless eyes. Sarah, in her white nurse's coat underneath which was a short, very short skirt: a precursor of swinging London fashions in her part of town.

Sarah, my future mum.

Gabriel was so flabbergasted that he lost track of everything. He was helped by the fact that she was carrying a small case marked with a red cross. A memory of three months earlier came back in a sweet pang. Their first and only meeting. Sarah had been doing work experience in the ferry's infirmary all that year. Three days a week she was on board for ten hours—four crossings— and she had to deal with the various incidents that cropped up. Seasickness, someone slipping on the deck, Scottish truck drivers brawling in the bar . . . nothing too serious. Despite the hassle of having to sleep three nights a week in a pension in the port of Dover, she found it quite a relaxing job. At that very moment, for example, with the boat at the mercy of the storm, she was calmly walking around handing out seasickness pills to the passengers.

Their first meeting had taken place in the summer during a smooth crossing. The waters were calm, Bundó and Gabriel had avoided the hordes of people by taking refuge in the bar and were fleecing the Frenchman in a game of cards. The pregnant girl was up on deck, basking in the faint sun that lit up the Channel on cloudless days. Then she fainted. A passenger half caught her as she fell and left her lying on the deck. Those nearest to her soon crowded around, and everyone had something to say. At her side, someone was trying to revive her, saying they had to let the air in, but the air was already there. The girl didn't regain consciousness. An overexcited passenger set off the alarm, and one minute later nurse Sarah appeared with her first-aid kit. She took the girl's pulse, looked up at the throng of people, and they all agreed it was nothing to get worked up about, but they'd take her down to the infirmary just in case. When they got there—two brawny Englishmen carrying her down—they saw Gabriel and Bundó coming along the passageway. After the alarm went off, the story had run the length and breadth of the boat. The infirmary was a minuscule room, and Sarah told them that only one person could come in. Bundó, who couldn't stand the sight of blood, disqualified himself saying he was too fat for such a tiny space. Thus it was that Gabriel and Sarah were left alone behind the closed door of the infirmary. With the girl who'd fainted, of course.

"We laid her on the stretcher bed"—my mother recalled—"and before I could say anything, Gabriel gave me to understand, with sign language and touching his belly, that the girl was pregnant. I asked, 'Are you the father?' His eyes went wide as saucers. I repeated the question, this time more slowly. 'No, no, no, no. I only driver. Driver.' He was driving with an invisible steering wheel as he spoke. 'To Londres. London. I . . . driver hospital. She . . . avortar in hospital.' He made another gesture, as if the girl's belly was a balloon and she wanted to make it explode. It was like playing charades. I nodded, letting him know I understood, giving him a soothing look. I have to admit that as soon as I set eyes on him and heard his babbling, he had me seduced. It's difficult to explain in any rational terms. When he wanted to speak, Gabriel shed that rigid look of his and became a stream of affection and concern. His gestures conveyed a kind of tenderness you never see in Englishmen. There was also a sort of Spanish machismo about him, something primitive and exotic and, I confess, I was doomed from the start. The taut muscles, suntanned skin, hot blood . . . When I looked at him, he made me think of a kettle full of cool water that, once on the fire, starts vibrating, showing its true temperament. There were so many stories about the impetuosity of Spanish men, and Gabriel seemed to be my one and only chance to experiment. I've always been one for trying everything."

When they met up again on the day of the storm, a crumpled memory of unbuttoned shirts, a raised skirt, and unbridled lust took Gabriel and Sarah back to the infirmary. It was so clear that it usurped the reality. In fact, nothing much had happened so they'd had to create the fantasy after going their separate ways. Now they were mixing memory and desire. The facts of the first meeting were as follows. That day, Sarah revived the pregnant girl by waving smelling salts under her nose. Then she took her blood pressure and pulse and, seeing that everything was fine, advised her to go back up on deck and get some fresh air. When the girl

left, still trembling with fright, Sarah asked Gabriel to stay behind for a moment to sign her report. Then, without further ado,
she shut the door and threw herself at him with predatory force.
After the first instant of surprise, Gabriel understood the situation
and went along with it (he always went along with any opportunity that came his way). Papers flew as they kissed, a box dropped
and pills rolled around on the floor, medical instruments fell with
a tremendous clatter, and, just as they were starting to get their
clothes off, three blasts of the ship's siren announced they were
coming into Dover. Loudspeakers summoned drivers downstairs
to the car deck to get their vehicles ready to disembark. They were
so steamed up that Sarah totally ignored it, but Gabriel was too
responsible. He immediately stopped, sweaty and disoriented, and
got dressed again as fast as he'd undressed. Before leaving, he gave
Sarah a long kiss. "Another day," he said, getting the English right
when he whispered the words in her ear. The warmth of his voice,
its soft tickling, had the effect of an anti-itch cream. Later, when
the truck drivers and the pregnant girl were on their way to London, Sarah, tidying up the mess in the infirmary, found a poker
card in one corner under the bed. As chance would have it, it was
the king of hearts. "That's a nice touch," she told herself. "These
Spanish lovers are in a class of their own."


This second time around, Sarah might have felt conned if she'd
known that Gabriel had another king of hearts up his sleeve ready
to be unleashed in the game, and this might have put an end to
the attraction she immediately felt for him, intact and even heightened by memory. Might or might not. Luckily for me (born nine
months later) we'll never know. What we do know is that Gabriel
totally forgot about the cards and the game and Monsieur Champion and went over to kiss Sarah. At the last minute she stopped
him. "Here no. Now no," she said in English, getting him to understand that the crew couldn't know about this. She quickly told him
her plan. She had to give out some more pills, and, in half an hour,
they could meet up in the infirmary and play doctors again (with

a wink from Sarah). Gabriel seemed baffled so she gave him a clue before leaving him: Taking one of the pills, she put it directly into his mouth, letting her fingers rest there for a few seconds. Then she removed them, put them in her own mouth, and, sucking them lasciviously, moved on along the passageway in search of seasick passengers.

The ferry's rocking as it sought to dodge an army of gigantic waves brought Gabriel back to an uncertain reality. He checked that the cards were still in place and returned to the cafeteria, trying to calm down as he went. At the entrance he found Bundó, who was about to go looking for him. He was extremely twitchy. Since he and Muriel had been courting, he couldn't stand being around Frenchmen because he saw a potential client of his girlfriend in every single one of them. It was tough on him. He only had to cross the border and the first customs official he sighted was a suspect.

"Where were you?" he asked testily. "This Frog's a cunning bastard, and he might smell a rat."

"It's all under control," Gabriel reassured him. "Leave it to me, just like always. When you see me loading up my bet, go for it even if you haven't got anything. The more money at stake, the more excited he gets. I've got his number."

Convinced that his luck was holding, Monsieur Champion was in a hurry to hang them out to dry and started to deal without saying a word. Ibrahim picked up the cards, fumbled, and one fell on the ground. He dived down to pick it up before the Frenchman yelled at him. He was tormented by the vision of Sans Merci suffering inside the horsebox. He might be dead. Only when everyone was holding his cards did Monsieur Champion break the silence as he puffed on his cigar.

"What a long visit to the men's room, *mon ami*. You must have had a nice rest."

"I've got a small bladder," Gabriel replied unfazed, "and I drink too much beer. I don't know what the problem's called in French, but I'm sure you know what I mean." A pause. "Bundó, you open, don't you?"

The first hand they played was a dummy run. Ibrahim won but the pot was negligible. The next four hands went to Gabriel and Bundó. The Frenchman gave them dirty looks, but then they let him win quite a good hand, and he relaxed. Gabriel didn't resort to his tricks until game eight. They'd been playing almost half an hour, and he realized he'd got back a ridiculously small amount. Between hands he was thinking about Sarah and keeping an eye on his watch. She'd soon be waiting for him in the infirmary. They'd better get a move on. Bundó dealt, and he got a couple of aces, hearts and diamonds. He had a hunch that the ace of clubs hadn't appeared. In the first draw, Monsieur Champion got rid of an ace of spades, suggesting that he held no other ace in his hand. With imperceptible sleight of hand, Gabriel produced the ace of clubs from his left sleeve. He bet high and so did the others. They showed their cards. Gabriel revealed his three aces, and it worked. The Frenchman cursed but didn't expose his cards. That was his right. Thenceforth, Gabriel kept winning without any need to revisit his shirtsleeve stash. He felt secure, and the cards were good. Luck always shuns the desperate. After a couple of hands, the ace of spades turned up again and he slipped it back inside his sleeve. From time to time, to avert suspicion, he gave the hand to Bundó or let the Frenchman win. Ibrahim was playing robotically. His mind was elsewhere. Hands were dealt, minutes went by, francs disguised as pesetas moved back to the truck drivers' side, and Gabriel picked up on something: Monsieur Champion's response was to bluff, one hand after another. He'd reached the point where he wasn't even studying the cards. It was as if he intuited that they were up to something and he was trying to bamboozle them by scrapping kings and queens at odd times. He was betting large amounts without rhyme or reason. It was crazy. Gabriel was watching his face, "Too many teeth," he thought. "You've got too many teeth and they're too white." Then the tic was revealed. Every time he was about to bluff, Monsieur Champion raised his upper lip, baring two rows of immaculate teeth in a strange stony-white sneer.

While Bundó was shuffling for the next round, Sarah appeared in the cafeteria with her first-aid kit. The ferry wasn't being tossed around so much now, but, all the same, she went over to passengers who were looking green around the gills and offered them a seasickness pill. She administered one to the Shakespearian actor, who swallowed it after throwing a few lines at her. Gabriel admired Sarah from a distance. As she moved around the boat, as lithe and sure-footed as an adolescent, she seemed to have the gift of turning the nightmarish crossing into an adventure on the Channel. Looking around for new patients, Sarah's gaze met Gabriel's. They locked eyes for a moment and looked away, fearing a short circuit. Sarah stood in the middle of the room and shouted with all the lung power of a fishwife in the market, "Last pills! Last pills! They're running out! Free! No more seasickness! If you change your mind and want one later, you'll find me in the infirmary . . . Free! They are free!"

Apparently ignoring her shouting, the four players concentrated on the hand that had just been dealt. Bundó, however, was trying to remember where he'd seen that face before. Ibrahim calculated that, with one bottle of those pills, there'd be enough to calm Sans Merci. At the first bet, Monsieur Champion attempted another bluff and his teeth gleamed like foam on a turbulent sea. They bet again, and Gabriel put an end to his bluff with a mere pair of jacks. The situation was verging on ridiculous. It only took ten minutes and one round to leave the Frenchman and his groom completely cleaned out. Gabriel's mind wandered back to the infirmary to summon up Sarah making obscene gestures at him.

"I think we'll be in Dover soon," he said. "Maybe we should call it a day, don't you think, *monsieur?*"

The look he got from the Frenchman would have done away with Captain Ahab himself.


The storm had changed the perception of time on board the ferry. The surging, rocking, lashing of waves, pounding of rain, seasickness, and boredom all came together in such a way that the minutes didn't tick by in an orderly fashion but in jolts. Some afflicted passengers felt as if they were riding an aquatic rollercoaster. Our card players took shelter inside a bubble of smoke and gambling. Under the effects of LSD, Anna, Ludovic, and Raymond wandered around the boat at a snail's pace. It had taken them all of half an hour to cover the hundred meters separating the cafeteria from their objective. Their progress through a mesh of passageways and doors was an expedition into the wilderness. Anna saw grass springing up under her bare feet, green, velvety, and fresh. The walls and metal banisters were sprouting thick branches, tropical vines, and intricate ivy that hid the path. Ludovic, brandishing a machete in front of her, was opening up the way. Behind her, Raymond was protecting her from the wild animals that were following hot on their heels. They walked in single file, frequently stopping to listen to the cries of distant monkeys and the trilling of birds in the depths of the forest. Some of them were rehearsing Beatles songs, and she'd been captivated by this for quite a while until a unicorn popped up in the middle of the path and presented them with a small round secret. They swallowed it before anyone discovered it (Sarah, seeing them so pale and stunned-looking, had made them take one of her pills). Now, thanks to the information that the secret had lodged in their brains, they reached the entrance to the temple without any problems. Well, a snake had bitten off and gulped down one of Raymond's arms, but he still had five left.

At the doorway leading into the car deck there was a sign prohibiting anyone from opening it during the crossing. As Anna stared, the letters turned into a bas-relief representing the palm of a right hand. She placed her own on top of it to make sure they fitted and the door miraculously opened. The brothers applauded. Another country awaited them on the other side. As they went down the stairs, the sedge was withering, and the steps crumbled into sand dunes. They were overwhelmed by the salty smell of the sea and realized that this underworld was warmer. Clothes were such a nuisance by the time they got to the bottom that they stripped naked without the least self-consciousness. In the distance they could hear the pounding of waves breaking on the shore, and their bodies were demanding water. They scampered uninhibitedly through parked cars and trucks, which appeared as huge rocks. Occasionally a sunbeam flashed in a rearview mirror, signaling that they were on the right track. Their feet sank into the sand. They took almost a quarter of an hour to negotiate the few parked vehicles and discover a blissful place tucked away in one corner. A crane-cum-coconut palm shaded them, and oil-coated crystalline water that had seeped in from the storm bathed their feet, leaving them with a phosphorescence of gasoline and coral. Anna understood that the experience was so unique that she moved silently over to the brothers, embraced them and set about fondling their genitals. The boys watched their instant erections turn into exotic fruit. Obeying a sign from her, all three knelt down and continued their caresses. The two brothers exchanged a look of conscious surprise transcending the effects of the drug, but the LSD lured them back into action. Anna lay on the ground and asked them to lick off the sand that was coating her body. Then, when Raymond and Ludovic had just got to work on the delightful task—one at each nipple—the horse's whinnying resounded through the car deck with the power of divine intervention.

"Be quiet. Silence!" Anna ordered. "This is Sans Merci calling us. It's the horse. We must free him at once."

She stood up, and the two brothers reluctantly followed. All three were trembling with cold. Their skin was camouflaged in a film of oil and grease—a lovely bronze suntan, they thought. Anna asked the boys to lift her and hold her aloft so she could survey the horizon.

Monsieur Champion's jeep and the horsebox, long, high, and narrow, were parked less than ten meters away from the tropical oasis. The car deck attendant, who was slumbering in his cab, had given them a spot that wasn't too close to other vehicles so they could maneuvre better. Traces of hay and alfalfa were scattered on the ground around the horsebox because Ibrahim had fed Sans Merci just before going upstairs. The horse whinnied again, and Anna identified the prison where he was being held. The three of them approached and, with an adeptness that can only come from a state of hallucination, slid back the bolt.

Hearing the metallic sound, Sans Merci fidgeted apprehensively, stamping and whinnying. Anna started singing a lullaby to calm him. Meanwhile, the two brothers carefully opened the horsebox door and lowered the ramp. The vision of Sans Merci's rump with his plaited tail and svelte bandaged legs transfixed them with sheer religious wonderment. The jittery animal plopped out a stream of golden manure, and its warm stench enveloped them. Anna kept singing, Raymond wished he had his guitar, and Ludovic started clicking his tongue.

*"Click, click, click, click."*

Hearing the sound, Sans Merci took a step backward, as he always did with Ibrahim, testing, trying to locate the ramp.

*"Click, click, click, click."*

Another step. Raymond slapped his rump, and the horse gained confidence. A few more steps and he was out. Sans Merci, somewhat startled, whinnied again, and Raymond kept stroking his hind legs. The horse was calmer now. Anna went into the horsebox and found some rope to make a bridle. She gently slipped it on and the horse acquiesced.

*"Click, click, click, click."*

Now they could see the whole animal, a real thoroughbred. The three young people felt humbled by its aristocratic presence. Then again, the effects of the LSD were starting to wear off.

"We only need to ride to the English coast, and then you'll be free, Sans Merci," Anna crooned in his ear. Then, adapting to the horse's pace, they set off to find an exit into the fresh air so he could run free under the sky without having to pick his way through the jungle.

Upstairs, at that very moment, Gabriel was asking, "So maybe you'd like to bet the horse?" After his earlier suggestion that they should end the game, the Frenchman had responded with a scoffing snigger, looking daggers at him.

"I'm the one who's losing so I'm the one to decide when we'll finish," he said, crumbling the tip of his cigar into an ashtray.

"But if you're almost broke and the English coast is in sight," Bundó replied, "there's no way you'll get it back."

"Deal and shut up, *nom de dieu!*"

They'd gone on to play two more hands, and Gabriel had wiped the floor with him in both. Cheating. The second time, Ibrahim had spotted him pulling an ace out of his sleeve but said nothing because he was longing to finish the game and go down to Sans Merci. Now there were no francs left to stake. Bundó had gathered up the cards and was stacking them neatly before returning them to their box.

"One last hand. All or nothing," Monsieur Champion said. His desperation wasn't about money but self-esteem. There was no way he was going to lose again to those Spanish truck drivers.

It was then that Gabriel, cool as a cucumber, put the question to him, unaware that all hell was about to break loose: "You're broke. So maybe you'd like to bet the horse?"

The Frenchman shook his head, pondering it for four eternal seconds.

"*Oui.*"

"*Non, non, non, jamais! Sur mon cadavre!*" Ibrahim screamed. He was beside himself. He wasn't seeing straight.

"Shut your trap, you," Champion came back with withering scorn. "I'm the boss here."

Ibrahim's reaction left them all astounded. Normally, cursing under his breath, he wouldn't have uttered a word, but this time his master had gone too far. He vaulted nimbly over the table and landed on top of the Frenchman. Groom and boss tumbled to the floor. Broken chairs cracked loudly. Cards fluttered like a host of feathers, and the coins that Bundó had not yet gathered up rolled around the floor. Ibrahim had totally lost it and now, perched on the Frenchman's chest, set about battering his face. They were childish slaps, more noisy than anything else, but Monsieur Champion had surrendered and took it, emitting a melodic mewling. One would have thought he liked it and that they were both well accustomed to it. Gabriel grabbed Ibrahim by the armpits and hauled him off his boss, who remained on the ground, covering his face with his hands. Attracted to the battle cries, the passengers and some crew members had congregated in the cafeteria. The actor decided on another line and bellowed it out at the top of his voice.

"Fury, Fury! There, Tyrant, there! Hark! Hark!"

Sarah turned up with her first-aid kit in case anyone was injured. Bundó, still counting the money, moved away from the scuffle and went over to the window, trying to find some peace and quiet. Then he looked outside—the ferry wasn't bucking so much now—and there before his eyes was an amazing, unearthly apparition, one that he'd go on to describe dozens of times and always with admiration. On the first deck, the widest one, a stark-naked girl was riding a charger. Woman and animal were moving so fast they seemed to be flying over the sea.

Anna was riding bareback, legs gripping the horse's flanks, hands clutching the bridle she'd put on before. Sans Merci was trotting rather than galloping but, with the blue ribbon of sea in the background, they seemed to be out to win the Derby. Bundó stared at the girl's small firm breasts but then he saw her face and realized it was Anna.

"Shit! Fucking hell!" he shouted. "Gabriel, it's Anna, that girl we're taking to London, and she's up there riding a runaway horse . . . She's going to kill herself!"

Though nobody understood what he was saying, interest switched from the brawl to the window. All the passengers came over and were mesmerized by the girl and horse. Someone was certain it was a reincarnation of Lady Godiva. As soon as he realized they were talking about a horse, Ibrahim broke free from Gabriel, spat on Monsieur Champion, and dashed up to the deck. Sarah followed. The onlookers in the cafeteria were then treated to a second impressive sight, the appearance of Ludovic and Raymond, dancing naked to the strains of a Celtic melody improvised by themselves. It wasn't clear whether they were chasing Anna and the horse or celebrating their passing. The floral erections still protruded from their groins.

~

When I'm feeling low, Christophers, or when I regress to my old bad habit of sniffing my fingers, I take refuge in this image of the naked equestrienne charging around the boat on her steed. It has the clarity of those recessive memories that help you, that top you up and save the day for you, but that can't hurt you because they didn't really happen to you. Ever since my thirteenth birthday when my mum told me about the adventure on the Channel, the image has stayed with me like a birthmark on my skin or a tattoo on my soul. Sometimes I think we should know what our parents were up to just before making us. I don't mean the moment of bonking or lovemaking—or whatever term they used—but just before that, the hours in the run-up. In fact, it wouldn't be at all bad if we were born with this information wired into our brains. That way, we'd understand more about ourselves.

In any case, that October day of 1966, the *Viking III* came into port five hours late, having exhausted its supply of seasickness pills. There were no victims to cry over. Anna, high as a kite, riding Sans Merci into the great blue yonder, was convinced they would leap over the prow and soar out across the sea to the white cliffs of Dover, but the horse showed he had more sense than his rider. When they got to the end of the deck he turned left, jumped over a low barrier and kept trotting, after which he dodged or hurdled every object that blocked his way. The ferry became an improvised steeplechase track. At the end of the second round, Ibrahim, running at his side, managed to stop him. The horse pranced for a few seconds. Ibrahim embraced him like a son and screamed at Anna until she dismounted, oblivious to her nakedness. She was shivering, her skin was damp and cold, and her lips were purple. Sarah swiftly bore her off to make sure she didn't have hypothermia, but the girl was young, and all the vital signs were in incredibly good shape.

Five minutes later Gabriel knocked at the infirmary door. He'd found Anna's clothes and was bringing them to her. The effects of the acid had almost totally worn off and now a sedative was battling to spare her mortification. Sarah helped her to dress. With feigned severity, Gabriel asked Anna if she would be so good as to go and find Bundó. He had to stay behind to sign some papers.

The ferry berthed in Dover, but Sarah and Gabriel took more than half an hour to emerge from the infirmary. They had lots and lots of papers to sign. All the vehicles left the ferry. Bundó settled accounts with Monsieur Champion. A large sum of French francs was burning a hole in his pocket, and he experienced the victory as his revenge against all the Frenchmen who'd ever passed through Muriel's bed. Sans Merci's owner had been ill-disposed to cough up the money but tried to act as if he didn't care, after which he swore that one day in the not-too-distant future they'd meet up again for the revenge game. "It's my right," he insisted. Meanwhile, Anna had said good-bye to the two French brothers, Raymond and Ludovic, wishing them lots of luck in their musical adventure (and we have no further news of them, not even whether they got to savor Carnaby Street's sweetest days). And then she fell asleep in the truck.

Thanks to the delay, Bundó and Gabriel had to do the move the following morning, a day later than scheduled. Senyor Casellas grumbled into the phone but Gabriel threw him the best possible excuse.

"We can drive the trucks faster but we can't struggle against the elements. With that storm we endured, Senyor Casellas, you should be paying us danger money."

Sarah, who had the next two days off, said she'd go with Anna Miralpeix to the clinic where they were going to perform the abortion. As a nurse, she'd be able to stay with her overnight, which, in normal circumstances, was something Gabriel or Bundó had to do. The next morning, after an especially placid night and while the two men were lugging furniture, a new Anna emerged from sleep. The mystical experience with the horse had awakened a hitherto unsuspected maternal instinct in her. Lying on the trolley as they bore her off to the operating room, she was beset by doubts.

Five months later, halfway through March, La Ibérica had another move across the Channel to London, this time without any abortive mission. Once on board the *Viking III*, Bundó and Petroli scoured the boat in search of Monsieur Champion and his easily won French francs. No such luck. Gabriel went directly to the infirmary and knocked at the door. When Sarah opened it, he saw the incipient roundness of her belly under her white coat—me—and knew without having to do the sums that he was the father. Since he had some experience—by this time, Christof in Frankfurt was toddling about and calling him Daddy—he responded more naturally. Gabriel and Sarah were closeted in the infirmary throughout the entire crossing, first talking and then signing more papers. Sarah, who wasn't daunted by the prospect of being a single mum, told him she wanted to have it (wanted to have me) and wouldn't ask anything of him. Gabriel asked for just one favor: that she'd let him come to visit from time to time. Ah, and choose the child's name. If it was a girl, he wanted her to be called Ann, like the girl who'd brought about their second encounter in the infirmary and, if it was a boy, Christopher.

"Why Christopher?"

"Why not?" was his enigmatic response.

Mum said she'd think about it, but she already knew she liked the mystery.

Gabriel's next trip to London was a reunion with fatherhood as well as with Sarah, who was no longer working on the ferry because she was on maternity leave. I'd been born a month earlier, in July 1967. Mum had phoned Dad at the boarding house to tell him the good news, and he promised to come and visit us soon. Would he have come if I'd been a girl? We have to give him the benefit of the doubt, but we'll never know for sure. In any case, that trip should be counted as an oversight in the La Ibérica timesheets. The last Monday of July, when they were closing down for a month's holiday in August, Gabriel sweet-talked the secretary, Rebeca, into giving him the keys of the newest DKV without Senyor Casellas's knowledge. That very evening and all alone, with no physical or human cargo, he filled up the tank and headed up through Europe.

About halfway through her pregnancy, Sarah had left the flat she shared with some other nurses and installed herself in a two-bedroom basement in Martello Street, behind the railway lines, not far from London Fields station. Dad turned up at the new address on Tuesday afternoon, as fresh as a daisy. He'd phoned as soon as he disembarked from the ferry in Dover, and Mum and I waited for him for ages in front of the house, counting the trains going by. As soon as he arrived, Dad took me in his arms (with an expertise that surprised Sarah) and whispered my name in my ear: Christopher... It's such a shame that these memories are stored under lock and key in some inaccessible part of my brain! I wish I could recall for myself what Mum told me later! Gabriel stayed with us six whole days. Six! A record. Christophers, it would have been the longest time we ever spent together. Fortunately, it was warm and sunny that first week in August, and we certainly made the most of it. It seems that we went walking in London Fields every day. As I slept in my pram, they had a picnic on the grass, and Gabriel tried to make sense of the choreography of a game of cricket that some enthusiasts were playing nearby. In the evening, before putting me to bed, we went to the pub, where they both enjoyed a pint of the black stuff. It was holiday time and the hours seemed longer. I like to think that during that week Dad came to sense the protective inertia of repeated days. I can say merely "sense" because at breakfast time on day six he told Mum he'd be returning to Barcelona that afternoon. He didn't offer any explanation, and Sarah didn't ask for any. Innocent and happy, still unaware of the privilege we'd just relinquished, Mum and I watched the van moving off down the street.

Now that we Christophers have got together, we know that Gabriel didn't go back to Barcelona that day but took a detour to Frankfurt where he visited Sigrun and Christof for four days. It's a strange sensation because the discovery of the lie brings with it instant forgiveness. Brother stuff, hey, Christophers?

And, as the actor in the ferry might have said, the rest is silence. The silence we're all trying to make more bearable.

# 10

# The World's Badly Divided Up

## CHRISTOPHE'S TURN

Let me give my chapter this title because it's true: The world's badly divided up, Christophers. Of all four brothers, take note, I'm the one who got to see our father most and am probably the one who received most gifts snaffled from La Ibérica clients. Paris was in the middle of many of their routes. He could talk to me because his command of French was passable. What a privilege, eh? Yet I've got almost no memory of all that. Less than three years had elapsed between my birth in February 1969 and the last time I saw him. It's not enough time. If I remember things it's because my mother kept telling me about them years later and because I can link them up with photos we still have of him. They're feelings more than memories. Once, half pushed into it by Mom, I went for a session of regression hypnosis with an Argentine psychoanalyst who lived in Porte d'Italie, and who'd been a sort of boyfriend of hers. I wanted to go back in time to the middle of that three-year period so I could dig up the first memory I'd kept of my father. I settled down on the couch and gave myself over to the whole ceremony. I started to count backward from a hundred softly. A hundred, ninety-nine, ninety-eight, ninety-seven...After a while, just when I was dropping off to sleep, I dived like a pearl fisher into the depths of my subconscious but surfaced with lost bearings and empty hands. Not a single secret memory, trauma, or unexpected image let itself be caught. I'm no good at these experiments.

Now here's a hypothesis: I was the first son that Gabriel really wanted. I'm not taking any credit for this, for the record. The first Christopher born of a single mother could be considered an accident; the second Christopher we might see as carelessness (sorry, Chris); the third Christopher must perforce have been the product of free will. (The fourth Christopher, in Barcelona, goes a step further and is born as fruit of an obsession, but the hero of that story will have his moment of glory later.) Whatever desire there might have been for my existence, however, was soon canceled out by my real father—a Gabriel who turned up when it suited him—and four putative fathers who, through accumulation and excess, demagnetized my filial compass. You see how the world's badly divided up? While you lot were spending long periods with your mothers, asking where Dad had gone and listening to outlandish excuses, I had four fathers who had no hang-ups about taking his place. There should have been one for each of us. Now that I'm an adult, I'm certain that these four friends of my mom's must have loved me and that I meant almost as much to them as a son of their own, but they never saved me from attacks of the horrible feeling that I'd been abandoned. You know what I mean, Christophers. We've talked about this at our get-togethers. It's that heavy feeling that came over us sometimes, like a kind of annulment of our existence that was only alleviated—with a bit of luck—by our mothers' attention or, more rarely, the announcement of a visit from Dad. Not even when it was clear that Gabriel was never coming back and I was (fruitlessly) trying to forget him did the four substitutes rise in rank. I never think about them any more. Must be genetic.

Since these secrets of mine might surprise you, I have to explain that when I came into the world Mom was living in a sort of students' commune in the Latin Quarter. Mireille was twenty, an idealist who was studying (in a manner of speaking) second-year French literature at the Sorbonne. She came to Paris at the age of eighteen from a village in Ardennes not far from the Belgian border. It was the fourth time in her life she'd been to the capital. The brightest little girl in high school came to the university with all the honors befitting a beauty queen who was going to represent the whole region. She says that shortly before her departure they organized a farewell in the local town hall, complete with a band playing music and second-rank dignitaries, and she'd recited two poems, one very lugubrious, by Apollinaire, and the other by Prévert to compensate for it. Thanks to a grant from the provincial government, her parents had got her into a pension for students in Rue de Vaugirard, very close to Boulevard Raspail. She could walk from her lodgings to the university, as if she were back in the village. The Saturday before her classes began they'd come with her to Paris and said their good-byes till Christmas. As she was an only child, they missed her and, trying to ease the pain of absence, took some comfort in an innocent scene, picturing her in the room they'd seen, studying at the table in the corner, twisting her long hair around one finger, or eating in the dining room with other girls just like her. The fact is that Mireille lasted only five months in the pension. At the beginning of 1968, after spending Christmas with her parents in the village, confirming yet again how its quietness stifled her and got her down, she went to her first university assembly, and that changed her life. Mireille described it with the energy that sometimes gets hold of her. When that happens she's unstoppable

"Look, when I landed in Paris, I was a match waiting to be struck. I had a head seething with ideas from all the books I'd read as a teenager, which helped me to cope with being alone and, yes, to survive, but they didn't clarify anything at that stage. I tucked them away inside my head, cramming them into the chaos, one after the other, so I didn't have to think about what was there all around me. There's nothing worse than the isolation of the provinces and, if you don't knuckle under, nothing worse than a winter's evening at home listening to those fake chummy voices beaming out from the local radio station. Your skin shrivels up out of pure loneliness, honest to God. You're so lucky you didn't have to go through that, Christophe," she said, jabbing her burning cigarette in my direction, a typical gesture of hers that harks back to her years of debates and discussions. "Your grandfather, as you

know, worked as a clerk in a furniture factory. Whenever he had a
free half-hour, he locked himself in the garage and constructed
miniature cars and trains. When he finished he gave some of them
to the kids of the furniture manufacturer's kids. I always thought
that he would have been happier if I'd been born a boy. Your grandmother was a long-suffering housewife. She suffered over everything and everyone. Without realizing it, I suffered with her. Once
I was in Paris, I always headed for the great avenues when I wanted
to go for a walk. The boulevards of Montparnasse, Saint-Germain,
Raspail . . . I walked miles. In those open spaces the suffering gradually left me. I loved hearing the rattling of cars on cobblestones.
I breathed in deeply, and, although I was alone, or precisely because I was alone, everything began to make sense. Then, one day
in January when I was killing time between two classes, half in a
trance, as if it were preordained, I walked into a students' assembly
in my department and the match was struck. *Rrrasss!*" In the absence of matches Mireille flicked on her lighter, providing the
flame for her onomatopoeia. "Don't think that I was converted into
an activist on the spot. What enchanted me in that first assembly
was the tumult of voices, the yelling, the warmth of all our bodies,
the students, like a cauldron turned up full blast, about to explode.
We all agreed on one thing: The fascist fossil General de Gaulle
was clinging to power, and we had to protest and get rid of him.
After that, though, the methods of protest and action diverged and
were even contradictory. The pandemonium that eventually broke
loose in the assembly hall was more or less pacified by four or five
student spokespersons. The views of one group were hissed at by
another and cheered by a third, but then you didn't know whether
they were really in agreement or just being sarcastic. One group of
boys giggled at every single proposal, and, when they did speak, it
was to call for sexual freedom as the only solution. 'Let's stop fighting and get down to fucking right now,' they shouted, taking off
their pullovers. None of the girls took any notice of them because
they were a pretty callow bunch. There were Marxists, Trots, anarchists, communists, textualists, and I don't know what else. Whenever somebody got up to speak, it only served to divide the protests

yet again. Half a dozen students, at the very most, declared themselves situationists and demanded that, before anything else, delegations should be formed to go and visit the factories and awaken the critical consciousness of the workers of France. Otherwise we'd be going nowhere. Anyone who wanted to, they claimed, could meet Guy Debord. Then one of the girls spoke up. 'Why would we want to meet Debord when we have Beauvoir?' Another cried, 'Beauvoir? Beauvoir and Sartre? Move on! Long live anarchist surrealism!' Or it might have been the other way around: 'Long live surrealist anarchism.' Mingling among the students, I spotted several of the lecturers, listening to their words and observing their exaltation with incredulity written all over their faces. Two boys who spoke with an English accent unfurled a banner attacking the president of the United States, a bastard who was called Johnson, or Johnston, or something like that, and calling for more worldwide protest against the Vietnam War. Everyone applauded, and they proudly raised their left fists. The others imitated them for a few seconds. After a couple of hours of this racket, the assembly broke up. There were no practical results that I recall, but we all felt that, with our joint efforts, we'd sorted out the world, or at least we'd tried to. At that point we couldn't have imagined what would happen four months later. As I left, I realized that this was the first time I'd ever played hooky, and I went back to the pension transformed. I hadn't talked to anyone. I'd just listened but I was really shaken up. I remember I locked myself in the loo, wet my face, looked at myself in the mirror, and let out a scream, half rage and half emotion. One of the girls tapped at the door asking if anything was wrong. 'No, no, it's nothing,' I replied, 'or everything,' but she didn't hear the last bit because I said it under my breath." Mom lit another of her Gauloises, took a long theatrical drag to prod her memory and went on. "At dinnertime, the girls in the pension looked like total wimps, a bunch of innocents with the stuffing knocked out of them, the replica of myself. I bolted down my food without saying a word and locked myself in my room. I remember that I read a few pages of a novel by Gide that we were discussing in class at the time, *Les Caves du Vatican*, I think it was, but my mind kept veering away from the text and getting lost in a tangle of other disjointed ideas. I had to put a stop to this. I wasn't the least bit sleepy, but I got into my pajamas, turned the light off and let my thoughts organize themselves. Then, in the compact darkness of that room, I couldn't stop thinking about my parents. I saw them as sacrificial victims. They lived in a borrowed reality, falsified by the government of de Gaulle and his gang. Slaving their lives away, trying to pretend that they actually liked the shitty existence that had been theirs to live after the war. I could see that my dad was a loser, just like the rest of them all over the country, someone who only got worked up over affairs of state (and, in particular, don't you dare touch his France, or his boss at the furniture factory, a god of personal achievement), and that my mom was a pathetic, indifferent extra, the walk-on always categorically taking his side. 'Things will never be as good for us as they are now,' she used to say when she sensed a family upset brewing . . . I mean, tiny little upsets, really. Her words bounced around my brain and made me totally depressed. Above all, let there be no changes, may the future not unsettle us. I realized that they'd be old very soon, well before their time. This revelation settled like a ball of lead in my stomach. It was the same pain I used to feel when they told me in their whining, blackmailing voices that they were missing me. Yes, go and study in Paris, they actually said, but come home to us so we can all be proud of it. I don't know if I cried that night . . . Yes, yes, I do know, what am I saying, of course I know, of course I cried, let's not deceive ourselves, first with a furious sob muffled in my pillow and then languid and tireless as a lullaby. It was so melodious that in the end I went to sleep." She closed her eyes for a moment, as if trying to summon up her interlude of sleep and, when she opened them again, she ran her tongue over her lips. "My mouth's dry from all this talking. How about bringing me a beer? There's some in the fridge." I brought two, one each, and she took up the thread again. "The next day I got up feeling giddy. My head was spinning as if I'd woken up in the middle of an earthquake. I threw on some clothes, skipped breakfast, and headed for the university. The sensation of shock stayed with me as I walked along the street. Then again, I remember that it was freezing cold, one of those winter days when the air ruffles the surface of the river, comes off even icier, and pricks your face with a thousand needles. I was walking but couldn't feel my feet. All of a sudden, my body decided that I was going to skip class again so I went into a café. Sitting in a corner, I asked for a latte to perk me up a bit and took my book out of my bag. I don't know which one it was, but that's not important. The prospect of spending the whole day in the café reading and smoking (I'd started a couple of months before) calmed me down, giving me a strange feeling of serenity. I'm not sure how long I was sitting there so engrossed—a couple of hours at least—before a girl came up to me and asked, 'You were at the assembly yesterday, weren't you?' The question must have jolted me out of some kind of daydream because she had to repeat it before I took it in. 'Sorry . . . my name's Justine. You were at the assembly yesterday, weren't you?' I'd seen that face. She was one of the few girls who'd spoken the previous day. I'd been awed by her when she'd talked without letting the others interrupt her. I said, "Yes, I was at the assembly," and asked if she'd like to sit down with me. Then we had more coffee and something to eat, and we talked till it got dark. Well, I talked and she listened. It was very easy, precisely because I didn't know her, and we were the same age. I spewed it all out: from the disgust I felt at my parents' passive desertion to the need to launch an assault on that fucking awful society so the same thing wouldn't happen to us. We had to change the course of history! I could hear myself parroting ideas that had impressed me so much the previous day, but now, coming out of my own mouth, they made me feel secure. Justine, who also came from outside Paris, nodded convinced, spurring me on. 'Our parents are the living dead,' I remember she said at one point. 'This is a country of the living dead. Is there anything more grotesque than all those daily parades of war medals? Leave this city, this neighborhood even, and everywhere you go you find the same thing: prematurely aged people working like beasts and getting dressed up on Sundays to go to the park and show off their medals. If their houses got flooded one day, they wouldn't rush to help their wives, children, or grandchildren first, but they'd save their fucking war medals . . .' I know that instant beguilement is one of the virtues of youth, or a defect if you like, and that it's often simple illusion, but I identified with Justine completely. When we said good-bye with a kiss on each cheek, it was as if we'd known each other all our lives. We arranged to meet in the same place the next day." Mireille paused. She looked tired. I told her that, if she liked, we could continue another time. "What are you saying?" she exclaimed. "The best part's yet to come! We met every day that week. We exchanged life stories. Our friendship grew more and more solid, like interlacing strands of a plait. On Friday she persuaded me to leave the pension and go and live at her place. Justine was right in the center of things, in the Latin Quarter, Place de la Contrescarpe, in a building of cheap apartments, made to measure for students and with the spirit of an intellectual commune. Counting me, there were four boys and three girls. (It would be unthinkable today: living in a commune like ours and in that zone, which is so expensive.) On the Saturday they helped me to move the few bits and pieces I had in my room. The very same day I phoned my parents and told them quite an elaborate lie: The woman who ran the pension had been arrested; some days earlier the police had discovered that she recruited girls, students, as prostitutes; the pension had been closed so they could carry out their inquiries. At the other end of the phone, my father heard me out with a look of stupefaction on his face, I imagine. I could hear my mother screeching in the background, 'What's happened to her? What's happened to her?' I calmed them down, begging them not to worry about anything. If I was phoning them, it was to tell them I was fine and that I'd managed to find another boarding house, a more suitable one and even closer to the university. Your grandparents, Christophe, died years later convinced that I'd always been a saint. I don't think I was very fair to them . . . Actually, I prefer not to think about it. The fact is that, thanks to Justine, my world expanded. As for the relationships between the seven members of the commune, I'll spare you the intimate details. A son shouldn't know these things." She grinned, soliciting my support, which she knew, in these matters, would be hard to get. "But, listen, I'd say that I've never lived as intensely as I did in that period. Not that I yearn for it these days, you realize. Justine's apartment, my new home, was a meeting point more than anything else. People were constantly coming and going, friends, rebel students like ourselves, looking for 'dialectics,' as we used to say in those days. The hours flew by. The heating in the apartment only worked erratically, and we were freezing. We'd all get together, crammed into one airless room, sitting on the floor wrapped in blankets around an electric radiator that someone had cadged from his parents. We passed the hat around to buy wine and cigarettes, bread and cheese, and argued till the early morning. We weren't always going on about politics—we were more attracted by the social struggle. 'Let us have justice for once and for fucking all! Let's open the eyes of our comrade workers!' we shouted, blurry with booze. Sometimes, inflamed by our proclamations, raging against the ruling class, we formed groups and headed out at midnight to cover the swanky neighborhoods with our slogans. We used to laugh so much! People who would later become famous filed through our apartment, for example Jacques Sauvageot, leader of the students' union, or a boy called Robert Merle who wanted to be a novelist. Or another fellow named Riesel, the leader of the situationists, but I don't know what became of him. That commune was the real university for me. By May, three months after moving in, I was totally ready to play my part in the revolution. Then, Christophe, one fine day you and your father appeared. Well, first Gabriel and then you, nine months later. That's the right order unless I'm mistaken."

So, here's the big joke, Christophers: I'm a child of the revolution. I told you before that the world's badly divided up. I was born in the blissful Latin Quarter. Mom wanted a natural birth assisted by a pioneering midwife and a bunch of hippies who, when I poked my head out, were in ecstasy over the cosmic communion that my appearance afforded them. The first smell to hit my nostrils on this side of the universe was that of marijuana. They swaddled me in sequinned Indian scarves, which I soon polluted with dribble and puked-up milk. Rocking me in my cradle, my wannabe fathers and mothers sang "Les Nouveaux Partisans" or "Le Déserteur" ("*Depuis que je suis né, j'ai vu mourir mon père, j'ai vu partir mes frères . . .*"). They sound like words wanting to predict my future, eh? Maybe it's the pendulum effect, but I've always had problems with the hippie flights and fancies of my mom and company. Not that I've gone to the other extreme, but I do value law and order and see myself as a pragmatic rationalist. That's why I studied science, I guess.

Sometimes when she's been in Paris visiting a friend from those days, or when she's smoked too much dope, or simply because she's having a regressive day, Mom phones me in the evening to have a chat (she kicked me out of the house years ago, as she likes to say). First, as an opening gambit, she tells me a bit of news, but she soon starts rambling on about how she's wondering where we'd be and what we'd be like now if we hadn't gone to live in the much more working-class neighborhood of the nineteenth arrondissement around Christmas in 1970. What would I, especially, be like if we'd stayed on in the commune? She's exquisitely polite, affably resigned, and shows no sign of resentment, but I'm sure that deep down, very deep down, she's having a go at me about something as if, entirely through my own fault, I missed the chance to be a better person and am somehow responsible for the way things turned out with Dad, and so on and so forth. I hear her out patiently and, in the end, always say the same thing: "Don't ask me, Mom, I wasn't even two."

I know I bore her to death and I don't do anything to spare her.

As I said before, Christophers, I've never been able to recapture all those events filed away in my perplexed little head. If we're going to reconstruct those days of wine and roses, I'll trust the memories of the lead players and go back a little more in time. I'd like to talk about the glorious entry—ahem—into Paris of La Ibérica's Pegaso. We'll leave Mireille stranded in the Latin Quarter commune. It's early in the morning. Cigarette in her hand, gaze

lost in the distance, her mind trapped between desire for insurrection and sleep, as she's just expressed in a yawn, she's smiling
as she contemplates the possible victory. Sitting around her, the
striking students are recounting their forays of the preceding days,
the police charges, and last Monday's meeting at the Arc de Tri-
omphe with some proletarian comrades. I look it up in the history
books—because it's history now—and read that the demands of
the demonstration were that the police should vacate the university campus, an amnesty for the detained students, and that the
Nanterre and Sorbonne universities should be reopened, but the
government ignored them. Mireille and her comrades are going
over their plans for future clashes.

That was the morning of Friday, May 10, 1968, and the first ray
of sun was about to light up the tip of the Eiffel Tower.

Meanwhile, more than eight hundred kilometers away, the
Pegaso had just got through the customs point at La Jonquera and
was now trundling along French roads. The previous afternoon
Bundó, Gabriel, and Petroli had loaded up the contents of an
apartment at the top end of Carrer Balmes. After a very early night,
they'd left La Ibérica at four in the morning. The move consisted
of transporting furniture and objects belonging to a young fellow
in the tanning business, who was opening up a branch in Paris.
Since his boy had married a Frenchwoman, Daddy had coughed
up and presented him with his very own luxury shoe boutique in
Rue Saint-Honoré.

As always, Gabriel was driving when they crossed the border.
Bundó had dropped off to sleep when they were level with Figue-
res, his head resting against the door. The gently rocking truck
was his cradle but, near Lyon, as regularly happened, he'd wake
up with a headache and then complain that his two friends hadn't
roused him earlier. Petroli, sitting in the middle, checked that they
had the keys and then leafed through the papers for the move. The
seven o'clock news on Spanish National Radio had just reported
disturbances in Paris. "The City of Light is under siege, is in darkness, and has become a war zone due to an uprising by students
and workers. The authorities are attempting to restore law and

order." He found the address: Rue de l'Estrapade. He'd locate the street on the map later. They still had hours of traveling ahead of them. They did a hundred kilometers listening to the radio in silence. Gabriel used to say that all their trips required a warming-up stage. During the first few hours, the coolest and the ones that went by fastest, they didn't waste their breath. There was no point in talking for the sake of it. The three men molded themselves into the seat and kept their eyes on the road, mesmerized by the monotonous landscape. Sometimes they looked for changes in it. They'd comment on them for a second and then lapse back into silence.

"That ad over there, '*Visitez la Camargue*,' was that there before?"

"I think so."

"I never noticed it."

"So maybe it wasn't there. I don't know."

"It doesn't look very new to me."

" '*Visitez la Camargue*'..."

They'd just passed Valence when Bundó woke up with a start. They'd agreed to stop for breakfast that morning on the Lyon road, a real sit-down, knife-and-fork breakfast for Gabriel and Petroli while Bundó used the time for a chaste encounter with Muriel-Carolina.

"Where are we?" he asked immediately, rubbing his eyes in an attempt to banish sleep and focus on the landscape. The other two laughed at his startled expression.

"We've just gone through Lyon, Dijon too. Carolina sends her regards," Petroli said. Still dopey, Bundó took some seconds to react, until he saw a sign saying 'Lyon—20km'.

"You two are just jealous," he said, relieved. He opened the glove compartment, took out the communal Dopp kit, which was stuffed with stolen goods, and started sprucing himself up. The operation involved running a comb through his tangle of hair, a dash of deodorant under his arms, a squirt of expensive cologne, and, finally, changing into a brand-new poplin shirt, very fashionable at the time. Bundó enjoyed doing this because he believed

he was making his two friends jealous. In fact, he was a bundle of
nerves and, with his curls and his ingenuous face-pulling in the
hand mirror, he looked like Harpo Marx. What's more, this time,
he was smartening up with some ceremony because he had a surprise for Carolina. Some days earlier, when he'd gone to the Monte
de Piedad savings bank in Barcelona to deposit his weekly pay,
the branch manager had told him about some new public housing
apartments in Via Favència. He had a leaflet with a plan of the
apartment, photos of the neighborhood, and a balance sheet showing the sums the bank had done for him. The conditions seemed
so favorable that Bundó had made up his mind—he only needed a
bit of encouragement from Carolina—to go ahead and buy it and,
without telling her, to put it in both their names.

Carolina was waiting for them outside when they parked in
front of the Papillon. In daylight, without the neon lighting and din
of cars coming and going, the big old building looked marooned
and so fragile that it might topple over with the next puff of wind.
Standing there, weary and as still as a statue after getting rid of her
last client five hours earlier, she fitted into the scene with painful
precision. Bundó was trembling when he got out of the Pegaso.
Gabriel and Petroli said hello to Carolina and went off to the gas
station cafeteria. They reminded Bundó and Carolina that they'd
be back in fifty minutes, not one second later. As they drove off,
Gabriel spied in the rearview mirror the tremulous image of a couple locked in a passionate embrace.

If I dwell a little on these moments, Christophers, it's not
because they are of any special importance in the coming epic.
Quite the contrary. They're only circumstantial details. I'm tran-
scribing them just as my mother related them to me—and Gabriel
to her—with the full weight of their triviality. I like emphasising
this because we, brothers, are heirs to this type of contradiction:
students turning out Molotov cocktails in a Paris commune and
three truck drivers stopping off on a side road to visit a prostitute.
Life's strange.

An hour later, a blast from the Pegaso horn reverberated
through that small corner of the world. The door of the upstairs

room opened and Bundó and Carolina emerged. The farewell was briefer and more mechanical than on previous occasions. Carolina waved good-bye from the landing, a woebegone send-off. Once in the cab, Bundó was his usual taciturn self but remained silent for a long time. He was the most temperamental of the three of them. His mood could change a hundred times in a single trip. He could just as easily be exultant with unwarranted joy or huddled gloomily in his seat. His brain was then a scramble of forebodings and misunderstandings. His relationship with Carolina had aggravated this emotional bedlam, and Gabriel and Petroli knew that when he'd been with her he always went through an unapproachable phase (and surreptitiously bet on how many kilometers it would last before he spoke).

That day, Bundó broke all records for silence. His friends tried, as usual, to cajole him out of his gloom with the odd cheeky comment, by needling him and teasing him, but he didn't respond. Gabriel, who'd witnessed these attacks of withdrawal both in the House of Charity and the boarding house, realized that this was an extreme situation. It was therefore better to get to the heart of the matter, without beating about the bush.

"Are you going to make us suffer, Bundó? What's going on with you two?" he asked. The question did the job.

"It's all gone down the drain." Bundó's words fell like a death sentence. He was still holding the crumpled Monte de Piedad leaflet. "Carolina will never come to Barcelona. It's over, boys. I showed her the plans of the apartment in Via Favència. I was so excited about it but when she saw what it meant she got really mad. Instead of being happy, she said that I'm taking too much for granted. She'll leave her job when she's ready to and not when I say so. I'm no white knight . . ." He made a strange, pathetic sound. His voice threatened to break into a sob any minute. "I know I'm no prince but I'm no jerk either. And she's no princess, fucking hell! It's all over. I'd bet my life she's got some client who waits on her hand and foot, one of these uptight Frog bachelors who wants to take her home, promising the world . . ." Petroli, at his side, patted his back to urge him on. Not that there was any need.

Now he'd started to let off steam, there was no way of stopping him. They were a captive audience for more than half an hour while Bundó delivered his monologue. When the list of grievances and complaints started becoming repetitive, his speech took an abrupt turn toward self-flagellation. Bundó took on the blame for everything. He was a miserable wretch...and she, poor thing, she did the best she could...How could he have not realized? Earning your living as a *cocotte* must be terrible. Now he saw it all clearly: He had to give her more freedom. So she'd feel more secure and, most of all, want to get back together. Gabriel and Petroli had switched off some time before they heard the last few words. "That's it! Now I've got it, lads. On the way back, if it's okay by you, we'll stop at the Papillon again. Ten minutes, that's all. In and out. I'll tell her we can forget all about the apartment, we'll tear up the prospectus, no more ties, and we'll go on just the same as always." He paused to catch his breath. "But I'm sure Carolina will beg me at the last minute not to do it. I'm certain of that. She's been doing that fucking job so long her feelings have frozen, but if anyone knows how to find the heart in that deep freeze, it's me. Maybe she doesn't know it yet, but we're made for each other. And when the time comes, you'll be at the wedding, won't you? Fucking hell, what am I saying? Of course you'll be there. Gabriel and you, Petroli, you'll be my best men."

At four in the afternoon they rolled into Paris through the Porte d'Orléans. Bundó had taken the wheel to get through the city. It was a good way to shut him up. Petroli consulted the street map and directed him, using their own pared-down language, like a driver and codriver in a rally. Second right. Straight ahead to the end, then first left if you can. Traffic lights, a roundabout maybe, then right if you can. They didn't say the French names of the streets because that would have complicated things. Gabriel, meanwhile, amused himself by looking at the city. He'd been in Paris several times, thanks to the accidental tourism afforded by the moves, and there was nowhere else he so wanted to stop the truck, forget the load, and go for a walk. He compared it with Barcelona, and it seemed to him that the view through the windshield was cleaner here. Another life was possible. "If I get lost some day, look for me in Paris," he used to say, but this didn't turn out to be true later on. As they moved toward the center, the traffic in the avenues was dwindling. It was Friday but it seemed like Sunday afternoon. After listening to the news in French and deciphering the situation, they'd expected a city swarming with people. On the contrary, the Montparnasse neighborhood was sunk in the silence of a curfew. A small smattering of pedestrians here and there; the café terraces, usually chocablock, practically deserted. They drove along a wide avenue to Port-Royal and then continued along Boulevard Saint-Michel but, when the Luxembourg Gardens came into sight, a gendarme made them take a detour. They were less than three hundred meters from Rue de l'Estrapade, very close to Rue Lhomond, but getting to the address they wanted required all kinds of twists, turns, and maneuvres. Some alleys were so narrow that the truck would have got stuck in the middle. The few people who were out and about stared at them as if they'd dropped in from outer space—and perhaps they had. Finally, they found a good parking spot at a crossroads. There was space to unload in front of the building and they stopped the truck.

Outside in the street, Petroli read out some graffiti painted on the façade of the house: "*Enragez-vous*! What the hell does that mean?" As if in response, the distant buzz of a beehive thrummed down the street. A jittery concierge was waiting for them at the entrance. He received them by throwing the doors wide open. Although they'd been duly instructed, he informed them once again that the owners wouldn't be arriving until Monday and they expected to find everything unloaded and deposited in the correct rooms, according to the floor plan he was giving them. Gabriel assented, saying he calculated that they could get the unloading done in five hours at the most, and then they'd head homeward. They wanted to be back in Barcelona on Saturday evening. That was the official line. The three friends had other plans, in fact. They'd agreed that if they finished too late and too tired, they'd sleep in the apartment. Who would turn down a night in Paris? They'd crash on the mattresses (no one needed to know), and the

next day they'd go on to Clermont-Ferrand. Thanks to his taste
for emigrants' social centers, Petroli had met some people from
Extremadura who'd been living in Clermont-Ferrand for fifteen
years. Now terribly homesick, about to retire, and with their two
children employed and off their hands, the couple had decided
to return to Spain. They'd bought a little house in Sant Vicenç
dels Horts. Since they wanted to take back the treasured furniture
they'd been accumulating over the years, almost as a testimony to
their efforts, Petroli had offered to do the move at cost price (without including it in La Ibérica's books).

Although the furniture only had to be taken up to the second
floor, the three men were delighted to find that the building had
a service elevator. After a long journey, the body was grateful for a
little physical exercise, for a loosening-up of the muscles, but after
that initial impulse, an elevator was essential. The bells of Saint-
Médard church were striking five when they opened the trailer
doors. If they wanted to finish before dark, they'd better hurry.
The last stroke intensified the silence. They could only hear the
muffled *click-clack* of billiard balls in a café on the other side of
the road. There was no need to say it, but all three of them felt
that, in their indifference to the world, those billiards players were
their allies.

While Gabriel, Bundó, and Petroli uncoiled ropes and shook
out blankets, closely monitored by the concierge, a few streets
away Mireille, Justine, and their comrades had stopped on a corner and were swigging from a communal bottle of wine to soothe
their throats. It may not have been a very scientific remedy, but
you've got to look after your voice. They'd been at it for hours,
bawling and screaming revolutionary slogans—and at times it even
seemed like an amusing competition to see who could be the most
original—and they still had hours of combat ahead of them. Today
was going to be a great day. In fact, it was a great day already. In
the morning they'd helped to paint banners and hang them all
over the neighborhood and then, seeing that the police were taking
up strategic positions, they'd set about digging up cobblestones.
Someone even assured them that they'd find a beach underneath.

Now they were on the corner of Boulevard Saint-Michel and Rue Soufflot and the clamor brought them out in goose pimples. Justine climbed onto the shoulders of one of the boys and said that the demo stretched as far as the eye could see, yes, it went on forever. The tide of people swept them along. One minute they were all arm in arm, spanning the street from one side to the other, and the next they let go and were leaping all over the place for a few meters, shouting in unison, "Amnesty! Amnesty! Amnesty!" Demonstrators bellowing through megaphones repeated that the peaceful occupation of the Latin Quarter had been accomplished.

At seven that afternoon, two hours later, Mireille's group once again reached the nerve center of the revolt, Place de la Sorbonne. It was expected that the student leaders would be speaking. They were going to demand that the government release the young detainees from prison. By then, the La Ibérica trio had emptied half the trailer. All the cardboard boxes—except for one they'd randomly separated, as if absentmindedly—were up in the apartment, together with the lightest and most fragile objects. What remained now were a few cumbersome pieces of furniture, spring mattresses, wardrobes, armchairs, appliances . . . Earlier, however, they'd very carefully transported upstairs the mirror that was going to grace the dining room. And what a mirror that was! It was two meters wide, set in a frame of gilded mouldings, and it weighed a ton. They removed the blankets in which it was wrapped so they could get a better grip on it and eased it out of the truck. Once it was in the street, the mirror flashed with a series of lurching images of the overcast sky of that May evening, of closed windows, old houses, and the paved street. Then, in the distance, a commotion of cars, sirens, and heavy boots shattered the calm. Intrigued, the three workers stopped to listen. Gabriel peered into the mirror and saw movement reflected in its depths. At the end of the street, coming along Rue Tournefort, a group of policemen, now trotting, was heading for the university. The line of men was endless and so highly protected with helmets and shields that they looked like an army of samurai warriors.

"*Vite, vite, vite!*" The desperate concierge nagged them from inside the building. The three friends felt like thieves about to be caught red-handed. The mirror tilted slightly and the battleground scene vanished. As they climbed the stairs bearing the enormous weight—it didn't fit in the service elevator—they heard a series of shots muted by distance.

The first tear gas bomb fell about a hundred meters away from the position taken up by Mireille, Justine, and their group in Boulevard Saint-Michel. Held aloft by one youth, a placard bearing a portrait of Ho Chi Minh took the impact. News came from the corner of Rues Bonaparte and Saint-Sulpice that the police were charging. They weren't expecting such a direct attack. Shortly afterward, another tear gas bomb was launched from Rue des Écoles. It spiraled down, from very high up, in a smoking orbit and people started pushing and shoving to get out of its range. They said that if you were unlucky enough you could get your face burned. Some of the young people caught in the thick of the smoke tried to disperse. Most of them covered their mouths with scarves and threw stones at the police, although they were only guessing at where *les vaches* had positioned themselves. In the midst of all the uproar, Mireille was scared for the first time, really scared. She could hear the booming voices of uniformed men on the other side of the street, and her legs felt wobbly. In order to take her mind off it, she forced herself to review the group's instructions. In her cell they'd decided that, come what may, they had to stay in the street. If they were separated by the struggle, they'd regroup at ten that night in front of a bistro they all knew in Rue Danton. They were not to return to the apartment in the Place de la Contrescarpe. The police had stationed their men everywhere, some of them in civvies, and might discover them. In the last few hours they'd become more brutal in their methods of detention and weren't fooling around, the bastards.

The whistling of another tear gas bomb scattered them once more. In the ensuing tumult the two girls lost sight of their comrades. The screaming was deafening, and Mireille couldn't understand what Justine was saying. Holding hands, they ran toward Rue Cujas but were suddenly caught up in an avalanche of people running from the opposite direction and were forced to separate. Justine, with more experience of demonstrations, turned tail and let herself be swept ahead by the human tide. Mireille struggled to follow a group of boys who were still moving against the tide and, like them, took refuge in the entrance to a building. Someone closed the door behind them. They crossed an inner courtyard and moved along a filthy passageway slippery with food scraps. She almost stepped on a rat that was hiding behind a bucket (and, full of revulsion, she had time to think, "Like me!"). At the end of the fetid tunnel, a girl opened another door a chink and peered out. All clear. Once in the street, they discovered that they were at one end of Rue Touiller. She breathed deeply, but no sooner had she filled her lungs than she again heard the sinister rumble of a police charge. "They're trying to encircle us!" someone shouted. Without knowing where she drew the strength from, Mireille ran across Rue Soufflot—glimpsing out of the corner of her eye the hulking Pantheon to her left, looming up like the back of a seated giant— and entered the first alley she found. She knew this territory and felt safer in its labyrinth. She was coming across fewer and fewer fleeing students. She thought about going back to the apartment, but a sense of loyalty pulsed through her and she started heading in the opposite direction. She turned into a street where time seemed to have stopped. She was tired and slackened her pace but was soon startled by a boy coming up behind her, yelling that she had to keep running. *Les vaches* were after them and would soon be at the corner. She started to run again, helter-skelter down Rue Lhomond and, before turning the corner, looked behind her. "Never look back," her friends had warned, but she couldn't help it. At the far end of the street a gendarme was yelling at her to stop and another was waving his truncheon. She ignored them and speeded up, zigzagging into Rue d'Ulm. The steps of the policeman echoed behind her. She turned into Rue de l'Estrapade, skidding, on the point of falling, her heart in her mouth, her brain deprived of oxygen. Dazed, as if she'd entered another dimension, she saw the La Ibérica truck parked just in front of her.

Gabriel and Petroli had just unloaded a two-door wardrobe.

Half a minute earlier, two students had dodged them and vanished down the street. Mireille stopped, not knowing what to do. She was panting heavily. Her terrified eyes fixed on Gabriel's. She wanted to say something, but the words wouldn't come out. She looked back again for an instant. Then he understood, opened the wardrobe doors and, with a theatrical gesture befitting a Milière comedy, ushered her in. Mireille forced a heroine's smile and leaped into the hideaway. Petroli was closing the doors as the silhouette of a gendarme shot around the corner.

With this fantastic trick, Christophers, Mireille entered Gabriel's world.

They were about to pick up the wardrobe—there was no time to be wasted—when the gendarme stopped in front of them. Pouring with sweat, his face twitching with rage, truncheon in hand, he asked where the girl had gone. Gabriel and Petroli shrugged, pretending they didn't understand, and this riled the cop even more. He repeated his question, shouting this time, giving the wardrobe a good thump with his truncheon (and, inside, Mireille shrank into the corner that seemed furthest away). Bundó now joined the group. He didn't really know what was going on, but he detested French police, more for being French than cops. He pointed at the wardrobe and said, "Yeah, right, man, bash it, why don't you! We've got people inside there, you reckon."

The gendarme looked him over with an expression of disdain. Gabriel and Petroli were petrified. Without deigning to answer, the gendarme whacked the wardrobe a few more times, not so hard now but as if marking the beat of his ruminations. Then, with perfect timing, the concierge appeared from behind the wardrobe and in conciliatory, very persuasive French, told the gendarme that the girl had run down the street and turned left.

"She was very tired. You'll catch her easily!" he drove his point home when the gendarme was already racing off. Then he aimed a killer look at the truckers and, clapping his hands, repeated his favorite refrain: *"Vite, vite, vite!"*

Soon they were enveloped in the same thick calm as before. Once again they could hear the chatter of billiard balls coming from the café on the other side of the street and the jolly *click-clack* of a cannon shot.

*Number 126. Barcelona-Paris.*
*May 11, 1968.*

*We got the box of sundries. There's one every move. It's always the last one the owners seal up. It contains all the odds and ends scattered around the house and things overlooked until the last minute. It tends to be knickknacks, but today it's not bad. Petroli gets a box of cigars and says he'll give the gold bands to El Tembleque, who collects them; he also gets a glass display case with six tropical butterflies, a book called* A Healthy Sex Life, *and a chipped ceramic statuette of dogs attacking a hunter. Bundó's taken a mat that says "Welcome" for the entrance to his apartment in Via Favència, a collection of university field hockey pennants—he'll hang them in his room and say he's well educated—and some sunglasses like the ones José Luis Barcelona wears when he's hosting that variety show of his on TV. Gabriel gets a new teddy bear and a battery-operated cassette player. It comes with tapes of María Dolores Pradera, Pau Casals, and Xavier Cugat and his orchestra. We also broke open a Domund Missions money box in the form of a black boy's head and we'll spend the fifty pesetas inside on a bottle of French brandy.*

How many times has my mother told me about the episode of the wardrobe? She closes her eyes, I guess to relive the darkness inside it, and now she's recalling it once more for you, Christophers.

It turned out that the three La Ibérica workers didn't release her from her hiding place. Afraid that another straggling gendarme might appear, or because some sense of propriety made them want to do the job properly, they didn't open the doors and let Mireille reemerge into the light of day, but carried the occupied wardrobe up the stairs. The trip didn't last long. "Twenty-six steps exactly, at a snail's pace. I counted them later, when I left." But it was enough for my mom to fall in love with Gabriel. Direct quote. Paralyzed by fear and embarrassment inside that sort of mobile confessional, she had her laywoman's epiphany: She'd been saved by the Working Class. While students like her were demonstrating for an egalitarian world where everyone can grow up with the same opportunities, those comrades had to keep working, enslaved to some bloodsucking boss. By saving her from the gendarme, she said, they'd returned the favor. So here we have the best possible example of the alliance between culture and labor that the students were demanding!

"Don't forget that I was only twenty years old with a head full of doctrines and proclamations," Mireille emphasises. "Inside the wardrobe it was so dark that I saw the light. That's all there was to it. Ah, yes, and one more thing you need to remember, which is infinitely more decisive: Gabriel was so attractive! Your dad was a seducer like few others, Christophe. What a pity you didn't inherit that quality. A passive seducer. Ask his other women if you don't believe me . . . Without the slightest effort, only with that half-inhibited presence of his, your father had me wrapped around his little finger in no time at all."

Upstairs in the apartment, Petroli opened the doors of the wardrobe, and Bundó gave her his hand to help her out. Mireille, dumbfounded, stared at the three men with all the bafflement of the noble savage contemplating other human beings for the first time. They asked if she was okay. Bundó did an imitation of the incensed gendarme, and they all laughed. Gabriel made the introductions. This was really the icing on the cake. Besides being oppressed truck drivers, these three Herculean creatures were Spaniards who eked out a living under the boot of the Franco dictatorship. They kept working, leaving her to her musings. By the time Gabriel came upstairs again, lugging a washing machine with Bundó's help, Mireille was in love with him. He took some time to realize it.

They finished the move as the clock struck nine. The three

men had a wash and changed their clothes. It had been a very long day for them, but their reward was waiting. *"Paris la nuit,"* they shouted in mangled French. The concierge came up to check that the apartment was all in order, signed the docket, and closed the door. Mireille wanted to stay with them for precaution's sake. She felt safer, she said. They went downstairs together. When the little man wished them a good trip home, each one played out his or her part, as planned. After an emotional farewell, Mireille went off down the street. The three drivers climbed into the Pegaso and left too. When they turned into Rue Lhomond, the girl was waiting for them, beaming from ear to ear. The truck stopped, and Petroli and Gabriel got out. Bundó had keys to the apartment. Now he'd go and look for somewhere to park—Mireille recommended the area around Montparnasse cemetery—and then come back on foot. The quarrel with Muriel that morning had shaken him up, and he was in no mood for fun and games. He might stop somewhere for a beer and a sandwich—maybe not even that. Petroli had his night planned. A while ago, some emigrants had told him about a bar that wasn't too far away, Le Buci, quite near the Odéon. They'd marked the spot with a cross on the map. If it had been a Thursday or a Sunday, he would have gone to Avenue de Wagram, which was where all the Spaniards got together. The other days of the week, Le Buci was the best place in Paris for hobnobbing with one's compatriots. He'd try to dodge the demonstrations, cross Saint-Germain and find the bar. Since he was very tired, he'd have a beer and come back straight away to sleep—unless, of course, some homesick lady from Córdoba or Salamanca claimed him.

Mireille convinced Gabriel to accompany her to the bistro in Rue Danton. If they hurried they'd be there in time for the ten o'clock regrouping. She was dying to show him off to Justine and the rest of them.

"With that parting in his hair, his wide-legged trousers and leather jacket, Gabriel was the living image of a unionist dressed up in his Sunday best for the strike," Mom recalled after I begged her to tell me the story. "He agreed to come with me but wasn't very keen. He wanted to do a tourist route through the neighborhood as far as Notre-Dame, but I told him that we were the tourists now, us, the students. While we walked along at a good pace, I told him all about the insurgency that afternoon and what we were demanding. I pronounced the words slowly so he'd understand. He nodded politely, but it was clear he wasn't interested. As we approached Rue des Écoles, the shouting got louder. We walked through clouds of smoke, which made our eyes sting. I wanted to convey to Gabriel the euphoria of being right there, right then. The importance of being there with him. Then floods of people started pouring around the corner from Saint-Germain. Without a moment's hesitation, I took him by the hand and we ran with them. I was exultant. After a few meters he stopped and pulled us into another street. 'Are you too tired?' I asked, feeling a bit let down. 'Yes, but it's not that. If the police catch me, I'll have problems. My passport says I'm Spanish. They'd send me back to my country, and I'd automatically be a political prisoner.' His fear touched me, of course. 'So why don't you stay here?' I blurted out in all my naivety. 'Don't go back to Spain. My friends will find you a job . . . You could stay with us. You even babble a bit of French.' He forced a smile and spent a few seconds searching for the exact words he needed. 'Thanks, but it's not possible. I'm one of those people who can't stay long in any one place.' His answer was so surprising that alarm bells should have rung, but I'd emerged from a wardrobe that evening, like someone coming out of a time machine into another dimension, and the only thing that occurred to me was, 'Let's go back and hide at my place, then. I live nearby. I'll show you the rest of the neighborhood on the way.' "

That's about it, Christophers. Chris needed reams of pages. I'm a bit more modest. I just have to tie up a few loose ends.

Yes, Gabriel stayed with Mireille till early morning. Just the two of them in the apartment. Don't get too worked up. Whatever comparison you were thinking of making between the ruckus that night in the Latin Quarter and what happened under the sheets in the commune in the Place de la Contrescarpe, I've certainly beaten you to it. As for Gabriel, our father, he was certainly a situationist! He had an amazing talent for being in the right place at the right time.

He went back to the apartment in Rue de l'Estrapade before daybreak. Mireille had only let him leave after making him promise that he'd think about emigrating to Paris—she called it going into exile. The streets wore an air of devastation. Uprooted cobblestones, broken lampposts, a lost shoe here, a singed placard there. Sirens and shouting could still be heard in the distance, coming from the direction of the Seine. Gabriel slipped around the edge of the battlefield, a fleeting shadow, like an agent provocateur. Not far from the building, another shadow started moving toward him. They stopped and stared at each other for a few seconds.

"Gabriel!" the shadow whispered at last.

"Fucking hell, Petroli, it's you," he replied.

This time she was from Murcia. He'd succumbed to the charms of a woman from Murcia.

At nine, after four hours' sleep and breakfast in a café on Boulevard Raspail, they went to get the Pegaso. Bundó, the most awake of the three, phoned Senyor Casellas, who was spending the weekend at his beach house in Caldetes. He informed him that the gendarmes had immobilized the vehicle all night because of the demonstrations but they'd be letting them go soon. He hung up in the middle of the boss's railing and cursing, savoring the privilege of getting him out of bed on a Saturday morning, and with bad news too.

Opposite Montparnasse cemetery, before they got moving again, the three friends divided up the box that had gone astray. Two and a half months later, on another trip to Paris one Saturday at the end of July, Gabriel rushed to visit Mireille. In his second visit to the commune in the Place de la Contrescarpe, Mom asked him again if he'd go into "exile" with her in Paris. Trying to convince him, she informed him she was pregnant. Her belly was still flat, and, with the flowing dress she was wearing, you couldn't tell.

"Is it mine? *C'est à moi?*" He asked at once, as excited as if it were the first time. They were with her roommates, sitting in a circle on the floor. Gabriel had just been introduced. He was preceded by his working-class fame, and Justine and the others, thrilled to bits, couldn't take their eyes off him. They were smoking and drinking wine. It was midday. The windows were open. They were listening to music on the radio. With summer and the end of term the student revolts had fizzled out, in Paris at least.

"Yes, it's yours," Mireille told him, "but you should know it's going to be everybody's. We'll all be the mothers and fathers of this baby. You too. It's a child of the revolution."

Mireille kissed him on the mouth, clinging to him as the others applauded. When she'd finished, Gabriel remained silent. He was listening to the radio, to a song that the presenter had just introduced. He raised a finger so the others would listen too. They all looked at him.

*Puis il a plu sur cette plage.*
*Et dans cet orage elle a disparu . . .*
*Et j'ai crié, crié, Aline, pour qu'elle revienne*
*Et j'ai pleuré, pleuré, oh! j'avais trop de peine . . .*

"This song . . ." he said, "this song is very beautiful. Let's do something, Mireille. If it's a girl, we'll name her like the girl in the song . . ."

"And what if he's a boy?" she inquired giggling.

"Well, if he's a boy, like the singer!"

Everyone laughed at the joke but, when I was born, Gabriel reminded Mireille of the conversation and, of course, she listened to him.

Yes, the song was "Aline," a hit at that time, and the singer was called Christophe.

Gabriel, the perfect situationist.

## 11

# The Last Move

And then," Christophe said with a mysterious air, "Gabriel woke up in his boarding-house bed. The sheets were wet and he realized that the whole Paris adventure was a dream."

" . . ."

" . . ."

" . . ."

"No. Hey no! It's a joke! Don't look at me like that, Christophers. Everything I've said is true. Honestly."

We're in the mezzanine apartment in Carrer Nàpols, in the middle of one of our "spiritualist sessions," as Rita likes to call them, and we're going crazy. Literally. Sometimes it's as if we're possessed by Gabriel's volatile spirit, as if these walls that protected him are taking over our minds. Each meeting of the Christophers Club only makes us more obsessed. We're reeling in our father, as detectives say in films, but we never nab him. The step-by-step description we have of his movements often leaves us wanting more. Although we include in our account all kinds of people that he dealt with—and there are a lot of them—we still can't make him any more three-dimensional or bring him any closer. On the contrary, Gabriel seems to enjoy disappearing into the crowd so that no one will notice him.

"Get back, get back, get back . . . to where you once belonged!"

It's not Chris singing these Beatles lyrics as one might expect, but Christof. Cristoffini joins in for the chorus and they're both out of tune. They're tiptoeing around the apartment (well,

Christof's tiptoeing, and Cristoffini's clinging to his neck as usual), opening doors with a flourish as if they're going to find our father hiding behind them. "Get back, come on, get back, get back, for once and for fucking all, to where you once belonged." You see? Even in the songs we choose we're directionless. If we're sure about anything, after so many months of reconstructing his life, it's that Gabriel never belonged anywhere. Most people need to have a place where they can put down roots. It might be in some isolated corner of the map, or in the chaotic center of some city, surrounded by pneumatic drills and traffic noise. Other people might be nearby or far away, but we always need some corner of the world where we feel alive. There are other people, in contrast, who are incapable of staying still, and their home ends up being movement itself, constant, routine flight with no destination.

"Like some species of sharks, which have to keep swimming. They even sleep while they're swimming because, if they stop, they suffocate and die," Christophe offers by way of illustration.

That's what Gabriel's like. From the age of seventeen when he left the orphanage and went to the boarding house with Bundó, he always kept a couple of suitcases under his bed. One of them, made of cardboard, had been a gift from the nuns, a sort of passport to his future. They were his special cupboards, you might say. There was enough space in the two of them for his childhood treasures, a few school exercise books he'd taken from the House of Charity, a novel or two, photos of us, and the treasure from the moves. He aspired to fit his whole life into two suitcases. This light baggage of his combined perfectly with the La Ibérica trips, which made him feel like a nomad, and his temporary accommodation in the pension. Now you see me, now you don't. Gabriel should have been able to embody perpetual motion with minimal wear and tear but then, one February morning, he was stopped in his tracks and was unable to move again for a long time. He had almost three months of total inertia, we calculate, which must have been an eternity for him. The exact moment of his coming to a stop, so physical and so Newtonian, happened with a deafening screech, the kind that challenges the sound barrier and shudders convulsively through you. The disaster meant that this was the last move. We'll try to stick with our story, which means we must now describe what happened without faintheartedness or faltering. It won't be easy.

~

*Number 199. Barcelona-Hamburg.*
*February 14, 1972.*

*A deep, narrow, rectangular cardboard box with the words "Very Fragile" written on top. Thanks for the clue. Since Petroli's stayed behind to live in Germany, everything suggests that this time it will be divided up between Bundó and Gabriel. Once opened, it turns out to be the typical box of large, flat objects that don't fit anywhere else. Bundó's keeping a gold-framed mirror for the entrance to his apartment, and two paintings of woods in the autumn, which are signed S.B. Since, coincidentally, they're his own initials, Bundó's sure to say he painted them himself. The mirror's wrapped in two towels, embroidered with the same letters. So the pictures have been painted by the gentleman of the house. They're nice but you can see they were done by an amateur. Gabriel will keep an atlas of the world, a wooden tray with etchings representing tropical fruits, and two Slazenger tennis rackets. There's also an envelope with a couple of dusty X-rays of a broken wrist: The tennis-playing artist must have slipped during a game and would have spent some time not being able to paint. Even though no one wants them, Bundó says the X-rays can't be thrown away because that will bring bad luck.*

What you've just read is the report from the last trip that Gabriel, Bundó, and Petroli set out on together. The Pegaso's last parade. As always, our father detailed the division of the spoils, little knowing there would be no more. Perhaps he was a little self-conscious as he wrote because Move 200 was coming up and everyone knows that round numbers demand respect, yet it would be absurd to scan his words for any sign of foreboding of what was about to happen, with the ink barely dry, a few hours later on the motorway. Then again, after coming at it from every angle, we Christophers are tempted to believe that, for quite some time, the three friends had unconsciously and reluctantly been heading for a point of no return. The future sucks us in with its uncertainty, but we call it destiny to simplify matters. When some calamity happens, we all do the same thing, don't we? We start looking for clues in the recent past in order to understand it, or even to justify it, as if we could somehow prevent the error or accident and go back to the natural order of cause and effect.

Sometimes, when we're together in the mezzanine apartment on Carrer Nàpols, we Christophers try to turn all these signs into certainties and branch out into all kinds of hypotheses. This, for example: It's highly probable that if the La Ibérica trips had continued that year, 1972, Gabriel would have moved heaven and earth to add another Christopher to the list. A little brother. This theory is supported by a certain biographical pattern: Christof was born in October 1965, while Christopher arrived in July 1967, and Christophe came along in February 1969. The rhythm tells us that every twenty months, more or less, our father was seduced by a girl and, after the nine mandatory months, these sporadic encounters brought forth another baby. We're sure, then, that sooner or later another European woman—Italian, Dutch, Swiss?—would have surrendered to his charms.

When we visited Petroli in Germany and told him about our theory, he thought it over for a few seconds and then, wrinkling his nose, countered it by saying that Gabriel had never planned to have children. These things happen, and that's that.

"Don't forget that your dad was a passive Don Juan," he told us. "Bundó always paid to feel like a Don Juan. I was the libertine Don Juan Tenorio when I was chatting up and sweet-talking my melancholic little Spanish ladies (and here he quoted, 'Down to the hovels I descended...up to the palaces I rose'). Your dad, however, obeyed the principle of least effort. In amorous matters, he simply couldn't say no. Ah, and he had an incredible ability to hit the bull's-eye, as your presence in the world confirms. In having kids—can't you see?—he was the very opposite of a Don Juan."

Okay, maybe he wasn't after a pan-European paternity, but we Christophers are certain that, wanting to or not, the passive Don Juan would have let himself get caught again that winter.

So, that's the situation before the disaster.

At the beginning of October 1971, after a delay of ten months and thirty panic attacks, Bundó was at last handed the keys to the apartment in Via Favència. On his first free Saturday he spent his small nest egg on some furniture, the most essential things. These items were delivered after ten days—by two moving men who, in the eyes of the international trucker were mere novices—and on the Sunday he and Gabriel took the DKV and moved in all the goods they'd lifted during the La Ibérica trips. Once the job was done, Bundó looked at the boxes scattered around the floor, the furniture still to be arranged, the bare bulbs, the curtainless windows, and, all of a sudden, these unprepossessing surroundings looked so familiar and cosy—he'd imagined them a thousand times before—that he decided to spend the night there.

"No sheets, just a blanket, I'll sleep on the new mattress, with the first ray of sun as my alarm . . ." he fantasized. "Like that time in Paris, remember? The welcome mat I got that day is packed in one of those boxes. It'll be the first thing I put in place because you'll always be welcome in my home."

Bundó's impulses. Gabriel went along with it for a while but saw he was so excited about his apartment that it seemed a better idea to leave him to it. He gave him the keys to the van so he could return it to La Ibérica the next day and said he was going back to the boarding house.

"It's eight o'clock," he said, looking at his watch. "If I don't get a move on I'll be late for dinner. You know how that puts La Rifà in a bad mood."

For all his composure, there was no way he could disguise the lame excuse. The situation wasn't easy for him either. Gabriel knew it was the natural order of things and told himself that things were fine, but now—amazingly—for the first time in thirty years, since they were toddlers in nappies, the two friends were no longer living under the same roof. For some time now, they'd been getting used to the peculiarities of the world, each in his own way, and life had embroiled them and swept them along unplanned paths. Of course it's no big deal because it happens to everyone and sometimes, late at night, they must have even joked about it, laughing so as not to cry: "Look at the fucking saints we turned out to be! One with three wives and three sons scattered around the world and the other courting a whore. Sorry, a *cocotte* . . . yes, *cocotte*: That sounds better." Given their background, it seemed inconceivable that Bundó and Gabriel would finally have to learn to live independently. It was as if Siamese twins, once separated, weren't twins any more, or even siblings.

When Gabriel left, Bundó went out onto the little dining room balcony and leaned over to look at the street. It was a seventh-floor apartment, and he immediately felt slightly dizzy. He gripped the rail. It was dark and, down below, the black, recently laid asphalt melted into the shadows of the night. The new street lights cast a patchy yellowish glow on the footpaths, which were still only half constructed. Tomorrow morning he'd be woken up by a cement mixer. A minute went by, and he heard the outside door closing, after which the figure of Gabriel moved off down the street toward the bus stop. He was walking with resolute steps. Bundó whistled a tune that had been their code since they were kids, another good-bye, but Gabriel can't have heard him because he didn't turn around. Trying not to think, Bundó looked for the van, spotted it, toy-sized in the street, and spat to see if he could hit it. The darkness engulfed his projectile at first-floor level. In the distance, toward the horizon, Barcelona's constellation of lights hypnotized him for a while. Carolina would be amazed when she saw it. It was cold. He went back into the dining room only to be ambushed by the stark realization of the change that he—and he alone—had brought about in his life. He'd been waiting for and fearing this moment for years and wasn't sure that he liked it. A strange uneasiness gripped his stomach, spread out everywhere and paralyzed him. His body immediately felt heavier, and the air around him thickened, pressing on him as if the house needed to make a mold of him in order to recognize him. Though it wasn't a painful sensation, he would have given half his life to have Carolina with him. He would have hugged her tight, and, together, they would have shattered the quiet.

Now we've come to a thorny question: Ever since Bundó had embarked on the process of buying the apartment two years earlier, Carolina had been stonewalling about coming to live in Barcelona. Every time he visited her at the Papillon they inevitably talked about the apartment. She said she was dying for them to be together, to wake up at his side every morning and to get those stinking Frenchman out of her sight for ever—at which point Bundó begged her, for the love of God, not to go into details. Yet she seemed in no hurry to bring an end to that stage of her life. When Bundó tried to persuade her to be impetuous, to seize the day, to climb into the Pegaso and ride off into the sunset together, she said it wasn't enough just to close the door and walk away from the neon red of the big old building. She wasn't sure exactly what she wanted, but things were never that easy.

It's worth recalling that Carolina turned twenty-five in the autumn of 1971, by which time she'd spent six years doing roadside service. She'd learned to live with Muriel, her own personal Doctor Hyde, and loved her as if they were one person. Thanks to her alter ego, too, she'd acquired a cynical outlook on the world. Sitting at the bar in the wee hours, with cheap champagne in her glass and a croaky voice, Muriel used to say, "There are no good guys or bad guys here. We're all wallowing like pigs in shit. And we like it. Not because it's squalid but because it's ours. There's no choice: Either you freely admit it or you might as well go and hang yourself from the highest beam." Recently, her status at the brothel had gained in prestige. With the arrival of new, untried girls, she worked fewer hours than before, which gave some solace to Bundó. Against the advice of the madame, she and a couple of coworkers had rented an apartment in Saint-Etienne and only went to the Papillon for the hours they were obliged to work. When there was a slack period, Muriel took aside the junior girls—among them two from

Spain, ingenuous, illiterate, and delightful—and instructed them in the art of faking it.

Nonetheless, this situation wasn't making her any happier. On the contrary. When the splendid, reserved Carolina, now well into her fifties, met Christophe in Paris, she talked about those decisive months without hesitation.

"Of course, it's very easy to say now," Carolina told him, "but I wish I'd gone with Bundó to Barcelona when he first moved into the apartment. My problem was dithering. It happened to all of us in the Papillon. You can't begin to imagine what it was like: The brothel routine was crippling. It robbed you of your life. You're young, you try not to think about it and, to justify it, you send money to your parents every month. In my case, I sometimes had flashes of lucidity, often just after a visit from Bundó, and then I realized that the millstone around my neck was Muriel. I couldn't take her to Barcelona or anywhere else, but I couldn't leave her there, all alone and waiting for reincarnation in the other girls. These doubts consumed me, month after month, like when you don't dare go to the doctor's because you're afraid of what the tests will say, and so on and so forth, until it's too late. Then, not long after the disaster (and because of it), when my life no longer had any value—this is no exaggeration—one clear-eyed morning I got out of bed, knowing exactly what I had to do." Carolina went quiet for a few seconds as if reconsidering what she was about to confess, but then continued in a more confidential tone. "I've never told anyone about this, Christophe, and I don't want it to go any further than you and if necessary your brothers. It was the end of that dreadful February, a weekday, midmorning, a time when I knew for sure that the Papillon would be closed and empty. I got up, after a sleepless night, my head teeming with thoughts, got dressed in my Muriel clothes, and phoned for a taxi. I put my Carolina clothes in a travel bag together with a few things I wanted to keep, especially gifts from Bundó. I wrote a note to my roommates telling them that a special job had come up in the Papillon (as sometimes happened) and that we'd see each other there that night. I got the taxi driver to take me to the gas station half a kilometer from the brothel, and then asked him to leave. I filled an empty container I'd brought from the flat with three liters of gasoline. The guys at the station knew me so I told them it was for a client's car: He'd paid me to go there and bring him back the gasoline. "Who knows what the bastard wants to do with it! There are all kinds of brutes running loose in the world . . . !" I told them. Walking along the side of the road, as I'd done with Bundó the night I fell in love with him, I reached the Papillon. There were no cars going by, everything was in silence and the building seemed to be sleeping. There was a window at the back that opened into the storeroom and a space where the garbage from the bar was kept. The madame always left that window slightly open to let in a bit of fresh air to combat the permanent stink (tobacco, room freshener, disinfectant, sweat). It was closed again at midday by a woman who went there to clean, wash sheets, and take out the rubbish. It was child's play to open the roller blind using an old broomstick I found lying on the ground. I got inside and went up to the second floor where the bedrooms were. I splashed the petrol where it would burn best: curtains, sheets, rugs. I plugged in one of the electric radiators so that it would look like an accident if anyone investigated. I used the remaining gasoline to pour a stream running downstairs to the bar, which was riddled with woodworm. Then I set fire to the house. The whole place went up. Destruction on a biblical scale. I only just had time to strip down and throw Muriel's clothes and things into the flames. The heat was searing but it felt good on my skin. Still stark naked, I escaped through the window and, once outside, got dressed as Carolina. Then I left, making my way through the fields, crouching and not looking back until I got to the next village, where I took a bus to Paris. Just as we were leaving, we were overtaken by two fire engines and an ambulance. The column of smoke was visible in the distance. That afternoon, when the fire had razed the building to the ground and everything inside it was burnt to a cinder, the police certified that there were no victims and the firemen attributed it to a short circuit. The premises had been crying out for renovation for ages. Since the madame was nobody's fool, she decided it would be best to forget

about me, grab the insurance money, and not get embroiled in fil-
ing complaints or investigations, which wouldn't have been good
for her at all. So everyone was happy. Farewell forever, Muriel.


Four months before Muriel's immolation, Bundó, putting himself
to the test of spending the first night in his new home, would have
been grateful for the warm embers of the Papillon. The apartment
in Via Favència had no heating, and he was freezing cold. Then
again, for his own psychological convenience, he covered up for
Carolina's absence by telling himself that the unexpected dread he
felt in the place wasn't because of loneliness but the glacial reception offered by the rooms. How ungrateful can you get! Couldn't
they see that he and Carolina would soon be filling them with
life? They might have been more considerate. Bogged down in his
excuses, Bundó went searching in one of the boxes and pulled out
a wall thermometer made to look like the Pole Star, lifted from
god-knows-who and god-knows-where. He left it on the ground
next to the window and watched how the strip of mercury plunged
to the bottom. Ten degrees! And the damp! At this rate he'd get
pneumonia. He'd have to buy a heater. The glass in the windows
was as flimsy as cigarette paper. He put on his anorak and stamped
his feet to warm them up. Then he went into what was going to
be the main bedroom and made himself a bed with a mattress on
the floor and makeshift bedclothes consisting of all the blankets
he possessed plus two bath towels. If he was still cold after all that
he'd sleep with his clothes on. When he'd finished he looked at
his watch and was surprised to see it was only half past nine. Time
didn't move in that igloo. He decided that the best fuel for his
body would be a glass of cognac, or two, and went out in search of
a bar. He recalled having seen one as he was driving by in the van,
further up the street on the corner of Carrer d'Almansa. When he
got there, the owner was wiping down the bar. There was nobody
else. He tapped at the glass door, making drinking gestures. The
stone-faced owner nodded, yes, he could come in.

An hour later, with the fourth Veterano in his glass—the last, too, because it really was closing time now—Bundó saw that there was a phone in one corner of the bar. He asked for a line and called Carolina. International phone calls cost the earth but he didn't care because he knew she wasn't going to pick up the phone. She'd be at the Papillon at this hour. He heard the beep on the line, the absence, but since the sound came from France, it made him feel closer to her. Then, without knowing why, he did something that wasn't remotely a good idea: He dialed the number of the boarding house. With the fourth ring Senyora Rifà picked up the receiver.

"Can I speak to Gabriel Delacruz, please?" Bundó said.

"Who's calling?"

"A friend . . . well, it's me, Bundó."

"Good heavens, Bundó! Have you got lost or something?" the landlady asked. "I'll put him on."

A few seconds went by. Through the earpiece he could hear some kind of racket in the background, an unusual hullabaloo for that hour of night in the boarding house. Then he remembered that the German mechanic, a lad who was setting up looms at the Can Fabra factory and was temporarily staying there, had told them he and his wife were about to have a baby, their first. He'd been on edge for some days but had promised them that when there was news they'd drink a toast to the new mother and his son or daughter. Bundó hung up before Gabriel got to the phone. He then managed to persuade the bar owner to serve him another cognac, come on, just one last one and then I'll go. He'd need it to deal with the cold. The night in the igloo was going to be a long one.

The next day Bundó turned up at La Ibérica, full of cold, with rings under his eyes and looking tired. Gabriel asked him about the call the night before, whether he'd hung up, or the line had been cut, or if it was a joke, but his friend didn't remember anything. A thick fog had fallen on the way back from the bar to the apartment. In the night, a burning in his stomach had countered the forlorn chill of the place.

The moves listed for that day had them running around Barcelona in the DKV. Petroli was off work with sciatica, which he'd had for weeks without getting much better. His replacement was

El Tembleque. The two friends were laughing at his drollness all day long, reliving their early days at La Ibérica when he'd entertained them and taught them everything they knew. About to retire and jauntier than ever, El Tembleque had a flirtatious remark for every woman he found along the way, be they old, young, or shop-window mannequin; he blasted the horn, whistled, shouted through the window, as cheeky as any Neapolitan skirt-chaser; he greeted traffic cops as if he'd known them all his life and they owed him money. When it came to unloading, they saw that time hadn't refined his art of bullshitting: eight years on and the same old excuses. If perchance he bent over to pick up some packet, his bad leg wobbled with its usual vigor but, now, the good one, somewhat the worse for wear, had contracted the malady. Every bit of him seemed to be doing the twist, all over the place, come on everybody, as if he had springs instead of limbs. The move was long and tedious because they had to go from one office to another   a successful lawyer was moving his office from Plaça Urquinaona to Plaça Calvo Sotelo—but, when it was over and they were back in the DKV, El Tembleque reminded them that he'd been their mentor in larceny. With a knowing wink and roguish grin he pulled, from inside his jacket, a box full of brand-new Bic pens that he'd snaffled and gave them three each.

"To write love letters to your girlfriends, lads. It's about time you got yourselves a missus."

Thanks to El Tembleque's irresistible center-stage presence, Bundó managed to keep a low profile that day and didn't talk much. Gabriel noted that he was a bit low and, when it came to saying good-bye, made a point of asking him what bus he had to catch to get from Poblenou to Via Favència.

"I'll come to the pension today," Bundó replied. "I'm paid up for the rest of the week, and it's a pity to waste that. Anyway, the apartment is too cold. I'm going to buy a heater on Saturday."

The words were balm to them both. After dinner, they went out for half an hour to have a coffee in Café Principal. They were done in, as they were every night, but going back to their old routine was a relief. Standing at the bar, they whiled away the time shooting the breeze: You know, El Tembleque was getting old, *Dicen* was sure that Barca was going to do . . . whatever it was going to do, and before you know it, it'd be time to get Christmas lottery tickets. Then, out of the blue, Bundó blurted that Gabriel should come and live with him in the apartment in Via Favència.

"Just a few months, eh? Only till Carolina comes. I'm thinking about you. You can save on rent and have a change of air."

Our father let him finish and answered at once, without the least hesitation. No; he wouldn't. He was absolutely sure. He was fine at Rifà's.

"I had to try," Bundó admitted and went on to change the subject as if he hadn't said a word. His thoughts must have kept marching on, though, because when they were walking back to the boarding house shortly afterward, and now not even trying to conceal his need, he promised our dad that at least they'd spend Christmas day together and eat at his place. A party for three: the two of them plus Carolina. He'd buy a Christmas tree and decorate it and—no need to be embarrassed about it—they could sing the songs the nuns had taught them. They'd give each other presents too.

"Heaven help you if you didn't invite me!" Gabriel answered.


When we want to picture our father at the end of that October of 1971, the most compelling image we have is that of a plate spinner in a circus. His chief skill is balance. He's holding a flexible rod in the palm of each hand, with one resting on his forehead and another on his chin. He keeps the rods upright with the plates whirling around and around the tips. They're slowing down. Slower . . . slower. His movements are so minimal that the audience is getting nervous. At the very last moment when everyone's sure they're going to crash, he gets them spinning fast again, one after another, and things liven up once more.

Gabriel had learned to pace his relationships with his three equidistant women and three sons and, like a good plate spinner, he seemed to keep his cool. Of course, the rules of the game were in his favor: He had his base camp in Barcelona, where he led a bachelor's existence and, thanks to the moving work, went to visit his families from time to time. He'd turn up about every three months—if we were lucky, more often. If one month it happened that he appeared twice, it suddenly seemed as if he was really living with us and the world was marvellous. It was hard to bear the waiting between visits, but our mothers learned not to carry on about it. They were young, brave, modern, emancipated. And they had us, the Christophers. In any case, we'd be naive if we thought that this family geography was ideal for our father and that he didn't suffer because of it. Rather, it was an unavoidable situation, although that doesn't free him from blame either. We, little kids of six, four, and two, cried when we saw him leaving and writhed with longing for him for hours on end—and he knew it. These were the arguments our mothers wielded over and over again to convince him not to get back in the damn Pegaso and to stay and live with us.

It wouldn't be unreasonable to imagine that since Gabriel was so neglected when he was small, this insistence only encouraged him never to change. It made him feel loved. Yet, how would the women have reacted if they'd discovered that Gabriel was a spinner of the same illusions with other women and other sons? Sigrun, Sarah, Mireille, and Rita (who appeared later, but she counts as well) prefer not to go into that. They finally learned the truth after its being buried under shovelfuls of calculation, suspicions, resignation, and then indifference for so many years that it seems far-fetched, like those articles that are calculated to inspire incredulous awe in newspaper readers. COOK MISTAKENLY SERVES GRANDFATHER'S ASHES AS CONDIMENT FOR SOUP, UNQUALIFIED LAWYER WINS TWO HUNDRED CONSECUTIVE CASES, MOVER HIDES FOR DECADES HIS RELATIONS WITH FOUR WOMEN AND FOUR SONS.

The reality, needless to say, far exceeded the limits of any sensationalist newspaper headline. It was much more complicated. Our father worked hard to keep the lie at bay. He spent a fortune phoning us on a fixed day every week, always in the evening when he got back from work. Thanks to his distinctive cocktail of ill-learned languages, his conversation always sounded like jumbled fragments from two very different international congresses. His only perfectly comprehensible sentences were those detailing places, days, and dates. "I arrive Londres, Saturday twelve in the morning, and go the Monday very early." "*Nous serons à Paris le divendredi quinze.*" Well, there were the intimacies of farewells too. Our mothers don't want to talk about them but admit they sounded sincere and loving.

Gabriel was meticulous in assigning a different day to each family.

"For us it was Tuesday," Christof said. "I remember that because we used to have dinner earlier. After I turned three, more or less, Mom taught me how to answer the phone and told me to say my name, 'Christof.' I used to hear Dad's voice, his laughter, and I became tongue-tied with embarrassment."

"Well, he phoned us on Thursdays," Chris said.

"Wednesday, always Wednesday."

We don't know whether our father jotted things down or whether he had a prodigious memory because nobody recalls him ever slipping up. Sigrun never heard herself being called Mireille, for example, and Rita was never turned into Sarah. Paris was never London and Christof was never Christophe, even though it was only a matter of a couple of letters and the intonation. From what our mothers tell us, his subconscious was equally orderly: He always knew where he was sleeping, and not even in his dreams in the different double beds did he ever betray himself by pronouncing the name of any of the women whose turn it wasn't.

However, Gabriel's cover was about to be blown, precisely because of the Christmas feast at Bundó's apartment. It was the first sign that the spinning plates could come crashing to the ground, and if one broke they all broke. In the years of his concubinage with Sigrun, Sarah, and Mireille, he'd managed to keep his Barcelona life a secret. You could say that, with a little help from Bundó and Petroli, he'd never expressly hidden anything from them but he had opted for evasion in some matters. He touched their hearts when he recalled his childhood in the orphanage. He spared no details when he talked about the job at La Ibérica: how he'd started to work there, how the owner ill-treated them, and how they took revenge by lifting stuff from the cargo they moved. They all knew that he and Bundó lived in a boarding house in the center of the city. He'd told them the telephone number but on the condition that they only phoned in case of emergency. He'd given them a fairly accurate portrait of Senyora Rifà, embellishing it only with a few years and a few kilos, and had made them laugh with his stories of stuffed animals. According to him, the other boarders were fossils too. Thanks to such trivia, Gabriel had been able to mask his life behind veils of generalization. As the backdrop to his words, Barcelona emerged as a sordid, boring, and inhospitable city. The streets were ill lit, the poor lived in hovels, the sea was faraway and dirty, and muggers robbed the few tourists that ventured there. "Spain is different!" he told them, echoing the regime's propaganda with a craftiness they were unable to detect. On the far side of La Jonquera, Gabriel turned into a more active opponent of the Franco regime, fulminating against the dictator with not very natural but highly convincing fervor.

Gradually, then, little by little, our mothers got the idea that Barcelona was a version of hell in which they never wanted to set foot. Through this prism, Gabriel's life at the boarding house could only be considered as a temporary arrangement, a waiting room en route to the future. The problem was that the future, and specifically the French future, got tired of waiting. One December morning, Mireille decided to get a bus ticket for Barcelona. This was a special service put on for Spanish workers who wanted to spend Christmas with their families, and the buses left mid-afternoon on Tuesday, the twenty-first. Mireille chose to leave Christophe with Justine, who had now hitched up with one of the old comrades from the commune. They'd both rocked his cradle when he was a baby and were well able to look after him.

"I was two years and nine months old. They had me dancing to Pink Floyd, and at night, after all the psychedelia, when I was totally hyped up, they gave me poppy tea with milk to make me sleep," the hero of the story wishes to note.

After hours and hours on the road, which gave her a better understanding of Gabriel's hard life as a moving man, Mireille arrived at the stop in Plaça de la Universitat at one o'clock on Wednesday afternoon. Since this was a difficult time of year, what with all the family reunions, the only return ticket she could get was for Saturday night. Three and a half days seemed pathetic but it would have been worse not to have seen Gabriel at all, and she hoped that her surprise visit would be his best Christmas present. She also hoped—in secret—that, finally, with this headstrong impulse brought on by some sort of faith in love, she'd be able to convince her man that they were made for one another and that his home was in Paris.

When she first set foot in the streets of Barcelona, the sunlight made her quiver with a strange feeling of optimism. It was ages since they'd seen such a sun in Paris. It had rained during the night, and, although the temperature was low, the light dappled the damp cobblestones and flashed gold from the buildings. She got into one of the taxis at the stand in the square and gave an address to the driver: Almogávares, 135. She knew the unpronounceable name by heart, after reading the Spanish version so many times on the Pegaso trailer. Seeing that she was a foreigner, the taxi driver treated her to a scenic tour of the city: He went along Gran Via, turning into Via Laietana, going down to the post office, after which he turned left toward Ciutadella Park. Along the way, Mireille absorbed every detail of the people passing by. Her gaze lingered on the sooty façades of the houses, the steamed-up windows of shops and bars, the streetlights crowned by a glittering long-tailed golden star, which was sure to be lit up at night. At the intersection with Avinguda de la Catedral, a policeman, decked out in festive regalia, was directing the traffic seated on a throne. Mireille marveled at all the gifts people were carrying in the street. The taxi driver saw her pleasure and smiled with something akin to pride in his city. He was tuned into a strange radio program, which seemed magical to Mireille: Children were ceaselessly singing a series of numbers—Christmas lottery results, as she later discovered—with the incantatory drone of prayer. As they passed Ciutadella Park she was enchanted by the pattern formed by the railings and the bare wintry trees behind them. A few streets farther on, where Poblenou morphed into a compact string of factories and warehouses, they overtook a mule-drawn cart laden with cabbages, lettuces, and sacks of potatoes. They stopped in front of La Ibérica at half past one. Despite the generous tip she gave the taxi driver, Mireille found the ride incredibly cheap.

Senyor Casellas was in the middle of delivering a few edifying words to the workers in the garage. Just as he did every year, he had assembled the whole staff on December 22nd and was officiating at the Christmas bonus ceremony. While he'd stayed in his office listening to the Christmas lottery results on the radio, the drivers had spent the morning cleaning the premises, washing the vans and trucks and decorating their hoods with holly and a few shiny ribbons. Then they arranged them in a semicircle, as in a trade fair, and set up a nativity scene in the middle with some enormous figures (Saint Joseph, the Virgin Mary, and Baby Jesus). Once the stage was set, Senyor Casellas summoned his workers with a blast of a horn and stood next to the nativity scene alongside his well-qualified secretary, Rebeca, and a priest sent by his sister from the orphanage. The show went as follows. In the affected Spanish they speak in the posh neighborhood of Bonanova, Senyor Casellas first gave them a sermon on the virtues of daily toil and the spirit of self-improvement, after which he reminded them that Christmas was a time of contemplation, family values, and thinking about Our Lord God. The priest nodded solemnly and then took the floor to lead the Hail Mary, which they all prayed aloud. Then he refreshed their memories, telling them yet again that these were Holy Days of Obligation. They were expected to go to Mass. Finally, with Rebeca's help, Senyor Casellas called out the workers one by one, wished them a Merry Christmas and handed over the envelopes with the Christmas bonus together with a Christmas box. Each one was treated to the usual paternalistic platitudes.

"How's that leg of yours, Tembleque? Still bothering you? It wouldn't be varicose veins, by any chance? Because we're at that age now . . ."

"This is for you, Petroli. Tuck it away good and safe. You never know what life's going to bring."

"Bundó, Bundó . . . let's see if he remembers the sisters at the Mundet home and gives them a little present. What could a paragon of modesty like yourself do with all this money?"

"Delacruz. Ah, Delacruz, here you are. If a banknote's gone missing, it must have got lost in some move or other . . . I'd count them if I were you."

Mireille, as yet unseen, witnessed the pantomime from the entrance to the garage, taking stock of the revulsion she felt for this man who, with those porky cheeks, could only be the fascist Casellas. Finally, priest and boss started to sing the carol "The Little Drummer Boy," which concluded the show every year, and the workers diffidently sang along. As the last "rum, pum, pum, pum" was fading, Mireille took a few steps, moving into the half-lit premises. Gabriel was the first to see her, silhouetted against the daylight with her bag on the ground, and recognized her immediately. He left the group and went over to her without making any attempt to hide his astonishment, but without getting flustered either. For years he'd been working out in his mind how he'd manage such an eventuality if it should ever arise. He hugged her and gave her a kiss. Behind him he could hear the shouts and whistling of his colleagues, with Bundó's voice in the middle of it all shouting, *"Oh, là là!"*

"Goodness gracious, Delacruz, you've certainly held your tongue about this," said Senyor Casellas as he came across. Holding out a limp hand with podgy fingers, he asked Mireille, "To what do we owe such an honor?"

Gabriel introduced them. The boss puffed up like a peacock in front of the girl but frowned as soon as he heard her name and realized that she was French. It was a curt, instinctive gesture as if in one tenth of a second he'd divined the source of all La Ibérica's problems on the other side of the Spanish border. Lost packages, delays, excuses, clients' complaints. Mireille's attitude, remote, with nothing servile about it, didn't help. A malign angel of silence flew overhead, its spell only broken by the pop of a champagne cork. Infused once again with Christmas spirit, Senyor Casellas scurried off to get a glass so he could propose the toast and invited Mireille to celebrate Christmas with them, with the great La Ibérica family. He made a mental note that, once the holidays were over, he'd interrogate Bundó—the most biddable of the three friends—about Delacruz's little French girlfriend.

When he left them alone, Mireille turned to Gabriel and, whispering in his ear with a tickly voice, asked, "Your boss doesn't know that Christophe exists, does he?"

"Are you mad?" Gabriel replied. "If he discovered that you and I have a kid out of wedlock, he'd get that fucking priest to excommunicate me on the spot. I wouldn't put it past him to sack me."

"Well, maybe I should have turned up with our boy and put on a show," Mireille said naughtily.

"Or maybe the solution would be for us to get married one of these days," he pronounced.

It was a risky response, a flight into the future, and Mireille burst out laughing. Ha! Get married! Never in her worst nightmares would she succumb to the temptation of this macho, bourgeois, outdated institution called marriage. One day they could live together, in Paris, Barcelona, or wherever, without having to give any explanations to anyone. If they were both committed that was enough. Didn't he agree? She lit one of her Gauloises in order to do something with her hands. Gabriel blurted out "yes" with no wish to stir things up. That was the end of the matter.

Today, Mireille sighs and remembers that moment. She feels flattered by the proposal, as if Gabriel had taken her unawares by entering through her emotional back door. Some time later, now back in Paris, alone with Christophe once more, a new thought started to niggle. "I wouldn't know how to describe it. It was that sense you have when you suspect that someone's pulling the wool over your eyes but there's no way you can prove it."

Apart from this initial folly, Mireille's stay in Barcelona went by serenely. Gabriel took her to the pension that afternoon and introduced her to Senyora Rifà. At first the landlady behaved with a severity and restraint that were bordering on offensive—or maybe she was jealous?—but she gradually softened up. She spoke quite good French as she'd studied and spoken it with the Claretian Sisters in Vic, and Mireille had the presence of mind to praise her after a couple of sentences. Senyora Rifà lowered her guard and soon took a shine to her. They conversed, leaping from one topic to another, from Edith Piaf to Grace of Monaco, from the

Eiffel Tower to recipes for hare *à la róyale*. Senyora Rifà gave her
a guided tour of the pension, telling her, now embellished with a
certain note of derision, the story of the gentleman from Logroño
and the stuffed animals. Mireille giggled, complicitly. Only French
women know how to laugh at the love woes of others without looking bad. She took a great fancy to the lustrous-plumed humming-
bird, now in its sixteenth year of captivity behind the glass of the
dining-room cabinet, and the landlady told her it was her favorite
piece too. At one point when Mireille excused herself to go to the
bathroom, Senyora Rifà lowered her voice and congratulated Gabriel. She liked the girl. She could see she had character. "A girl
you can bring home," she might have said if she'd been his mother.
Taking everything into account and in recognition of all the years
Gabriel had spent under her roof, the landlady made an exception
and let her stay. She would be the first woman in two decades who,
apart from Natàlia Rifà herself, had spent the night there.

Toward evening, when it was getting dark, Gabriel took Mireille
out to show her the neighborhood. They went first to the House
of Charity and walked around its high walls of blackened ashlars.
Most of the streetlamps were either not working or broken, and the
building loomed up with the horror of a medieval prison. It has triggered childhood nightmares in Gabriel more than once. (Mireille
embraced him.) Then, strolling along Carrer Elisabets, they reached
the Ramblas. A few strands of little colored lights had been strung
up across the street and, seen from the top end at Rambla de Ca-
naletes, they sparkled in the distance, conjuring up an image of an
endless marquee crammed full of people. They decided to walk
down to the bottom. Hundreds of people laden with bags and packages were heading for the top and they felt as if they were swimming
against the tide. A little lower down, now level with the Liceu opera
house, there was a sudden change of direction and, like them, everyone was now heading downward toward the statue of Columbus.
In some sections they were accompanied by the stirring strains of
a brass band. As they walked along, Mireille absorbed every single
detail of their descent: the painted panels illustrating the westerns
and cops-and-robbers films they were showing in the cinema nick-

named Can Pistoles; the shouts of the shoeshine boys—*¡limpia!*—
and the startling sight of the local drunk known as the "Sheriff of the
Rambla" who, by that hour, was well and truly sozzled; the newspaper kiosks; birds cheeping in their cages; the flower sellers . . . They
stopped at Café Moka for a beer in memory of the revolutionar-
ies—Mireille had read Orwell not long before. They strolled along
hand in hand and, for the first time in his life, Gabriel felt an inner
calm. The company of his French girlfriend suddenly made him feel
that his milieu wasn't totally alien to him. He was enjoying showing
it to her, as something that was his. Near the end of the Rambla
they turned into Carrer Escudellers and went to have dinner at Los
Caracoles. Mireille was full of admiration for the display of spit-
roasting chickens at the entrance and went over as if to warm her
hands. A charming waiter with glossy hair and a stained apron assumed they were both French tourists—Gabriel had no wish to set
him straight—and invited Mireille to choose the chicken that most
appealed to her. The waiter immediately marked its thigh with a red-
hot poker so they'd recognize it when it came to their table.

La Ibérica was closed for the holidays on the Thursday and,
of course, Friday, which was Christmas Eve. These were days
for company accounting, for closing the year's books, and people
weren't moving house. Mireille and Gabriel divided the daylight
hours between the Falcon Room and walks around Barcelona.
Mireille, who's never since wanted to come back, has only a blurry
memory of what she saw in those two days. Too many experiences
to recall them all. She'll only say they stopped in a market, but
she doesn't know if it was La Boqueria or Sant Antoni. She'll say
they went up a mountain (Montjuïc or Parc Güell?). She'll say they
walked through a square with palm trees and went to drink ver-
mouth in a bar (Glaciar? Ambos Mundos?) and then—and this she
does remember—they walked to the zoo because Gabriel wanted
to show her a white gorilla, so cute, just like a giant teddy. She also
remembers going to a Christmas street fair and, since they must
have been feeling guilty, they bought presents for Christophe.

They used Thursday night to run an errand. Some months earlier, Justine, Mireille's best friend, had met a boy from Barcelona

at the university. He was spending some time in Paris, was smart, long-haired, a voracious reader of Lukács and the structuralists, highly dialectical, and wasn't sure whether to become a filmmaker or literary critic. Justine had attended a seminar discussing the divergences between Marxism and Maoism, and he'd been there too. The young man, a rather incoherent blusterer, had challenged a view she'd forcefully expressed. On the way out, she wanted to give a more nuanced account of a couple of points and the discussion adjourned to a bar. By the end of the night, since there was no way they were going to agree, they'd moved the debate to the area called praxis—in other words, between the sheets, in a room he was renting. Two days later, he'd had to return to Barcelona for family reasons, and Justine was dying to know what had become of him. So she asked Mireille if, in exchange for looking after Christophe that Christmas, she would take some books to the Barcelona dilettante and engage in a bit of busybodying.

Even now, thirty years on, Mireille gets exasperated when she remembers this story.

"Justine jotted down the address on a bit of paper. The boy had told her that, if she ever came to Barcelona, she'd find him in that bar every night before dinner." We Christophers made our inquiries and discovered that it was the Boccaccio. "Gabriel had seen the name in the society section of some newspaper. It was in the swanky part of town, well away from the everyday world, and it was hard to imagine it as the kind of place where students met. As soon as we went inside and felt the eyes of the room turn and stare, we got it: This was a bar for trendy, pampered, daddies' boys! Some of them had even reached the stage of being daddies of daddies' boys! We've got them in Paris too: eternally young scions of good families playing at counterculture but, come the hour of reckoning, they have church weddings. That night, the progeny of Barcelona's elite were arranged around a long bar and draped on red velvet sofas. Seen from a distance, they all looked like versions of George Peppard and Audrey Hepburn in *Breakfast at Tiffany's*. We asked a waiter if he knew Justine's friend. He jerked his head toward the back of the bar. The subject of our search was sitting with a group of boys and girls holding forth. It must be said that all of them, and especially Justine's friend, radiated a natural optimism that you might describe as inherited. It was extremely easy for them to ignore the fact that they were living under a dictatorship. Maybe that's why they were dressed in a style that seemed to be de rigueur: the girls in vaguely oriental tunics, floaty dresses and miniskirts, and the boys in Lois jeans, Shetland wool sweaters, cotton shirts and, in some cases, a knitted tie. They laughed at everything and guzzled gin and tonic as if they'd just walked in from the desert. Two of the girls were smoking extra-long cigarettes. Gabriel opted to stand at the bar having a beer. I went over to the group and they all fell silent. I said the boy's name and handed him the packet of books saying, 'From Justine in Paris.' He put two and two together and thanked me. One of the girls sitting next to him assumed an expression of boredom. The boy opened the parcel and, without paying much attention to its contents, handed the three books to his friends. He read the note inside the parcel. 'Ah, so you're the famous Mireille,' he said. 'Justine told me a lot about you ... and that must be your Barcelona truck driver over there. Tell him to come here. Come on, let me invite you to a drink.' I went to get Gabriel. They made a space for us, and we sat with them for a while. I was the only foreigner but they were more than happy to switch to French. Now they were intrigued. They stared at us and asked questions, which someone translated into Spanish for Gabriel. He didn't say a word. The conversation was a string of banalities. They were trying hard to be brilliant and cosmopolitan, speaking in affected French, which made them come across as effete and pedantic. They'd been in New York not long before and were dropping Andy Warhol's name all the time. They told me, without a hint of a blush, that in Barcelona they were known as the '*gauche divine*.' Yes, that's right. In French. Just imagine! I asked them about the political situation and the latest student revolts. One of them raised his glass and very seriously proposed a toast to some comrades in the anti-Franco front called 'Assemblea de Catalunya,' but the others seemed rather lukewarm. They followed suit mechanically. The choral clinking of ice cubes provided the clue: They'd installed

themselves in a fictional world and thought that their Boccaccio
was the Flore, or Deux Magots, the meeting place of the intellectual vanguard of the left. It's true that every social class has its
own forms of evasion. This made me want to wind them up a bit,
to start asking about their families, what they did and if Franco had
caused them any suffering, but someone butted in, saying we could
go to dinner at another of their favorite haunts. A chic restaurant
where they served omelets. How about that? Gabriel and I saw our
chance to escape, and we left them to their little show. They were
the masters of seduction and would soon find someone else to
worship them. We wished each other Merry Christmas and knew
that they would have forgotten all about us after a minute or two."

"Lucy in the sky with diamonds..." Chris sings. His interrup-
tion makes sense. It's his crafty way of reminding us that we have
yet to deliver the final detail of that evening. Gabriel and Mireille
were at the door of the bar saying good-bye to Justine's friend when
a girl came up from behind them and tapped Gabriel's shoulder.

"Hey, what are you doing here?" she asked. "Don't you recognize me?"

Gabriel had to dredge up the identity of the thin, angular face
and cropped blond hair from the depths of his memory. He went
back six years, to the ferry taking them to England and then recap-
tured the fleeting form of a naked girl riding a horse. Yes, it was
Anna Miralpeix. It turned out that Anna was a cousin of Justine's
friend. All in the family.

"What did you have in the end, a boy or girl?" Gabriel asked.

"A little girl. She's called Llúcia but we call her Lucy. She's
five now and the cutest little thing in the world. Well, she's a bit
naughty and never keeps still, that's for sure."

"She must take after her mother. Does she like the sea?"

"She prefers animals, especially horses," she said, winking.

The encounter with the "divine left" of Barcelona was offset, or
at least found its antidote the next day, with Christmas dinner at
Bundó's apartment—or perhaps we should say Bundó and Carolina's apartment—even if it's only for the first and last time. If Gabriel
and Bundó had been alone they would have had a Catalan-style

Christmas lunch on December 25th, but the presence of the two girls meant that they celebrated with a dinner on Christmas Eve instead. Carolina had arrived the day before, also by coach, and had taken possession of the apartment in a matter of a few hours. Gabriel couldn't believe his eyes. This bore no relation to the desolate place he'd left on the verge of depression that first night. It had only taken a few finishing touches and a dash of good taste to transform it. Bundó, of course, was exultant. Still in her apron, Carolina emerged from the kitchen to greet them, as if she'd been doing it all her life. The smell of chestnut-stuffed turkey browning in the oven wafted through the apartment, perfuming it with a kind of domestic warmth that all four of them—for different reasons—identified with an idea of happiness. Since this was something unknown to them and they weren't oppressed by nostalgia for earlier Christmases, they forged a special bond over the course of that night, so unique and unrepeatable that they never experienced it again. If they believed in some god, it would have been the essence of that Christmas.

They were ablaze with happiness all night. Carolina and Mireille took to each other immediately. They were both wearing *minijupes* and high boots. They smoked the same brand of cigarettes. They'd grown up in fits and starts. They spoke French together, and when Bundó and Gabriel moaned about not understanding them they carried on like a pair of affluent expatriates, teasing them and treating them with exaggerated haughtiness. Behind the fun and games, however, if the friendship gelled it was thanks to the secrets kept by their boyfriends: Bundó had never told Carolina that Gabriel had two other women and two more sons in England and Germany.

When the turkey was reduced to a carcass, they had the mandatory Catalan *torrons* for dessert and proposed their toasts with French champagne nicked by Gabriel and Bundó on a recent trip. Some days earlier they'd agreed to buy gifts. As they opened them, Carolina and Mireille joked that they couldn't accept anything that came from a move. It wouldn't be ethical at Christmas, they chided. Then Bundó, who'd drunk more than the others, started singing carols, making up the words if he didn't know them, and Carolina and Gabriel joined in. Mireille tried to remember something in French, from her childhood, and Carolina joined in with her too. They turned out the lights and sang in the subtle flickering of candles and disco-style flashes of the Christmas tree lights. Lacking the traditional *zambomba* drum to accompany the carols, Bundó was in such high spirits that he improvised by grabbing a bottle of anis and kept the beat going by rattling a knife up and down the knobbly glass. The two girls couldn't stop giggling and had tears pouring down their faces, to which Bundó responded by clowning even more. He was out of control, prancing around the living room, sweaty, with his shirt hanging out, scraping away at his anis bottle. He was the picture of contentment. The victory of the present.

Gabriel, more contained, was also laughing at his antics. Later, when only memory remained, of all the Bundó's he'd known, he'd remember precisely that Bundó of that Christmas Eve. Day after day after day. The only way to bear the pain was by celebrating past happiness.

We've been going on too long, haven't we? We Christophers do go on too long. So what else is new? We've been putting off the Pegaso's last ride for a while now, as if the fact of not talking about it could change the course of history, but that's enough beating about the bush. We're now so well schooled that we could reconstruct in real time—on a scale of one to one—everything that happened between that Christmas Eve and that February 14th, that sad Saint Valentine's Day. But this isn't a good idea. If we want to make progress in our search for our father, we'll have to go back to that awful time for once and for fucking all. We'll need to take a few shortcuts in order to get ahead. For example, although they became great friends that Christmas Eve, Mireille and Carolina never saw each other again.

The next day, Gabriel and Mireille spent a lazy morning in the Falcon Room. They'd woken up with brutal hangovers, and every word they pronounced echoed in a drum-roll crescendo in their heads, *rum pum pum pum.* The throbbing alcohol-steeped nausea demanded darkness and silence, and they didn't speak any more about their future. If they'd known that these were going to be the last hours they'd be together as a couple, they probably would have made better use of the time.

As the afternoon advanced, Senyora Rifà heard that they'd got up and offered them a couple of plates of noodle-and-meatball soup left over from Christmas lunch. The broth was warming and hearty, and it revived them a little, if only enough to get them to understand that the coach was leaving for Paris in a couple of hours, at eight o'clock. As Mireille was packing her bag, Senyora Rifà knocked at the door and presented her with the stuffed humming-bird. She'd dusted down the iridescent feathers, and the vibrant patina of colors brightened up the farewell and the journey home.

"Take good care of it for me," the landlady said in French. "Ah, and come back for Gabriel some day. I love him a lot, but if he stays in this house too much longer he'll end up as a dried animal like all the rest."

The hummingbird at least still resides in Mireille's house in Paris. As for our father, well, as you'll understand, we don't know how he reacted to her absence. This was the first time he'd tasted the medicine he'd so often doled out to our mothers. For the first time, he was the one who said good-bye, the one who stood there quietly and went home to face loneliness. We Christophers imagine that this new situation caught him unawares. To cap it all, a few days later he had to deal with another tricky situation. Carolina had stayed in Barcelona for a whole week, until New Year, and went back to France on January 1st. The Papillon needed Muriel. At the beginning of her stay they'd agreed, and she'd promised too, that she'd come to live with him in Barcelona very soon, but Bundó took her departure badly. The commitment Carolina had made soon amounted to nothing. He was unmanned by his fear that she'd go back on her word and was consequently tormented by renewed attacks of jealousy over all the Frogs who were paying for her favors. It made him ill.

"She didn't even leave a toothbrush," Bundó raved as Gabriel tried to calm him down.

After the holidays, in their first week back at La Ibérica, Bundó's doom and gloom only worsened. He was convinced that he absolutely had to go and visit Carolina at the Papillon, but there was no foreign move planned at the time. They were doing jobs around the city instead or, in some cases, going to other parts of Spain. Every day that went by without seeing her, Bundó feared that Carolina was moving further away from him. Distraught, he phoned her at night but the minute he heard her voice he didn't know what to say and hung up. After the third call, Carolina started to insult the *putain de connard* that was harassing her. In the middle of all this exhausting folly, Bundó came up with a tailor-made solution. Carolina needed an incentive to come to Barcelona. She was terrified of being lonely and bored. If Mireille was here too, and since they were friends, it would be easier for her to adapt. Therefore Mireille had to come and live in Barcelona. Bundó set out on a crusade against our father's complicated love life and tried to convince him that he had to put his energies into making Mireille happy. In Barcelona. He abruptly deserted their lifelong, mutual, respectful discretion and started attacking him from every flank. Gabriel had to choose one woman—Mireille—and forget about the rest. This mix-up wasn't good for him. He nagged him to leave the boarding house—couldn't he see that La Rifà had set her sights on him, wanted to abduct him?—and get himself an apartment in Via Favència. "Everyone needs a family, Gabriel, but only one. That's enough, so let's not have any more fucking around about that." "Surely you don't want to die all alone . . ." Stubborn as he was, Bundó never missed a chance to lay siege to Gabriel. When they were driving around in the truck, when they were unloading an extra-heavy wardrobe, when they were having dinner together after a gruelling day. He didn't care if Petroli witnessed his harangues. On the contrary, he was a friend and Bundó sought his support. Right, Petroli? True, eh, Petroli? Don't you agree, Petroli?

"Bundó, poor boy, really lost it for a while," Petroli recalled when we went to see him in Germany. "It was terrible to see him so obsessed. His whole temperament changed. He wasn't eating, which was incredible for him, and it was almost worse when he was silent. He withdrew into himself. His jealousy was preying on his mind and we were scared stiff about him driving the Pegaso in that state. In those days, people didn't take it seriously but now the psychologists would say he had a galloping depression."

Gabriel knew Bundó like a brother—well, he was his brother, our uncle, dammit—and, when it started, was very patient with him. It'll pass, he told himself. This is just one of his fits. At the end of January they did the first international move for 1972 (Barcelona-Geneva, Move Number 198), and, at last, Bundó found a way of meeting up with Carolina. But the two-hour visit to the Papillon didn't help. On the contrary. Carolina received Bundó with tenderness and devotion as always—she'd missed him so much those three weeks!—but he was in such a state he didn't notice, was too blind in his zeal to convince her, and she ended up retreating behind her usual doubts and forms of evasion. Bundó climbed into the Pegaso feeling like he'd taken a step backward. The world was falling apart. The next day he was so down that he couldn't even go to work. He didn't have the phone turned on in the apartment so they couldn't contact him. Halfway through the morning he got on the bus, went to the boarding house, and asked Senyora Rifà if she had a room free. He wanted to forget about the apartment in Via Favència and to be near Gabriel. Showing very good judgment, Senyora Rifà made him a cup of linden-blossom tea and told him she had no vacancies, after which she sent him back home, making him promise to find some distraction and then go to work in the afternoon. When he got back to Via Favència, with the intention of staying in bed until Carolina came to rescue him, he found Gabriel and Petroli waiting at the door. They carried him off to do a move—Senyor Casellas was enraged—and that night, fearing he might do something stupid, Gabriel stayed in the apartment to sleep. In those four weeks without Carolina, the place had turned into a nest of dirt and neglect.

The spiral went on and on with no end in sight. Then came the trip to Hamburg, which changed everything.

After years of international haulage, Gabriel, Bundó, and Petroli had got into the habit of comparing every trip with climbing a mountain. It was Petroli's idea. He'd done some hiking when he was young. The climb was always the slowest, hardest part: loading furniture, leaving first thing in the morning, ensuring the delivery time set by Senyor Casellas was met . . . Once they got to the destination and had done the unloading, which was the equivalent of planting the flag, things got easier and more agreeable. Europe was the downhill run. The Pegaso rolled along more lightly, they divided up the booty, invented excuses to take a break and, whenever the route permitted, stopped off to visit the family—interpret the word as you please. To stay with the simile, the journey to Hamburg was their Everest. The longest possible route within La Ibérica's radius. They'd only done the trip on one previous occasion and had a doleful memory of it. Hamburg, they'd found out, was at the northern edge of Germany. Just looking for it on the map made them feel cold.

"We're going almost all the way to the Arctic Circle," Bundó announced with his usual flourish.

That first journey had been relentless and, since it was also in winter, they'd faced every kind of inclement weather. Rain and snow, and more rain and more snow, and driving with chains on the wheels, and police checkpoints every couple of hundred kilometers, and jam-packed motorways, and cab heating that kept breaking down . . . The truck was getting old and couldn't handle such extreme ordeals any more.

Two years later, the Pegaso was the same old grumbling heap, Hamburg was still in the same place on the map, and all three drivers had a dwindling spirit of adventure.

They began the ascent in the very early hours of Saturday morning, February 12th. Senyor Casellas had calculated twenty-four hours on the road to cross France and Germany, taking turns to sleep on the bunk, after which they'd do the unloading on Sunday the thirteenth first thing in the morning. At that rate, they could be back in Barcelona on Monday night and ready for work again on Wednesday morning. All three knew that these tight schedules never worked, but what intimidated them was the move itself. In addition, the Pegaso was chockablock: They were taking the furniture and all the mementos of a recent window who was going back home forty years after having fled from the Nazis. Since then, she'd married a Catalan nationalist banker, gone through some lean times during the Civil War, and raised four children, who now wanted her out of the way.

Just after they crossed the French border—with Petroli driving—the first contretemps arose. Bundó had been unusually quiet and pensive. Now he broke the silence.

"Now, soon," he said, "when we're going through Clermont-Ferrand, we need to stop for a moment at the Papillon. In and out. Ten minutes. I have to talk to Carolina."

He said this in the calm, falsely naive tone of a kid begging for a gift knowing the answer will be no. Gabriel and Petroli were afraid this would happen. Before leaving, the three of them had agreed that they wouldn't be stopping anywhere on the way up so they could get to Hamburg as fast as possible. They'd gain time that way and then, on the descent, they could take it easy. Gabriel responded.

"You know that's not on, Bundó. You say ten minutes but it will be longer. We all know each other. We can't waste time this trip. This is Everest."

"Why do we always have to do what you two say?" Bundó replied. "You know what, just drop me off and go on without me." His friends laughed at the joke. "No, I'm serious. I'm off. I'll find something. I'm leaving La Ibérica. You two can tell Senyor Casellas. Bye-bye. I've been thinking about this for a while. I'll buy a van and do my own transporting. What with the shit wages we get . . ."

"Think before you speak, Bundó," Gabriel countered. "On the way home you can spend as long as you want with Carolina. Anyway, I don't know why you're carrying on like this. She's crazy about you. Just seeing the two of you together on Christmas Eve was enough to know that."

"No, it might be too late on the way back. I have to see her now. I need to convince her to leave that fucking job of hers and come with me. Tomorrow, if possible. I have to tell her that one day Mireille will be in Barcelona too."

"You know you can't say that. That's never going to happen." Gabriel was red with rage.

"Well, then I'll tell her something else. How would you like me to tell her that you've got a woman in Frankfurt and another one in London? And two more sons, to tip the balance." He paused. "I've always been obliged to lie for you, Gabriel, to protect you, and I don't get anything in return!"

Our father—and this we know from Petroli—remained quiet and shot him a pitying look. Bundó forced a guilty smile, shocked at his own temerity. He would have understood it better if his best friend had thumped him, and hard. Behind the steering wheel and out of the corner of his eye, Petroli witnessed the silent massacre of thirty years of friendship and tried to stanch the bleeding.

"Okay, we'll stop for ten minutes at the Papillon," he pronounced. "Ten minutes and that's all. Just time for a fag. If you take any longer, Bundó, we're leaving without you and you can go to hell."

Bundó thanked them in a tiny voice and went back to his brooding. They covered the remaining kilometers to the brothel without saying a word. Gabriel was still in a state of shock, staring ahead empty eyed. Trying to drown the silence, Petroli tuned into the international service on Spanish radio.

"Ten minutes, Bundó. Six hundred seconds," Petroli repeated as they pulled up in front of the Papillon. "We're timing you."

Ten minutes later he started the truck, and Bundó shot like an arrow out of the brothel door. As they were having a smoke, Gabriel had thanked Petroli. Carolina waved at them from the top of the stairs, looking completely bewildered.

"She's giving me a date when I see her on the way back!" Bundó shouted as the Pegaso got underway. He was so excited his face had changed.

"Did you tell her?" Gabriel asked without looking at him. He was staring at the road.

"What?"

"Have you told her anything? About Sigrun and Sarah and Mireille and the boys?"

"Of course not! What do you take me for? A traitor?" Bundó exclaimed. "My friends, Carolina says that on the way back she'll give me a date. You understand? The exact day she's coming to live in Barcelona! We miss each other too much and we can't go on like this."

He was so wound up he couldn't keep still. Without further ado, he hugged Gabriel and ruffled his hair. It was his way of saying sorry. Our father broke free with a conciliatory shove, and Petroli gave three blasts of the horn.

Once that stumbling block was behind them, the ascent to Hamburg was accomplished with a fairly typical series of difficulties and distractions, no different from those suffered during the best of times. When they reached Strasbourg the truck broke down and they had to stop to change the fan belt. In Germany, nearing Karlsruhe, they had dinner in a roadhouse that served venison stew every day. It was one thing after another.

We Christophers would pay a fortune to be able to go back in time and witness one of those roadside dinners, to be with them inside the cab of the Pegaso, on a long trip. To join in with the chat, the rows, the jokes, to smell the stuffy stench of the cab and moan about that despot Senyor Casellas, to doze off and dream about the naked calendar girls. In short: to be one of them.

We tell ourselves that with all the hours we're spending tracking down our dad and his friends, we're saving on psychologists' fees. By learning about his circumstances, maybe we'll be able to understand ourselves a little better. Anyway, if we are not to go on too long about this last journey, we'll now take another short cut: As incredible as it may seem, that very day Petroli stayed behind to live in Hamburg.

The last hours of the last move were especially punishing. After Hanover, the snow covering the motorway had frozen over and the truck made exasperatingly slow progress. They got to Hamburg at midday on Sunday, five hours later than planned and it took them another hour to locate the building where they had to unload. They'd been on the road for more than thirty hours. It was always the same thing, however: They could be at dropping point but the sight of the peak gave them a lift of new-found energy, which they invested in their final effort. That day in Hamburg, luck smiled on their final exertions: The German widow had contracted two

strapping fellows to help them unload. Full of the Olympic spirit
of Munich '72, they demonstrated that they could have earned a
place in the German weightlifting team. Between the five of them,
then, they finished the job after dark, but still early enough to find
a restaurant open. Observing the ritual that always marked the
end of any move, they took off their work gear, had a quick wash,
and got into some clean clothes. Before taking their leave of the
brawny Germans, they asked if they knew of a good place nearby
where they could eat and, out of some kind of proletarian intuition, the men told them how to get to the Asturian Center. Petroli
couldn't believe his luck. That one didn't appear on any list!

Christof and Cristoffini have got ahead of us here, but now
it's time to go into detail. While Gabriel and Bundó dived into
a trucker-size dish of Asturian pork-and-bean stew, the famous
*fabada*, Petroli preferred to sit at the bar, have a glass of cider and
enjoy a bit of conversation. Whenever his radar detected Spanish
emigrants in his vicinity, all hunger and weariness vanished. Then
someone introduced him to Ángeles and, in a space of a few seconds, his life changed. Completely.

It must be said that the bedazzlement was mutual. Ángeles
and Petroli spent two hours gazing into one another's eyes and
engaging in mutual seduction with tales from the post-war years.
(After that night, they swear, they were immune from the past and
it was never again a topic of conversation. It was no longer necessary.) Meanwhile, Bundó and Gabriel, their bellies fit to burst, collapsed into two armchairs in a corner and nodded off. Eventually,
Petroli came over, woke them up and, without any preliminaries,
informed them, "I'm staying, guys."

"What do you mean?" Gabriel asked.

"What I said. I'm staying. I'm not coming back with you. I've
met the woman of my dreams. I've been trawling through places
like this for years and now I know why. No, no, I'm not drunk. I
know you won't believe me but that lady over there (no, don't turn
around now!) is called Ángeles and we're made for each other. It's a
gut feeling and you know I'm not into that kind of stuff. If it doesn't
work out, I'll find my own way back. Please go without me."

He spoke with such conviction that there was nothing they could say. Petroli was no braggart and neither was he desperate like Bundó, who'd been about to pull the plug on everything for his ten minutes at the Papillon. Petroli knew what he wanted. He called Ángeles over, introduced them, and then they rode off into the sunset . . . et cetera.

As Petroli confirmed, that night was the last time the three of them were together.

Bundó and Gabriel slumbered in the armchairs like a couple of angels. Petroli had paid the bill and asked the Asturians not to disturb them till closing time. After sweeping up, the last waiter came over and shook them awake, which took a while. They were fast asleep and, even when they opened their eyes, were slow to work out where they were. Then they remembered what had happened just before they dropped off: Petroli's decision. Did they dream it or was it real? The waiter politely turned them out and advised them that if they wanted a nice snug spot to spend the night they should go to the railway station—"the *Hauptbahnhof*, it's called"—which was very close, and the bar was open all night.

The air outside was so cold and damp that it woke them up like an icy-cold shower. After midnight and not a soul to be seen. They had to tread carefully to prevent slipping on the footpath.

"Is there blood coming out of my ears?" Bundó asked. "I can't feel them!"

"Hamburg is our Everest," was our father's response.

They were walking huddled over in their too-thin anoraks and scarves. Though they'd been snoozing for four hours, their legs were heavy and their muscles felt as hard as rocks. They had two good strong coffees at the station in the company of three globe-trotters and a gaggle of hippies. Then, half compelled by tradition, they rather listlessly opened up the rectangular box that had "gone astray" in the move. They divided up the loot as usual, and our father spent a few minutes updating his inventory in the notebook. Then they went back to the Pegaso.

Gabriel offered to drive. Now they were on the descent, he calculated that they could be in Frankfurt at about nine in the morning, just in time to have breakfast with Sigrun and Christof. A surprise visit. In the first few kilometers, until the heating came on full, Petroli's absence was very noticeable: It was much warmer with three people squeezed up together in the cab. Bundó didn't take long to fall asleep and, with his snores as the soundtrack, our father gripped the steering wheel good and tight. Every motorway on earth looked ghostly on winter nights. He tuned into a German radio station. The announcer's voice kept him company and, though he didn't understand a word, he was under the impression that he was practising his German.

At half past six the sun came up in a gray sky heavy with low clouds. Shortly afterward Gabriel woke Bundó.

"Time to wake up," he said. "We've just gone through Kassel. Frankfurt's not far."

Bundó squirmed in his seat.

"No, no, no, we can't stop in Frankfurt. If we do that we won't get to France on time. Do you know what day it is today? It's the 14th of February, Saint Valentine's Day, lovers' day! I promised Carolina I'd visit her. You can't let me down!"

Gabriel took a few seconds to consider whether to fight over it or not. In the end, without answering except for a reluctant nod, he put his foot down on the accelerator. A few kilometers farther on, they drove past the Frankfurt exit. He hadn't had time to tell Sigrun he wanted to drop in so it wasn't all that serious. How many times in the future would he go back to that moment of doubt? How many times would he curse it?

He kept driving.

"We'll pull over at the next service stop and have some breakfast if you want," he said, "and then you can take the wheel."

Bundó snored in response. He'd dropped off again, so quickly that Gabriel wondered if he'd heard him speak just a moment before. After about twenty kilometers of a straight downhill run, the Pegaso was flying along, a winged horse. Gabriel noticed something like a grain of sand in his field of vision. An irresistible heaviness tipped his head forward. Then he fell asleep.

Beyond the windshield, it was snowing heavily again.

*Part II*

ARRIVALS

# 1

## At the Airport

In the spring of 1968, Barcelona airport's hallways and departure lounges gleamed with the deceptive luster of ice. Although the Minister for Civil Aviation had inaugurated the new El Prat international terminal only a few weeks earlier, every day brought some new hitch. When the doors opened in the morning, the night-waxed marble floors dazzled, reflecting the walls stuccoed in the official beige of the time. However, when the passengers arrived, running for planes or wandering around bored by delays, dragging bags and suitcases and dropping smouldering cigarette butts, the floors soon lost their shine and began to show the wear and tear. By midday, the busiest areas put one in mind of a neglected tombstone, and the terminal took on the hostile feel of a vast, dingy mausoleum. One of the regime's officials must have noticed it during a stopover, or wandering nervously around waiting for some VIP (vanishing footsteps and dark glasses), and the management very swiftly contracted three men with one sole mission: to sweep, mop, and make the airport shine as if it were going to be inaugurated by the Generalísimo himself every day.

The trio were called Sayago, Leiva, and Porras, and the first time they laid eyes on each other was in the manager's office where a calendar on his desk, advertising Iberia Airlines, showed Friday, June 21, 1968. Unprompted, the three workers stood in line, straight-backed, as if the shifty-looking manager were a

239

commander about to inspect his troops. He spent five minutes instructing them how to do their jobs, informing them in passing that he'd once wanted to be a poet, and then ordered them to go and start cleaning at once. Yes, he knew they'd been told to start on Monday, but an Italian cardinal was arriving en route to Jerusalem that afternoon, and all kinds of religious and political dignitaries would be here to receive him. They had to give the airport's marble floors the same spiritual aura as the Vatican basilica. It was their baptism of fire.

Leiva, Porras, and Sayago ran off to get changed and attacked the cleaning with such zeal that they earned their ticket to heaven and eternal salvation that very same day. As it turned out, His Eminence didn't set foot in the terminal, but that's another story. When they knocked off that evening, they went to have a beer in the airport bar. They were completely done in, with cramps in their wrists from so much mopping. Like a shared secret, the exhaustion of their first day united them in brotherhood. Although they'd never met before, they lost no time in discovering their shared biographies. Sayago and Leiva were in their forties, lived in the Magòria neighborhood and had come to Barcelona at about the same time, some ten years earlier. Gradually, on their meal breaks or going home by bus, they discovered that they had both been born in the province of Jaén, in villages separated by just twenty kilometers of stony ground; that their wives worked as seamstresses for the same despotic mistress; that, with time, their homesickness had become increasingly abstract, although present in the same way that a distinctive freckle or birthmark you might have been vaguely proud of once was now so familiar that you didn't notice it when you looked in the mirror.

Sayago, who sported a bushy moustache and well-trimmed beard as a kind of personal trademark, loved unearthing things he had in common with Leiva and could be a pain in the neck with his barrage of questions. "So what was the name of your teacher at school? It wasn't that bastard Paredes, was it? In those days the teachers went from one village to another . . ." No, no, he'd grown up with señorita Rosario and she gave them aniseed sweets when they behaved—at least during the six years he'd gone to school. Leiva was grubby but a good fellow. He ran his hand through his long, greasy hair and forced himself to dig up details of his life that the present had managed to bury beneath a large shovelful of reality. Sometimes, out of sheer laziness or not wanting to disappoint Sayago, he lied: Yes, of course he remembered that family of actors that came through the provincial villages every spring, with that girl who was more of a woman every year and showing more and more thigh, with her father keeping an eye on her from the stage . . .

Porras was a lot younger. He'd just turned seventeen. He was of slight build and somewhat lackadaisical, as if thinking was too much effort and he'd rather let himself be guided by fate. He lived—or rather slept—in the Verdum neighborhood, on the other side of Barcelona, with his mother, two brothers, and a sister. They'd been in a rented apartment for four years, ever since they arrived from Murcia. Porras was fed up with getting clobbered at school by a bunch of misfits who'd made him their scapegoat and by screwed-up frustrated teachers, so his older brother, who was working in the airport as a bartender, got him a job there as well. Every day, they got up at seven and crossed the city on the brother's Vespa, which he'd bought with his first pay packet on July 18th.

Despite their difference in age, Porras got on well with Sayago and Leiva from day one. Since he had no dad, they treated him with paternal concern but without the responsibilities imposed by blood ties. More than a son, Porras was a younger version of themselves, and they occasionally flirted with the possibility of starting life all over again, without the dead weight of so many forgettable years. Moreover, there was another detail that united them: None of them had ever traveled by plane. Every day they witnessed dozens of planes taking off and landing, heard them jolting along the runways when they hit the ground, the fleeting whistle when they lifted off. But, for them, these mammoth inventions were as fantastic as prehistoric animals.

I love these three guys! Leiva, Sayago, and Porras. My mother was with them at the airport for about ten years. They were very good friends. From the booth where she attended irate passengers who'd lost their luggage, Rita saw them going past her window from time to time and, when she didn't have any clients, she beckoned them over to gossip.

She told me that by February 1972, which is when this story really gets going, the officious airport manager was pushing up daisies after a sudden heart attack, and his books of poems were selling at cost at the Sant Antoni market. The three friends were still sweeping and mopping Barcelona airport from one end to the other, striving for perfection. The ties of friendship had become inextricably knotted. It was almost material for the final scene of a tragicomedy. It was some time since Leiva's and Sayago's wives had left their nasty boss and set up with their own sewing machines. In addition, the two couples went out dancing together every Sunday afternoon. Many Mondays the men had nothing left to talk about, but that didn't worry them in the least. Sayago had stopped interrogating Leiva, who'd put on twelve kilos, three per year, and still didn't bother to comb his hair in the airport changing rooms when they got ready for work or to go home. Sayago's questions were now aimed at Porras, who was courting his seventeen-year-old daughter. Every afternoon after work the boy got on the Vespa he'd inherited from his brother, went to pick her up at the household-goods shop where she worked, and took her home a couple of hours later. The following morning, Sayago, taking advantage of running into him in a corridor, or deliberately seeking him out, would corner him with a barrage of questions. Where had they been the previous evening? What were they doing in the bedroom and why had they closed the door? Did they have any plans? He was terrified at the prospect of becoming a premature grandfather, and you could tell when he was nervous because he kept touching the tips of his moustache. Leiva, meanwhile, looked on from a distance, thanking God that he and his wife had only had boys—two—and no daughter.

I'm telling you about these three exemplary gentlemen, Christophers, not because I want to get off track but because there was a moment when their intervention was crucial to our lives. Yes, yours too, so take note. These three, Leiva, Sayago, and Porras, were important. And with all their scams they certainly deserve walk-on parts in this story. It will all come out in due course. Let me tell you now about the first time I set eyes on them. I must have been about seven. One day I was with Mom walking past Niepce's, the photographer's shop on the corner of Carrer Fontanella and Via Laietana, and we stopped for a moment to look at a big black-and-white photo, about a meter by a meter twenty, which was exhibited in the window.

"Come on, where am I?" Mom said, showing me the photo. "Let's see if you can find me."

I stared at the three rows of people, all of them very neat and tidy, without much idea of what she wanted me to find, but my eyes flew straight to the pale, ecstatic-looking face, almost like a candle flame, at the end of the top row on the left. A child's fingerprint smeared the window.

It was a carefully posed photograph of the airport workers, some fifty men and a dozen women, all dressed up in their Sunday best. Not long before, one of the bigwigs in the Ministry of Civil Aviation had announced his retirement and someone aspiring to succeed him got the idea of having the commemorative photo taken before the speeches took place and snacks were offered. They must have been very proud of the photograph at Niepce's, or maybe they were obliged to show it through some personal commitment, because it remained in their window for years. It almost acquired the status of a public monument and became part of the city's geography, like the sign for Werner's music shop a couple of doors away, or the huge thermometer of Òptica Cottet in Portal de l'Àngel. My mother's photo was surrounded by an unvarying constellation of studio portraits that were uniformly boring for most passersby: a class of law graduates from the University of Barcelona, all decked out in the mandatory gown and mortarboard; a pudding-faced Miss Barcelona 1977 wannabe wearing a tartan skirt; the sugary bliss of a laughing bride and groom on their wedding day.

Studying the airport workers' photo was one of my childhood

pastimes. Whenever we were near Plaça Urquinaona I begged Mom to take me to Niepce's so I could find her in the photo. For my entertainment, or perhaps because she felt compelled to do so, on our third or fourth viewing of the photograph she told me about Leiva, Sayago, and Porras, the three men fixed in the center of the middle row, just behind all the dignitaries flashing their medals.

"You see that boy with the naughty face, just like yours?" she asked, and I nodded even though I couldn't single out the one she meant. "That boy's called Porras, and he worked with me at the airport. He used to come by motorbike every day, a Vespa, and, in winter, what with the cold and the wind in his face, his eyes would be teary all morning. As soon as he got to the airport he'd change into his working clothes and then come to see me in my booth. Sometimes, as a joke, he used to say he was crying over me because I didn't love him and wouldn't give him a kiss. But that's not true: I did love him."

"Was he one of those friends who used to keep the lost suit-cases?"

"Yes. Porras and the other two next to him, Leiva and Sayago."

Leiva, standing behind the airport manager, seemed to be slyly examining his bald crown. The young Porras had his mouth slightly open as if he couldn't contain his laughter, and, at his side, Sayago, of course, had subjected his moustache to some serious primping and was gazing into the camera with the gravitas of a great leader. Every time we stopped in front of that window—and it was often months between one visit and the next—Mom filled me in with a few more details about the lives of her three friends, or her own life at the airport.

I was growing up and the photo was growing yellower.

I don't know when they removed that sun-bleached relic from Niepce's window. One day, years later, I went past the shop, in-stinctively sought it out and realized it wasn't there any more. My heart skipped a beat and feverish nostalgia flared inside me. You might think it's absurd, but I stood there transfixed for ages. I longed for that photograph like you long for your favorite child-hood toy, with that incredible power memory has when it completely swamps the present. I'm not trying to be dramatic, but that image of the airport formed a direct link with my previous state of darkness, the obscure eternity before I was born. Frozen at that particulat point in time, the photo contained a latent anxiety—my mother's—the encoded, tentative knowledge of what was at stake for her now, and this had become my own special treasure. Also, behind the assembled group you could glimpse the airport corridors, cleaned and polished by Leiva, Sayago, and Porras. Those gleaming spaces would later reflect the disoriented footsteps of my future father—our father, Gabriel. A brief yet decisive moment, another sort of treasure.

I'm not trying to be dramatic, as I said. When I got home that evening, I immediately told my mother that they'd taken the photo out of Niepce's window. I expected her to be upset, that she'd share my dismay and that we could get indignant together but she wasn't bothered at all. Her only response was to open one of the cupboards and poke around until she found a tin box in which she kept a lot of old papers: It turned out that she'd kept a smaller version of the photograph. They'd all been presented with a copy some days after the farewell party—their reward for having taken part in the farce—but she'd never shown it to me because she wanted to preserve the magic of visiting the shop window. Then she'd forgotten all about it. Years later, it looked at first glance like one of those images of pilgrims going to Lourdes: a flock of people, all of them crippled, ill, or in mourning, anointed by the holy light of the Virgin Mary's blessing and having their picture taken to record it. Crutches, candles, and clerics. My mother, up there in the top left-hand corner, could have played the role of a levitating Virgin perfectly. I told her that, and she let out a dry laugh tinged with bitterness, the product of passing years and disappointments. And two glasses of whisky a day.

I went back to the photo and looked again at her once youthful face.

"How old were you here?"

"You know very well."

"No, come on, how old were you?"

"Work it out. Twenty-one or twenty-two. With a head full of mad ideas."

Her face looked so different from all the others. I stared at the group. Four bosses with brilliantined hair in the front row and a contingent of mousy men around them, all doing their best to conceal aching feet, worries about bills waiting to be paid, and the disagreeable taste of tap water. And in the middle of them all Mom's three friends: Sayago, Leiva, and Porras.

When she saw how curious I was, she took the photo from my hands and stared at it. Then she said, "Do you know that you're kind of here too?"

"Me?"

"Yes, it was that very morning that I realized I was pregnant. Just before they took the photo I threw up in the bathroom. That's why I'm so pale. The next day I went to the gynecologist . . ."

I kept the photo.


"To the airport! To the airport! Hurry up!"

They're my brothers and they're impatient. They've been bugging me for a while now with their cries and their cursing, half joking, half serious, prodding me at every step because I'm younger than them and they think they can get me to do what they want. Now that I'm at the wheel, they want me to speed through this story like a lunatic taxi driver, skidding around corners, taking short cuts down side streets and racing through red lights. Faster, faster, we'll leave you a good tip. Come on, spare us the details and get us to the airport. Hurry, hurry! But our father's adventures can't be hurried. On the contrary, they're stuck in the gray calm of a February morning on the tarmac next to an airplane. And, what's more, my brothers know it.

All of us want to come up with the improbable mathematical formula for one father and four mothers dotted around Europe. Fine, but it's my gig now. You've had your turns, Christophers, and you've certainly made the most of them. Now it's me, brothers, son of Rita Manley Carratalà, who decides how far back we have to go.

You can be choir and orchestra. My applauding audience. Once again, we have to do the run-up so we can jump, and that's why I'm going back to April 1967 (and earlier if need be), when Rita had just turned sixteen and her room—off-limits to her parents—was a teenage chamber of horrors. Her hang-ups, dreams, disappointments, fantasies, and demons resided there day and night and, if you weren't immune, as her friends were, five minutes in that bedroom would have your head spinning. She decorated its walls with a collection of photos of her musical idols, stuck up all over the place at odd angles, striving for a more funky effect. Here in the privacy of her den, she listened nonstop to a Zenith radio with the volume on full blast and a bent antenna that struggled to pick up the sound waves by leaning toward the light coming in through the window, as if it worked by photosynthesis. Dozens of perfume samples, eye shadows, lipsticks, and other makeup products stolen from Wella and Avon demonstrations were neatly arranged into a miniature glass-and-plastic city on top of an old writing desk. Languishing in one corner with a few dusty balls of wool was a knitting machine that had been loaned to her when she'd signed up for one of the long-distance learning courses offered by the Center for Culture and Knowledge. It had kept Rita amused for six whole weeks the previous winter, as attested by fifteen centimeters of a red pullover hanging from its jaws (two centimeters before the white deer that was supposed to adorn it grew legs).

With the door of her room slightly ajar that Saturday morning, Rita was lolling in bed, savoring the chaos of her parents flapping around the house. They were opening cupboards, shoving clothes in suitcases, arguing incessantly over stupid things blown out of proportion by overwrought nerves. It was music to her ears: This was the first time that her parents were going on a trip without her, and they were leaving her alone for seven whole days. From Saturday to Saturday—168 hours—10,080 minutes—604,800 seconds of adult freedom that she was already starting to breathe through the chink of her bedroom door. These seven days were a chance for Rita to get up to all the mischief and sins she could possibly imagine—all in fact very innocent—and she'd still have time for the misdeeds she hadn't dared to dream up. Who would have thought it? Her friends envied her for having such modern-minded parents, and she, only daughter of only children, pampered and overprotected to the point of pain, was enjoying the potential of their absence for the very first time.

One evening her father had come home from the shop beaming from ear to ear. At dinnertime he opened a just-in-case bottle of champagne he'd been keeping in the refrigerator and extracted from his pocket two plane tickets to Paris plus a reservation at the Hotel Ritz in Place Vendôme. His hands trembled with excitement, and, as always when he was worked up, his face took on a mulish expression that made him look like one of those stuffed toys in a firing-range booth at a fair. Then he explained what it was all about. His main wig supplier, a Paris wholesaler, wanted to express his gratitude with this luxury getaway because he'd bought wig number two thousand with his last order. Rita's parents—my grandparents—Conrad Manley and Leo Carratalà had never been out of Spain. Their honeymoon, twenty years earlier, had taken them to Valencia and Alicante to visit a whole string of her relatives. A wooden key ring from the Ordesa National Park, hanging at the entrance to the apartment, was a memento of holidays a decade ago in the Aragonese Pyrenees. That was about it. For them, Paris had always been their dream city, a romantic idyll summed up in four clichés: the Eiffel Tower, Versailles, the Louvre, and the wigs of Louis XVI!

Lying in bed, Rita listened intently to the upheaval as she leafed through the most recent issue of *Garbo*. In the living room, her father was busy combing two wigs, the one he was going to wear and the one he was going to pack in his suitcase as a spare. On the mannequin's head they were both combed in the same way, with the parting on the left, but the spare wig was more daring because the hair was four centimeters longer and ended in tiny curls that were very difficult to achieve. More Belmondo and less Delon, let's say. Combing away, as carefully as if it was his own hair, Conrad Manley was talking to himself, raising his voice from time to time.

"Ah, if only that damn fool father of mine was still here!" he cried sarcastically. "I'd tell him to his face, 'Look where wigs are taking us! They're taking us to Paris!'"

Every time he referred to his father, his dome—shiny and baby soft thanks to all the creams and lotions he applied—tensed and then turned scarlet. Even when he was "dressed" in a wig, as he liked to say, and you couldn't see it, the skin underneath took on the purplish hue of a young eggplant, just visible at his false hairline. This wasn't surprising, however. My grandfather Conrad and his father Martí loathed one another, compulsively, and judging from my grandfather's words years later, the hatred endured beyond Martí's death. It seems that their mutual dislike began very early, when my grandfather had to leave school and was put to work, and it was so intense that they ended up as physical opposites, night and day.

Now, Christophers, be warned, here comes another flashback. On his return from the war—where he'd pretended to be fighting with the Republicans until it seemed better to go over to the Nationals—my great-grandfather Martí went to work in a barber's shop on Ronda de Sant Pau near Avinguda Paral·lel, in the same establishment that my grandfather turned into a wig shop years later. Before the war, Martí Manley had worked delivering merchandise for some of the stalls in the Sant Antoni market but, when he was sent to the front, he'd learned to skive off by becoming a barber, having a lot of fun killing lice with a safety razor and shaving heads as if he was getting rid of a few dead leaves. The soldiers didn't complain. By the time he got to shave and cut the hair of some of the top brass, he'd learned to keep a steady hand and to govern the scissors, avoiding any disasters that might have sent him directly to the lockup.

The military experience wasn't very useful except when it came to showing who was boss in the barber's shop. He was secretive and tight-lipped at home, as if his time at the front had left him emotionless, but with scissors and a comb in his hands he was quite a different man, one who'd mastered every register of futile conversation. He spoke to his clients, looking them in the eye in

the mirror, knowing how to crack a joke and how to concede they
were right about everything without coming across as an ass-licker.
Sometimes the particular shape of a skull, an ear, a shaven nape,
or the trusting client who tipped his head back offering a clear
shot at his carotid reminded him of the fraternal bond he'd known
at the front. It was such a natural, innocent feeling that he'd spend
the next few minutes missing the war.

Three years after he started work the real boss retired, and
Martí Manley bought the business at a very low price, although
he did sign a document promising he'd hang a photo of the former
owner on the wall so his oldest clients wouldn't forget him, and
did offer him all the services of the establishment free of charge,
including the final tidy-up before he was buried. Instead of paying
an apprentice, Martí made Conrad leave school and start at the
barber's shop one Monday morning. To make it less traumatic, my
great-grandmother Dolors, who secretly abhorred her husband's
decision, bought Conrad a white coat and had his name embroidered on the pocket. It was 1944. My grandfather Conrad was
fifteen with a downy moustache and beard that grew in patches,
making shaving difficult. Quite a portent.

The business was slowly making a name for itself in the neighborhood. Not a day went by without some stranger coming in for
the first time, and often returning after a few weeks. Since it was
near the theaters in Avinguda Paral·lel, Martí soon acquired some
very elegant clients, gentlemen who dropped in before a show for
a trim, a shave, or to get their sideburns touched up. They often
appeared in magazines, and their signed photos were starting to
keep the old owner company on the wall. When they went out
into the street, coiffed in a cloud of hair spray and wafting a trail
of scented lotion behind them, Martí Manley puffed out his chest
and shot a quick self-conscious look at himself in the mirror. He
was a happy man.

Then, only a year and a half after he started to work as an apprentice, due to heaven knows what variety of genetic plot, Conrad Manley's hair started to fall out. At first, like all maladies, this
one manifested itself with a few random symptoms. Four jet-black

hairs on a pillow when he woke up; a tuft tangled in a comb; a clump blocking the drain in the bath. Soon, however, its virulence spread all over the crown of his head, denuding the whole region in a matter of weeks. When he realized what was happening, Conrad tried to cover it up by combing his hair backward because he knew his father would feel betrayed by the wasteland. Martí was convinced that a great part of the business's success was attributable to the image offered by the barber—an aesthetic model to emulate—and every day, before opening, he attended to his mane of hair with morbid devotion. Nature had been generous with him, and a great lock rose above his forehead, a lordly presence evoking the glass canopy of Hotel Colon. It inspired respect.

For all Conrad's efforts to hide the calamity, the ravaged zone kept growing. Surprisingly, a potion bought from a pharmacist in Carrer Unió, stinking like a sewer and fecal yellow in color, which he had to slather over his head and cover with a hairnet before going to sleep, gave him not only an assortment of ill-smelling nightmares but also three weeks' hope. Once the respite ended, though, his hair seemed even more panicked and opted for mass suicide.

Soon, when it was impossible for him to hide the alopecia, Martí started to give his son black looks. First, he criticized his bizarre hairstyles, but it didn't take him long to start mocking—mercilessly and in front of the clients—his shameful adolescent baldness.

The scene is more or less as follows: Martí is giving the final touches to a client's hairdo, scissors busy in pursuit of a couple of elusive hairs that are still sticking out. He gets them with a dry snap, slicing the air. The mirror, occupying a whole strip of the wall, reflects a humdrum scene with the smug-looking face of the client in the foreground, apparently levitating under its own steam as if there were no body sitting beneath the white cape; the never-still figure of Martí holds a small mirror so the client can contemplate his own nape, saying, "Yes, thank you, that's exactly what I wanted"; and, finally, Conrad's bald head, a saintly crown, emerges behind the other two as he sweeps up the spread of sacrificed hair.

MARTÍ: That's right. Go ahead and sweep up now ... Let's see if all this shifting of other people's hair will make a few stick to you, for God's sake!

CONRAD: ...

CLIENT: So young and such a naked skull. You don't take after your dad in that, my boy.

CONRAD: ...

MARTÍ: Not in that or in anything else.

CONRAD: ...


The mutual detestation between father and son kept fermenting in Conrad's resentment-laden silences. The scene was frequently repeated with scant variation. Perhaps prompted by the chill of the razor on their necks, the clients tended to agree with the father but, occasionally, somebody would show compassion for the boy and send him an encouraging glance in the mirror, a compassionate lifting of the eyebrows. Conrad limited himself to responding with a shriveled smile and a shrug. One gentleman, a regular who came to get his tobacco-yellowed moustache dyed, cheerfully proposed the solution of a wig.

"Never! Not in my lifetime! Don't even mention it!" Martí cried, shaking his head so violently that his forelock, compact and glossy as Bakelite, looked as if it might crack. "Wigs are the work of the devil. They're false. They're disgusting. They're dead hair! Never trust a man who wears a wig!"

Over time, the youth's craven resignation turned into a sort of pride. As Martí's scorn bounced higher and higher off his crown, Conrad's character grew stronger, nourished by ever-deepening loathing for his father. At night, when Martí was asleep, Conrad conspired with his mother. They mimicked him, portraying him as even more grotesque than he really was, a Nogués-like caricature, and their nocturnal whispers often exploded into muffled laughter. I imagine it was their only resource when forced to live with such a raving lunatic. Worse, for some time now, Martí had been throwing tantrums over the slightest thing and always dragged his bald-headed son into the thick of it. Everything was his fault, and, more than once, in the middle of all the screaming and shouting, it escaped his lips that Conrad didn't even look like his son. His wife, emboldened by the accusation, then asked whose he was if not his own and he, completely beside himself, purple with rage, ordered her to investigate every branch of the family tree to see if she could find a bald head. Just one would be sufficient.

My theory is that the barber Martí was right and grandfather Conrad wasn't his son, but there's no way of proving it. This is just conjecture, or maybe a desire, based on nothing more than a family history replete with miscalculations and frustrated expectations. On the maternal side (only children of only children of only children, throughout) freethinking and somewhat eccentric characters prevail. So, a simple adulterous liaison in the Barcelona of the 1920s—or, more specifically, at the end of June 1929 during the World Fair, according to my calculations—could almost be seen as a duty for my great-grandmother Dolors.

The Christophers agree to my telling the part of the story that isn't about their bloodline. But they do so too mechanically and without much interest, only to keep the story rolling. They want me to take a leap forward, getting them back to the airport again, but I'm ignoring them because there are some crucial moments that can't be left out. For example, the day my grandfather Conrad turned seventeen, when his mother gave him a wig without his father's knowledge.

That night, when Martí went off to sleep, Dolors took Conrad into the bathroom. She told him to stand still in front of the mirror and keep his eyes shut. Then she placed the wig on his head, covering the bald patch and even some of the hair on the sides of his head. With his eyes closed, Conrad felt as if it was his mother putting a small hat on his head, a beret maybe, but then he could feel her fingers, like a comb running through hair, and he smiled. When he opened his eyes, however, the first impression was one of horror. The person reflected in the mirror wasn't him. He felt ridiculous mainly because the wig was too big—it wasn't made to measure, of course—and it suddenly brought back childhood feelings of anxiety, like the time when Dolors had dressed him up as a hunter-trapper, a sort of Daniel Boone. The photo of that pale, stressed-looking child with a synthetic fox tail wrapped around his head was still lurking in one of the drawers at home like an overlooked prophecy.

Conrad touched the wig and tried to rearrange it. The faint rustle of fake leather made the hairs on the back of his neck stand on end.

"Don't worry, we'll fix it," Dolors said from the mirror. "It just needs a few snips here and there and a bit of something to stick it on. But the color's just like yours."

The picture that my mother has created of her father over the years is that of an idiot, sometimes loveable and sometimes incredibly annoying. She says he didn't know until much later that the wig had belonged to a dead man. Three or four doors down from their apartment in Carrer del Tigre lived a family of espadrille sellers whom my great-grandmother frequently visited. They were older than Dolors and had been a great help to her and her son when Martí Manley was at the front. Once the hard times were over they'd reopened the shop, now well stocked, and they even had a disabled old uncle to keep them company. He'd lost the power of speech after a stroke but, from his corner where he was parked in a well-upholstered armchair, he didn't miss a single detail in the shop. He seemed to follow the conversations with his small bright eyes rather than his ears. He was a bachelor with the ill-concealed mannerisms of a coy young lady, as his relatives admitted, but little was known of his life because he'd always been something of a rebel. He'd been a bohemian, and vain about his appearance before his stroke, and enjoyed reminiscing about his nights of absinthe and cabaret with his friend, the artist Santiago Rusiñol. His relatives looked after him in the hope (illusory) that some hidden inheritance would be revealed when he died—a painting of hanging gardens, a drawing of a languid woman, or some unpublished play by his friend—and every morning, to make him happy before taking him down to the shop, they dressed him up in a suit and tie and put on the wig he'd always worn. Even toward the end of his life, when he was increasingly senile, the mute old man in the armchair still had a proud and dignified bearing, a presence that fascinated everyone who entered the shop.

The day the wig finally came to perch on Conrad Manley's head was the culmination of my great-grandmother's three-month campaign: three whole months, first of worries, calculations, insinuations, and then direct propositions until she came to an agreement with the espadrille sellers. The old uncle had another stroke, this time more serious, and the doctor warned his family that there wasn't much hope. He was sleeping all the time and could barely move, so they stopped taking him down to the shop. He's only got a few days, his family whispered, but the few days dragged on and multiplied. Dolors offered to look after the sick man on Fridays and Saturdays when there was more work in the shop. They no longer bothered to put on his wig and, left alone with him, she studied him on the sly, measuring his cranium with all the fervor of a phrenologist.

As agreed, once the uncle was dead and buried, the wig was the relatives' reward to Dolors for all her help. She'd confided her plan to them, and they were pleased to give it to her. If Conrad wore it, they said, a bit of their poor uncle would still be alive.

Although he didn't wear it for very long, Conrad never forgot that first wig. He talked about it in the same way you remember your first dog: its way of fawning over you, letting itself be stroked, its utter devotion, and the strange pain you experienced when it died—an untimely death of course. But Conrad's first wig was more than good company. It gave him security. On Saturday nights and Sunday afternoons he'd go out on the town with his friends. They'd walk down Carrer Viladomat to Paral·lel, go into some bar with table soccer or hang around outside the Arnau Theatre an hour before the variety show began, checking out all the dancers and leading ladies who went in through the back entrance. Conrad and his friends knew who they were from their photos hanging next to the entrance, listed them according to their charms and hypothetically shared them out. It didn't take much to imagine

them stripped of their loose-fitting everyday clothes, squeezed into
sheer body stockings, their nakedness covered with sequins and
strategically draped boas, and a feathery cap on their heads. Of the
whole group, Conrad was the only one who dared to venture an indiscreet remark or a whistle of admiration, which the girls tended
to respond to with a disdainful smile. That adolescent boldness
was the opposite of the faintheartedness that, only half an hour
before, had been such a source of anguish to him at home when he
told his parents he was going out with his friends. Without looking
at him, Martí emitted an indifferent good-bye from his armchair.
Dolors gave him a kiss and a wink and furtively patted his shirt.
This was their secret. Closeted in his room, Conrad had tucked
the wig under his shirt, making sure it didn't bulge. Once in the
street, having walked far enough away from his neighborhood to
feel safe—the hair tickling his stomach with every step—he went
into a café and asked if he could use the men's room. After locking the door, he put on the wig and tidied it up with a few strokes
of the comb. He knew the movements by heart since he'd repeated
them so often and, out in the street again, with his newly acquired
self-esteem, he was close to being a different person.

Since Conrad couldn't bear the idea of his father seeing him
in disguise, he and his mother resigned themselves to enduring
this life of fearful deceit, furtive wigs, and café men's rooms for
years, until Martí died or, if they were unlucky, until some client remarked on it in the barber's shop, unwittingly setting off a
bomb. Nevertheless, the happy ending came long before anyone
imagined: my great-grandfather kicked the bucket alone and unnoticed one Saturday evening when his son had been wearing the
dead neighbor's wig for two years, and, except for him, the whole
neighborhood was party to the secret.

It would have been eight o'clock at night. He'd closed up the
barbershop and spent some time replenishing the bottles of Floïd
aftershave, just as he did every week. When he applied the lotion he put on a great show, patting it briskly on his clients' faces,
flapping a towel to fan them if they complained it was stinging,
and they all believed this was a proper massage. In fact, my great-

grandfather used a concoction he bought wholesale. A chemist in Poble-Sec distilled it in his own garage, and every few weeks Martí climbed up to the foot of Montjuïc with two empty five-liter glass flagons. It seems that the blend achieved by the Poble-Sec chemist was very similar to the real Floïd, the main difference being that the counterfeit aftershave contained more pure alcohol.

When Dolors found him that Saturday at midnight, Martí was lying dead on the floor with his mouth twisted and eyes wide open. At his side lay one of the flagons, smashed to smithereens. The fake Floïd had spread across the floor, infusing the premises with its virile sickly-sweet fragrance.

"It stinks like the boxers' changing rooms at El Price," remarked one of the Civil Guards supervising the death scene. "At least the gentleman's had a perfumed death. Every cloud has a silver lining . . ."

The forensic surgeon determined the cause of death as alcohol poisoning and cardiac arrest but no one ever found out what really killed Martí, the heart attack or excessive inhalation of his dodgy aftershave. Whatever the cause, it's a pity it was all so prosaic because, in hindsight, a frenzied death in a fit of rage after discovering the secret kept from him by his wife and son would have suited him better. I imagine a completely over-the-top scene, something hammed up by a bunch of amateur dramatics enthusiasts. I see my great-grandfather coming home from the café one Saturday evening—no need to change the day—walking past the La Paloma dance hall in Carrer del Tigre. I see Conrad, who's about to go inside with his friends, and I see the famous wig on his head, gleaming and drunk with hair spray. I see Martí looking at that head of hair from a distance with certain professional admiration and how, closer up, he sees that it's fake. His look, now one of revulsion, goes from the mane of hair to the face of the wig's owner, and then he realizes that it's Conrad, his son. I see the veins in his neck swelling and his eyes popping out of his head. I see how his legs and his whole body start trembling when he goes up to him from behind, reaching out his hand to tear the wig off. Now I see Conrad's look of surprise when he turns around, I see how the wig flies after being grabbed by Martí, and I see Conrad's hands at his father's throat. And when the man falls to the ground, suffocated by his son, I hear the famous last words from a mouth twisted in a grimace as he loses consciousness: "Never trust a man who wears a wig!"

"Facts! Facts! Get to the airport!"

My brothers are complaining again because I'm having a ball inventing amazing death scenes. They're all worked up, shouting (as if they'd never blathered on) and demanding that I get to the point. Cool it, Christophers, I'm wrapping it up now. My great-grandmother Dolors didn't cry much over Martí's demise, just shed a few tears when receiving condolences and that's it. When the death notices were distributed around the neighborhood, the news spread fast and the apartment filled up with barbers from the guild and clients who came to pay their last respects. Conrad had also hung up a notice saying "Closed Owing to Bereavement" on the door of the barber's shop. No one knows whether he was devastated or happy.

Some memorable moments from the wake have been passed down to us thanks to Dolors's reminiscences. The barbers' guild printed an obituary notice to be distributed around the neighborhood and other barber's shops. Under my great-grandfather's name, like a family shield, they'd placed an emblem consisting of crossed scissors and comb. The former barber's shop owner, for whom Martí was a disciple, asked to view the body. He wept when they opened up the coffin but, seeing Martí lying there before him, couldn't resist whisking a tortoiseshell comb from his pocket and tidying up the corpse's venerable forelock, which was starting to wilt. It seems that there were mutterings about the funeral too. Conrad had at first decided to attend wigless in deference to his father's memory, but my great-grandmother was a very stubborn woman and didn't let up until she convinced him to wear it. After all, Martí was dead, and Conrad's wishes came first now. Martí's barber friends considered it a provocation, and, coming out of the

Our Lady of Carmen Church to express their condolences to the family, some of them looked askance at the wig, unable to disguise their contempt and anger.

This happened in 1949 when my grandfather was twenty years old. Now he only needed the reason for my mother's birth. Martí's sudden death was a big relief to Conrad and, as they say, he never had to take his wig off again. Three months after the uncomfortable funeral, and with the black mourning armband still in place on his left arm, Conrad sold his father's shampooing equipment, the mirrors, and the chairs to a barber who was setting up in Carrer Tallers, and opened a wig shop in the former barbershop.

He called it "New Samson Wigs," and it sent shockwaves through the neighborhood. In the early days, Conrad received several anonymous letters threatening to scalp him of his leather pelt just like Indians did to palefaces in John Wayne films. The former owner of the barbershop, who now felt like an abandoned orphan with no chance of getting free haircuts in any other establishment, kicked up a huge fuss about this "betrayal of history" and demanded that Conrad return his signed photograph. The parish priest of the Our Lady of Carmen Church, in Carrer Sant Antoni, a faithful servant of the National Movement, stalked into the shop one afternoon and, with a crow-like expression of disdain and in a sinuous voice that would do justice to a Richelieu, informed him that the name of the shop was heresy, maybe even anathema or cause for excommunication. Conrad explained that, quite the contrary, the reference to Samson was his homage to the Holy Scriptures, and he won the day by promising the priest free wigs for Jesus and the apostles when the Easter Week procession came around.

In their zeal to erase any trace of Martí, Conrad and his mother transformed the old barbershop from top to bottom. It was as if the cut hair that was once been strewn around the floor had colonized every corner of the place: There were wigs in the front window, majestically crowning the heads of mannequins that looked like royal busts, wigs on the shelves, wigs on the work table ready to be combed, wigs of every size, with golden curls, long jet-black tresses, or white powdered hair. The only thing mother and son had failed to eliminate was the cloying smell of fake Floïd, which, since the Saturday of Martí's demise, had seeped into the walls. Despite all the changes, the odd absentminded client occasionally wandered in and asked for Martí. In his wig palace, Conrad had toughened up, and he couldn't stand being reminded of the old days so, brandishing whatever wig he happened to be working on right then, like a guillotined head, or Samson's locks in the hands of Delilah, he went berserk and kicked him out, yelling from the door, "Here we don't keep anybody's hair. Here we sell hair!"

In that 1950s city of soot and rags, in that diminished and fearful city called Barcelona, most people saw the New Samson wig shop as an extravagance that would soon be pulling down its shutters for once and for all, but, just when it had lost the gleam of novelty and people forgot all about it—when it blurred into the life of the street—business started to pick up. Conrad was affable to the point of being unctuous and, once he'd sussed out what kind of client he was dealing with, whether the person was timid or vain, he'd come out with one of his lines.

"As I always say, every wig in this shop has a head waiting for it."

"Well, we're not meant to go around with our heads exposed to the elements."

"Whatever way you look at it, a wig makes a gentleman."

One October morning, the props manager from the Romea Theatre turned up to buy wigs and false beards for *Don Juan Tenorio*, which was opening on All Saints' Day. They were very happy with Conrad's service, and the word got around in the profession. The theatres on Paral·lel soon became regular clients of New Samson. The dandies who'd once come to Martí's barbershop for trims now returned to the shop, less conceited and more decrepit, sneaking in as if they were smuggling something and asking for a toupee to cover up their incipient bald spots. The same variety show stars that Conrad and his friends had spied on at the Arnau or El Molino now came to buy hair extensions for a number starring the Queen of Sheba surrounded by a gang of Solomons in diaphanous tunics, or for shows featuring some innocent little Valkyrie who, covering her bosom with long blond ringlets all the way to her waist, laid waste to a risqué song. With trembling hands and trying to stay calm, Conrad Manley combed their tresses in front of a mirror but, come Saturday, he put on a show of bravado for his friends, telling them tall stories that sounded like vaudeville scripts. Dolors, who kept him company in the shop in the afternoons, watched him attending to the girls and detected his lustful thoughts. Once they were alone, she tried to flush them out.

"If you want my advice, son, don't get tangled up with one of those little ninnies. What sort of a woman gets up at midday and drinks champagne for breakfast?"

Conrad leaped to their defense. "I'll listen to all the advice you want to give, Mother, but you know the client's always right." As he got to know them better, he'd discovered that behind their capricious façades these women were simple, rather unsophisticated girls who giggled at everything and were easy to talk to. They'd come from places like Úbeda, Ponferrada, or Albarracín and their worldly airs were nothing but a shield.

In any case, Dolors's advice was futile, and Conrad finally fell into the claws of one such aspiring chorus girl. Her name was Leonor Carratalà, Leo, "a lioness seeking a tamer," as she liked to present herself, and she'd come from Alcoi to triumph on Paral·lel. Her father owned a hatter's shop, which Conrad took as an omen.

"Everyone knows that wigs and hats form a lasting alliance. There's nothing like a good Panama hat, a straw hat, or a top hat to ensure the stability of a wig," Conrad explained to his mother the day he introduced Leo.

Conrad courted Leo for some months under Dolors's inquisitorial eye. The mother dreaded the day when she'd be gathering up the gnawed bones of a son who'd been devoured by a lioness. She only breathed freely again when they announced they were getting married. Leo left the stage, the boas, and the dance steps—it seems she wasn't very good—and reserved her cabaret numbers for conjugal nights.

The photos that Rita has kept of the two of them are eccentric, even charming: a bow-legged, tense-looking little man with something like a newly landed flying saucer on his head standing next to a good-looking, buxom, wide-eyed woman several inches taller than he is. They might be the doppelgangers of Secret Agent 86—Maxwell Smart—and his wife.

"In a nutshell, my father was a pain in the neck and my mother a nitwit who did whatever he wanted," Rita says when I force her to look at the photos. "They were only wig sellers but they had such airs and graces. Their feet never touched the ground. Dad said he'd fallen in love with Mom because she looked like Hedy Lamarr, who'd played Delilah in one of those old films. As if he bore the slightest resemblance to Victor Mature! There were times when their inanity was funny but, I assure you, there were other times when it was unbearable, especially for a spoilt brat like me. Anyway, perhaps they were made for each other. So it makes sense that they died together."

On days like this my mother talks as if her life had been suspended in that April of 1967 when she'd just turned sixteen, as if she hadn't known what to do with it after that. She's back in her adolescent bedroom where we left her before, lying in bed, flipping through the latest issue of *Garbo*. Rita Manley Carratalà is turning the pages. Her parents Conrad and Leo are packing their bags. Meanwhile, Christophers, if you want, while they're saying good-bye, we can fill in the first sixteen years of Rita's life. (The Christophers are ecstatic but perhaps they're being ironic.) Let's begin then.

*1950.* Conrad and Leo get married in the Our Lady of Carmen Church. Three days earlier Leo makes her last appearance in the Victòria Theatre where she's a dancer in the show *Madness of Love*.

*1951.* Rita is born nine months later, almost certainly conceived in a Peníscola hotel. Fatal coincidences: my great-grandmother Dolors dies a week later (shower, slips).

*1953.* The wig sales continue apace. My grandparents buy new dining-room furniture. On Sundays they have lunch in a restaurant and go on excursions to Sant Joan les Fonts or, at Corpus Christi, to Sitges.

*1956.* Rita Manley Carratalà starts school, instructed by Sacred Heart nuns.

*1964.* Young people have long hair but it doesn't affect New Samson. On the contrary, Conrad prefers to think that all those hairy people are turning up their noses at the barbers. It won't be too many years before a couple of them, seborrheic singers, turn up at the shop looking for a wig to cover their premature baldness.

*1967.* April. For the first time in its history, New Samson closes for holidays, taking in the Easter break. Conrad Manley and his wife Leo Carratalà are going to Paris. They are booked into a room at the Ritz in Place Vendôme, and are going on a tourist trip around the City of Light. The Louvre, Versailles, the Seine by *bateau-mouche*. Then, after kissing them good-bye, their daughter Rita hears the front door closing. She's still leafing listlessly through the latest issue of *Garbo*.

~

Rita kept leafing listlessly through the latest issue of *Garbo*. It was ten o'clock Saturday morning, and she didn't know how to start spending her new-found freedom. The extraordinarily agreeable silence of the apartment urged her to stay in bed till midday. She could go back to sleep if she wanted, and, this time, her mother wouldn't wake her up with the fuss she usually made on Saturdays—a symphony of raised blinds, dazzled protest, and screechy scolding. She tested her new situation by lazing around a bit more but eventually decided that she had to tell someone about it. She got out of bed and went to the table by the front door to phone her friend Raquel. As she was asking for the number from the operator she saw, lying next to the telephone, an envelope showing the name of a travel agency. She dropped the receiver back in its cradle, opened the envelope, and found her parents' tickets inside: "Flight IB 1190. Barcelona-Paris," she read. She cried out in surprise. She was barefoot and could feel the coldness of the tiles rising up, paralyzing her legs. She tried to work out how she could fix things, but the mere idea that her parents would miss the flight and mess up her week banished all possible thinking. Then she heard keys in the lock, and the door was flung open. It was Conrad. His face was contorted, lopsided, which always happened when he was in a state. Drops of sweat squeezed out from under the Alain Delon wig and ran down his temples.

"We were at Plaça d'Espanya, and the taxi had to turn around!" he shouted. "What a disaster!"

Before Rita could say a word, he grabbed the tickets from her hand and shot off again without closing the door.

"Hurry. You've still got time," she called from the landing. "Bon voyage."

"Oh, oh, oh, oh, oh . . .!"

The hysterical wails of her father faded away in echoes rising up the stairwell. Rita shut the door proprietarily. Now the apartment was hers and hers alone. She returned to her room without phoning Raquel and flopped on her bed. The image of her parents making a scene in the taxi came to her and, as on so many other occasions, she saw them as a couple of twits. The conventional, drab world of their house contrasted with the elegance and good taste she rediscovered in *Garbo* every week. Tony Franciosa, Ira von Fürstenberg, Sylvie Vartan, and Princess Soraya hadn't been a good influence on her with their breezy responses to intrusive questions or their willingness to be photographed on the beaches of the Côte d'Azur. Rita was tormented by images of her parents wandering around the streets of Paris. She pictured them losing their way, or sitting in some modestly luxurious restaurant while Conrad, who thought he spoke French because he could say "seevooplay," asked for the menu with the minidictionary in his hand like the buffoon that he was.

As an antidote to these thoughts, Rita went back to leafing through the magazine. In its first pages, a soothsayer called Argos offered his weekly horoscope in two parts, His and Hers. She looked up her sign first—Cancer, the "Hers" part—and read the text. Argos recommended that she shouldn't give up hope—a generalization, certainly,—and then declared that her week was clearly going to be very rich in affection and gifts. Rita took this mumbo jumbo very personally and then went to check what was happening with her parents. She'd always been amused by the fact that her mother, who was called Leo, should be a Leo. The horoscope was so vehement and apocalyptic that it startled her. "Jupiter is, right now, vexed with you ladies. Be as pleasant as possible. Avoid all family misunderstandings. Do not write. Keep away from anyone who might depress you. Do not travel." The final warning made a terrible impression on Rita and, to allay it, to shoo it out of her mind, she turned the page and looked up Conrad's sign, Gemini, the "His" section. It said: "Period of instability that you will manage with your prompt initiative. Avoid anything that could agitate you or upset you. Do not get discouraged. Ask your loved ones for advice. Enjoy yourself but without traveling far." The two horoscopes fitted together like two halves of an orange.

"This Argos must be joking," Rita told herself, and the fear that had frozen her blood for a couple of minutes slowly melted into the silence enfolding her. One of her neighbors who'd set about spring cleaning started to sing one of Adamo's songs, about putting his hands on somebody's waist.

*Y mis manos en tu cintura . . .*

As so often happens, as soon as adolescence hit, Rita had begun to scorn the boundless love of her parents. She needed space to breathe and so ripped apart the family cocoon. The same antics that had her roaring with laughter as a little girl, when Conrad used to play their special game with his wig, putting it on back to front or doffing it like a hat to greet her, now seemed so childish and corny that just thinking about it made her cringe. Leo's solicitousness when she had to do her homework (not nagging like other mothers, and even helping her), or her tenacity in taking her daughter's side against Conrad when Rita wanted more fashionable clothes—advantages that had made her daughter stand out from her friends some years earlier—had, more recently, started to look like signs of weakness—a weakness that Rita exploited. Rita's inner life needed these minimal insurrections for its own survival and, on her more negative days, she succumbed to an ardent desire that her parents would suddenly die, both of them together. That they'd leave her to her own devices. Once the funeral was over, and the weeping done, she'd know how to take care of herself. These thoughts usually took the form of a euphoric but rather vague whim and were soon banished with a good dose of down-to-earth guilt. However, that Saturday morning, the coincidence of the horoscopes let her shrug off the guilt and play more freely with the idea. The stars have predicted it, she told herself.

Back in bed, Rita tried to get up but sloth got the better of her. Then, to banish her parents from her mind and feel she was part of the glittery world depicted in the magazine, she did something she remembered playfully years later: She took off her nightdress. The warmth of the sheets had her skin tingling with excitement.

I know that, for once, you won't ask me to spare the details, Christophers, but I can't get under the sheets with that ingenuous, wayward, naked Rita because even then, somehow, she was already my mother (the future is contained in the past, they say) so we'd be verging on incest, even if it's only literary incest. And although nothing scandalizes today's Rita, the Rita of those days might feel offended by so much disclosure. I'll only say that, after a while, her eyelids began to droop and she went back to sleep. The wished-for death of her parents was diluted in the ether of her dreams.

Three hours went by. In those days, winter Saturdays in Barcelona advanced with the muffled calm of a geriatric home. Occasionally, the snuffling of a blocked vacuum cleaner two floors down or the sharp crack of a motorbike with fouled spark plugs in the street broke the silence for an instant and then accentuated it further. When Rita woke up hungry, with a rumbling belly, it took her half a minute to relocate herself in the world: This was her room, she was naked, and she was alone. She yawned three times in quick succession, cutting short the third one when a glance at her alarm clock revealed how late it was. She felt gleefully rebellious and undisciplined.

When I ask my mother to share those moments with me—she gets out of bed, walks around the apartment naked and confident, has breakfast and then a shower—she always says that they come back in a blur, as if everything happened underwater, in the depths of the sea, or behind frosted glass. It's not surprising. Before getting under the shower, Rita turned on a portable radio that Conrad kept on one of the bathroom shelves. Every morning he shaved to the eight o'clock news on Radio Nacional, and Rita had to tune into another station to find some music. After a while she emerged from the bathtub—one of those old-fashioned truncated ones with a ledge—and dried her hair with a towel. The steamed-up mirror offered a foggy reflection of her face. And then, in the middle of this vapor-filled atmosphere, the announcer interrupted a song for an urgent newsflash.

"By courtesy of Kelvinator and the program 'I Like Life!' we now bring you an important news bulletin. A few minutes ago at Barcelona's El Prat Airport, and due to circumstances that are as yet unexplained"—the voice announced, suddenly mournful—"an Iberian Airlines aircraft left the runway as it was taking off and caught fire after colliding with a delivery truck. According to airport sources, the flight concerned was Iberia 1190 with the destination of Paris Orly Airport in France. It is not yet known whether there are any survivors. The airline company, now working with the Red Cross, has asked relatives and all those affected to contact the authorities at the following telephone number..."

From those blurry moments Rita is only able to recall one detail with any precision: In the midst of the chaos, the impact of the news, and as her eyes filled with tears, she wrote the telephone number in the condensed steam on the bathroom mirror so she wouldn't forget it. Some minutes later, as the numbers were dripping away, she called Iberia and shrieked the names of her parents.

"Excuse me, could you spell your father's name, young lady?" a Red Cross voice asked. "*N* for Navarra...*A* for Alicante..."

"No, no! Manley! Conrado Manley. With *M*...for mortal, *A*...for accident, *N*...for...nobody..."

2

# In the Cage

Instead of their romantic dream holiday in Paris, Conrad and Leo's destination was the Montjuïc cemetery of Barcelona, a humbler but equally beautiful Père Lachaise. Christophers, if you feel like visiting it some day (and it's only a suggestion), ask for section one at the entrance and then look for the tombs of the anarchists Durruti and Ascaso. Turn to face the landscape of pines and trucks dissolving in a haze of sea mist with the commercial port in the background. Then walk twenty meters to your right and you'll find the niche containing the coffins of my maternal grandparents. Read the tombstone: Those names and dates are their only material presence in this world because almost nothing was left of their bodily trappings—as the spiritualists might say—after the accident.

My mother says that a dozen people died and about a hundred were injured. In those days planes didn't have black boxes so the official version of events was constructed from the testimony of survivors—the pilots among them—and data supplied by the control tower. The authorities established that, just when the plane began accelerating to take off, a tire burst and the plane skidded across the runway. The pilot managed to regain control by reducing the speed but, at the last minute when it seemed that the whole thing was going to be no more than a fright, its tail end hit a tanker that appeared from nowhere. It all seemed to happen in slow motion, but the plane broke in two as a result of the impact—a clean break, as if chopped by a guillotine—and the tail immediately burst into flames. "Amid general hysteria," the journalists reported, "the explosion instantly engulfed the unfortunate passengers sitting in the rear seats." Grandfather Conrad, on the advice of some know-all neighbor, had moved heaven and earth to make sure that he and my grandmother were sitting in the tail section. "He says it's the safest place because it's farthest from the engines. This business of aerodynamics is very complicated," he pronounced, trying to reassure himself.

The first phone call after she came out of the shower gave Rita little cause for hope. Choosing her words carefully, the woman from the Red Cross told her not to despair but her parents' names were on the list of more-than-probable victims. Rita provided the necessary details and waited for news. Confined to her room out of some sort of superstition, she lay on her bed listening to the radio. The phone rang several times, but she had neither the will nor the strength to take any more calls. Some hours later two policemen knocked at the door. It may sound like a cliché, but my mother remembers them as a pair of grim old men in crumpled uniforms, with the mandatory moustaches. One, apparently the more affable of the two, spoke to her in a fluting, childlike voice, informing her that her parents had been in a plane accident at the airport and that, as she now knew, they'd "gone to heaven." Rita had spent the whole afternoon telling herself she had to be strong, but the policeman's words made her feel like a little girl, and she started to cry.

They did their best to console her. They offered her a handkerchief, stroked her hair, and told her she had to be a big strong girl. Rita was sixteen, and it was clear she was no longer a little girl. She was secretly cringing with embarrassment for everyone, her parents included. She resolutely dried her tears, for which the policemen were grateful. The other one, hard-boiled and with a gruffer voice, opened up a folder, took out a sheet of paper, and asked her if she had any brothers or sisters. No. Grandparents? No. Uncles or aunts? No. With each negative response, the good cop's eyes grew misty. Distant relatives? Couldn't she remember the name of some distant relative, even if they hadn't met for years? There was no one, of course there was no one, but Rita suddenly realized that the question had the anxious ring of a last chance. When she hesitated for a few seconds, the good cop urged her on, reminding her that she was still a minor and that she couldn't be left alone under these circumstances. There had to be somebody.

"I've got a great-aunt who lives in Sagunto," she lied. She chose Sagunto because she recalled that her grandparents had lived there years before. "She's very old, but I phoned her this afternoon and she's arriving by train tomorrow at midday."

The lie worked, and the policemen heaved a sigh of relief. They then asked her for a photograph of her parents and took her to Raquel's, her best friend's house. In recent months she'd slept there a couple of Saturday nights, and Leo and Raquel's mother used to shop at the same stalls at the market. For Rita, the following days passed as if she were acting in a play. She remembers the show of mourning, the black clothes, the outpouring of sympathy, and how neighbours and friends fussed over her. Raquel's parents treated her like a daughter, taking care of the formal procedures of grieving, and her friend behaved like a jealous sister.

Since they had to wait for official confirmation of the deaths, the funeral didn't take place until the Friday, six days after the accident. On the Thursday, the two policemen came back and handed Rita a document signed by the judge and covered with official seals. Then they asked her an odd question.

"Now, dear, could you tell us whether, on the day of the unfortunate event, your daddy was wearing a wig or a hairpiece?"

It happened that the only vestige of Conrad left after the crash was a scrap of his Alain Delon wig. The passengers' luggage was burned in the crash or destroyed in the ensuing chaos but, several hours later, when the on-site investigators were trying to recover human remains that might help them to identify the victims, a fireman found a small piece of the wig. It was eighty meters from the wreckage, stuck to a charred patch of tarmac. He picked the thing up very carefully, believing at first that it was skin with hair on it, but when it was subsequently analyzed in the laboratory they found it was synthetic skin. Rita never got to see the singed tuft, but that final scrap of paternal vanity inspired her to pay one last tribute to her parents. One of the few decisions Conrad had taken with an eye to the future, and for which Leo always scolded him, had been to sign up for a life insurance policy with Union and Phoenix. There were no bodies to bury but, since the coffins and funerals had been paid for in advance, Rita wanted a proper ceremony. Just before the two empty caskets were taken from the apartment to the Saint Lazarus chapel where the funeral Mass was to be celebrated, she took her father's collection of wigs and arranged them carefully in the upholstered interior of his coffin. There were ten all told, including the first one, which looked like a cross between a crash helmet and a trapper's cap, and the splendid wig he'd bought for his wedding day. Thus displayed, they were like an exhibition representing the different stages of his life. Then, to honor her mother, she cut out a photo of Hedy Lamarr and Victor Mature from one of her back issues of *Garbo* and placed it inside Leo's coffin. The new Samson and Delilah.

After the funeral, Rita took stock of the fact that she was all alone in the world. Now that it was imposed on her, the wish she had so often flirted with, longing for it to come true, suddenly lost its charm. She was the perfect orphan, and it took her more than a year to get used to her new circumstances. When she finally did, she was a different person.

The big blow was dealt by her father. Not wanting to go to university, Rita had left school at fifteen. Since then, she'd hung around at home claiming she was seeking her vocation in the various courses she'd enrolled for, including teach-yourself knitting, teach-yourself French, and a correspondence course for congress and trade fair hostesses. She was so spoiled that everything bored her. However, the deaths of Conrad and Leo put an end to her idleness, and at nine o'clock one morning she opened up the doors of New Samson.

"Neither of my parents left a will, and I inherited the business, didn't I? So the most logical thing was for me to take the helm," Rita recalled years later. "All the fuss of the first few days bewildered me, and then it spurred me on. I'd helped out in the shop on occasion, but now I had to deal with all the ins and outs of the trade by myself. Clients came to pick up their orders, and I had to move half the storeroom to find them. The suppliers took advantage of my inexperience to palm off stock. Inside those four walls my father's voice droned on, giving me nonstop advice. 'The secret is to comb the wigs every day so they sit proudly on the heads of the mannequins,' he said. 'It's very important to make sure that men, especially the older ones, lose their fear of trying on a wig. Leave them alone in front of the mirror. Give them privacy.' I was so baffled and worried the first two weeks that I didn't have time to decide whether I liked the work or not. The only thing I knew for sure was that when I cashed up before going home in the evening the numbers never squared. I studied the notebook where my father wrote down all the sales and purchases and didn't understand the first thing. 'You'll have to take on an accountant,' I reassured myself. One Friday, a formally dressed man with a briefcase— a salesman, I thought—came into the shop and, luckily (I can say it now), that was the end of it. It turned out that the gentleman wasn't a salesman but a solicitor. He introduced himself and asked to see Senyor Conrad Manley. I told him that my father and mother had died very recently. He looked at me doubtfully. 'This isn't a joke, is it?' I said no, it wasn't. I was Conrad Manley's daughter, and I was running the business now. He expressed his condolences and, looking even more serious, held out a piece of paper and then dealt the blow, 'Senyoreta Manley, I suggest you find a good lawyer. I understand that you are in no way to blame, but your father, with all due respect, was a swindler. You will be served with the summons very soon.'"

Oh, grandfather Conrad, what an imposter he was! Calling him a swindler, Christophers, is giving him kudos he doesn't deserve. It would be more to the point to call him a bullshitter or even an utter crackpot. Rita was never really scared of her father. She knew him too well, but she had grown up with the fits of temper and attacks of fanaticism that would consume him for several days, after which he'd forget all about it with equal fervor.

"Actually, I was a chip off the old block if you think about my fixation with starting dozens of correspondence courses and never finishing any," Rita admits. "Completely out of the blue, for example, he'd get it into his head to make yogurt, and he'd fill the fridge with fermenting cultures. Or he'd spend a couple of weeks sending letters to all the newspapers complaining about the terrible state of the streets. Then there was a time when he sat down in front of the typewriter every night to work on his memoirs (which didn't get past page twenty but he already had the title: *Not a Dumb Hair on His Head*)."

A few days later, when the subpoena was delivered, Rita went to Raquel's house and told her parents what had happened. Raquel's father, who worked in a bank, found her a lawyer the following day. That afternoon they both came to New Samson to study the account books, the summons, and the suppliers' bills of the past few months. Rita could hear them discussing the situation and arguing as they did the sums in the little office at the back. When they finally came out, the compassion on their faces betrayed them.

The two gentlemen explained to Rita what the figures revealed. The wig business had been heading for disaster for more than four months. Instead of looking for a reasonable solution, Conrad had opted for suicidal folly: He'd asked for a loan from the bank and had put up the shop as collateral. Maybe he'd intended to clear up his debts but, from what they'd seen, he hadn't settled a single one. He'd spent almost half his remaining money on plane tickets and the hotel reservation in Paris. A travel agency bill they'd found crumpled up in the waste paper basket confirmed their suspicions.

Conrad, as I've said, was impetuous, one of those people who is always all over the place, but this time his mental mayhem had got the upper hand. You could, perhaps, appreciate the touch of sick irony: The famous wholesaler who, he claimed, had invited them to Paris was in fact his biggest creditor.

The lawyer's conclusion was that Rita was set to lose everything. On his advice, therefore, she sold as much as she could, at a loss, before the month was out. An amateur dramatics group took the wigs, practically as a gift. A junk dealer from Carrer Tamarit bore off the furniture, the shelves, the mannequins, and the New Samson sign (and two decades later, in the early nineties, its luminous letters turned up at the Miró Foundation as part of an installation by a conceptual artist). By the time the judge ordered the premises to be sealed and handed over to the creditor bank, the space was only a nostalgic memory for a few nearby residents and clients, first as Martí Manley's barbershop and then as Conrad Manley's antagonistic New Samson. When she surrendered the keys to the bank officials, Rita wondered what would have happened to New Samson and to her and her parents after they returned from the trip to Paris. What would have become of them? What calamities would Conrad's follies have brought about? A subversive idea, this time unintentional, began to take shape in her mind. Maybe the accident was a blessing in disguise.

Meanwhile, in order to escape being sent to an orphanage, Rita had cultivated and embellished the lies surrounding her great-aunt from Sagunto. As the days went by, she learned to imagine her and to give her a body, a face, a name (Aunt Matilde). At first, she referred to her in conversations with the neighbors or when she was with Raquel's parents, always portraying her as old and decrepit. "She's got pains in her legs, and only goes out when she's seeing the doctor," Rita declared. "She came here to look after me, and now I'm the one who's looking after her," she claimed. The next step was to give her a voice. She practiced it when she was walking in the street so it would sound more natural at home. Aunt Matilde spoke Spanish and was deaf. Therefore the neighbors could hear her shouting through the open windows of the inside patio. Rita learned to invent conversations, trivial remarks, and even the odd argument. She'd position herself by the open kitchen window and yell, "What shall we have for lunch today, Aunt Matilde?" "Go to the market, dear, and get what we need for a chickpea stew . . . Bring me my purse." If the phone rang, Aunt Matilde sometimes took the call and then handed the receiver to Rita. My mother never told anyone her secret, not even Raquel, as she was convinced that the smallest crack in her story would be her undoing. Anyway, Aunt Matilde kept her company and helped her to stay active and stave off loneliness.

The farce lasted almost six months, until the autumn. Rita got by with the money from the New Samson sales plus some savings that Leo had kept in a drawer just in case, but that didn't amount to much. She knew that when she came of age she'd get the money from the life insurance policy, a considerable sum but, meanwhile, she was poor or, more precisely, needy. Trying not to spend money, she stayed at home getting bored in front of the TV and eating only two meals a day, breakfast and dinner. Her reflection in the mirror stared back frail, wan, and exhausted. In her lowest moments she realized that if this went on much longer she'd be found out. Maybe that was what she needed. Then, when she was on the point of cracking up completely, a surprising stroke of luck stopped the downhill spiral and changed her life.

Her guardian angel was the lawyer who'd informed her about the subpoena. And, yes, we should give his name. After all, although his turning up in the story is circumstantial, he did play a decisive role.

"What was he called, Mom, do you remember?"

"Of course I do. He was called . . . he was called . . . Carlos Bravo. It sounds like a singer's name. But I called him Senyor Bravo. He had an office in Carrer Provença, near Rambla de Catalunya, above the Mauri pastry shop. He wasn't far off retirement."

In his long, arduous journey through the courts, Senyor Bravo had become accustomed to dealing with charlatans and rotters as wily as sewer rats. Rita, the poor young girl who'd been left helpless and alone, was an exception, a victim, and he was fond of her. Not long after New Samson was impounded, Senyor Bravo phoned her one morning and asked her for a few details about her parents. If she gave him permission, he told her, he'd try to get some sort of compensation from Iberia or the airport. After all, somebody had to be responsible for the accident. Rita hung up and discussed it with Aunt Matilde—who told her to light a candle to Saint Rita, her patron saint and granter of impossible wishes—and never gave it another thought. Summer came, the August holidays went by, and one morning at the beginning of September Senyor Bravo phoned again.

"Do you remember me, Senyoreta Manley?" he asked. "Carlos Bravo. I have good news for you, I believe. I've been making some inquiries and telephone calls to see if we can get compensation for what happened to your parents, but we haven't had much luck. Iberia will pay some indemnity for damages, but, I warn you, it's a pitiful sum. It's better than nothing, of course, but I hoped to get you a lot more. In any case, I spoke to the people at the airport's legal services, and, although they're under no obligation to pay anything, they were moved by your case and they've come up with a proposal. It happens that, with the extensions they're doing to the terminal at El Prat, they need to fill some new positions. If you're interested in applying, and I most heartily advise you to do so, you have a job. I don't know what area it is in but they've assured me that the salary is adequate and there are good possibilities for promotion."

Thus it was that, a few months later, just before her seventeenth birthday in January 1968, Rita started work at Barcelona airport. It was a tender age, which possibly worked in her favor since her job was to deal with indignant passengers at the Lost Luggage Office.

As for Aunt Matilde, she packed her bags that very afternoon, and without saying good-bye to anyone, not even to Rita, she went back to Sagunto for the rest of her days.

Thanks, Christophers, for allowing me to rescue these family dramas and antics from oblivion. Scissors and wigs. And now that we've left Rita working at the airport (we're getting closer and closer, as you can see) and with a brighter future ahead of her, we have to go back to Germany again. I know we don't want to return there, but that Saint Valentine's Day morning of February 14, 1972, is calling.

It was snowing heavily again, right? Bundó was asleep. The Pegaso driven by Gabriel was roaring down the motorway . . .

Months later, after he'd met my mother and was still unsure about whether to pick up the pieces of his life, Gabriel poured out the whole story of the disaster. How long must he have been asleep at the wheel? Eight, ten seconds? Ten seconds at the most. Close your eyes and count to ten, Christophers. It's nothing, but it's also an eternity. It was enough for the truck to veer to the right, leave the road and, borne along by the thrust of its downhill run, hurtle about fifteen meters down a wooded slope. Gabriel remembered opening his eyes in the middle of a tremendous din, sounds he'd never heard before, and screaming in terror. The first image he had when he relived that moment was of a torrent of water washing over his face with supernatural force. Before the accident, our father had dreamed one night that he and his friends went off a bridge and fell into a river with the truck. The smashing of glass, the cracking of branches, the rain of mud, the confusion that had sprung from nowhere ... In the accident itself, all these elements eclipsed the nightmare.

When the Pegaso finally came to a halt, in an almost vertical position with the cab squashed underneath, Gabriel took some seconds to get his thoughts together. His left arm, trapped between two creases in the buckled door, sent out the initial jabs of pain. He understood they'd had an accident. Fucking hell, he'd gone to sleep. While his brain was gaining consciousness, his right hand automatically groped for the ignition key and he turned the engine off. A wheel stopped revolving in emptiness. Then he understood the all-pervading silence, the false, intrusive, grotesque silence and immediately realized that Bundó was dead. He couldn't see him. One of his eyes was veiled with blood. He shouted.

"Bundó! Bundó! Wake up! Fuck!"

The right side of the cab was less damaged by the impact. Though his posture looked uncomfortable, Bundó lay with his head resting on the door, the way he usually slept. Eyes closed. Three or four small cuts on his face were bleeding. Only one detail was different: the strange position of his neck, an impossible angle. Gabriel shook his friend's body three or four times. Submitting to defeat, he clutched Bundó's hand, trying to transmit life to him. Then he, too, was still.

He didn't deserve anything more.

Incomprehensible shouts, coming closer and closer, briefly shook him from his concussion and kept him hazily awake.

Thank goodness for the snow, Christophers. It was seven o'clock in the morning and there wasn't much traffic. A minute after the Pegaso left the road, a Turk driving a worn-out Mercedes understood the meaning of the lines traced by wheels on snow-covered asphalt. For some kilometers, for safety's sake, he'd been trying to keep his wheels on the thick constant tracks made by the truck's tires, but the straightness of the two parallel lines suddenly ended, swerving gracefully off toward the hard shoulder and disappearing into nothingness. He braked in time, resisting the impulse to follow the lines to the end, and stopped his car by the side of the road. Then he saw the wreck of the Pegaso beneath him, a dark patch smoking among the trees, and he ran down along the path the truck had opened up.

"*Alles in Ordnung? Hören Sie mich? Sagen Sie was!*"

In the retelling, Gabriel wasn't sure whether he lost consciousness at this point, but the last thing he remembered from inside the truck was the face of this man, shocked, or numb with cold, looking at him through the window with his head upside down, opening his mouth to say something. The next thing he knew he was on the motorway, in an ambulance, surrounded by cars and emergency lights. A male nurse from the Red Cross was immobilizing his left arm—broken in two places near the elbow—and another one was cleaning the wounds on his face and neck with alcohol-soaked cotton balls. His forehead, nose, and one cheek were scored all over with scratches and cuts from shards of glass. The circumspect silence of the two nurses presaged the terrible news but, lying on the stretcher on his way to hospital, he asked one of the nurses about Bundó.

"*Mein Freund?*"

The nurse shook his head.

He spent all that day and the next in a hospital in Kassel. First they took X-rays of his arm and set it in a cast. Then they kept him under observation. Frankfurt wasn't far away, and we don't know if he thought about phoning Sigrun or not. The fact is he didn't. As I see it, Christophers, if he had phoned her we probably wouldn't have come to this point, which we can now interpret as the very first sign of Gabriel's long period of inactivity. Meanwhile, another ambulance had taken Bundó along the motorway to the hospital morgue. A crane had recovered the wreckage of the poor Pegaso, and the German police checked the vehicle's papers. They identified the transport company, phoned Barcelona, and informed Senyor Casellas of the accident.

Halfway through the afternoon when Gabriel was starting to feel cut off from everything, he was visited by the secretary of the Spanish consulate in Frankfurt. The man looked familiar. They'd done his move a couple of years earlier. After expressing his condolences over Bundó's death, the secretary informed him that the consul—another former client of La Ibérica—had received a call from Senyor Casellas asking for help and advice. Naturally, Senyor Casellas wished to convey his support, express his sympathy because he knew Bundó was Gabriel's best friend—and wish him a swift recovery. The secretary also informed him of some practical matters. The consulate had arranged for the German branch of La Ibérica's insurance company to take charge of the wreckage of the truck, which was a complete write-off. If the doctors confirmed that he had no internal injuries, as they hoped, they'd reserved a seat for him on a Lufthansa flight from Frankfurt to Barcelona the day after next, on February 16th, in the morning. If he had no objection, the body of Senyor Scrafí Bundó would be repatriated on the same flight and, needless to say, the consulate, prepared for such matters, would also supply an emergency coffin for the occasion.

Gabriel heard the secretary out, agreeing mechanically or answering in monosyllables. Although he hated the situation he was in, the pen-pusher's diplomatic smoothness was a help. The painkillers they'd given him were making him groggy, and his brain was grateful for the rest. Not thinking. Letting go. When the consular underling had taken his leave, however, memory crept into the lonely hospital room. When the secretary and his family had moved to Frankfurt, the three La Ibérica movers had mislaid a bag containing sports clothing. The shared booty was meager, mainly tracksuits, sneakers, tennis socks that nobody wanted, and swimming goggles. Although it was hardly his size, Bundó got it into his head that he wanted an apparently brand-new and aristocratic-looking man's dressing gown, in navy-blue toweling and decorated with a shield on the breast pocket. Now, when he recognized the original owner, tall, slender, and mournful-looking, Gabriel had a flashback of Bundó wearing the dressing gown. He'd worn it for a while when they were living at the pension. He put it on when he came out of the shower or over his pajamas at night and the effect was hilarious. Since he was shorter than its original owner and on the tubby side, the dressing gown was a tight fit so he couldn't quite keep it together with the belt and the two front corners trailed on the floor. When he was walking around in it, Gabriel used to say he looked like a king in a cape, a medieval king fed up with the rabble and about to condemn all the boarding-house riffraff to death. The vision brought a painful smile—tugging the stitches of one of his cuts—and then he slept, out of pure exhaustion.

A day and a half later, on the Wednesday morning when they came to take him to the airport, he was no longer befuddled. Without the painkillers turning his brain to mush, reality kicked in with piercing force. Every second without Bundó at his side drilled through his temples like Chinese water torture. The guilt tormented him. Under such a sky, the future could only get worse. He'd never been on a plane, but this fear was engulfed by other fears. A contest of fears. And it was only eight in the morning.

From the hospital door, dressed in clothes they'd supplied, he saw two black cars pulling up. One was the hearse that had just picked up Bundó's coffin. The other was driven by the consulate chauffeur, who got out and opened the back door, but Gabriel gave him to understand that he wanted to sit next to him in the front seat. He was no big shot. Once he was in the car, the chauffeur gave him a folder bearing the emblem of the Spanish consulate in Frankfurt and a black canvas bag. He opened it. Inside he found a few personal effects of Bundó's and other things retrieved from the Pegaso, like a bottle opener and his sunglasses, still intact. They'd been useful once but now they made him angry. There was also a shirt and trousers belonging to Bundó, impeccably washed and ironed thanks to the good offices of the consulate staff. They were the clothes he'd changed into after the move to Hamburg, and Gabriel had some trouble identifying them. Bundó was a slave to his own fads, and that had been his favorite shirt for some months. They'd nicked it from a move to Bonn (Number 188), and he liked it, he said, because it had the three great qualities a working shirt should have in winter: Being made of flannel it was warm, it let him move freely because it was loose on him, and it didn't show the dirt. That third reason wasn't objective. Bundó was always covered in food stains, but he didn't care. When Gabriel or Petroli pointed it out he laughed at them and started looking for geographical shapes in his stains—a tomato-sauce Italy, an aioli Iberian peninsula, a chocolate-ice-cream Africa. The flannel shirt was black-and-white herringbone, modern and very eye-catching, and the stains were fairly well camouflaged. Now, the sight of that shirt, so soft and neat with a starched collar, crushed Gabriel even more. It was as if they'd stolen the essence of his friend.

To keep his mind off it, he opened the consulate folder. Someone, maybe the secretary himself, had put his plane ticket inside and, in a neat pile, the documents they'd been able to rescue from the cab. He found his passport and Bundó's, the waybills, the Pegaso papers, his international driving licence, postcards nobody had written on, a few maps ripped at the edges (Bundó always folded them badly), a crumpled leaflet about the Via Favència apartments, Petroli's list of Spanish emigrant centers, and several other documents. He flipped listlessly through the papers and was once again caught off guard by Bundó's presence in all of them.

Gabriel recognized his own handwriting on one scrap of paper. On it were a few sums from the day when they distracted themselves as they traveled by calculating how many kilometers they'd covered together in the Pegaso. Another newer sheet of paper bore the La Ibérica letterhead with its drawing of a truck crossing a map of Europe. Here, Gabriel read a series of dates, times, and doctors' names. It had been typed up by the secretary, Rebeca, and, taking in the details, Gabriel felt the thrust of their perfidious dagger. They projected a future that would never exist for him and Bundó. Every two years La Ibérica's drivers had to pass a medical checkup

confirming they were fit to drive the trucks. The checkups were
done in the insurance company clinic, and Rebeca arranged them
two months in advance to fit in with the moving schedule. Bundó
and Gabriel always did their checkups together. Senyor Casellas
insisted on this, to kill two birds with one stone, he said, and to
make sure they didn't forget. The day they were getting ready to
leave for Hamburg, about to commence fatal move number 199,
Rebeca had called Gabriel into the office and handed him copies
of her list.

> *Dates of medical examinations of Gabriel Delacruz and
> Serafí Bundó*
> (Yes, I know it would be better to do it all in one day but it's
> impossible.)
> *Place:* Transport Insurance Company. Clínica Platón, Calle
> Platón, 33.
> *Thursday, April 20, 9 a.m.* Blood test. It has to be done on
> an empty stomach—and that means no breakfast, Bundó.
> *Friday, April 28, 10 a.m.* Oculist. Doctor Trabal.
> *Friday, May 5, 10:30 a.m.* Ear, nose, and throat. Doctor
> Sadurní.
> *Monday, May 8, 9 a.m.* General checkup. Doctor Pacharán.

Gabriel was gripped by the strange power of the papers, so
painful yet so reassuring, and couldn't stop fiddling with them
until the car got on to the motorway. Then he took out the plane
ticket, his passport and Bundó's, and returned the folder to the
black bag. A few kilometers farther on, when they were nearing
the scene of the accident, Gabriel asked the driver to stop there.

"*Zwei minuts,*" he said. "*Es importante.*"

Slowly, finding it hard to keep his balance because of the un-
wieldy cast, he went down the slope alone. The chauffeur watched
from the top. They'd taken the Pegaso away the day before, and all
that was left now was a strip of razed vegetation and churned-up
ground. Flattened bushes and a smattering of glass indicated the
spot where the truck had stopped its downward slide. Beyond that,

a layer of frozen snow covered everything. He went down a little farther. Here and there were scraps of metal, a fragment of a tire, a splinter from the rearview mirror. Why did he want to return to the scene of the accident? Three weeks later, still unable to cry, he told himself it was his first attempt to summon the tears. On the day itself, however, he tortured himself with a scathing thought: "The killer always returns to the scene of the crime." The driver whistled from the top, signaling for him to come up. They were going to miss the plane. Gabriel lingered a moment longer. It was a bright day and the snow was melting in patches. Something was missing... With the tip of his shoe he poked at the ground among the fallen leaves. The chauffeur whistled again, now impatiently, and just as he was about to desist, to begin the retreat, his right foot hit something soft. That was it. He picked it up, pleased to find the black oilcloth notebook, the record of their thefts, the truest biography of his adventure on God's earth with Bundó and Petroli.

He got back into the car, and the funeral procession made its way to the airport.

That's what you wanted, wasn't it, Christophers? "Facts!" you were saying. Well, now you've got facts. One after another, linked up and synchronized as if orchestrated by some capricious and mocking god. And we're not done yet. Not by a long shot! Gabriel and Bundó's body are flying to Barcelona. It's the first time our father's been on a plane, but he's so overwhelmed by the facts—the facts!—that he's not aware of anything. Meanwhile, at the airport, Rita's well into another day at work in the Cage, as she called it.

If you do the sums, you'll realize that, by this February 16, 1972, Rita had been working at the airport for more than four years. Conrad and Leo were slowly filling the space she had reserved for them among her other memories. They had priority, of course, but they remained cut off, fixed in time, and mythologized somehow, as you'll soon see. Along the way, motherless and fatherless, she'd discovered the security afforded by daily routine and a salary at the end of the month. Her working hours at the Lost Luggage Office had, from the very start, given momentum to her sense of independence. She was now used to waking up early and getting up by herself, for example. At seven she took a bus to the airport. Once there an hour later, she donned a uniform that made her feel like an air hostess and applied the lipstick that would frame her smile when, scrupulously following the instructions she'd been given, she began the day's work of dealing with irate clients. Rita started as a novice but had mastered all the tricks of the trade within a couple of months. They'd chosen her for her youthful innocence and sweet angel face that disarmed the most belligerent members of the general public. Like everyone else who worked in the office, her first duty was to be the target of their wrath. The scapegoat. She had to listen to the passengers' complaints and demands and make them believe that they'd been very unlucky, that such a thing rarely happened.

"Early in the morning," my mother told me, reminiscing about those times, "I used to get the more fuddled, better-mannered passengers. They'd just staggered off a transatlantic flight, disoriented with jet lag, not knowing whether it was day or night, and then they discovered that the company had lost their bags. As I tried to get them to understand that their luggage was still in Buenos Aires or New York, and that it would come without fail the next day, on the next flight, they slumped over the counter and answered listlessly. Their eyes were half shut with fatigue. It was incredibly difficult to get them to fill out the form, but, after that, most of them wandered off, resigned and uncomplaining. You have to understand, it was different then. Now any Tom, Dick, and Harry can travel, but not in those days. The tickets were expensive, and the passengers got princely treatment from the airline companies . . . The businessmen started arriving after eleven, most of them with a young secretary. You could tell from their mood if the girl was also on bedroom duty. If they were foreigners, one of my colleagues who spoke a bit of English took my place. If they were South Americans or Spanish, I dealt with them. Needless to say, I always got the worst ones. Such airs and graces these idiots had! It was so obvious that the Franco regime had filled their pockets, and I say pockets because they didn't even carry a wallet but went around with bundles of notes held together with a rubber band. Uptight and boorish, they were escaping for a few days from their dingy cities and towns, believing that they'd be met in Barcelona with a red carpet and everyone bowing and scraping. Often, the only way to calm them down was to solicit the support of the secretary. "I wish to apologize in the name of the airline company, Mr. So-and-So. I cannot tell you how much we regret the inconvenience caused to you and your wife,' I used to say and, if necessary, resorted to the double whammy. 'Goodness me, you wouldn't be on your honeymoon, would you? You seem so much in love . . .' The men always went red or got tangled up in a thousand explanations, and then the women took over. Without denying anything, they gave me the name of the hotel where we could send the luggage once we'd recovered it and graciously accepted the vanity case we presented them with. Some of them even winked at me when they said good-bye, like coconspirators. After midday, tourists and other travelers who'd had to come to Barcelona for whatever reason replaced the businessmen. These were people who'd boarded the plane with a problem and who, on disembarking, found they had two. Lunchtime was coming up and, instead of being in a restaurant or back at home, they had to line up to reclaim a lost suitcase. These were the most difficult hours. The atmosphere in the terminal was charged, and everybody was more irritable. Then, if someone raised his or her voice unnecessarily, or insisted on calling the Guardia Civil, I had to resort to my secret strategy, my private commemoration of Leo and Conrad. 'Please don't let it upset you so much,' I'd quietly tell the complaining individual. 'It could have been worse . . .' At this point I threw in a dramatic pause, adopting my orphan's pose, after which I added, 'Like with my parents.' The rest of the sentence was left dangling in the air, and the client, without fail, took the bait after a couple of seconds. 'And what happened to your parents, young lady, may I ask?' By now the tone had mellowed. Then I only had to mention the accident (which everybody remembered), sparing no gory details, and ending with a stagy lie. 'You might remember me because I appeared in that news program about the accident. I was the lost-looking girl in the cemetery while the voice-over announced that the disaster took a large number of innocent lives and left a trail of disconsolate orphans in its wake.' The news program never existed, of course, but I always won them over, I can assure you."

The claims office was hidden away in an ill-lit corner of the airport, on the ground floor behind the baggage carousels. It had two windows and a desk for attending to the public. Inside, behind a permanently closed door, was a large room crammed to the ceiling with lost suitcases, boxes, bundles, and all sorts of mind-boggling things. Four people worked each shift, two attending to the passengers and two in the storeroom. Rita called the office the Cage, not so much because of the daily claustrophobia and confinement but because, for her, it evoked the animal kingdom.

"When we're attending to the passengers we sound like parrots," she used to say.

After some months of dealing with the public, she was instructed in the other two occupations of the Cage, which took place in the back room. First, they had to put in order and write a description of the ownerless bags, which Rita thought was the most boring task. When an item was left behind, dizzy after a hundred rounds on the carousel, one of the airport workers picked it up and delivered it to the Cage. The person in charge that shift then produced a basic description: size, color, weight, and other external details that might help with identification. If the piece bore a label with a name and address, or if it was claimed by telephone the same day, the next flight took it to wherever it had to go. However, if it was still unclaimed after a week, it went into the storeroom and was then ready for an "autopsy," as the denizens of the Cage called it.

Opening bags and suitcases was the job Rita liked most. Often it was sufficient to undo a buckle or a knot, but sometimes they slashed open a fabric suitcase or even smashed the odd safety lock with a hammer. Then the contents were laid out in an orderly fashion on a long table in the hope of finding some sign of who the owner might be. Some of the Cage workers were revolted by the autopsy, put off by the unfamiliar smells emanating from a bag, or the strange ways of packing clothes, some of them dirty, or the chilly accusations from possessions whose privacy was violated. For Rita, in contrast, the operation was fascinating. It made her feel like a trainee detective. If no useful document was found in the luggage, she had a natural gift for turning up data that might be useful in the long run: a prescription matching a bottle of anti-depressants in a first-aid kit, an owner's name inside the cover of a novel written in Italian, an ashtray and towels nicked from a hotel in Acapulco . . . If really valuable objects like watches and jewelery turned up, or if any bundle looked suspicious, they had to inform the Guardia Civil, who then took charge of the luggage until the owner was found.

Rita confesses that her inspections didn't often end successfully, but she was certainly entertained by the task. She could regale us with a whole string of anecdotes that include, for example, cassocks and suspender belts in one bag (never reclaimed by the priest), a mummified monkey fetus and other articles of black magic, and then there was the gentleman from Galicia who'd emigrated to Chile and was going back after his holidays at home with a box full of dry bread for his chickens. She also recognizes now, all these years later, that her effectiveness was limited because she herself sabotaged it. As you'll soon see, if the contents of a suitcase looked valuable, she returned it to the storeroom without a word to anyone, thus condemning it to oblivion in the depths of the Cage. Oblivion so absolute that, in the end, the piece of baggage melted away for ever.

Now, as you see, Christophers, Rita had no problems in adapting to a working existence. She threw herself into it with an enthusiasm that her workmates in the Cage found hard to explain. Her salary was nothing to write home about, but she could certainly get by while she waited to turn twenty-one and thus become eligible to receive the bounty of her parents' life insurance policy, a tidy little pile.

Anyway, this portrait of Rita on February 16, 1972, just before Gabriel turns up in her life, would be incomplete if we didn't take her off-duty hours into account. Since starting her job at the Cage, her private life had suffered. Inspecting suitcases satisfied, in an illusory way, the longing for adventure that befitted her age. Her timetable didn't help either: She had to work one weekend in three and she wasn't seeing her old friends so often. When they did go out together she realized that their priorities had diverged. She didn't want to run away and travel the world like Raquel, who was now studying at the University of Barcelona, and neither did she dream of marrying the first fellow who crossed her path and having lots of children. "You're okay. Your life's sorted," the more conformist among them said with a touch of envy that she never quite understood. Furthermore, stranded in the seclusion of her orphanhood, she hadn't been able to change any aspect of her life. It was as if time had dropped anchor in that definitive Saturday afternoon, as she slumbered in her adolescent's bedroom. In the early days of her solitude she emptied the wardrobes and took her parents' clothes to the parish church, but that's as far as it went. Too many memories and too much dust to get rid of. She kept the main bedroom shut off and in darkness, as if amputated from the rest of the house. When she cooked herself dinner she ate it sitting in the chair where she'd always sat.

"The truth of the matter," Mom says, "is that I was twenty years old and about to become a premature spinster. Luckily your father turned up to save me."

Or not so luckily. It had more to do with *Garbo* than Gabriel, I tell her. She accepts the provocation and responds with a wry smile. Within a few months, the job at the airport with all its ruses, fiddles, and pillaging had helped to ease the burden of being alone in the world. However, it didn't encourage romance. Her workmates in the Cage were family men or too old and, as I said, her friends were either too mindless or too daredevil. Under these circumstances, the pages of *Garbo* became her only other escape. Every Friday afternoon she spent five pesetas on the new issue. Then she sat down for a snack in the bar La Valenciana, on the corner of Gran Via and Carrer Aribau, losing herself in its glamorous, starry world. Farah Diba spent all winter skiing in Saint Moritz with Maria Pia of Savoy doing her bit as friend and confidante, while Raquel Welch modeled *the* hairstyle for anyone who wanted to be fashionable. Rita wasn't dreaming about white knights and neither was she naive enough to believe everything she read about that heavenly world. Nevertheless, these privileged women did reinforce her growing intuition that life is a battle of random forces and it's better to meet it full on than try to run away.

Then again, there was the matter of the horoscope. Not long after her parents' funeral, as she was flipping through a new issue of *Garbo*, Rita recalled the exactitude with which this so-called Argos had anticipated the accident and her parents' deaths. She read his predictions for Cancer and was amazed once again. "Days of unexpected changes. Be strong and the future will reward you," he advised. She immediately wrote a letter to the astrologer congratulating him on his psychic powers. The man or woman hiding behind the pseudonym didn't answer, but that didn't discourage her. When she looked up the magazine's address, she discovered that the editorial office was very close to home, in Carrer Tallers, number 62, and she turned up there one free afternoon asking to speak to "Senyor Argos." The receptionist soon got rid of her. No, that was impossible. Nobody except for the director knew who was hiding behind the enigmatic name. Argos sent the copy by post every week but never put a return address on the envelope.

This aura of mystery only encouraged Rita and she obsessively analyzed her horoscope thereafter. On Fridays, even before leaving the kiosk, she opened the magazine at the horoscope page and read what he had to say about her life. Argos's words were a fine example of an oracle's wisdom: sufficiently imprecise and yet sufficiently personal to speak to her desires without provoking too many doubts. She gradually broadened her field of interest and asked her colleagues at the airport what sign they were. If she could see Porras and Sayago arguing over some stupid thing, or that Leiva was dragging his broom around in a way that looked too taciturn, she consulted the horoscope and always found a plausible explanation.

As tends to happen with such fixations, there came a time when *Garbo*'s weekly horoscope was no longer enough. Since she'd begun work at the airport, as Argos had predicted ("Professional News"), her life had become increasingly complex. Now she was dealing with more people than before and talking to strangers every day, so there were more possibilities for chance to play its

part. She needed to be prepared for this, but *Garbo*'s soothsaying
fell short of the mark.

One winter Saturday she stumbled upon the help she needed.
Not long before, she'd lost her house keys—probably after dropping them in the street—and she decided to get the lock changed
because she was worried about thieves. She wanted to make a
copy of the new keys and then remembered that her mother always went to a locksmith in Avinguda de la Llum. In case you
don't know, Christophers, this was the name given to an underground gallery beneath Carrer Pelai, right next to Plaça de Catalunya. Clustered together in the artificial glare of its fluorescent
light were the entrance to the railway station, a bar, a cinema
and a few shops. Rita went down the steps next to Carrer Ber-
gara and entered Avinguda de la Llum. Although it was Saturday
afternoon there weren't many people around. The air was thick
and sweet, mingled with the aromas of fresh-baked biscuits and
soot. Nicotine-yellow columns on either side made the long narrow corridor look like a burial crypt. Or the interior of a dinosaur's
trachea. She dodged the stragglers leaving the cinema, their eyes
still adjusting to the light, and looked for the locksmith's booth.

After getting her copies of the keys, she hung around for a
while longer looking in the display window of a corset shop. Then,
when she was about to exit at the other end of the tunnel, she
noticed a man sitting at a fold-away table next to the last pillar.
He was very tall, had long hippieish hair, and was dressed in a
silvery-lilac tunic with a pendant in the form of a five-pointed star
hanging around his neck. In front of his table a sign proclaimed
"Jorgito the Magician. Know your future . . . now!" Rita didn't think
twice before asking him how much he'd charge to do her horoscope. The magician looked her up and down and, unfolding a
chair he kept stashed under the table, told her to get comfortable.
The price wouldn't be a problem. He immediately informed her
that good horoscopes had to be based on a birth chart. Anything
else was bullshit. Had she ever had her birth chart done? No?
Well, to begin with, she'd need to tell him the exact date and hour
of her birth. She told him. Jorgito the Magician then took a book

out of his bag, opened it to a page with an intricate astrological chart, and blathered away while he was doing his calculations on a bit of paper, uttering words that sounded very professional to Rita: the position of the planets . . . the ascendant appearing on the horizon . . . the lunar sign, the solar sign, and so on.

Rita returned twice more to Avinguda de la Llum. Jorgito the Magician needed to study her astrological profile. We don't know how much she forked out for the whole thing—no doubt more than she should have—but she eventually came to see it as a good investment. The magician divided his predictions between three different areas: health, money, and love. Rita wasn't concerned about health and money. However, she did want to know more about this very ambiguous, very strange thing called love. Therefore, after her third visit, she had a slightly better idea of her emotional fate. With his reading of the mutual attraction between certain signs of the zodiac and the planets influencing the ascendant, Jorgito the Magician was able to give her a detailed profile of her ideal man. A roaming adventurous spirit (the magician knew by now that Rita worked at the airport), without family ties (he'd been informed she was an orphan), born in Barcelona, or in Stockholm, Paris, or New York (all with direct flights to El Prat—what a coincidence) or within a hundred kilometers of these cities and, above all—and this was highly important; this was crucial!—his birth date had to be between November 10 and December 7, 1941. These two dates guaranteed perfect symbiosis between the ascendants of her and her future suitor's zodiac signs.

No, Christophers, if you're thinking I'm going to say that fits with Gabriel's birth date, you're dead wrong. That's too easy. Chance isn't so easily manipulated.

The following Monday, after her final visit to Jorgito the Magician—I can hardly bear to pronounce such a ridiculous name!—Rita had memorized the dates almost to saturation point. Her brain was running amok, repeating them again and again like some pop song you can't get out of your head. When the first male client of the day approached the Cage, she went through the standard procedure and asked for his passport in order to fill out the form. He was a pleasant man, handsome, athletic-looking, about thirty years old, of reserved character, and Rita's eyes raced to discover his date of birth. On seeing that it didn't match her dates, that it was more than a year out, she was hit by the first of the day's disappointments. There followed so many more, caused by so many men that, eventually, she almost took perverse pleasure in the experience. The mere possibility of success was the prize.

In the first months, until she got used to the recurring frustration, Rita was in a state of constant emotional turmoil. When she saw that the passenger's birth date coincided with the days of November or December specified by the astrologer, even if the year was wrong, she prolonged the proceedings and delved into his personal life. Sometimes she got so carried away that she lost control and asked inappropriate questions.

"Oh yes, and are you married?" she'd say, adopting a scientific air, at which point her workmates looked up. Some observed her in amazement while others laughed at her boldness.

"No, I'm not married," the passenger replied indignantly. "And, frankly, I don't see what that's got to do with my lost luggage."

"Indeed it is connected," she answered. "If you were married, it's quite likely that your wife would have packed the bag and put an address tag on it. Women are always more farsighted."

Every comment, every reaction helped her to construct the image of her ideal man. To yearn for him, too, without even knowing him. One day, for example, she attended to a young woman from Mallorca who'd lost her bag. She asked for her identity card, as she did with everyone, and automatically checked the date of birth. November 11, 1941! With a fluttering heart and in a state of great agitation, she treated the woman so effusively that she took fright. Rita says she'd never been so close to her target and immediately felt attracted to the stranger even if she wasn't a man, but she lost her chance to probe any further because the woman went off somewhat confused and with the uneasy sensation that she'd revealed half her life to a stranger. Two days later the bag turned up, and Rita dealt with it personally. She locked herself in the autopsy room and examined its contents with great care: two floral dresses, underwear, a makeup bag with beauty creams, some beach shoes, an Ursula Andress–style bikini, a novel by Françoise Sagan . . . Rita stared at it all with idiotic devotion but suddenly understood that these things didn't make her feel any love for the woman. On the contrary, like the belongings of an older sister who'd had better luck in life, they only aroused uneasy feelings of unjustified envy. She put everything back in the bag before getting it sent to the woman's address but, at the last minute, she had a slight change of heart and kept the bikini. Out of spite. When she got home that evening she tried it on. It looked good in the mirror, tailor-made for her, but when she mimicked Ursula Andress's goddess pose in that James Bond film (she'd cut out the photo from an old issue of *Garbo*) her bravado collapsed into pathetic farce. She felt sorry for herself.

Rita kept waiting for the man the stars had decreed for her, but a thousand similar obstacles and disappointments lay ahead. Within the security of the Cage she learned not to get excited about it. Her fantasy lost some of its luster with each setback. The tricks of the calendar seemed less cruel, and, in time, some near misses even brightened up her day. Then, without any warning, as tends to happen with tempests, tragedies, and miracles, the glorious day of February 16, 1972, came along.

The plane slowed, the wheels touched the ground with a shudder and Gabriel inhaled deeply several times, as if he'd been holding his breath for the two long hours of the flight. Never again. It was the first and last time he ever traveled by plane. His truck driver's body was accustomed to the vibrations of engine and asphalt, when the wheels transmitted to his legs the throbbing of the road, gravity and movement and his hands gripped a steering wheel. How can you drive a vehicle that's suspended in the air? Really, how could anyone want to do that? They'd given him a window seat next to the right-hand wing. He'd never liked birds.

The melodious voice of one of the hostesses welcomed them to Barcelona airport. Now that they were returning home, the image of Bundó lying in his coffin came to him again. They'd closed his eyes and concealed his wounds with makeup. The German customs police had made Gabriel identify him and then sign the necessary papers. Nevertheless, over the last few days, from the moment of the accident and, in particular, in the hospital Gabriel had not really faced up to the reality of his friend's death. Now that they were coming back to the point of departure, the origin of it all, he noticed how this new absence weighed on him and how differently he felt. The plane came to a stop. An unbearable heaviness churned in his stomach, like a bag of cement in a mixer. The last move to Hamburg, their final leave-taking from Petroli, and even the peaceful image of Bundó sleeping in the cab were distant memories with all the incongruence of make-believe. The passengers around him prepared to disembark, but he was paralyzed. He'd never be able to get up from that seat. A hostess tapped him gently on the shoulder. He was the last to leave the plane. Outside, he could see two members of the Guardia Civil and a hearse waiting for him on the tarmac.

Repatriating a corpse means entering a bureaucratic nightmare. The two men of the Guardia Civil were accompanied by a notary sent by La Ibérica's insurance company and someone from the funeral home. On that dark, overcast, typical February morning, the four men stood motionless next to the black hearse, a sinister tableau that would bring anyone out in goose pimples. It was as if everything had been prepared for a duel in which Gabriel had been challenged to fight. The notary requested the copies of papers given to Gabriel by the German police and, after checking them and signing them, handed them to the Guardia Civil. He then informed Gabriel that Senyor Casellas had come to meet him. He was greatly distressed and waiting at the international arrivals door. Given the absence of any family members, if he had no objections, they'd decided that Bundó's funeral would be held the following afternoon in the El Vendrell parish church. Gabriel said yes to everything. After the service they'd go to the cemetery and lay him to rest next to his parents.

On the evening of that first day in the hospital in Kassel, Gabriel, in a moment of lucidity, realized that he had to phone Caro-lina. It had to be him, had to be his voice that pronounced the dreadful words.

"Something terrible happened this morning, Carolina. We had an accident. I'm so sorry. Poor Bundó is dead."

Carolina went mute. Gabriel clung to the receiver with a trem-bling hand and waited in silence. He could picture her. She'd been waiting all day, a nervous wreck in her room at the Papillon, fearing the worst. She'd been counting the hours, listening for the engine of the Pegaso rumbling into the parking lot, hoping Bundó would arrive before Saint Valentine's Day was over. After a minute, her desperate sobbing got louder. Then, much later, came the tearful question: Where was he? She needed to see him. She couldn't bear a single minute more without seeing him. Gabriel finally con-vinced her to go directly to Barcelona. On Wednesday morning they were going to take Bundó to Via Favència so they could keep the vigil in his home, as was right and proper.

Shit, Christophers. What a terrible thing. Sorry it's such a sad story, but it had to be told and now it's done.

Airport workers and the young man from the funeral home took the coffin off the plane and put it in the hearse. Then, prompted by the notary, Gabriel gave the driver the exact Via Favència ad-dress. Carolina would probably be in the apartment by now. When the notary and hearse had left, the two men of the Guardia Civil accompanied our father to the baggage collection area. In Frank-furt, they'd made him check in the black canvas bag containing Bundó's personal effects and other items rescued from the Pegaso. They went to pick it up from the carousel, but it wasn't there. All the passengers from his flight had gone. The red tape involved in getting the coffin out of the airport had taken up almost an hour, and the two policemen escorted him to the lost luggage office. The bag must have been taken there.

Gabriel followed them robotically. He was so bereft of will-power, so knocked out, that he would have followed them all the way to hell that morning. As usual, the two Guardia Civil flirted with the girl in the office, telling some crude joke or other. Then

they informed her that this gentleman had arrived on the flight
from Frankfurt, after which, touching their three-cornered hats in
a salute, they returned to their sentry box. Rita treated the passenger with professional formality but soon realized she wasn't getting
through. The man was in a bad way, consumed by some unidentifi-
able problem. His movements were sluggish, suggesting that any
moment now he might stop in his tracks and never move again. The
cast on his arm only accentuated his fragile appearance. She asked
him to describe the bag. Gabriel was correct in saying it was black,
black cloth. She made a note of that on the form and then asked
for some document. It could be his passport or identity card. Then,
with some support from his immobilized arm, Gabriel opened the
folder containing the documents, some of which spilled on to the
table. Rita picked up the first passport she saw.

It was Bundó's.

She opened it at the page she needed and, as always, her eyes
rushed to the date of birth: November 29, 1941. The world stood
still and she almost screamed. She looked up, stared at the face of
the vulnerable man, and read the date again: November. 29. 1941.
She felt like somebody checking the numbers on a winning lottery
ticket. Stifling her emotion, she flipped through the pages of the
passport and saw all the customs stamps. To cap it all, he was a
traveler. By the time she turned the last page she was all his. She'd
do anything to get to know this stranger.

Gabriel was totally out of it. Rita gripped the passport hard,
without even looking at the photo—why would she need to if he
was standing right in front of her?—and wrote down the name
of the man of her dreams: Serafí Bundó Ventosa. How delightful
it sounded! Her writing was wobbly, which made her realize she
wasn't paying enough attention to the man himself. She had to
speak to him, hear his voice, learn more about him. Of course,
the address! What if he wasn't from Barcelona? She asked for his
address, and Gabriel hesitated. He was so far away from everything, it was hard for him to collect his thoughts to the extent of
knowing where he lived. If, indeed, he was still alive. Finally, he
gave her the boarding house address. Ronda de Sant Antoni, num-

ber 70. In Barcelona? Yes. As she jotted it down, Rita realized it was very close to home. They were neighbors. "Less than two hundred steps apart," she thought. To hide her excitement, and also to hurry things along, she said, "Ah, we live in the same neighborhood . . . I could bring you the bag myself, tomorrow, when it turns up." Distracted, Gabriel agreed although he'd imagined they'd give it to him right away. Rita respected his shyness. She was dying to ask him more but, what with the turmoil of her emotions, nothing came to her. For the first time ever, she was afraid of intimidating a passenger. Trying to play for time, she asked him to sign the form. Gabriel produced some unintelligible scrawl and, before her astonished gaze, reclaimed the passport, turned on his heel with a mumbled good-bye, and shambled off. Rita took a while to react, and, when she did, calling out his name, he didn't hear her. Instead of despairing, she took the form, reread the name and address, and let him go. It didn't matter. She had the token. It was written in the stars that the black canvas bag would bring them together when it turned up the next day.

Gabriel followed the arrows pointing to the exit. On the other side of the terminal, the farthest point from the Cage, he walked past the last carousel. A lonely bag was going around and around. He went over. Although it looked the same, it wasn't his bag but, at the time, his mind wasn't functioning properly. He recognized it only because there was no other bag. Not understanding anything, not wondering about anything, he picked it up and went outside to be met by Senyor Casellas. The two men of the Guardia Civil saluted him awkwardly from their sentry box.

# 3

## Mysteries and Swoonings

*Vati*. Daddy. *Papa. Pare.* Is that what we called him? Did we ever get used to it? Did we stop thinking about him all those years ago? Our work's piling up. We have to trust our mothers' word. When we ask them about it, they say Gabriel liked us calling him that, was proud of it, asked for it, but admit that we almost always referred to him in the context of his distance or absence. Where's Daddy? Daddy's coming tomorrow. Come on, listen to the telephone. Daddy wants to say hello. No, Daddy's not here now. You want to know when Daddy's coming, little one? We could make a list of all the excuses and lies our mothers had to invent once he'd stopped visiting us, but those pages would be too sad.

Yes, our work's piling up. It could well be that our zeal for pinning down the past is an instinctive reaction to our loss, our protection against the uncertainties of the future. Now that we Christophers have got used to hanging around in February 1972— "mea culpa," Cristòfol concedes—the present is rebeling and wants a share of the limelight. We fixed the date for our next meeting in Barcelona. At two o'clock on Friday we met for lunch in Can Soteras, a restaurant on Avinguda Diagonal frequented by Senyor Casellas thirty years ago when he wanted to impress some client or other. After that, we walked down Passeig de Sant Joan to the Arc de Triomf and then to Carrer Nàpols. It was a long time since we'd been in the mezzanine apartment. The weekend plan was to follow the trail of Gabriel's movements around the neighborhood. While we were having lunch, Christof came up with some news that

298

impressed us all: He and Cristoffini had located a truck cemetery on the outskirts of Kassel. Thanks to the Spanish license plate, they'd then discovered the poor Pegaso's wreckage on the edge of the dump. After more than twenty-five years, the cab was more or less holding its own. It was full of rust holes, and the inside was a forest of moss and dead leaves. Its wheels, windshield, lights, and steering wheel were gone. Rain had rotted the seats. Naturally they took photos of it. They even climbed up inside it and, contorting themselves, squeezed into the driver's seat and touched what remained of the gear stick. They rummaged around and found almost nothing. The truck cemetery owner said that if they wanted what was left of the Pegaso he'd give it to them. Cristoffini was all for it, but Christof's good sense won the day and they left with the license plate, a miraculously intact 1972 Pirelli calendar, and a cracked hand mirror that had well and truly used up its requisite seven years of bad luck. How many times would it have reflected Bundó's face when he was sprucing up to visit the Papillon?

We were still amusing ourselves with our speculating when we got to the mezzanine floor. Cristòfol opened the door. We went in and spread out around the apartment as if it was ours. Christof went to the bathroom, Chris raised the blind of the dining-room window, Christophe went into the kitchen, and Cristòfol went into the study to get some papers. Perhaps not in that exact order, but it doesn't matter. The point is that the apartment suddenly went quiet. We regrouped in the dining room a moment later. We walked on tiptoe and we all looked as if we'd seen a ghost. We had no evidence—no dirty plate in the kitchen sink, no ashtray with a couple of butts in it in the study—but we were all certain that somebody had been there. I don't know what it was but there was something, some detail we'd picked up at a glance, some strange noise . . . As if we needed confirmation, Christophe put a finger to his lips, "*Ssh,*" then pointed at the bedroom door. Closed. We always left an inside window half open to ventilate the rooms, but there couldn't have been any draughts. And doors don't close by themselves. We looked at each other and all thought the same thing: Had we finally found our father, now, and here? We were loath to admit it, but the idea didn't appeal. We'd spent so many hours rewriting his biography that we imagined a rather more dramatic ending.

Chris, the most unflappable brother, carefully opened the door. The rest of us peeped in from behind him. The light filtering in through the curtains gradually revealed there was no one in the bedroom.

Our subsequent exploration of the apartment led us to the conclusion that the intruder had been Gabriel. Who else, otherwise? The front door was intact, nobody had forced it and, since he was such a solitary soul, we surmised that only he had the key. It looked as if he'd spent a night here, or at least a few hours, because the blanket was slightly rumpled although the bed was still made (he might have slept in his clothes). The wardrobe door was shut, and its bare interior revealed that he'd taken all his clothes, including the cardsharp's jacket and shirts. Now other questions were begging to be asked: Had he really decided to leave for good? And right now? Yet it was difficult to believe that he'd forsake his belongings. Those objects that our father kept as his treasure (or a life sentence) had always been with him and, paradoxically, had given him the only anchor he'd needed. Once again, we sifted through the boxes and folders he kept in the study to see if we could find some clue as to his fate. Everything was in order, in place, hadn't been touched, and the only items we found to be missing were his new packs of poker cards, still wrapped in cellophane. In our inventory that first day we'd counted twelve and now he'd taken the lot.

More clues. We Christophers had taken over an empty shelf in the junk room where we kept everything that our inquiries yielded. There was a notepad detailing the La Ibérica trips; papers and letters from Carolina; a tape recorder with the tapes we'd made with Petroli; the objects we'd so despicably lifted from Petroli's house . . . At first it looked as if Gabriel hadn't moved anything. Then it seemed—but this was impossible—that the things were tidier, dusted, as if he'd seen to it himself.

More clues, more clues. On our previous visit to Carrer Nàpols, we'd left an envelope with our photos in it on the dining-room table. We'd taken them the summer that we'd met up in London.

There were photos of London Fields, the house where Chris and Sarah lived in Martello Street (which our father visited several times), of us four toasting each other with pints in the pub. We'd made some extra copies and planned to send them to Carolina and Petroli as a thank-you for helping us. From the dust marks on the table and the position of one of the chairs, we deduced that our father had sat down to look at them. We checked to see if any were missing and, although we weren't sure, we suspected he'd taken one featuring the four of us. Or was that wishful thinking?

Over dinner that evening we pooled our ideas. Okay, we weren't certain that the intruder had been Gabriel, but it seemed the most logical explanation and it helped us to believe he was alive. We had no choice but to cling to our theory. In that case, he knew that we four brothers had met up and were looking for him. He knew that we were crazy enough to get together every so often in Barcelona. That we'd turned the mezzanine apartment in Carrer Nàpols into the headquarters of the unlikely Christophers Club. We considered all the facts and told ourselves we were on the right track and yet, since this was about our father, we also knew it would be a good idea to nip any optimism in the bud. He was the one who'd started it all by leaving a list of our names on the bedside table, right? It looked like a calculated decision aimed at making sure everything would proceed step by step. That's why it would be naive of us to expect that he was going to pop up all of a sudden, just like that. Right from the start we'd understood that our father hadn't disappeared overnight—Abracadabra!—but had crumbled apart, little by little. So, maybe the reverse was happening now, and, instead of suddenly turning up, he was sending us signs, enticing us with clues to keep looking for him.

Mixed up with all the tension of the day, the exhaustion—and a few bottles of wine—these conclusions had us all waxing lyrical. We wondered what would happen to the Christophers when we found our father. Would our lives change? Would we go on seeing each other? It might be better to let the whole thing go and just celebrate our friendship. To hell with Dad. Christof, the most melodramatic (and drunkest), gabbled on about how we had to have a brothers' pact but didn't specify what that meant. Chris retired to a solitary corner as if he could conjure up through silence some idea of the future. Cristòfol wondered what was more important, the quest itself or success, the end or the means, and Christophe wound him up by expounding on theories of risk and consequence.

Feeling the need to banish gloomy portents, someone had the good sense to propose a toast to our mothers.

That night the four of us went to sleep well and truly addled, Cristòfol at his place and the visiting Christophers at the hotel where we always stayed. The next day, Saturday, we overplayed our hangovers—come on, admit it—and pretended to forget our fit of psychodrama. The new developments were pushing us to act. At breakfast time, Christophe came down from his room with a surprise that, what with all the chatter the day before, he'd forgotten to show us. It wasn't as spectacular an offering as Christof's wreckage of the Pegaso, but it immediately became very important. A friend of his from the University of Paris, in the Department of Computer Applications in Physics, had been working on a project to create highly accurate computer-enhanced portraits. Their precision was so impressive that the French secret services bought the program. Christophe had given his friend a photo of our father, the most recent one we had, from 1975, and the computer came up with a sketch of how he might look today. The friend had handed him a sealed envelope on which he'd ironically written "Top Secret," but Christophe preferred not to look at it until we were all together. It was quite a surprise. We decided to open it with due solemnity, after breakfast, and in the meantime we nursed our headaches with strong coffee and puerile conversation.

"Will we recognize him, do you think? I've imagined him so often . . ."

"The facial structure doesn't change much, my IT friend tells me."

"Yes, but don't forget he turned sixty in 2001 . . ."

"So, now he'd be about to retire. That's if he ever went back to work."

"What if he's got white hair?"

"What if he's got fatter?"

"Or thinner . . . Maybe he doesn't eat much."

"You're so annoying! The computer can't know all that. It just does a sketch of the face. The program starts out from the logical evolution of the three most prominent features. Nose, ears, mouth . . ."

"Ah, I get it: It'll be like a prison mugshot."

"All computer-enhanced portraits look like prison mugshots."

Since the conversation was going nowhere, Christophe asked for silence. Then he opened the envelope, and the portrait was revealed.

The impression it made on us was enormous. It was him and it wasn't him. We looked at that face, with so little that was personal about it, and were fascinated to recognize Gabriel in it, although his proximity was unsettling. But it was him, yes. He would certainly look like that. Together with aging his features, the computer had cleverly given him a gentle stare—the elusive warmth the four of us had known when we were little. He gazed at us out of the sheet of paper, as if trying to convey how bad he felt about the situation.

We made photocopies of the portrait. We went back to the mezzanine apartment—where everything was as we'd left it the day before—got out a map and divided up the neighborhood. The grid layout of the Eixample zone made the task easier. Our idea was to go into shops and bars and ask people if they recognized this man. It was quite likely that they'd seen Gabriel, that he'd been walking these streets in the last few days, and any information they could give us, however tenuous, would be a great help. We separated at the street door, agreeing to meet up in the same place in two hours' time.

"Let's synchronize our watches," Cristòfol said. We were acting like kids pretending to be detectives, so excited by the game that our hearts were thumping.

Most of the people we spoke to looked at the portrait and said they'd never seen him. We asked them to try to remember, to imagine him: a tall, thin man of some sixty years, retiring by nature, a good man. Perhaps he used to come to the shop a while ago, or maybe they'd seen him recently. Some gave it a bit more thought, as if they were doing us a favor, and then said no. When they realized we were foreigners—except for Cristòfol—a few people started asking questions. Is he a terrorist? Did someone kill him? Has he disappeared? Are you from Interpol?

Not everything turned out to be so predictable, however. Chris spoke with the man from a kiosk in Passeig de Pujades, near Carrer Nàpols, and he recognized our father as an old client. He bought a newspaper every Saturday and Sunday. Only the newspaper? No, there was a time when he was buying a BBC English course in installments (Chris smiled), but he'd tired of it after some months. When had he stopped going there? A year ago, the kiosk man guessed, maybe more. He offered to stick the portrait up in his kiosk so people could see it, but we preferred to keep it private.

Cristòfol stumbled upon the most promising clue—or, let's just say, another piece of the mystery—in a greasy dive in Carrer Sardenya. Even the name was prescient: Bar Carambola, the "stroke of luck" bar. When he went in, a minute or two before midday, they'd just opened and there were no drinkers. In the depths of the bar, two little girls were sitting in front of a television set watching cartoons. A bartender was restocking the fridges. The owner was leaning on the bar flicking through a sports paper. His eyes were puffy and ringed with dark circles. Cristòfol showed him the portrait of Gabriel. The man made a strange sound like a snorting horse—*bruuf-f-f-f*—and looked even more loutish, at which point the toothpick fell from his mouth to the floor.

"He used to come here on Friday nights," he said. "He met up with a group to play cards. They'd be at it for hours. They used to begin with low stakes, but the betting always heated up after a while."

The oafish bar owner remembered Gabriel. He remembered him because he had a very peculiar way of playing, holding his head high and always looking dour. He'd gone up in smoke all of a sudden.

"If he's still alive, he'll certainly have problems. That's why you're looking for him, isn't it? I knew he'd end up badly. The way he concentrated so hard on a game of cards ... Either he ended up in the clink, or someone rearranged his face." He went quiet as if he had nothing else to say but then added meditatively, "The fact is he knew how to win, the fucker."

Making it clear that he didn't want to talk, the bar owner inserted another toothpick and went on turning the pages of the sports paper. Cristòfol asked for a coffee, out of courtesy. The bartender, badly shaven and about thirty years old, served him with a wink. When he raised his cup, Cristòfol found a folded paper napkin underneath. He picked it up and glanced over at the bartender. The bartender pretended to look away but nodded his head. The owner was still absorbed in the sports news. Cristòfol cupped the note in the palm of his hand and read it. There was a nine-figure number and the words "Phone me tonight." Then he paid for his coffee and left without saying good-bye.

Back in the mezzanine again after we'd met up at the agreed time, Cristòfol was jittery, and the bit of paper was burning a hole in his pocket. We shared the results of our inquiries and, once again, confirmed what we already knew: Our father had the ability to lose himself in a crowd, to pass unnoticed. And the place where he really excelled at anonymity was in the house where he lived. We spent the afternoon consulting the other residents in the building, and the results were shockingly meager. In three of the nine other apartments they wouldn't even open the door to us. Three other neighbors denied knowing him or even having seen him on the stairs (since he lived on the mezzanine, Gabriel wouldn't have used the elevator). Two chatty old ladies who lived in next-door apartments on the first floor opened their doors together, like a pair of coconspirators. They studied the portrait and assured us that this man was the "ghost" who'd hidden himself away in the mezzanine apartment some time ago. This creature, they informed us, had died about a year ago. They themselves had called the police to report a terrible smell coming from the apartment. Behind the whole thing, they said, was some murky story, some high-level affair of state, because the government pretended that nothing had happened.

"He must have been a Russian spy. Or American. A leftover from Franco's times."

"Or an extraterrestrial. They kidnapped him without making a sound so they could analyze him."

"Sometimes we heard him speaking foreign languages."

"He was communicating with his superiors. Somebody doesn't want that to be known, but that's the whole truth and nothing but the truth."

"We're not giving up on this and we're still in a state of high alert. We've been hearing voices from the mezzanine again, for some months now."

"It's always at weekends. Something's going on there."

We said they weren't mistaken and asked for their help. We didn't want to disappoint them. If they heard any noise in the apartment during the week, or more conversations, they should inform us. They were so thrilled we feared they might have a seizure.

The woman in the mezzanine apartment on the other side of the wall separating it from our father's was an Italian called Giuditta—which we knew from her mailbox—and she was the most interesting resident in the building. The first time Cristòfol went to the apartment in Carrer Nàpols, she heard him arrive, came out, and called to him from the landing. They chatted for a bit. She knew about Gabriel's disappearance and was very sorry about it. The police had questioned her a couple of times before registering him as missing, but unfortunately she didn't know anything. Gabriel had never been given to chatting with neighbors, had he? Then she offered to collect any mail that might arrive.

This time, when we Christophers knocked at the door, she opened it just a crack so we could see her only as far as the chain allowed. Cristòfol thought she was more aloof than on the first occasion. We said we needed to talk to her. Had she heard any noises recently? We suspected that her neighbor . . . She asked us to wait a moment and closed the door again. She took two or three minutes (running around the house, tidying up, turning off a radio, banging a door) and then opened up again, and this time was slightly more communicative. She'd changed into a dress and put on a bit of makeup, but neither the rouge on her cheeks nor a touch of lipstick concealed the fact that she was rattled. She seemed uncomfortable.

Somewhat stiffly, she invited us into her living room. She didn't offer us anything to drink, probably because she wanted us out of there quickly. The living room was a colorful, baroque version of our father's. The floral curtains and sofas gave it a slightly shabby British touch, like the Fawlty Towers dining room. Her wall-to-wall carpet was in different shades of brown that would have been perfect in a bingo hall. The walls were completely covered with two shelves of books (most with brightly colored spines), paintings of different landscapes, and photographs. Since we were obviously gawking at everything, she told us that she liked reading two very different sorts of books, romantic novels and atlases. Christophe pointed at a black-and-white photo on the wall. A spotlight was shining on a girl hanging upside down from a trapeze, and you could make out some of the structural elements of a circus tent in the background. The girl's feet were hooked over the trapeze bar and she made it look easy. Her life depended on the tension of those two feet, yet her face transmitted angelic calm.

"Excuse me, is that you?"

"Yes, that photo . . ." She sighed. "I wasn't even sixteen. Imagine. I look at it sometimes and don't believe it's me."

Senyora Giuditta was over fifty. She still had the svelte, tucked-in figure of a trapeze artiste but her face had the markedly ambiguous expression, halfway between forced happiness and real fatigue, of someone who's had to pile on makeup every day of her life, of a woman who's grown old in the circus. Without waiting for us to ask for further details, she was quick to tell us she'd grown up in a circus family—the Cherubini Brothers, as advertized on a framed poster—and had been singled out for the trapeze from an early age. After retiring, she'd stayed on with the circus, working with her family until one day about ten years ago, when they were doing a season in Barcelona, she'd got fed up with her nomadic existence and put an end to it. Shortly afterward, a school employed her as a gym teacher, and she was still working there.

Tension crept into her voice when we told her that we'd come to see her because someone had been in the apartment the previous day and everything seemed to suggest that the intruder was Gabriel Delacruz himself. He'd taken some things with him. Had she heard anything? The other neighbors... She seemed to be listening to us out of courtesy, or because she'd suppressed any desire to talk. Her answers were now short and tetchy. We shouldn't trust the other neighbors, she said. The two old ladies on the second floor had pinecones for brains. Senyora Giuditta spoke Catalan shot through with Italianisms, which elevated her words into something almost lyrical. Cristòfol translated them into our own idiolect. She hadn't spent much time at home recently. No, she hadn't heard anything the day before. In fact, she'd only seen Gabriel on very few occasions. If they met on the stairs or taking rubbish down in the evening, they had very brief conversations. They talked about the weather, criticized the other neighbors or recommended the odd television program. Sometimes, if she was away, he took delivery of the occasional packet from her book club. We showed her the portrait, and she confirmed that the drawing was quite a good likeness of Gabriel. From what she remembered. Now it must be, let's see... more than a year since she'd seen him. No, she had no clue as to where he might have gone.

"I can't tell you anything more, really I can't." She stood up to indicate that our time was up. Yet you would have said she enjoyed talking about Gabriel. When we stood up too, she couldn't resist asking us a favor.

"Could the four of you sit down together on the sofa? Just for a moment, that's all."

It was a reasonably long comfortable sofa but still quite a squeeze with all of us sitting there. We waited for Giuditta to say something. It was clear that she wanted to look at the four of us all lined up like the Dalton Gang.

"You're Gabriel's four sons, aren't you?" she finally said but didn't wait for us to confirm it. "You're very alike. When you started coming here at weekends, that's what I guessed. One day Gabriel opened up more than usual and told me he had four sons. From

four different women. In four different countries. He said it like
it was the most normal thing in the world. I didn't believe him, of
course. At the time, I thought he had a very strange way of com-
bating his loneliness, with his dry sense of humor. 'He's laughing
at himself so as not to despair,' I decided."

After thanking her, we said good-bye and went downstairs.
Back on the street, we each drew our own conclusions.

"I'd say she couldn't stand our father," Christophe began.

"Well, I think she was secretly in love with him, and he didn't
want to know about it," Christof said.

"Maybe . . . but did you notice one thing?" Cristòfol asked. "She
said that she and Dad talked about TV programs . . . but Dad hasn't
got a television set."

"I don't know what to say, really," Christopher mused. "But I
don't trust her. While we were piled up there on the sofa, my fingers began twitching and started feeling around. It's one of my
tics. You know how the nether regions of sofas, those yucky spaces
between cushions and grooves, are always a treasure trove of surprises. My fingers found this."

He pulled his hand out of his pocket and flashed a crumpled-
looking poker card. It was the joker. Careful examination of the
card revealed that somebody had drawn a little spot on the front
of it, a mark.

After our unhelpful conversation with Giuditta, we went for
a walk around the neighborhood and then for a beer. Taking a
roundabout route we approached the Carambola. It was open and
noisy inside, but we gave it a miss because we didn't want to put
the bartender in a tight spot, if he was still working at that hour.
We had our beer in another bar and argued for a while about the
definition of "night," the time we were supposed to phone him. At
nine on the dot, as the result of our democratic vote, Cristòfol got
out his mobile phone to call the number that was going to bring us
a little closer to our father.

"I want you to get one thing clear from the start: This conversation never happened. Remember that please," implored a boyish
voice, which immediately conjured up the bartender's scared face.

"Now listen. The owner of the bar is a shithead called Feijoo, with a double *o*. This morning he clammed up like the bastard he is. He used to play too, in those poker games, and he still plays every Friday. They pull down the metal blind and lock themselves in there till daylight. You saw how sleepy he was, didn't you? I think it's against the law to play for money like that, but a retired cop from the Guardia Civil comes along too. He's called Miguélez. Remember that name. Feijoo makes me stay on Fridays to serve them drinks, clean up, and keep an eye on the entrance. Remember I haven't said a word, eh?" he repeated. He spoke slowly, anxiously, as if what he was saying had been bottled up for a long time. He didn't allow any time for a response. "That man in your drawing, Delacruz, they called him, always cleaned them out. One way or another and without any fuss, every Friday he turned up he went away with a lot of money. They all lost to him, some more and some less, but they were really pissed off. No one remembered who brought him along in the first place or whose friend he was. He drove them crazy because he wasn't a show-off and he didn't drink or carry on like they do when they win a good hand. They tried to distract him by winding him up with their insults but it didn't work. This Delacruz only drank cognac. He wet his lips and that's all, always after putting down a card. A glass lasted him a couple of hours. Once Feijoo made me serve him some cheap cognac. It was off and would have made any barracks drunkard throw up, but Delacruz didn't complain. He asked for a bathroom break and the others said he could go. They were laughing their heads off, but the guy came back after five minutes, a new man. Then he bled them dry once again. You're still listening, aren't you?" He paused.

Cristòfol just managed to say, "Yes, yes, I am," and the bartender spewed out another torrent of words as if they were burning on his tongue. "I haven't said a thing, okay? Then one of the regular players started telling Feijoo that this Delacruz was cheating for sure, and they had to catch him at it. Feijoo spent the whole week after that going on and on about it. 'This Friday's not going to go by without us catching him red-handed.' He was like a cracked record. Friday came along, and the other four players turned up in the bar ten minutes early. They brought new cards and marked every joker with a felt-tipped pen, a tiny black spot between the eyebrows, like the third eye of those Hindu gods. Every time you got a joker in your hand you had to look at it carefully. If you got one without the dot, that meant he was using some trick to switch cards. That's what they suspected. While they were getting ready for the game, Miguélez pulled out a pistol—he put it in his coat pocket. I remember him saying, 'It's not loaded but, if necessary, we can give him a nice little fright.' " Cristòfol tried to interrupt but, once again, the bartender wouldn't have it. Seeing that this was going to go on for a while, he clamped the phone to his other ear and signaled to us other Christophers to be patient. "Anyway, I don't know whether Delacruz was cheating or not, and I don't care. I liked him because he was taking money off those jerks. That night, I left them drinking around the table, ready for the game, and went outside. I pretended to be sweeping up around the entrance. Ten minutes later I saw Delacruz coming along Carrer Almogàvars. When he was near the door I muttered that he should take care. He stopped, looked at me in surprise: Why and what was the danger, he asked. 'The boss and his pals have got their knickers in a twist today,' I said. 'They put their heads together and they're out to get you.' He thanked me. 'The cop's even got a pistol, but don't worry, it's not loaded,' I added at the last minute. He strolled into the bar like he didn't have a care in the world. So sure of himself. After a while, when I went back inside, they'd started playing. Delacruz sat with his back to the bar as usual, and I couldn't see his face, but his presence always inspired respect. So concentrated and still, you would have sworn he had a blindfold over his eyes and was facing a firing squad. I put his glass of cognac on the table, but he didn't look at me. I watched the game for a while, coming and going with rum and coke for the rest of them. They were playing in silence, concentrating hard, jumpy as hell and smoking like chimneys. They were all on the lookout. With each game the notes were piling up more and more in the center of the table. It was about an hour before they chilled out and started laughing. They were all winning except for Delacruz, and he was losing and

losing, hand over fist. Everything I'm telling you is true, right? I'm
not bullshitting. By about two in the morning, they'd cleaned him
out. We're talking big money because the starting stake was always very high, about seventy or eighty thousand pesetas. He told
them he was pulling out. They'd bled him dry. But Feijoo said no
way. They'd all had bad nights and they'd all hung in till the bitter end. Now it was his turn. For me, looking on, it was clear that
Delacruz was losing on purpose, but those jerks didn't get it. They
were blinded by the winnings they were going to be sharing out.
Delacruz said that wasn't in the rules of the game. Everyone knows
that when you lose everything you can call it a day. To their amazement, he gulped down his cognac, got up, and started to put his
coat on. When he turned around to leave, Miguélez yelled, 'You're
not going anywhere till I say so! Sit down again, you son of a bitch,'
and pointed the pistol at him. Delacruz turned around and saw the
gun. He raised his hands as if this was a holdup and his gesture
made the situation even hairier. One of the players called for calm.
'Get back to the table,' Feijoo ordered. 'I'll write you an IOU so you
can keep playing, but you'll be paying me interest, and you'd better
swear in your mother's name that you'll repay me tomorrow morning, right down to the last peseta...' 'You mean so he can keep
losing,' Miguélez interrupted, and they all laughed.

"I was watching Delacruz, full of admiration for him because
he had the situation under control. He knew it would turn out like
that, just as he'd planned. He sat down again, signed the note,
and took Feijoo's cash. Then he went on till daybreak, losing everything like some kind of bonehead, and the game came to an
end. The next day... no, the same day, I mean Saturday, Delacruz
didn't show up. Of course he didn't. No way. Feijoo was foam-
ing at the mouth and, as the hours went by, he was more and
more aware that he'd cocked up. More than the money he'd lost,
what really pissed him off was that he'd been taken for a ride. He
kept taking the note out of his pocket, looking at the scribble that
passed for a signature, and asking aloud who this Delacruz was.
Where he lived. What he did. Being met by silence got him even
more worked up. That night, at closing time, Miguélez the cop ap-

peared. He dropped in to make a big deal of himself, bragging that he'd spent his winnings on taking his wife out to lunch by the sea in Barceloneta and a classy whore after that. When he saw Feijoo in such a foul mood he said he'd sort it out and not to worry. On Monday morning, no problems, he'd drop into the cop shop and get Delacruz's address.

"When you bring it to me,' said the boss, 'bring me the gun too, with bullets this time, and we'll pay the bastard a visit.' I don't know what happened on Monday, or during the rest of the week. What I know for sure is that Delacruz didn't show up for the game that Friday, and he never showed up again."

The bartender stopped his monologue, at last, waiting for questions, but Cristòfol couldn't think of what to say. The deluge of information had left him flabbergasted. Circling around him, the rest of us Christophers were laughing at the stupefied look on his face.

The bartender, however, was still wound up. "Don't come back to the bar, please. I've told you everything now. Don't come back, or if you must, for whatever reason, don't give me away. Feijoo . . . Well, I know what he's like. He'll get someone to beat me up, and then get the cops to arrest me on some pretext. I couldn't deal with that. He's the one the police should lock up. If Delacruz's disappeared off the face of the earth—and I don't know for sure that he has—but, if he did, I'm certain that Feijoo and Miguélez had something to do with it. You saw the way he was talking about him this morning, like he was shit . . . Look, so you know I'm being straight with you and this is no joke, I'm going to tell you something, what my interest is in all this. But you've got to keep it secret. I'm going to let you in on my secret, okay?" Cristòfol had no time to react. "I've been in love with Feijoo's wife for more than a year now. She's called . . . well, never mind what she's called. I'm crazy about her, and the little girls too. When you came today she wasn't there, but you'd only have to see her for two minutes to know that the shithead doesn't deserve her. He treats her like a slave, for one thing, and he does it in front of me. I can't do anything about it, but one of these days I'm going to lose it. You get what I'm saying, right? If we could prove that Feijoo's killed Delacruz, or he's at least an accomplice, we could get him sent to prison, and then everything would be different for us. I'm telling you, if you want to know what happened to Delacruz, you've got to get on the track of that retired cop, and Feijoo (with a double *o*, I'm not sure if I told you). And now good-bye. I've got to go. I wish you the best of luck."

End of conversation. He hung up. Cristòfol hadn't opened his mouth but was exhausted from listening so attentively. We immediately called him back, if only to thank him, but this time the bartender didn't answer. Not that night, or the next, though we tried several times.

In what remained of Saturday, and over the course of Sunday until the Christophers went back to their respective countries, we analyzed every aspect of the bartender's story. We agreed it rang pretty true, and the cardsharp angle fitted Gabriel's profile, but there were still a few points that remained unclear. For example, the bartender was trying to make us believe that Feijoo and Miguélez had killed our father, but we were sure that wasn't the case. We wanted him alive. His secret visit to the apartment had really built up our hopes. Who knows whether that fateful card game was the detonator, the turning point that had made him decide, in the best pulp-fiction tradition, to go to ground for a while. But "a while" turned out to be indefinite. After all, we agreed, our father had plenty of experience in living a clandestine existence.

All this speculation took us down new, less playful, less agreeable paths, but what were we supposed to do about that? We thought that Cristòfol, since he was nearby, should start going to the apartment once or twice a week to see whether there were any changes, or if the Italian neighbor would decide to give us any more clues. From time to time, he could also check out what Feijoo was up to in the bar, especially Friday and Saturday nights.

Meanwhile, we told ourselves, the best way to get a sense of Gabriel's present was to continue exploring his past. You might think we were just playing for time. That's okay. We don't mind. Moreover, we know that everything's cyclical, time repeats itself, and sometimes the present and the past get mixed up. For example, we're looking now for Gabriel, clinging to uncertain clues, and, twenty-five years ago a girl called Rita got off on the wrong track (thanks to an erroneous astrological ascendant) when she was desperately looking for him too.

All right, go ahead, Cristòfol. The floor's all yours.


Very well. We left things on February 16, 1972, the day when, thanks to a passport blunder, Rita fell in love with Gabriel thinking he was called Serafí Bundó. That Wednesday, then, after she left the Cage, Mom went to look for the stranger's house. It was only a first step. All morning, she'd thrown body and soul into finding the mislaid bag, but it remained mislaid. However, he'd given her his address, she knew they lived near one another, and she thought this would snip a bit off the distance that united them. Take note, Christophers, I say "united" them rather than "separated" them: Even then, Rita was convinced that nothing and nobody would be able to separate them. It was just a matter of time. If the stars had led their paths to cross, who were they to contradict them? Today's Rita would find a thousand convincing answers, but that Rita, aged twenty, single, and a devout believer in horoscopes, didn't give it another thought.

She got off the bus at Plaça de Catalunya and headed for home via her usual route. She went along the Rambla, turned into Carrer Elisabets and continued in the direction of Carrer Joaquim Costa. When she got to Carrer del Tigre, though, she walked past her street door and kept going toward the Ronda de Sant Antoni. She reached the door of number 70 after counting exactly 192 steps from her house, only to discover that this man Serafí had given her the address of a pension. The half-witted optimism to which she was in thrall promptly suppressed a suspicion that maybe someone had taken her for a ride—pensions, like airports, are only places of transit—and she steered her plan back on track. On second thought, she told herself, it was better that he didn't have a place of his own. Plants without roots are more easily moved. She walked to the edge of the sidewalk and examined the façade of the building. In other circumstances, she would have thought that the scruffy aluminum street door was cheap and nasty, but now it was practical. She looked up at the glassed-in balcony on the second floor where she imagined the pension was. Behind the window she could see two men sitting in armchairs, chatting animatedly as they drank steaming cups of tea. Although the balcony wasn't lit and the two figures were silhouetted in semidarkness, she was sure that neither of them was Serafí. They looked too active. Meanwhile, a petite, well-groomed lady in a black dress emerged from the door. They exchanged glances, and then the lady tottered off with a *tap-tap*ping of high heels. Rita saw her chance and slipped inside before the door closed. She couldn't help herself: Anything to do with Serafí served as bait. She went up the first flight of stairs and stood outside the pension door. From its vantage point on the wall, a stuffed goat's head observed her like a learned professor. What if she knocked at the door and asked for Serafí? What was she going to say? That they hadn't found the bag yet? She wanted to see him again, away from the airport, on his own ground, but the goat's head made her feel ridiculous so she turned and ran downstairs. Then she spied on the house from the street.

It's a pity that Rita didn't go into the pension that afternoon after confronting the oracle goat. She either lacked the willpower or suffered an excessive attack of reverence. If she'd done it, if she'd knocked at the door and asked for Senyor Serafí Bundó, she might have spared herself some of the anguish, weeping, swooning, and misunderstandings that were in store for her, starting the very next day. One way or another, if she'd spoken to the boarders who lived in the pension at the time, prize busybodies all, Rita would have put two and two together. But she didn't do it. A fit of prudence pushed her into retreat from her usual impetuousness.

While Rita was keeping an eye on the pension window with the furtive excitement of a Mata Hari, the lead players were in a less traditional neighborhood of Barcelona. It would have been enough for her to trail Senyora Rifá when she left the house in such haste. She would have got on the bus with her and crossed the city to Via

Favència. There she would have followed her hesitant footsteps (it was the first time she'd come to such a faraway part of the city) to Bundó's apartment.

In the morning, when he'd at last left the customs people behind him and had come out with the wrong bag, Gabriel found Senyor Casellas and his secretary, Rebeca, waiting for him. Casellas, who was wearing a black armband, held out his hand and declared that, at such a difficult time, he had wanted to come and meet Gabriel in person. Then he expressed his condolences, throwing in a few platitudes (however, it should be acknowledged that, as a good Catholic, he did try to sound sincere). A distraught Rebeca embraced Gabriel and burst into tears. Her tears were real. She'd always got on well with Bundó: She thought of him as a teddy bear, cuddly and tender-hearted, an ally among that gang of uncivilized men.

A taxi took them directly to the apartment in Via Favència. The hearse should have arrived at Bundó's by now, Senyor Casellas informed him. The funeral home employees had been instructed to transfer the body to another coffin, a better-quality one than that provided by the consulate in Germany, paid for by La Ibérica in gratitude for all his years of service in the company.

Gabriel, still sunk in misery and responding in monosyllables, let himself be led. Each new stage of the nightmare crushed his willpower even further. The only time he really made an effort to put on a brave front was when he walked into Bundó's apartment. Carolina had arrived by train from France that morning. For the last half an hour, since they'd brought Bundó's body for the vigil, she'd been sitting stupefied on the bed where her man lay in repose.

Christophers, now you have to try to imagine the drama. It's awful for me to have to reconstruct it. Imagine—and it's not difficult—the wreaths, the cloying smell of chrysanthemums, long faces, workmates patting each other on the back or standing around with their hands in their pockets, not knowing what else to do with them. Imagine the heartfelt and pathetic words of El Tembleque (who'd knocked back many a *sol y sombra* since the previous night in Bundó's honor). Imagine, too, the conversations that filled the silence, anecdotes whispered with too much solemnity to do justice to Bundó's contagious cheerfulness. Imagine Senyora Rifà consoling Gabriel like a big sister, and Carolina like a mother. Imagine a destroyed, bewildered Petroli, who'd also just arrived from Germany, trying to avoid Senyor Casellas and having to give him explanations, and wanting to speak privately with Gabriel; imagine him looking like a lost dog, haggard, guilt ridden ("I should have been driving that truck . . . He'd still be alive . . ."). Imagine, finally, the moment when everybody left and our father and Carolina were left alone in the Via Favència apartment, keeping one another company, talking in the darkness without turning on the lights, summoning memories of Bundó like people taking medicine to stave off depression. It wasn't even two months since that Christmas Eve when Gabriel had had dinner with the two of them and Mireille, and their laughter had filled those rooms with life . . . What was left of that now?

Well, Christophers, don't be shy. You can say that life's a pile of shit if you want, and you won't be wrong, but that would lead us down a dead end—and we all know that truck drivers prefer an open road with good visibility (sorry about the motorway metaphor; it slipped out). Anyway, experience teaches us that, more than anything else, life's a black comedy. If you don't think so, look at what happened to Rita. We left her standing guard in front of the pension, starting to feel cold but still attentive to all the movement inside it. She watched the place for ages. She checked out all the men entering and leaving the building, keeping herself amused with a string of fantasies about her life with Serafí. It was as good a way as any to be thinking about him. At eight, the lady she'd seen earlier came back (she had to give her lodgers their dinner). By ten, one of her legs had gone to sleep. She was hungry so she went home.

The next morning when she was on her way to catch the bus, she took a detour past the pension. Just in case. Nothing. What with running late and her state of nerves, she forgot to have breakfast. Thus began the day in which she was going to pass out twice.

As soon as she got to the Cage, she ran to have a look at the file they kept on incoming and outgoing lost luggage. Having confirmed that her item was still missing, she calmed down and started attending to irate clients. She asked her questions automatically, without getting involved, waiting for a break so she could go and have some breakfast in the cafeteria. Her eyes no longer sought the date of birth on the passengers' passports. Their disagreeable comments didn't bother her any more. She'd embarked on a new stage of her life. Serafí Bundó didn't know it yet (for him, it was still only written in his stars), but that was the second day of their life together.

A new traveler came over to the Cage and, like all the rest, wanted to reclaim a lost suitcase. Rita could never remember any feature of this particular man, whether he was tall or short, young or old, ugly or handsome. She had no idea of his face. When she thought about him—and she would think about him often in the days to come—the only thing that came to her was a casual (or, she wondered, maybe not so casual) movement of his hands and the intriguing sensation of not being sure whether to be grateful for the favor or to curse him to hell and back.

The passenger in question had flown in from Madrid and had lost his bag. Rita wrote down his details on the form and, as was customary, asked him to confirm them and sign the form. The man picked up the yellow sheet and read it. His right hand fumbled for a pen in the inside pocket of his jacket. It must have been a brand-name pen and very delicate (or maybe he was very fussy) because, in order not to damage the nib, he laid a newspaper on the counter and put the form on top of that before he started writing. The newspaper was *El Correo Catalán,* and he'd read some of it and then folded it. They must have given it to him on the plane. The crossword was half done. The pen signed the bottom of the form and the hand held it out to Rita. The newspaper was visible again. Before the man took it away, Rita saw that it was open at the obituaries page, and with the speed acquired over her months of spotting dates, her eyes flew straight to a box at the bottom of the page, in the center, to a discreet death notice. It said:

SERAFÍN BUNDÓ VENTOSA
(1941–1972)

These things happen.

Rita's brain took too long to react. It was like the seconds that separate the clap of thunder from the flash of lightning. The man had walked away, taking the newspaper with him, still fretting about his lost luggage, and she was left behind, paralyzed, clinging to the counter, trying not to collapse. Seeing her standing so still, one of her colleagues asked if she was all right. She heard the voice but didn't have the strength to answer because she didn't understand the question. Her gaze was fixed on the newspaper, the hand of the man who was walking away. She'd soon lose sight of him. Her blood slowly began to flow again. No, it can't be, she said. This is a joke. This is really bad taste. And she let out a hysterical titter, only one—*he-e-ee-ee!*—which immediately turned into a wheeze of despair. On the other side of the baggage claim area, the man threw the newspaper into a bin, and that revived her. In a couple of strides she was out of the Cage, running to rescue the newspaper and, standing right there next to the bin, she read the death notice again. Serafín Bundó Ventosa. Was that him, the man destiny had handed to her just yesterday? She checked the date of birth. 1941, yes. Again: 1941, yes, definitely. A hundred times she read and reread that name, written in bold black death-notice letters, and relived the encounter with her Serafí, the false Bundó, Gabriel, the man with his arm in a cast. Call him whatever you like. Her head was spinning in hopeless confusion, and she fainted for the first time that day.

Christophers, I'm telling you all this in my own words because my mother doesn't want to know about it. Even today, she's ashamed, embarrassed about the whole thing, as if she were guilty of something.

Publishing the death notice in *El Correo Catalán* had been the secretary Rebeca's idea, probably behind Senyor Casellas's back, as he only read *La Vanguardia*. The text said that Bundó's colleagues at the La Ibérica transport company announced their "heartfelt loss" to the readers, asking them to pray for his soul. It also said that the funeral service would take place that Thursday at four in the afternoon, at the Sant Salvador parish church in the town of El Vendrell in the Penedès region.

Porras and Sayago, who happened to be cleaning and buffing up the marble floor nearby, were the first to come to Rita's aid. When she came around—lying on the floor with Sayago fanning her with the same damn newspaper—the first thing she asked was what time it was. They helped her to get up. It was ten in the morning. The two maestros of cleanliness accompanied her to the Cage and, true to form, exaggerated Rita's fainting fit, blowing it up to romantic-heroine proportions. She tried to explain it away by saying she'd skipped breakfast, but, seeing how wan and ill she looked, her boss told her to go home. Rita needed no second bidding. She put away the file of the man with the newspaper and made her way to the bus stop. As she walked past Sayago, pretending to dither in order to disguise her haste, she heard him say, "You wouldn't be pregnant, would you, girlie?"

"If only I were," she answered with tears in her eyes. And anyone would have thought she really meant it.


That was the start of Rita's long journey to Bundó's funeral. A workers' bus took her to Barcelona where she got out at the Passeig de Gràcia stop, went into the station, and bought a round-trip ticket to El Vendrell. She jumped on the train as the doors were closing.

While she was looking for a seat, an old man grumpily asked her if they had women ticket inspectors nowadays. She'd left the airport without changing out of her Cage uniform. She sat down in an empty compartment and removed her jacket in order to avoid further misunderstandings and so as not to feel so out of place. As always in winter, the heating on the train was turned up full blast and she was grateful for the hospitable warmth. As she calmed down, the tears and confusion returned. She was trying not to think about bad luck because that wouldn't be fair to Serafí. Then again, if she concentrated on him, her head began to fill up with questions. How had he died, for example? Who had found him? She'd seen he was a wreck the day before, but he wasn't that bad. What if she was the last person he'd spoken to? What a useless honor. In short, she told herself, she was in mourning again, just like when her parents died. It was a strange kind of mourning, a sort of indirect mourning, and it brought to mind the words "We began the house with the roof..."

What with the warmth and the rocking of the train, Rita nodded off, still assailed by her thoughts. She didn't wake up for a long time. She opened her eyes because the train had stopped at a station and her sleep was invaded by high-pitched cheeping. In Vilafranca del Penedès two countrywomen had come in and sat beside her. They were carrying a basket full of chicks.

"Is it far to El Vendrell?" she asked.

"It's this stop, young lady! You'd better hurry..."

She leaped off the train with the last whistle. She heard the curses of the station master while the two women applauded her from the window. The platform clock said three minutes past four. Following the directions of a passerby, she took another five minutes to walk down an attractive rambla, cross through a market, and go up a narrow street before reaching the church square. The funeral service had already begun by the time she entered the church. The sickly smell of burning wax made her feel dizzy. The casket had been placed before the altar. The priest was praising Serafí, a native son of El Vendrell who, in accordance with the designs of Our Lord, had led a life marked not only by hardship and the vicissitudes of fortune but also by his iron will and determined efforts to stay on the path of righteousness. His mellifluous voice, redolent of Montserrat choirboys, echoed inside the baroque church. Rita counted only thirty people, all huddled over against the cold. She sat in the second-to-last row and looked at the backs of the necks in front of her. The men were on the right of the altar and women on the left. A pious tableau of three nuns was conspicuous in the first row on her side. Sitting next to them were the lady she'd seen coming out of the pension in Ronda de Sant Antoni the previous afternoon, and a blond girl who couldn't stop crying. She was inconsolable and kept shaking her head. Rita preferred to believe she was Serafí's sister and not his widow. There were more men than women and it was difficult for her to work out who was who on their side of the church. She imagined they were his workmates (and we now know that all La Ibérica staff members were present under the captainship of Senyor Casellas). Who would go to her funeral, if she died, she wondered. Her workmates at the airport, her neighbors, her few friends, and that was all. A lot of people wouldn't even know for weeks or even months, which is what had happened with her parents.

Distracted by these thoughts, she just about survived the ceremony. From time to time she looked over at the coffin. Her Serafí was lying in there, she reminded herself. She'd get into the habit of coming to visit him at All Saints, every year without fail, bringing him a bunch of flowers. She'd come by train to El Vendrell. It would be her secret. She saw herself as an old maid, decrepit, not easy to pigeonhole. She'd play bingo with her friends using chickpeas instead of coins and, over afternoon tea, if some widow asked her if she was lonely, she'd summon up an old love of her youth. "A tragic story," she'd say, "too tragic to talk about," and then she'd go quiet.

When the priest dismissed them with the last amen, Rita followed the other mourners out of the church. An altar boy handed her an In Memoriam card, and she read the name again. Once outside, everyone took up positions on either side of the entrance and steps, leaving a corridor for the pallbearers. The hearse was waiting with its back door open. It was a cloudy day, but a peekaboo sun was warming the square when they came out. Rita glimpsed a few men inside the church raising the casket and resting it on their shoulders. They had to be friends and workmates. Soon the priest came out, murmuring a prayer and followed by the altar boy. The pallbearers followed. They walked slowly and carefully. Rita watched the scene transfixed. Everything had happened so fast that nothing seemed real. As the coffin passed in front of her she was dazzled by a ray of sun and shielded her eyes with her hand so as not to miss a single detail. Then, right there, in front of her, she saw Gabriel, her Serafí, alive, grieving as he'd been the previous day, but alive, having some difficulty bearing the coffin using only his right arm and shoulder (as his left arm was in a cast). What a shock! The supernatural vision made her shudder violently, and she cried out in fright. Like all the other mourners, Gabriel turned to look at her but didn't recognize her. Of course he didn't. Rita was so overwhelmed that she started to shake. Then she buckled at the knees and fainted for the second time that day. It was one swoon responding to the other, a swooning competition.

Two women who worked in a knitting-wool shop in the square and who'd been watching the funeral proceedings brought her around by getting her to drink the standard remedy for attacks of hysteria, *aigua del Carme*, made by Carmelite nuns. Meanwhile, the funeral procession moved on to the cemetery. Of all the mourners, only Natàlia Rifà, who had a thing about graveyards, remained behind with the young lady in the strange uniform. She'd spotted Rita watching her building the previous evening for heaven knows what reason, and now she recognized her. Her curiosity was killing her.

Rita felt drugged by the holy remedy. Her head was spinning. Her first words were to ask whether the dead man, Serafí, had a twin brother. She'd seen the arm in its cast, of course, but at this stage she didn't believe her own eyes. Natàlia Rifà gave her a maternal smile and cleared up the matter by telling her that her Serafí's real name was Gabriel Delacruz. They went into a café, and she told Rita about the accident, Bundó's death, and all the ups and downs in the lives of the La Ibérica truckers. The airport misunderstandings gradually began to untangle. If she'd paid proper attention, she would have seen that the death notice in *El Correo Catalán* said that Bundó had died three days earlier.

The next train departing from El Vendrell took them to Barcelona. Despite her uniform, Rita was in such a state that no one took her for a ticket inspector this time. On the way back she confessed to Gabriel's landlady about her obsession with the horoscope, the predictions of Jorgito the Magician, and the coincidences at the airport. Talking about her troubles brought some relief, and Senyora Rifà lapped it up. She saw in Rita a version of herself some twenty-four years earlier when she'd come to the city to take over the pension, a young woman fizzing with vitality, somewhere between naive and reckless. She therefore enjoyed telling Rita everything she knew about Bundó, his relationship with Carolina, and all sorts of stories about his years in the boarding house. He and Gabriel had arrived when they were seventeen. They were still children. She'd been looking after them for almost half their lives, so to speak. It wasn't that she'd been a mother to them, but she nearly had, especially with Bundó, who was needier.

She suddenly remembered that she had a photograph of him in her bag. She'd picked it up before going out in case they wanted to put it on the headstone, but Carolina told her they already had one. She showed it to Rita. It had been taken three months earlier, and Bundó had given it to her as a memento when he went off to live in Via Favència. Although it made her feel decidedly strange, Rita gazed at the stranger she'd never seen before but with whom she'd fallen in love because of his name. His chubby cheeks made him look like a cute, mischievous little boy, but, at first glance, she felt she could never have fallen in love with someone like him. What's more, he was wearing a horrible shirt. It was made of some black-and-white material in a flashy weave that hurt her eyes just looking at it and, even worse, he seemed proud of it. An hour earlier she would have paid a fortune to discover the slightest detail about Bundó, but now she was doing her best to forget him.

Walking home, she realized that her next task was to tidy up the chaos left in the wake of the earthquake and settle a new guest in among the ruins . . . Gabriel Delacruz, was that his name? The stars and the horoscope were a rip-off. She'd just have to listen to her own feelings. Besides, there was the matter of the lost bag. The next day, Friday, or whenever Lufthansa handed it over, she'd take it to the boarding house and try to get to know this Gabriel. She'd express her condolences over the loss of his friend and the whole story would start all over again.


That afternoon, after the funeral, Carolina and Gabriel went back to Barcelona in Senyor Casellas's car. Our father's wish, Christophers, was to stay in the pension and not come out for a good long time. It was five days since the accident, and his head was all over the place. It was like arriving in an unfamiliar city without a map. This was something he'd experienced on other occasions, but, if the solution once lay in keeping moving and trying an exit at random, now he only wanted to stay still. Luckily, or unluckily, with his arm in a cast, he'd be on sick leave for several weeks and he could put off any decisions.

Senyor Casellas left them in Plaça Calvo Sotelo and headed for his affluent neighborhood. Gabriel offered to go with Carolina to Via Favència, and they hailed a taxi. Now that Bundó had died, the apartment was hers. Gabriel imagined that Carolina would break for ever with Muriel and her French past. At the entrance, however, Carolina asked the taxi driver to keep the engine running. She took the keys out of her bag and handed them to Gabriel.

"I'm not going up," she said. "Everything I need from Bundó I have with me. I couldn't even spend five minutes in that house. The memories we didn't get to create . . . the constant trap of what couldn't be would make my life unbearable. I'm taking the train back to France tonight, Gabriel, to see if I can start all over again. I'll write to you or phone you. Here, take the keys and do whatever you want with the apartment. Live there, if you like. We'll sort out the legal stuff later. It'll take no time at all because there's nothing more I can take from there."

That night, Gabriel slept in the Falcon Room. Well, rather than sleeping, he waited till morning. Then, at breakfast, he informed Senyora Rifà that he was leaving the boarding house.

"I'll be away for a long time," he said.

Even in his most desperate moments he only thought about a provisional change of address (but, in fact, he never went back there). Then he phoned El Tembleque and asked him to help him move his few belongings. That's how he ended up living in Bundó's apartment. He didn't know why, maybe it was like repaying a debt, but he had one clear goal. He would never go out unless it was absolutely essential. Once again, Christophers, irony did a dazzling double somersault. The very day that Rita decided to spare no effort to find the man of her life, he finally stopped moving.

Barcelona was too big a city for playing hide-and-seek.

# 4

## Reclusion

Gabriel's retreat lasted eighty days. The day it ended . . . well, the day it ended, Christophers, my mother appeared in his life for the third time, ready to stay for ever. But there's no need to get excited about that just yet. It'll all happen soon enough. As for what happened during his lengthy (two Lents!) reclusion, we now have a paradox: While our father was running around in the Pegaso, we could easily stay on his trail but when he finally stops in one spot, we lose track of him.

All we know of that period is what he revealed to my mother during pillow talk. His withdrawal into the apartment in Via Favència couldn't have been more prosaic. It's not as if he rolled down the blinds, for example, believing that his solitude should be steeped in darkness or, worse, exposed beneath the interrogative glare of a bare light bulb. He wasn't moved by mystical or esoteric impulses; he didn't want to purge his pain like an anchorite; he wasn't trying to communicate with Bundó's spirit (though he would have liked to). Neither did he want to take his friend's place even though Bundó had once suggested that they could live there together. No, Gabriel locked himself away in his new home out of instinct, a simple reaction to his own state of mind. Yet we might say that, in his isolation, Gabriel respected Bundó's wishes.

The apartments in that building—and, in fact, the whole neighborhood—seem to have been designed to blight the private lives of workers, to make them yearn for the factories. In sixty square meters, counting dead space and off-kilter walls, there were two bedrooms, a kitchen, a living-cum-dining room and a bathroom. I know that because, when we first started to look for signs of our father, I went up to Via Favència one Saturday morning to see Bundó's apartment. I rang at the street door. After taking me for a Jehovah's Witness and then an encyclopedia salesman, the lady who's now living there decided I was a journalist and let me in. My heart sank when she opened the door. It was a desolate sight. Thirty years after the building went up architects had discovered structural deterioration typically associated with high-alumina cement. A forest of metal props temporarily underpinned her ceiling. The lady ushered me into the apartment through a sort of tunnel.

"It might smell of mildew because of the damp," she warned. "I don't notice it any more."

Hiding my excitement, which would have been unseemly, I walked around that bunker, room by room. For a few frivolous seconds I was tempted by the idea that all this ruin emanated from our father's unhappy days, a kind of affliction brought on by delayed grief. With admirable poise, no doubt a by-product of two years of enduring life on this building site, the lady made coffee, which we had in the living room. It was like being in an abandoned coal mine. The only relief came from a yellow canary warbling in its cage and a radio-cassette player from which issued Antonio Machín's boleros. "Right here, on these very tiles," I thought, "Bundó was capering and dancing around like a man possessed on the last Christmas Eve of his life."

The lady, a widow in her sixties, wanted me to have a look at the title deeds. She always kept them handy, tucked away in a plastic folder ready to show visiting journalists or building inspectors. I recognized Carolina's signature on them. The date on the contract of purchase for that slum was June 1979. I would have paid a fortune to know the terms of the agreement between Gabriel and Carolina. What was clear was that the apartment remained in Carolina's name for the seven years Gabriel lived there.

I asked the lady if she recalled the person who countersigned the contract, but it had been a long time, and her memory was no longer what it used to be. What she did tell me is that when she and her husband moved in they found a collection of things left behind by the former occupant. Most of it was junk, but they'd taken a fancy to two or three items. I asked her if she could show me any of them, and she pointed at two pictures, still hanging on the wall. They were the autumnal landscapes, the bad Olot School imitations claimed by Bundó in the divvying up of the last move, Number 199. He hadn't lived to see them on display, so I deduced that Gabriel must have retrieved them and hung them up. Ah, and before leaving, Christophers, I indulged in a bit of mischief that you'll like. I told the lady that they were by a very good painter who hadn't been properly recognised in his lifetime, informing her, too, that the initials S.B. with which they were signed concealed a man called Serafí Bundó.

"That name rings a bell . . ." the candid soul said, not knowing how happy that made me.

In the few months he was living there, Bundó had fixed up the apartment to his liking but had left the smaller bedroom empty, the only room he hadn't wallpapered. He always said it would be for the kids. When Carolina reminded him that she didn't want to have children, that she'd told him so a thousand times, he corrected himself and referred to it as the guest room. That was our father's refuge. It was about nine square meters with a window opening onto the light well. Since it was a seventh-floor apartment, halfway up the building, this window had to be kept closed all the time because of the smells drifting up from the downstairs kitchens. Before moving in, Gabriel bought a mattress, a bedstead, and a bedside table and set out his possessions just as he'd done when he was in the boarding house. You might say only the falcon was missing.

You mustn't—please don't—confuse this conduct with any kind of temporary insanity. What I want to say, and I'll try to clarify this, is that when it suited him, Gabriel's withdrawal was sometimes more psychological than physical. He spent whole days without going out, but this wasn't because of dogma, and it didn't make him a Carthusian monk either. When the larder was bare, he'd go out for an hour or so in the morning, call into the bank, get a bit of money out of his account, do some shopping at the corner shop, and stock up at the tobacconist's. On one of these expeditions, two weeks after shutting himself away, he went looking for a pay phone and called La Ibérica. Although he was still on sick leave, he told Rebeca he'd decided to call it a day. Advising him not to rush into it, the secretary spared him the conversation with the boss. They'd talk about it again when they took the cast off and he was fit to work. He agreed but on condition that she never revealed to anybody where he was. Nobody. Rebeca went along with it.

"You're still living in that pension, aren't you? One of those places where people come and go without having to give any explanations . . ."

They say the past is a foreign country where things are done differently. During that period of reclusion, Christophers, the saying would have applied quite literally to our father. Bundó, Petroli, and the moves in the Pegaso had been his main link with the world. For him, being alive meant being on the move, nonstop, savoring the lightness that came with crossing the border, and tinkering with the schedule so he could visit his three sons and their mothers. The accident stole all that from him, in one blow, with the appalling shock of pain. All of a sudden, alone in Barcelona, obliged to stay put, he could see the present fading before his eyes. You and your mothers became a point in the past, a tangle of relations that were too complicated for him to maintain at a distance without hurting somebody. This is our main beef with our father, I think. Was he so unaware, so naive that he'd never foreseen this? Was it possible that he didn't realize that his amorous rounds couldn't go on for ever and that one day it would all go askew and collapse like a house of cards? He's the only person who can answer that. Without wanting to excuse him, it's likely that he counted too much on your mothers: young, free, and with an independence of spirit that wasn't acceptable in Franco's Spain. It's also probable that, immured in his solitude, he longed for the family protection of Sigrun and Christof, or Sarah and Christopher, or Mireille and Christophe . . . But that, of course, would have meant choosing one family, and he was in no condition to choose anything.

In the light of this speculation, then, we shouldn't be surprised to discover that Gabriel went to ground in the Via Favència apartment. Once Carolina had renounced it, the place became a no-man's-land, a desert island for a voluntary Robinson Crusoe. Visionaries might say that Gabriel was waiting for some sort of epiphany to bring him out of his isolation. They'd be wrong. This self-inflicted solitary confinement is monotonous, inviolable precisely because it has no ambition. The only possible epiphany is the dullness of everyday life: The sun rises, the sun sets, another day gone.

As I noted, we know very little about Dad's confinement. We can confirm, however, that he became a TV addict. At the end of December, a few weeks before the accident, Bundó had gone to Pont Reyes and invested his Christmas bonus in a Philips television set, cash down. He'd put it on a small wheeled table in a strategic corner of the dining room and set up a Nativity scene underneath. Unlike Bundó, Gabriel wasn't remotely interested in TV. He'd never been able to spend more than half an hour looking at it without getting bored. At most, he occasionally glanced at it out of the corner of his eye if they happened to be broadcasting a soccer match on a Sunday afternoon when he was having a beer at Café Principal. He was more of a radio man, listening to news, sports programs or some nighttime serial. Senyora Rifà was the same. She'd always refused to install a television set in the pension because she didn't want her lodgers to settle down in front of it and lapse into an after-dinner stupor.

Strange as it may seem, Gabriel turned the TV on because he was freezing. It was a Tuesday night at the end of February and Barcelona had been hit by a cold snap. Just before dark, he'd gone out on to the balcony to check the thermometer and discovered it was four degrees below zero. Sitting on the couch wrapped up in a blanket, he recalled something Bundó had said just after he moved in. "The only problem is there's no heating and it's fucking cold."

Gabriel had closed the living room and left the butane heater on all day, but the walls kept oozing damp, and the icy air squeezed in relentlessly through cracks in the window frames. Insulating tape was completely useless. Then he got the idea of turning on the TV to see the weather report on News at Nine. He was sure that a new ice age had arrived, and he wanted the meteorologist to confirm it. In addition, he told himself, the screen might add a smidgen of warmth to the room.

The weatherman reported on the polar cold wave, but his forecast of a huge anticyclone building up in the Azores brought some comfort. By the end of the news it didn't seem quite so cold. The new warmth encouraged him to leave the TV on for a while longer. There were a few minutes of ads, a riveting war film, more ads, a shorter news report, and then an inordinately serious gentleman took his leave of the viewers until the morning. It was midnight, and Gabriel had sat through it all without once getting up from the sofa. The screen filled with randomly flickering snow. Then his body started to freeze again. The television, he realized, kept him company.

After that first night Gabriel's new hobby became an evening ritual. Six hours every day. The first step was to turn the TV on just before six in the afternoon. The children's programs came immediately after the test card. With their jolly dulcet voices, the presenters of these educational slots reminded him of the nuns at the House of Charity when they were organizing games. He watched them without really wanting to, just for the hell of it, a sort of warm-up session to distract him while he was waiting for the films to come on: a horse from the Wild West, a naughty kangaroo, some astronauts lost in space. The Pink Panther made him laugh for the first time in ages, and the next day he unconsciously hummed the music while he was making coffee. As the days went by, he refined his viewing habits, shaping the rhythms of his life to the TV. At half past seven they broadcast "Buenas Tardes," a current affairs program. If he didn't like it, he went to make himself something for dinner, which he ate watching the daily episode of *Persuasion*. After that came the news program. It was the only thing he watched out of obligation, like a sort of compulsory road toll. Apart from the daily fare of Franco propaganda, he was exasperated because there was hardly any news about what was happening outside Spain. It seemed as if Spain was the only country that existed in this black-and-white world. He never checked the TV Guide and liked being surprised by whatever film or series turned up on the screen at night. He especially enjoyed the moments when the credits appeared and a male voice-over announced the title. "Tormented." "Ironside." "McMillan & Wife."

Things were more upbeat on the weekends, and these mood changes on the TV cushioned his routine. There was the Saturday rugby game, for example, which they called the Five Nations Tournament. Although it was hard for him to understand the game, he wallowed in those fields of England, France, and Scotland. He repeated the names aloud: Twickenham, Murrayfield . . . He saw the grimacing faces of players huffing and puffing like bullocks, and they reminded him of some of the characters he'd met when he was driving around those places in the Pegaso.

One evening, when he was trying to turn up the volume on the television set, he pressed the wrong button and another channel came on. What a surprise, what a wonderful thing! He felt like he was entering a parallel world. The film they were showing was set in Paris, but the people were speaking fluent Spanish. The streets and people of the city were so wonderfully reproduced that they tricked him into feeling nostalgic. He was glued to the TV right to the end, and, when the announcer said goodnight, he confirmed what Gabriel already surmised: This was the second Spanish channel. It was called UHF. Thenceforth, his devotion to television was increasingly complex. He couldn't watch everything so he had to choose, which wasn't so bad. Every evening he got up from the sofa a hundred times to change channels. These gymnastics soon encouraged him to be more selective. He stopped watching the news and tended more toward UHF's less predictable programming. The window was now opening onto another kind of landscape. His favorite program was on Sunday nights. It was called "Un Domingo en . . ." and offered reports about cities in other parts of the world. Budapest, Berlin, Amsterdam . . . London! With his eyes glued to the screen, his feet were braking and working the clutch while his hands sometimes gripped an invisible wheel. He was on the move once again, if only in black-and-white.

Mourning is a process, they say, and each person channels it the best way he or she can. The weeks were rolling by, and Gabriel hadn't shed a single tear over Bundó's death.

The night of the first Monday of April, which turned out to be Easter Monday, he was watching an episode of *Hawaii Five-O*, one of his favorite programs. There was a scene in which two masked delinquents beat up a parking lot guard and steal a luxury car. Shortly afterward, Detective McGarrett interviews the guard, who appears with a black eye, bandaged head, and arm in a cast. Gabriel recognized himself. He looked at his own cast. Since it didn't hurt or bother him, he'd completely forgotten about it. His body had grown used to it like a wristwatch or a new haircut. He stared at it. It was filthy with accumulated dirt, really disgusting. He hadn't used the sling for days, and, thanks to the blows it was getting and his scratching inside with a knitting needle, it had been crumbling and chipping. He always wrapped it up in a plastic bag when he was having a shower but the water had softened it and it looked quite mangy. He got out a calendar and counted the days since the accident. It should have come off two weeks before.

The next day, Tuesday, he asked for an appointment with the orthopedic specialist provided by the insurance company. When they broke open the shell, a defenseless white arm emerged. It stank. Gabriel carefully cradled his wrist with his other hand. His weedy arm felt as floppy as a newborn kitten.

"Since I see no one's drawn or written on it, I won't ask you if you want the cast as a memento," the doctor commented as he dropped the debris into the garbage bin. Gabriel didn't answer. It was the first time in a month and a half that he'd ventured beyond his neighborhood. "You'd be amazed at the stupid things people write on a cast nowadays. Sometimes they carry political messages and, depending on the policeman that discovers them, you can be sent straight to prison."

The nurse washed his arm and the doctor then examined it, bending it up and down several times. Before Gabriel left he suggested that he should do some weightlifting, to strengthen the muscles, and then he signed the medical discharge papers. Gabriel could return to work on the following Monday.

Needless to say, come Monday, Gabriel didn't go near La Ibérica. No way. The visit to the orthopaedic specialist and the removal of his cast—like shedding dead skin—encouraged him to get out on the streets a little more, even to go for a walk every morning, but not to get into a truck. The same day another significant event contributed to his rebirth, if we can call it that. Gabriel remembered that once, in the division of spoils after a move to Munich, Bundó had kept a set of hand weights. At first, he'd left them in the Pegaso and, when it wasn't his turn to drive, he did biceps-strengthening exercises, twenty lifts at a time, counting aloud, as they rolled along.

"I'm losing muscular mass," Bundó would announce, panting, and his two friends would laugh at him, telling him he was losing brain mass.

"Stop this weightlifting and carry a few more boxes by yourself and you'll see how your muscles grow," they challenged him. In the end, fed up with their teasing, he took the weights home.

Gabriel turned the apartment upside down looking for them. He rummaged methodically through cupboards and drawers, inspecting Bundó's possessions, forcing himself not to load them with meaning or memories of his friend, but the weights didn't appear. Then he realized there was still one place to look, the main bedroom. That's where they had to be. In all the time he'd been living in the apartment he hadn't been in there once. In his own way, trying to survive, he'd managed to strip the whole place of past associations, except for the main bedroom. After pondering it for a while, he grasped the door handle, breathed in deep like a diver about to plunge into the depths of the sea, and went inside. Everything was just as it had been on the day of the funeral, the same shadows, the same silent, accusing stillness. Moving fast, Gabriel knelt down by the side of the bed, lifted up the bedspread and looked underneath. Sure enough, the two weights were there, cowering beneath a shroud of dust. He knew Bundó's habits and peculiarities as if he'd given birth to him. He pulled them out and, just when he was about to retreat, a black object, half tucked away in a corner, caught his eye. He went in for a closer look.

In the semidarkness he recognized the cloth traveling bag he'd brought from the airport. Someone, most likely Gabriel himself, had dumped it there on the day of Bundó's wake. Then, after coming back from the cemetery, things had moved so fast, what with Carolina's renouncing the apartment, his moving in, his subsequent reclusion, and so on, that he'd erased it from his thoughts ever since. He picked it up and, taking it over to the dining room table, realized it hadn't been opened since that day. He thought he remembered what was inside, but now it seemed heavier.

When he opened the zipper, Gabriel was met by a gust of sweet, illicit air and instantly knew it wasn't his bag. He'd been plundering other people's baggage for many years and knew all about unfamiliar smells. He slowly unpacked the contents and laid them out on the table. Then he examined them. There were several items of male clothing, very good quality and, once, well ironed. Their owner had packed two of everything: shirts, trousers, T-shirts, underwear, and a couple of discreetly elegant ties. A belt and shoes in the same kind of leather with a British brand name. Two gifts in kids' wrapping paper turned out to be a Lego set and a wooden grasshopper. A sealed white envelope at the bottom of the bag contained what seemed to be a sheaf of papers. Intrigued, he opened it and found two porn magazines. They were Swedish or Danish. Pooling funds with Bundó and Petroli, he'd bought a few on their trips to Germany and France, but he'd never seen photos like these. Sex between men and women, and women and women, appeared with stunning naturalness as scenes from paradise on earth. He continued his investigation. A delicate bronze reproduction of the Little Mermaid confirmed that the owner of the bag must have returned from Copenhagen, most probably after a week-long business trip. A small case revealed that, besides being well off, he was diabetic: There were five ampoules of insulin, two syringes, and a rubber strip.

His inventory of these objects made him recall how euphoric the three of them used to become when they opened up the pilfered boxes. How they used to laugh! How happy they were! And how they used to fight too! Gabriel cast a practised eye over the items before him and immediately imagined their hypothetical distribution. Bundó would have kept the clothing, of course. It was more or less his size and, as tended to happen, he would have ended up mistreating it. Gabriel could just see him unloading furniture in those dreadfully expensive pullovers, carrying on and cussing like some disinherited nobleman because his cashmere had got snagged on a nail sticking out from a piece of furniture. Petroli would have wanted the toys, the bronze mermaid, and maybe one of the ties. Gabriel would have kept the belt and shoes but would have been too embarrassed to wear them since they were so classy. He would have given the little case to a workmate at La Ibérica who was also diabetic, and, as for the two smutty magazines, there was no doubt about that: They would have remained in the Pegaso for the personal, solitary pleasure of all three of them and then, one day, they would have disappeared. (When he got bored with them, Bundó used to sell them to some workmate or other at La Ibérica, the ones that only did moves within the city or to the provinces, thus earning himself a bit of a bonus.)

*Another life is possible.* That afternoon, as he always did when they divided up the booty, Gabriel chewed on those words at length, breaking them down and savoring them. Another life *was* possible. Then, again as usual, he knocked back the idea. Trying to stave off dark thoughts, he concentrated on the bag again. What should he do with it? The most natural thing would be to return it to the airport and try to recover his own bag, but his heart wasn't in it. However, he did get out the old notebook and wrote down the imaginary sharing out of Number 200. It seemed the right and proper thing to do. Then he put Bundó's items in his wardrobe with the rest of his clothes and parceled up Petroli's things. If they ever met up again he'd give him the packet. He kept the magazines for himself. He put on the belt and new shoes and went out into the street. When he'd gone about twenty steps along Via Favència, he realized they were slightly tight. He'd end up with blisters, for sure.

The passenger from Copenhagen must have tried to reclaim his luggage several times, perhaps appealing to the sentimental value of the toys for his children (without a word about the magazines), but he never got it back because Gabriel never gave it back. In the Cage, ninety days after its disappearance, they considered the bag definitively missing, and the airline paid out a paltry sum in compensation. It wouldn't even pay for the shoelaces.

When a piece of baggage disappeared for ever, as that one did, Rita used to say it had gone to heaven. She liked to portray the Cage as a kind of purgatory in which the destiny of those gone-astray souls was decided. Most of the pieces went back to their owners, to an active existence after a period of uncertainty. (Life, therefore, represented hell.) This cosmology—which Gabriel, Bundó, and Petroli could have applied to their La Ibérica thievery—didn't answer to any spiritual criteria: The lost luggage heaven was simply a way of justifying and embellishing the criminal acts that Rita perpetrated with Sayago, Porras, and Leiva.

Rita acquired a taste for felony shortly after she started to work at the airport. We might say she inherited it from her predecessor in the Cage, a little soul from the working-class neighborhood of El Clot who retired just before she arrived. The lady's name was Carola, and she was a spinster. Of fragile appearance and with perpetually moist or teary blue eyes, she'd become a fully fledged institution within the Cage. She worked there for more than twenty years and could be described as its founder, its brain, an inspiration. At the beginning of her career, when there were few commercial flights, she was the only person employed to attend to passengers' complaints. The stories she told from those times were worthy competitors for a Berlanga film. Later on, when air transport expanded, the management put her in charge of reorganizing the department along the lines of the system they used in Madrid's airport. The little soul went off to the capital, studied the meth-

ods, adapted them to the more modest needs of Barcelona, and
created an effective, apparently unimpeachable office: The Cage
had just been born. It happened, though, that behind her timorous
façade—so very Saint Francis and so very useful with regard to
the public—a great strategist was lurking. Without anybody sus-
pecting, not even her co-workers, Carola had hatched a plot to
line her pockets. The regulations decreed that every three months
without fail all unclaimed baggage had to be taken on a regular
flight to a depot in Madrid where it would be destroyed, burned,
or whatever. "All that work for nothing," the little soul muttered
to herself and, having identified the problem, preferred to save
the company headaches: Not a day went by when she didn't bear
off, hidden under her overcoat, in her handbag, or in her lunch-
box, some more or less valuable object yielded by those ownerless
suitcases. Sometimes, for example, if the clothes she found in a
bag were for a woman and they fitted her, she'd lock herself in the
ladies' room and put them on under her own clothes. She'd then
head for home, asphyxiating, her peaky face pearled with sweat.
"Hot flashes, it's the hot flashes . . ." she would exclaim if anyone
gave her a questioning look. With all her busy-bee thefts, the bags
went off to Madrid half empty or half full and nobody was any the
wiser. At the other end of the chain was one of her brothers, also
unmarried, a stallholder at the Els Encants flea market. He sold
the stolen goods.

When Rita came to the Cage some years later, progress had
forced the little soul from El Clot to expand her business and
spread the profits. After the renovation of the airport in 1968,
when the Guardia Civil installed their sentry box inside the terminal and there were twice as many workers, plundering became
much more difficult. Moreover, she was getting old. She'd almost
been caught a couple of times—in her old age she sometimes got
distracted—and once she'd almost had a heart attack. It dawned
on her that she needed help. After meticulously studying everyone around her, the fads of her fellow workers and taking note of
any lazy tendencies, the little soul decided that Leiva, Porras, and
Sayago were the ones. The selection process adhered to her cri-

teria of remaining in control, but it also deferred to a pious streak because, of all the airport staff, the three cleaners were the most needy. At breakfast on one particularly slow day she asked them to join her in a corner of the terrace of the café next to the runway and told them of her plan. She spoke in a mysteriously detached tone, and the sounds of planes taking off and landing drowned out her words... Every two or three days. Sweeping the terminal. She'd give an agreed-upon signal. One of them would come over with the biggest garbage bin. He'd start cleaning the passage behind the Cage, a spot where no one went. They'd wait a few minutes out of caution. She'd open the back door. An unclaimed bag would get in his way. He'd do his job and pick up the rubbish, the obstruction. Stow it in the garbage bin. Till the end of the day. They all knocked off at the same time. One would carry the bag. Concealing it. They'd share out the contents in the bus shelter, equal shares, according to their needs. But she'd always have first choice. She was the group's ideologist.

Porras and Leiva agreed to the plan without a moment's hesitation. The watery gaze of the little soul, brimming with benevolence, had them convinced they weren't breaking the law. They'd be heirs to Robin Hood. They'd steal from the rich who flew around in planes and give to the poor who went on foot, which is to say they'd keep the goodies for themselves. Sayago caressed the tips of his luxuriant moustache and announced that he wanted to think it over. For moral reasons. The little soul, who knew that the three friends were inseparable, said no. In or out. Now. Say yes and you won't regret it. The woman's energy disarmed him. Anyway, his younger daughter's first communion was coming up, and he'd invited relatives from the village. He couldn't stint. The lunch was going to be in a restaurant in the capital city. In Barcelona. Yes. In.

Bovine-natured Leiva, a run-of-the-mill fellow, performed the first mission, a trial run with an empty suitcase, and it came off just as the little soul had planned. The subsequent missions were also accomplished without any problems, and they soon discovered the joys and benefits of the project. Whenever one of the three cleaners was pushing his broom in front of the Cage, the little soul flashed him a conspiratorial smile. If she'd been twenty years younger she would have fallen for Leiva and his slightly rustic parsimony. Porras was fast. He acted with the brazenness of someone who knows how to hot-wire and steal a car and was unfazed by the risk of getting caught. This made his two workmates very jumpy, but the little soul was proud of him. Sayago, in contrast, drove her crazy. When he was shifting the bag inside the bin everything went wrong and he kept fumbling and stumbling. Him and his badly dyed moustache! The man looked like a walrus.

One day, the brother of the little soul from El Clot gave up his stall in the Els Encants market. Thenceforth, she kept plundering out of habit and as a sport. She gave her part of the booty to Caritas. Her unlawful suitcase trade made her feel alive. By the time she retired, Porras, Sayago, and Leiva were sufficiently well trained to keep the pillaging fires burning as an old Cage tradition that wasn't to be lost. So they had to look for a replacement.

Not long afterward, when the unclaimed (and unplundered) luggage was beginning to pile up dangerously in the Cage's storeroom, the three friends chose Rita. They could see that she was innocent, slightly wild, and as malleable as soft bread. She'd just replaced Saint Carola from El Clot and hadn't yet bonded with her workmates. Porras, young like she was, befriended her with a few jokes and then reeled her in. Rita accepted without giving it much thought, as if looting lost luggage was part of the Cage's job description. She'd been on a rollercoaster for some months now and wasn't bothered by vertigo. Didn't pastry cooks eat all the cream they wanted; didn't tailors' children have free clothes? Well, it was exactly the same thing as far as she was concerned.

The cleaners phoned Carola to inform her of their choice. The next day, the little soul from El Clot conscientiously came out to the airport to visit her old friends in the Cage. She missed them so much! They had no idea how bored she was at home! The lachrymose eyes got even more waterlogged, two pools of sadness. She'd brought a box of Birba cookies and a bottle of Aromes de Montserrat liqueur. They called over the three cleaners and the two men of the Guardia Civil and drank a toast out of plastic cups. Somebody introduced Rita as her replacement. The little soul, still angelic, looked her up and down and asked a few courtesy questions. Rita held her gaze throughout. Ten minutes earlier, she'd come across the wizened old lady in the ladies' room. She'd been standing in front of the mirror, lips tightly compressed in a grimace of pain as she poured a liter of eyewash into each eye.

The little soul was all smiles. In front of Leiva, Porras, and Sayago, who were hanging on her every word, she said, "You'll do a very good job, Rita. Dealing with people, colleagues in the terminal . . . This is very enriching work." She smirked, looking straight at Rita.

That evening, when she got home and took off her coat, Rita felt something in her pocket. It was a bottle of eyewash.

Christophers, in defense of my mother, I hasten to say that she never resorted to eyewash to soften up pissed-off passengers. Rita, as I said before, had sufficient character to update the little soul's methods and was well able to wring out the pity with her own tragic tale. Yet she was a worthy successor in the business of lost luggage. I can attest to that because I have personal experience of it. My childhood wardrobe mainly came from suitcases that had been flown in from half the countries around the world. Since Leiva's and Sayago's offspring were quite a bit older, Mom took all the kids' clothing. I remember some Tyrolean lederhosen; a T-shirt with a drawing of the Aristocats orchestra with the English words "That's Entertainment," which Dad translated for me; some extremely shiny patent leather boots, which the kids at school said were girls' boots (and they were probably right); a sailor suit; a tweed jacket with very long sleeves that made my wrists itchy; some Nike sneakers, the ones with the blue stripe, straight from the United States, which made me the most popular kid at school for a time.

Rita felt fulfilled with her daily exploits at the airport. More than a job, it was her life. Proof of that was my birth. At first she decided not to keep working and that she'd devote herself body and soul to raising me. Gabriel's intermittent presence at home, especially during my first weeks in this world, nourished the fantasy of having a family, and she told herself that this was what she wanted. Soon, however, the scales fell from her eyes. After a period in which she was entirely content with contemplating me sleeping, boredom loomed and she moved heaven and earth to persuade her boss to let her go back to the Cage. In this era of earth mothers, more than one of her female workmates thought she was irresponsible and a bad parent. She disarmed them by singing the praises of powdered milk, which had come into fashion thanks to the younger pediatricians. Bottles freed women from the bondage of breastfeeding! The fact is that Rita went off to work early in the morning secure in the knowledge that I wouldn't be going hungry. The days when Dad had slept at our place he looked after me. Otherwise Mom left me with a dependable neighbor. More than a couple of times, when all else failed, she had to bring me to the Cage. Then she went into the back room, opened up an unclaimed suitcase, improvised a bed with the spare clothes it contained as a blanket, and settled me down to sleep. It seems that I didn't protest at all and slept even more soundly there than I did at home. When I woke up crying and hungry, Mom got some water boiled—the men of the Guardia Civil had a portable gas burner in the sentry box—and gave me my bottle while attending to fractious passengers who'd lost their luggage. My blissful expression helped to placate them.

Perhaps it's because luggage occasionally doubled as my cradle that one of my earliest memories, from when I was tiny, was Mom coming home with a suitcase in her hand. The mere sight of it made me drowsy, and I'd start to yawn. Although she always brought it with her from the Barcelona airport she could have been returning from a journey anywhere in the world. She'd put the bag down in a corner, take her shoes off, sit down with me on the sofa, and cover me with kisses. There were some weeks when unopened suitcases piled up in the entrance. Then, when Dad came to visit us, they had fun opening them together. Mom already knew what was inside—she'd previously divided up the stuff with Leiva, Sayago, and Porras—but she liked to ratchet up the excitement so she could pass it on to Dad and me. Years later, as an adult recalling what I'd taken to be a cosy family atmosphere, I realized that it had another dimension. For those two, the game of opening suitcases was sexy, suffused with eroticism, foreplay, if you like. I'm serious about this: After all, what had brought them together in the beginning was precisely a piece of lost luggage.

Now that we're talking about the eroticism of suitcases, let's get back to Rita and Gabriel again. Shall we return to February 1972 when Rita was pining for a black cloth bag, just one bag, the object that would take her straight to Gabriel?

So let's do a recap.

I wasn't born yet.

Christof was six, living in Frankfurt with Sigrun and, when he felt lonely, he shared his troubles with a ventriloquist's dummy. They were almost like brothers: Either they were inseparable or they were scrapping over any stupid thing. On the latter occasions, the dummy used to torture Christof by telling him his dad was never coming back.

Christopher hadn't seen Gabriel for three months. He was four and a half. At nursery school he made a clay figure, which he later presented to Sarah. It was meant to be a moving truck, with a very big trailer and two little figures—him and his mom—in the cab and ready to go.

Christophe had just turned three. Mireille had spent the previous Christmas in Barcelona. Sometimes when she was missing Gabriel she'd settle Christophe in her lap and tell him things about the city. They'd go and live there one day. She could get a job in the French bookshop. When daddy came back, soon, yes, soon, she might suggest it to him. Christophe didn't understand what she was going on about, of course, but says that kids interpret these things in their own way.

I wasn't born yet, as I say. They hadn't conceived me. Mom and Dad hadn't even met. If I could imagine myself as some object, or could be endowed with some sort of physical presence before the idea of my existence actually took shape, then I was that ownerless bag. Or, to rephrase it, that bag, on its way through heaven knows what airport, contained a good part of Rita's future.

On the Friday, the day after Bundó's funeral, Rita went to work as if nothing had happened. She was never ill and, if she'd wanted to, she could have phoned in to say she still felt weak after her fainting fit and was going to spend the day at home. They would have understood. But she was driven by her need to retrieve Gabriel's bag. She'd woken up earlier than on other days, unable to go back to sleep because she was so keyed up. Standing in front of her open wardrobe, about to get dressed, she was beginning to get some idea of what was happening. So should she wear black in mourning for poor Serafí Bundó or choose something bright and cheerful to celebrate the fact that her Gabriel had risen from the dead? The two feelings canceled each other out. She chose a bit of each, and headed for the airport.

Having to change into her drab navy-blue uniform soon brought her down to earth. First of all, of course, she checked the register to see if anyone had turned in the damn bag, but there was no sign of it. She wasted the whole day fruitlessly looking for it. She pretended she was cataloging newly arrived pieces of luggage, but actually she was checking all the bags in the storeroom, one by one, in case someone had put Gabriel's bag in the wrong place. At midday, beside herself, she phoned the Lufthansa office in Madrid. She recited the claim number (she knew it by heart), and they assured her that the bag had been sent two days earlier and they should have received it in Barcelona by now. She rudely hung up on them.

There's a problem with the past, Christophers: It's untouchable, and nobody can change it. Since we can only observe it from a distance we are, however, granted the gift of omniscience. So, we might be mere spectators but we're everywhere at once and able to admire the artful designs of crossed paths. We now know that while Rita was getting dressed that morning, trying to recover from a difficult night, only three hundred meters away Gabriel was waking up for the last time in his boarding-house bed, under the steely gaze of the stuffed falcon. While Rita was rummaging through dozens of pieces of alien luggage, Gabriel was trying to stuff all his belongings into his two trusty suitcases, plus a couple of bags and a few cardboard boxes. While Rita was returning home with disappointment written all over her face, Gabriel plonked the last box into El Tembleque's van, and the two of them climbed up through the streets of the Eixample, up, up, up, on their way to Via Favència. While Rita . . .

The clock struck five, and Rita left the airport. Sitting on the bus taking her into the city center, she told herself she couldn't go on like this. With or without the bag, she had to go directly to the pension, speak to Gabriel, and clear up the misunderstanding. Were you in any doubt, Christophers? She walked down Carrer Tallers and then Carrer Valdonzella till she got to Ronda de Sant Antoni. She strode along with all the verve of someone who knows she has a plan. The dying February sun smoothed over the angles of the houses, aging their façades. With its windows still in darkness, the pension building looked dilapidated and uninhabited. The door was open, and she slipped inside the ghostly house. Someone from the top floor turned the stairway light on and started coming down whistling the march from *The Bridge on the River Kwai*. She rushed up so as not to meet him. The mountain goat received her with an irked expression as it had done two days earlier, but this time she wasn't going to be intimidated. She rang the bell. Without the bag as a foil, she'd rehearsed all kinds of excuses so she could speak to Gabriel but didn't get to put them into practice. Senyora Rifà recognized her at once and invited her in.

"I was expecting you," she said. Untrue, perhaps, but her words made uncanny sense. Rita suddenly felt uncomfortable, as if someone were spying on her from a hiding place, Senyora Rifà turned on the hallway light, revealing the gallery of stuffed beasts. "Come in, do come in. Let's have a cup of coffee and chat about Bundó and Gabriel."

"Is Senyor Delacruz in? I need to see him right away." Rita was speaking softly as if she was in an old folks' home. She was walking close behind the landlady. The floor vibrated and expensive glassware tinkled in display cabinets. One of the hallway doors was slightly open, and, walking by, she glimpsed a man lying on a bed. He was reading a newspaper in this improbable posture, and she couldn't see his face.

Senyora Rifà's only answer was to stop in front of a door and throw it wide open. The room was empty.

"Gabriel's flown the nest, dearie," she said laconically. You could hear a quaver of disappointment in her voice. "It was high time he moved on to warmer climes, if you want my opinion. As far as I'm concerned he could have stayed here till he grew old but, for him it's better like this."

Rita went into the room and stood quietly in its shadows. "The nearer you get, the farther away you get," she dared to think. From the threshold, Senyora Rifà went into room-showing mode and turned on the light. The space, so stark and bare, made Rita shudder. That afternoon, things were getting clearer and clearer in the form of a string of disappointments. The wool mattress, rolled up like a cannellone, was waiting to be beaten. The wardrobe door swung halfway open, all by itself, in a gesture of surrender. On the bedside table, several thick rings testified to a bleary night. Cognac for sure. There was nothing else, no other sign of life that might lead anyone to imagine that somebody had slept in that lair the previous night.

"That must have taught him . . ." Rita ventured, pointing at the stuffed falcon over the wardrobe. Senyora Rifà pulled a face, not understanding what she was getting at. "How to fly, I mean. That big bird must have taught him to fly. Has Gabriel gone very far?"

"I can't answer that," Senyora Rifà replied, pleased to be able to make the most of a juicy bit of gossip. "I asked him, of course, as you can imagine, but with Bundó's death he's gone strange and doesn't want to talk. I told him a hundred times not to dwell on it but he feels guilty. If he's always been tight-lipped, well, you can guess what he's like now. He just said good-bye and that he'd drop in and say hello when things settle down. He was in a hurry because a friend of his was waiting downstairs with a loaded van. When he was on his way down, twisting half sideways because of his arm being in a cast, I called out—Gabriel!—and asked if he was going to live in Bundó's apartment. He looked up at me through the stairwell and nodded good-bye again but didn't say yes or no. Look, we were close but, well, dear . . . Anyway, if he did go to Bundó's apartment, I hate to say it but he's going to die of sorrow up there among all those Spanish migrants who never speak a word of Catalan."

Rita didn't stay for coffee. Five minutes later, she was in the street again, back on the job and happy to be so. She'd left the pension with an address written on a bit of paper and a promise that, if there was any news, Senyora Rifà would let her know at once. It was Friday evening, and she had the whole weekend free for finding Gabriel. Nothing was going to stop her now. Nonetheless, she had trouble getting to sleep that night. She couldn't get the stuffed falcon out of her head. She could still see its piercing enigmatic eyes and envied it the thousands of hours it must have spent spying on what went on in that room.

It was drizzling when she went out the next morning. She got the Number 50 bus and crossed half the city until it left her at one end of Via Favència, after which she walked through the neighborhood looking for the apartment into which Gabriel had apparently moved. Some streets were still under construction, dirt tracks that, with the rain, had turned into puddle-strewn bogs. Rita was overdressed and walking on tiptoes trying to keep her shoes clean. By the time she found the building in question it had started to rain more heavily. A lady with a shopping cart held the door open for her, and she dived inside. Alone in the vestibule, she read the names on the mailboxes but couldn't find the one she was looking for. In a glass display case used by the residents' association, the notice of Serafí Bundó Ventosa's death was stuck up with a drawing pin. She checked the floor and number of the apartment and climbed the stairs.

Gabriel—we now know—was certainly at home, and he didn't open the door when Rita rang the bell. Another wasted opportunity. He was curled up under the bedclothes, stunned by the upheaval of the past few days. He'd woken up very early (that's if he actually slept) and felt unable to do anything. The paralysis that

had just begun—another thing we know—was going to last more
than two months. Rita didn't give up and rang again, three brief
friendly chimes, trying to convey that she was someone he could
trust, but it didn't work. She then stuck her ear to the door and
listened for ages to the heavy silence emanating from inside the
apartment. "If he opened the door now," she thought, "there could
only be a brick wall on the other side." A neighbor from the same
landing, coming up the stairs laden with bags from the greengro-
cer's, interrupted her reverie. Puffing with exertion, he startled her
with a curt hello and told her that nobody lived there, that the
owner had died a few days earlier. He then waited for her to go
downstairs before he went into his apartment.

Back in the street, Rita moved a few meters away from the
building to take in the whole thing. She didn't believe what the
man had told her. She counted the apartments and worked out
which balcony had to be Gabriel's. The blind was up. On this gray
day with a lowering sky paved with dense clouds she could see no
light shining through the window. This first failed attempt didn't
discourage her, however. She went into a nearby bar for breakfast
but didn't lose sight, not for a single moment, of the people coming and going along the sidewalk. Their umbrellas made it difficult
for her to keep watch, however, and as soon as she'd finished she
went back into the street. Stationed under a balcony with the cold
creeping into her bones, she spent the whole day there. Shortly
after lunchtime, she saw the surly neighbor leaving the building
and heading into the bar. She used this opportunity to rush upstairs and ring the doorbell, once again without results. Then she
scurried back to her surveillance position. The hours went by, it
stopped raining, night fell and the few streetlights came on. The
balcony window remained in darkness. For a long time it was the
only black window in the whole façade, like a blind eye. Rita could
make out a tiny flickering light, the hint of a candle, but then realized it was the reflection of starlight on something in the air. Her
neck ached from looking up for so long. At half past ten, when
the owner of the bar pulled down his blind and everyone seemed
to have gone home, she sneaked inside the building again. This

time she didn't ring the bell but just put her ear to the door. The automatic light switch went off, and then she seemed to hear a cavernous metallic noise coming from the other side, like a pulley heaving up a bucket of water from a well. Under the weight of silence, the ear invents the most peculiar sounds. She took fright and ran downstairs. She hurtled down, three steps at a time, her leaps muffled by television sets blaring in every apartment. At midnight, seeing that all the windows were darkening, she gave up. Her feet were frozen and, when at last she reached Plaça Virrei Amat, she was able to hail a taxi.

The next day she woke up with a fever and aching bones, but she repeated her mission exactly as she'd done on the Saturday. The results were the same, a shitload of hours hanging around and all for nothing. Now that we know that Gabriel was actually in the apartment, the story is even more disheartening and dramatic but, for those two days, it was all he could do to survive. Bed, bathroom, bed. Bed, kitchen, bed. Not once did he leave his burrow to enter the dining room and go over to the window. The outside world (including the door, the bell, and the finger pressing the bell) had ceased to exist.

Going home on the bus on the Sunday night, Rita might have felt very sorry for herself. However, she preferred to see those hours as proof of her resistance vis-à-vis everything that she was yet to face. How far was she prepared to go? The question had arisen in a weak moment that evening. Words aren't sufficient, but I can try to answer . . . She'd look for Gabriel as long as was necessary. She'd look for him as long as she didn't stop feeling the imperative need to do so, as she did right now. The bus came down Passeig de Sant Joan and crossed Avinguda Diagonal, leaving behind the statue of the poet and priest Jacint Verdaguer, and, as wide-eyed as the owl on top of the Rótulos Roura building, she stared at the people in the street. Night vision. Any one of them could be him. She only needed to look out for the signs: tired steps, an arm in a cast, an absent air. Or maybe he'd appear now that they'd turned into Gran Via from Plaça de Tetuán, for example. Two men were arguing while they waited at a red light; a very elegant gentleman and lady walked hand in hand toward the Hotel Ritz—but, of course, that wouldn't be her man!—a group of boys and girls, looking snug in duffle coats and scarves, emerged from the depths of a bar called El Viejo Pop. When the bus came to a stop, she turned to check out the people who hadn't got on. Then she looked over the ones who had. Everything was an opportunity and, as long as the emotion lasted, as long as the city kept giving her some cause for hope, it would be worth it.

Christophers, don't think that Rita was naive. It wasn't that. It's just that she was very lonely.

On Monday she phoned La Ibérica from the airport. The secretary, Rebeca, took the call and, when Rita asked for Senyor Delacruz, told her that Gabriel was on sick leave. She didn't know when he was returning to work. It would be a long time.

"We're phoning from the airport because we need to deliver a bag of his that was mislaid," Rita lied. She'd been spending a lot of time moving heaven and earth to find the bag but still with no results. "Do you know where we might locate him?"

"Gabriel lives in a pension on Ronda de Sant Antoni . . ."

"He no longer lives there," Rita cut her off. "Well, that's what they've just told us. You don't know where else he might be? With some relative?"

"No," Rebeca replied. "He has no relatives. He only has his workmates, but they're not in the picture right now. Being who he is, he could be anywhere . . . Wherever."

"Wherever?"

"Yes, but I'd say he's in Barcelona. I don't think he's in any state to go anywhere, to tell the truth. He broke his arm in an accident. I don't know if you know that. And he had a bad experience recently. His best friend, his soul mate, died. Go and check at the pension again. Or if you like, bring the bag here to La Ibérica, and we'll get it to him . . ."

"No, no, that's impossible," Rita countered. "The delivery must be made in person."

Then she hung up.

Wherever. Wherever, yet in Barcelona. Since she had no other

alternative, Rita took Rebeca's words as a challenge. That afternoon, coming back from the airport, she bought the Barcelona city
guide, an updated 1972 edition. Looking through it at home, she
read on one of the first pages, "Contains 10,006 streets," but instead of letting the enormity of this fact get her down, she thought
about limits instead. There's nothing like being in love. That incredibly lengthy list of streets boiled down to only two hundred
pages of maps! She'd never realized that Barcelona was so small.
Which is the best approach if you want to find someone? Staying
still and waiting till he walks by, or running around all over the
place? The answer was obvious because, after talking with Rebeca, she suspected that Gabriel was stranded somewhere. She
was going to unstrand him. Starting from tomorrow she'd devote
every free moment to finding him, page by page. After work, she'd
take the Metro to wherever she had to go. She had to be system-
atic: She'd start with page one and she'd comb the city, neighborhood by neighborhood, if fate didn't help her run into Gabriel.
If she got to the end without unearthing him, she'd go back to
page one.

It's clear there was no future in this method. Indeed, Rita herself admits nowadays that not even she believed in it. "You can't
travel the world without a rearview mirror," she says enigmatically,
but she also recalls that her plans distracted her then and helped
her not to think too much. It never so much as entered her head
that she might have wasted a whole lifetime—two lifetimes, even,
or a hundred—without ever coming across Gabriel. Humans are
like that: We're attracted and moved by love stories that are born in
the most unlikely, adverse, and even absurd circumstances but forget that, for each happy ending, there are a million that will never
prosper. Right, Christophers? Maybe that's why we're reconstructing our father's steps. Because of his remarkable character. Like
those people who win the lottery twice, or get struck by lightning
in three different storms and live to tell the tale, he had the odd
blessing of getting himself chosen by four women. Not one. Four.

# 5

## Waverings

Rita didn't know it, but when she was roaming around Barcelona and working her way through the pages of the city guide, as if she could thus rule out streets, there was one factor that went in her favor: Gabriel attracted coincidences. From the moment that an unknown woman had dropped rather than brought him into the world, chance took a shine to him, like a cat playing with a mouse, to such an extent that if he went back over his thirty-one years of existence, he had the feeling that, however intensely he appeared to have lived, he'd never made a single major decision for himself. Things just happened to him because that's how it was or because others wanted it like that, starting with the inaugural gesture of the salt cod seller at El Born market who'd heard his squalling and put him to her breast. Even the one firm wish of his life—staying on in the boarding house—could be seen as antivolition, another passive move. Rita sought coincidences obsessively; for Gabriel they became inevitable. That was the difference that united them.

Following this line of thought, we can assume that Bundó's death—which Gabriel might have prevented if they'd stopped in Frankfurt, or if he'd obliged his friend to take over at the wheel of the Pegaso—changed him overnight. In the first two months of his seclusion in the apartment in Via Favència he resigned himself to

353

living without a destiny, as if he'd already died, but then something as arbitrary and imposed as being named Gabriel sneaked into those shadowless days and pushed him to make a real decision.

Gabriel's retreat—as we've seen—was sabotaged for the first time the day the orthopedic surgeon removed his cast. Many people experience a sort of reverential fear when they go to the doctor. In the waiting room, whether they've come to get their flu diagnosed or a prescription for some antibiotic, even the most serene or simple-minded individuals are infused with a feeling of solemnity that automatically evokes death. It has something to do with that white silence, the serious faces of the other patients, the calculus of the pain of others. In Gabriel's case, the visit had the opposite effect: He arrived there so alone, so without hope, so alienated that this atmosphere somehow managed to revive him.

Thenceforth, every time he had to go out and buy something, he took the occasion to go for a stroll. He put on his English shoes, which had now molded themselves to his feet, and wandered around the neighborhood. April had finally brought good weather, radiant mornings in which bare-legged girls welcomed the sun in short skirts, licking the first ice cream of the season. In the afternoon, if the good weather held out, Gabriel went down to spend an hour in Guineueta Park. Like a statue bearing witness to the passage of time, he sat on a bench with the pensioners and listened to their ailments (which made him feel better) and at the same time watched the children playing on the swings, studying their expressions and looking for them repeated in the faces of the mothers who were keeping an eye on them.

He was spending less and less time in front of the TV, which had now lost its novelty, and he was plucking up the courage to venture farther afield. In those days, the Canyelles neighborhood was still under construction, especially the part next to the mountain, Roquetes. If he felt like a bit of exercise, Gabriel picked his way through the havoc of Via Favència and headed up to Carrer Alcántara or Carrer Garellano, going higher and higher. Most of the streets were still dirt tracks, dusty in summer and perpetually boggy in winter. Solitary towers raised in the middle of vacant ground carried power cables spreading out like a menacing spiderweb to supply the buildings. Some residents—most of them from Andalusia or Murcia—had cemented the few square meters in front of their houses, embellishing the little patio with the trilling of a caged goldfinch and a geranium planted in an old five-kilo olive can. At nightfall, now that spring was well advanced, they took some chairs outside and sat in the fresh air. The men smoked black tobacco and pretended they didn't give a damn about anything, and the women shrieked hysterically when they saw the shadow of a rat fleeing down the hill. Then they dashed to close the front door while their menfolk burst out in full-throated, complacent laughter.

Twice a week, midmorning, a van drove into the middle of one of the vacant lots. Two Gypsy women set out boxes full of clothes and loudly proclaimed their wares to customers. A bit further on, a few callow school-age kids mucked about with a ball while their older brothers hung around smoking and arguing about which motorbikes were easier to steal, the Bultaco or the Montesa. When he went on his walks, Gabriel gave all that a miss, heading farther and farther uphill till he reached the edge of a small pine forest. While stopping to catch his breath, he smoked a cigarette and contemplated the city. Rising ever higher, the cranes in the foreground loomed over the few hovels that were still hanging in there, while the skeletons of two or three blocks under construction cast threatening tiger-striped shadows over their corrugated asbestos—cement roofs. Beyond Via Favència, way below, the social-housing buildings lined up like domino tiles or a cement rib cage, their contours blurred in the pollution.

When he tired of this route, Gabriel went farther afield. He never used public transport. He was drawn to three squares that he could reach on foot, all of them named after places in the Balearic Islands. He walked to Plaça Llucmajor or continued further down to Plaça Sóller and, on a few occasions, even strode through Horta, going up Turó de la Peira and down again to Plaça Eivissa. The return route was always quicker. He was like a pup that strays beyond his regular patch and suddenly feels lost, but the walk left him with a very agreeable aftertaste of adventure. These were parts of Barcelona that he'd seen in passing from the van, but he'd always had to keep a close eye on the traffic. Now he was like a foreigner mapping unexplored terrain.

Gabriel's forays into the outside world (which could also be seen as incursions into the inner world) frequently had a sentimental side: He saw himself as Bundó's surrogate, tracing out his routes in what would have been his natural habitat. He observed these places with the voracious eye of his friend strolling, let's say, arm-in-arm with Carolina one Sunday afternoon, and felt consoled. It was one way of not feeling like an intruder.

Immersed in his new routine and with the same ease with which he asked for a coffee in a bar, or greeted neighbors, or hung out his washing, Gabriel began to contemplate suicide. He wasn't an impulsive person, and the idea didn't appear out of the blue in a moment of weakness but slowly grew inside him like pebbles and sediment settling in a riverbed. In the end, on one normal, humdrum day, they block off the flow of water. Not even he would have been able to pinpoint the moment when the idea first came to him. In fact, looking back, it seemed to him that it was predestined. "Something like a factory defect," I recall my mother saying when I asked her what that meant.

What happened was this. Late one afternoon at the end of March, El Tembleque came to visit him, and they had a beer in the bar downstairs. Besides bringing him up-to-date with the news from La Ibérica, his friend brought him a message from Senyor Casellas: The appropriate amount of time had now gone by since the accident, and they knew at the company that the doctor had given him the all-clear. If he didn't show up at work the following Monday he could consider himself dismissed. Alone in the apartment again, Gabriel weighed up the situation and realized that if he put going back to work on one side of the balance, there was something weighing more on the other side. He didn't immediately identify it, but it didn't take him long to work out what it was: nothing. In other words, he thought it would be easier to wipe himself off the map.

His eventual decision to kill himself took shape in ways that, if anything, were banal. Gabriel smoked a carton of Ducados every seven days. His cigarette consumption had gone up since he'd begun leading a sedentary life, but he tried to exercise some restraint by buying his supplies on a fixed day. Therefore, every Monday morning he went down to the tobacconist's to get the week's rations. The man in the shop, a Valencian who'd lost an eye in the war, always bent his ear for five minutes, clearly intent on rhapsodising over the latest deeds of Franco (who observed them from a photo hung up behind the counter), and then wrapped up his Ducados in a sheet of newspaper. The man read *La Vanguardia*, and that Monday he used the Entertainment page. Since he hadn't smoked since Sunday, Gabriel unwrapped the carton and lit up as soon as he got home. Then, ensconced on the sofa, he took the half-crumpled newspaper page and read this headline:

## THE ACTOR JORGE MISTRAL COMMITS SUICIDE
### *He had been living in Mexico for some years*

Although he didn't have much memory for names of actors, he knew who Jorge Mistral was, and the news gripped him. During one of their last moves in the Pegaso, the name had come up in a conversation with Bundó and Petroli. A news item on National Radio referred to the actor in reporting the death of his newborn daughter. After chatting about the tragedy, the three friends started talking about his films. Petroli had seen *Love Madness*, in which he appeared when he was very young and was what they called a promising actor. Bundó remembered one time when the House of Charity nuns had taken them to the Goya Cinema. They would have been about eleven or twelve and had seen *Anchor Button*, in which Jorge Mistral had a starring role and, after that, all the boys in the orphanage played at rescuing sinking ships and proclaimed that they wanted to be sailors when they grew up.

The newspaper, Gabriel noted, was from a few days earlier, Friday, April 21st. Jorge Mistral had killed himself on Thursday the twentieth. When he read the article he found that Jorge wasn't his real name. He was actually called Modesto Llosas Rosell. He'd shot himself in the head. He was fifty-one years old. He was Spanish but had lived in Mexico for many years. He'd left three letters, one for his wife; one for a friend, also an actor; and another for the coroner.

This information rekindled Gabriel's suicidal ambitions. He now began to imagine his disappearance and subsequent absence, although without yet introducing the gloomier logistical aspects of the story. What if that page was a sign? Years earlier he'd learned about his birth thanks to a newspaper page that had turned up by chance. These things happen. Well, now the page might be showing him the way to go. There was a certain symmetry in the whole thing that appealed to him.

That afternoon, he went back to the tobacconist's and asked the disabled veteran if he could leaf through the weekend newspapers. The man, who suspected everyone, looked at him out of the corner of his remaining eye but went to look for the back issues. A customer was a customer after all. On Saturday, *La Vanguardia* reported that the deceased Jorge Mistral had cancer but hardly anyone knew, not even his wife. On Sunday, a new article talked about all the messages of condolence from the actor's friends. It seemed that his will stipulated that he wanted to be cremated, but the family had preferred to bury him because, that way, they said, they could take flowers to his tomb. Gabriel asked the tobacconist if he could have the two pages—if necessary he'd buy more tobacco—and the man gave them to him.

On Tuesday he went down very early to get *La Vanguardia*. Standing there next to the kiosk, he opened up the newspaper and flipped through it looking for the Entertainment page, but there were no further revelations. He went back to buy it again on Wednesday. He wanted to know what Jorge Mistral had said in the letters he left behind. He read the Entertainment section attentively but found nothing and, having got through that, kept turning the pages. In the News in Brief section he found a headline that froze the blood in his veins:

## GEORGE SANDERS TAKES HIS LIFE IN A
## CASTELLDEFELS HOTEL

Another actor. In this case, more space was given to the news, three columns accompanied by a photo of George Sanders with that bearing of his that had brought him so many roles as the enigmatic, always affable yet distant gentleman. The actor's face looked familiar, but Gabriel couldn't remember any of his films. The article included a reproduction of the note he'd left: "Dear World, I am leaving because I am bored. I feel I have lived long enough. I am leaving you with your worries in this sweet cesspool. Good luck." Another note, in Spanish, said. "Tell my sister. There's enough money to pay for everything."

He'd written his good-bye in English, the writing slightly wobbly but still bearing a calligraphic beauty, and someone had translated it for publication in the newspaper. Gabriel pored over every word of the article, a man interpreting an oracle. George Sanders had killed himself in Room 3 of the Rey Don Jaime Hotel in Castelldefels. He'd washed down five phials of barbiturates with the help of a bottle of whisky. He'd arrived two days earlier from Palma de Mallorca—after selling his house there in January—and was to have left for Paris the following day. It seemed he'd hit a rough patch, was in low spirits, and was toying with the idea of buying a house by the sea in Castelldefels. (Who knows whether the palm trees along the coast, leaning at their half-wild angles, reminded him of Santa Monica or Venice Beach, or some other seashore near Los Angeles?) The news item was rounded off with a biographical note and a list of films that had made him famous. Gabriel recognized two titles—*All About Eve* and *The Picture of Dorian Gray*—but he wasn't sure whether he'd seen them. The next few days he'd keep an eye on the television programs. Sometimes when a famous actor died, Channel Two paid homage by showing a film.

In the next few hours he reorganized the facts to establish some kind of framework. Was it coincidence that George Sanders and Jorge Mistral were actors and had the same first name? He didn't know where—most probably on the radio—he'd heard that one suicide often leads to another, like an epidemic. Perhaps George Sanders had made his decision—because it was a decision, a brave act—after hearing about the death of his colleague. If that was true, who would be next? What sign should he wait for? The next few days he was irresistibly drawn to the News in Brief pages. He was now buying *El Correo Catalán* as well as *La Vanguardia*. He sat at the dining-room table and read the two newspapers from start to finish. Over the next couple of days he was still gleaning new details—the pills Sanders had taken were Nembutal and Tranxene—but then the story dried up. With their callow pretensions of documenting the present, newspapers are the best proof yet that time is a tyrant that punishes with oblivion.

Not yet satisfied, he took the train to Castelldefels on Saturday and went to the Rey Don Jaime Hotel. He'd put on a jacket and tie, hoping to slip by unnoticed, but someone in reception was on to him at once and threw him out, shouting that they'd had enough of journalists. If he wanted to know anything else he should go to the police. Twenty minutes later, concealed in the middle of a group of German tourists, he came back in and slipped down a side corridor. When he got to Room 3, he found it was sealed off with yellow tape. He hesitated about whether to try to open it or not but then thought better of it. On the way home he mulled it over. What would have been the point? He'd never been a busybody and wasn't going to change now.

In short, his suicidal predisposition didn't go away. On the contrary, it was unrelenting and able to exploit these moments of weakness to conquer a little more of his spirit. He calculated that five days had passed between the announcement of Jorge Mistral's death and that of George Sanders. It wouldn't be altogether stupid, then, to suppose that in another five days—Monday—the newspapers would report a third suicide. If he was wrong about that, perhaps he should start thinking about whether it was his turn.

It happened that Monday fell on the first of May, Workers' Day and a public holiday. It was hot, and the city had been so empty over the long weekend that any news seemed impossible. The previous day the newsdealer had informed Gabriel that he'd be closed on Monday and reminded him that *La Vanguardia* wasn't coming out either. This meant that he stayed home and didn't read any newspapers. Abstinence was good for him, and the hours went by without any upsets, but he had trouble getting to sleep that night. A new question took shape, a clot forming and refusing to dissolve in the liquidity of sleep: When the time came, how was he going to go about it?

He was as yet unaware of it but Tuesday brought further respite. He went out to walk for a couple of hours in the afternoon and bought three newspapers, from the kiosk on the way home, almost grudgingly and as if under duress. He opened *La Vanguardia* at the Obituaries page and the headline of a half-column report immediately jumped out:

### ON THE DEATH OF THE POET GABRIEL FERRATER

The text didn't specify how Gabriel Ferrater had died, but the fact he was a poet alerted Gabriel. "Poets have always been killing themselves," he thought. Then he read the article and, although the text was full of euphemisms, he saw it quite clearly. Shortly afterward, a less-inhibited newspaper confirmed that it was suicide.

Of the three deaths, Gabriel Ferrater's made the greatest impact. He even had the same name! Could there be any doubt now? First a Jorge had inspired a George and now a Gabriel was calling upon another Gabriel. The poet had killed himself a few days ago, Thursday, he calculated, but they hadn't found him till Monday. He lived alone in Sant Cugat. Besides being a poet, he was a teacher at the Autonomous University. He hadn't yet turned fifty. Gabriel trawled all the sources of news but didn't come up with any more substantial information. He didn't know, for example, whether the poet had left any note or message.

Gabriel pored over the story, which took him some hours to digest. By the time he looked up it was night. It was that time of the evening when, without really knowing why, he went out on to the balcony to smoke the second-to-last cigarette of the day (the last one he kept for just before going to bed). It was eight, the colors were fading high in the sky, and, down below, the city had a morbid, vaporized look about it. The panoramic view was one of the reasons why Bundó had decided to buy the apartment. The sun slowly went into hiding behind the Collserola hills, and Gabriel amused himself by imagining how, with the light now behind him, the shadow of his slim body was sufficient to cast the whole of Barcelona into darkness. If he raised an arm, he could eclipse an entire neighborhood. In the midst of such distractions he looked down at the street and was once again surprised at how high up he was. Seven floors before hitting the pavement. An idea took shape in his brain: Taken one at a time, every instant of every day made its own sense but, if they were all put together, the result was meaningless.

Let me say it again, Christophers. You can be sure that these arguments that were pushing him to kill himself were not cast in a tragic light. The proof is that while Gabriel was doing something as mundane as getting undressed that night, putting his pajamas on or cleaning his teeth, he was trying to work out when it would be his turn. If he counted four days from getting the news about the poet, he'd have to do it on Saturday. Yes, Saturday wasn't an especially bad day. Yet this advance planning seemed excessive and unnatural and, moreover, it made him understand something evident: He wouldn't be appearing in the newspapers. No journalist would write an article titled FURNITURE MOVER COMMITS SUICIDE IN . . . If he really wanted to insert his link into the chain of suicides, and if his grand act was going to make sense, he'd have to look for a public place that everyone knew. The Sagrada Familia Expiatory Temple. The lions in the zoo. The airplane in the Tibidabo funfair. A touch of eccentricity that would put him on the front page.

Now, at the hour of reckoning, he was being capricious.

In the end, after much rumination, he chose the Christopher Columbus monument, which appeared on page 27 in Rita's city guide. He was playing with the symbolic idea that his last route would be traced by a leap from the feet of such an illustrious traveler as this voyager. He'd do it on Saturday afternoon at the time when the citizens of Barcelona came out to stroll along the Ramblas, when the florists lowered the prices of their half-wilting wares, and the prostitutes scored their first gentlemen on the corner of Carrer Escudellers and in the inner reaches of Carrer Conde del Asalto. He'd pay to get into the monument, take the elevator up the column to the lookout directly beneath the statue at the top and, when no one was looking, he'd throw himself off, embracing the whole city with his last gaze or perhaps, heeding Columbus's finger, he'd look where he was pointing, out to the open sea. The seafarer wouldn't bat an eyelid when he hit the ground. Isn't it true that all the big monuments, from the Eiffel Tower in Paris to Big Ben in London, have their own particular stories of a suicide that adds to their prestige? Well, his would go down in history as the "Columbus Suicide."

Although he'd planned it quite well, Christophers, Gabriel never jumped from Columbus's feet, didn't get to say hello to the elevator driver or even buy the ticket to go up the monument. However surreal it may seem, his soul mate Bundó saved his life. He did it with an intervention from the grave that amply compensated for all the patience and favors our father had bestowed on him ever since they were little kids.

Furthermore, the intercession in extremis of a transmigrated (or, given the form it took, would it be more apt to say "transliquified"?) Bundó was doubly fortunate because, by then, Rita had already ruled out the possibility of Gabriel's hiding on page 27 of her guide. She would never have turned up at the bottom of the Columbus monument to save him in the nick of time.

In fact, Rita's intentions of looking for Gabriel on the map of Barcelona had lapsed overnight. She had abandoned her highly idiosyncratic methodology thanks to a major new development that had come about more or less when Gabriel was discovering the chain of suicides and weighing up his chances of joining in.

For some weeks now, Rita, the queen of tenacity, had turned her quest into compulsive routine. The first thing she did on arriving at the airport every morning was check to see whether the black canvas bag had turned up in the Cage. The negative response didn't deter her in the least, and some of her colleagues thought she'd lost her mind. They repeatedly urged her to forget about it. The fucking bag was never going to appear. Lost luggage was everyday fare and she, precisely, knew that better than anyone. Then, one April day, the long-awaited revelation came.

Although she'd imagined the scene a thousand times, the black bag didn't simply pop up as she'd expected but appeared piecemeal. What happened was as follows. She was in the Cage, sitting on her stool at the counter, and had just seen to a passenger, the last in the line before the next batch turned up. Since she'd been notching up a considerable number of kilometers around the city every day after work, her legs had become more muscular but the soles of her feet hurt. It was one in the afternoon and nothing was happening. The boss had gone to lunch. In the absence of passengers, she should have gone to the storeroom to sort out the lost luggage that had come in that morning but, right now, she didn't feel like it. The figure of Leiva and his mop materialized in the distance. Rita recognized his pachydermal silhouette. He'd been off work with the flu, and she hadn't seen him for several days. As he mopped and buffed up the shine on the marble floor with his particular art of zigzagging like a slalom skier, Leiva was moving closer to the Cage. Rita yawned.

"Are you better now?" she asked when he came within earshot. Their friendship was based on controlled, ironic condescension toward one another. They knew how to take a joke to the limit without ever causing hurt. With Porras, on the other hand, the relationship was all about saucy innuendo that she rebuffed, calling him a bighead. With Sayago, it was that of hysterical father and rebellious daughter (with conversations tending to end up with a little-girlish "Yes, Daddy" from her). Leiva was the one she had most fun with as some months earlier she'd started to speak to him in Catalan: "How was your vacation?"

"So-so," he replied, disguising a grimace. She'd passed the yawn on to him: delayed effect. He raised his hand to his forehead to check his fever and immediately tore it away as if burnt. He dropped the mop.

"What's the time? Tell me it's two. Tell me a lie if you must."

"It's two." She waited a few seconds for it to sink in. "No, it's one on the dot. Aren't you wearing a watch?"

"Of course I am. It's the Festina from when I got married," he said pushing up his sleeve to flash a gilded wrist. "But it stopped when I was sick, and I have to get it fixed. Anyway, I put it on because I can't be without it. I feel naked."

"Better for everyone, then, that you never take it off."

They both laughed. Leiva had now leaned his entire weight on her counter. He was one of those people who can't stand up straight. He pulled a packet of chewing gum out of his pocket and offered it to her.

"You don't want one, do you?"

"No, thanks, it'd probably poison me," Rita shot back, but took one anyway. Then she looked him up and down, feigning scientific objectivity. "Have you lost weight? You look skinnier."

Leiva, a good fellow, didn't understand she was messing with him. His blue work coat was too tight as usual, straining over his belly.

"Maybe I have," he said smugly. "It's because of the flu, but I'll soon put those kilos back on, I can assure you."

He gave emphasis to his words by undoing one button of the coat and pulling it open as if it were about to explode. It was then that Rita noticed the shirt he was wearing underneath.

"That shirt . . . Let's see. Take off your coat, Leiva. Please."

Leiva needed no further encouragement and revealed a flannel shirt in a moiré black-and-white herringbone pattern so garish that it hurt the eyes.

"You like it, eh? It's the first day I've worn it. And the last. It makes me sweat too much."

Rita recognized in a flash the horrible shirt that Bundó was wearing in the photo she'd been shown the day they buried him. There couldn't be two the same. That was inconceivable, and Leiva was wearing it with exactly the same sloppy indifference.

"Where did you get it?" she demanded.

Leiva moved a little closer and lowered his voice.

"Here. You know. Our business . . ." and he winked, not knowing how otherwise to hint at their shared secret.

"When was that? I don't remember . . ."

"Must've been three weeks ago. It was one of those days when you were so busy with other bags and you told us you didn't want anything, that it was all ours."

"It wasn't a black canvas bag, was it?"

"No, I don't think so . . ." Leiva was evidently unsure of himself and scared of blowing it. After all, Rita was the boss when it came to stray luggage. He ran his hand over his greasy hair in an effort to recall. "No, now I remember. It was one of those khaki bags, like those big army ones. I don't know if you remember it . . ."

"Sounds familiar. Yes."

"It looked full but, the thing is, when we opened it up, it was almost empty and inside there was . . . yeah, that's right, there was another bag inside it. And it was black. I remember it now because when we discovered it, Sayago came out with one of those sayings of his: 'The big fish has eaten the little fish.' The Lufthansa people didn't give a shit and shoved it in there, I suppose, to save space on the plane."

"And why didn't you tell me the next day?"

"You were so hot and bothered dealing with your own stuff that we didn't want to worry you, girl. You'd passed out, as I recall, and you looked very peaked. And there was nothing valuable in it anyway. Useless stuff like a rusty bottle opener and some old sunglasses. You know. This shirt was the best part of the loot!"

"And what did you do with the bag? Weren't there any papers? Or some address?"

"Yes, I'd say so. But I reckon we threw the whole lot away, like we always do . . ."

"Poor you, if you did!"

"No, hang on. No, of course we didn't!" Leiva immediately exclaimed, wanting to set things right. "Porras kept it. There was a folder, just like some minister would have, from the Spanish embassy or something like that in Germany, and we were so impressed we couldn't throw it into any old wastepaper basket. I think he's still got it in his locker."

"Well, you can just go and look for him and tell him to bring it to me right now!" Rita was beside herself and Leiva barely recognized her. "You've got no idea what I'd give to have that folder!"

Rita's words, of such surprising vehemence, rained down on her partner in crime like lashes from a whip, and he scuttled off like a man possessed to go and find Porras.

Within ten minutes Rita had the consulate folder in her hands and was caressing it with a despot's greed. The black canvas bag had been lost along the way, dumped in some anonymous garbage bin, and the objects it sheltered had met a similar unfortunate fate. They were the inevitable losses, the victims of friendly fire, leaving more space for maneuvre in the operation of closing in on Gabriel.

Now a few words about Rita. When I push her into the torture chamber of memories—because, yes, I do that to her and am a bad son—my mother admits that she spent the energy reserves of half a lifetime in that period. She puts it like this:

"My natural state then was wakefulness, vigilance, being on the alert, a state of ecstasy that drove me day and night, a courage I've never known since. It's because I was living in the future and not in the present (the present was only a springboard), and, as everyone knows, when you pine for something it's quite easy to get your imagination to come up with the five extra letters you need to turn pine into happiness. When I was walking up and down that toy-size Barcelona I never doubted, not even for a single second, that I'd end up bumping into Gabriel. I knew he wouldn't run away from me. It was enough to have looked into his eyes during those five minutes at the airport."

"This business of love at first sight, without knowing the person...it makes me think you were in love with love," I tell her. "There are people like that. Maybe Gabriel was just a screen onto which you projected..."

"No, no, it's not like that at all," she cuts me off, very sure of herself. She doesn't like me interrupting her with silly theories. "The proof is that I never again repeated the same error. I was in love with Gabriel and that's that. In love with a future with Gabriel. Not all love stories have to be conventional, do they?" I can see she's getting upset. "So you think I never had any other opportunities? I was twenty-one with a personality forged to struggle against family misfortunes and loneliness and I don't know which was worse. I'd learned to take care of myself. More than one traveler with a stuffed wallet (which they showed me without the slightest embarrassment!) proposed to me on the spot, at the Cage, standing there at the counter five minutes after laying eyes on me for the first time. Maybe I should have taken them up on it...Who knows where I'd be now. You, nowhere, my little one, that's for sure. You wouldn't be anywhere."

Okay. I get the hint—I always get it—and hold my tongue. At the age of fourteen or fifteen I begged her never to say "my little one" ever again, but on these occasions it's her secret weapon.

When she finished at the airport, Rita bore the folder off to her apartment. She carried it with extreme care, like a chaste student pressing it tight against her breast, wary of anyone who went near her. She could have opened it on the train but she didn't dare to look at it in public. Once she got through her front door, caution flowered into adoration. She left the folder on the dining-room table ready for examination. First, however, she got changed, went to the loo, and fixed herself a cup of hot milk and some chocolate, which is what she did when she wanted to watch a good film on TV or read the last chapter of whatever novel she was into. Nothing was going to disturb her. There was no hurry and she was enjoying prolonging the suspense. Destiny had promised her and then withheld so many things, she told herself, that it had no right to disappoint her this time.

Two months earlier, in the car that was taking him to the airport, Gabriel had put the contents of the folder in order. Now, in reverse, trying to roll things back, Rita set about correcting that past.

Inspecting the Pegaso papers was fascinating because they brought her physically closer to Gabriel: Most of the sheets were marked with greasy fingerprints, some of which had to be his. The international driver's licence and the route plans seemed cryptic and of little interest. The publicity leaflets for the apartments in Via Favència confirmed she'd been spying in the right place but didn't stir up any nostalgia for that weekend mislaid between wretched coldness and wretched coldness. It was obvious that the remaining papers were boring company circulars, crumpled receipts from moves dating back five years (but to her starstruck eyes they became autographs penned by Gabriel, who had frequently signed them), instructions and addresses at which loads of furniture were to be delivered . . . She went through all these items somewhat dejectedly, like an archivist on the point of retirement, until she detected a more recent one. It bore the "La Ibérica Transport and Moving" logo, and, on reading it, she let out a cry of happiness. Rita had before her the sheet of paper that Rebeca had given to Gabriel and Bundó just before the last move, the one with the dates of their medical checkups. The message couldn't have been more definitive. It was as if someone was communicating with her, giving her instructions.

*Dates of medical examinations of Gabriel Delacruz and*
*Serafí Bundó*
(Yes, I know it would be better to do it all in one day but it's impossible).
*Place:* Transport Insurance Company. Clínica Platón, Calle Platón, 33.
*Thursday, April 20, 9 a.m.* Blood test. It has to be done on an empty stomach—and that means no breakfast, Bundó.
*Friday, April 28, 10 a.m.* Oculist. Doctor Trabal.
*Friday, May 5, 10.30 a.m.* Ear, nose, and throat. Doctor Sadurní.
*Monday, May 8, 9 a.m.* General checkup. Doctor Pacharán.

The dance of figures and days intoxicated and muddled her. For a moment she seemed unable to interpret the jumble. What day was it today? Friday, already? Thursday? Thursday, April 27? Yes it was, wasn't it? One of her colleagues at the Cage, a woman called Montse, had brought them some cakes from Tortosa in celebration of her name day. Or was that yesterday? She didn't have a calendar at home and cursed herself for being so susceptible: One Saturday at the end of the year, she'd gone shopping in the market and, when she was paying, the butcher presented her with a pocket calendar with a photo of cute little kittens. It was ridiculous, cheesy, and she'd thrown it in the wastepaper basket, even knowing that she'd need it one day. The same thing happened every year. Now, all those dates had her completely flustered. She went out on to the landing and knocked at her neighbor's door. A lady opened, wiping her hands on her apron. She must have been cooking dinner.

"What day is it today?"

"What?"

"What day is it today, Mariona?"

"Thursday, love."

"And what's the date?"

"Thursday, the twenty-seventh of April, feast day of the Virgin of Montserrat. But, tell me, Rita, what's wrong? Come in. I've got a potato omelet cooking . . ."

"No, thank you. Bye . . ."

The words faded away along Rita's hallway. She'd forgotten to close the door, as she'd done on so many other occasions, and the neighbor closed it for her. Meanwhile, Rita was calculating her chances of success. One of the dates was gone, history, but three more dates lay ahead, three more glorious chances—April 28th, May 5th, and May 8th—and all the calendars in the world should have them marked in red as holidays.

The next day she phoned the Cage and told her colleagues that she'd woken up with an extremely swollen eye—a sty, that's what it's called, isn't it?—and she had to go to the eye doctor. The lie, masquerading as half-truth, cheered her up and got her in the mood for coincidences. We might say, Christophers, that it was the Stanislavski System applied to the theatre of work. Bundó and Gabriel's appointment with the eye specialist was at ten that morning. By half past nine, Rita had patrolled up and down past the clinic twenty times. At quarter to ten she went in, asked where the oculist was, and sat down in the waiting room. Three men were there ahead of her, but none of them was Gabriel. Or Bundó (that would have been the last straw). A receptionist asked what her name was in order to check her appointment time, and she explained that she was there to help a girlfriend.

"She phoned me this morning and asked me to come," she invented. "She's not here yet. She says she's got a swollen eye, I'm not sure if it's the right or left one and, depending on what Dr. Trabal says, I might have to take her back home."

The receptionist believed her. Rita had brought all the papers— at last she had the perfect excuse to talk to Gabriel—and she was so nervous that she started picking at the plastic on the corners of the folder and peeling it back. The next few minutes went by with her attention oscillating from folder to door, door to folder as if she were watching a game of tennis.

All the patients in the waiting room went in to see the doctor, and new ones arrived but Gabriel didn't appear. At ten past ten, the receptionist stuck her head around the door.

"Serafín Bundó."

She repeated the name. Since no one got up, she read another name.

"Gabriel Delacruz." Pause. The other patients looked at each other. "Gabriel Delacruz?"

Rita felt so identified with the name that she was about to shout "Here" and go in to see the doctor herself, but then they called the next name on the list, and a girl got up. She waited ten minutes more, just in case, and then crept out with her tail between her legs. Unlike her other disasters, this new disappointment had her in despair. Like an actress who has trouble coming out of character after the show, she left the oculist's office with blurry vision. Although the sun was shining, the outside world had

turned into a diffuse melange of colors in which grays predomi-
nated. If she managed to focus, allowing things to recover their
natural form, it was because she still had two bullets left to fire, on
May 5th and 8th. In a flash of pragmatism, she promised herself
that if Gabriel didn't turn up on either of those dates she'd forget
about him forever.

She walked up Carrer Muntaner, trying to persuade herself of
these arguments, when she thought she recognized him sitting on
a bench in Plaça Adrià. He had his back to her, and she couldn't
see his face, but the appearance of the man—bony back, short hair,
longish cranium—fitted with the image she had of him. Instant
conjecture: Maybe he'd gone to the clinic and then had second
thoughts; maybe he'd lost the address and didn't know what to do
now; maybe . . . Recently, before Rita had got her hands on those
crucial dates, the city had been full of Gabriels, and these appa-
ritions had become a constant in her everyday existence. In her
walks around Barcelona, she could spend half an hour following a
Gabriel candidate, or studying him until something convinced her
it wasn't him. Restrained by some sort of superstition she never
directly approached them to ask their name. Now it seemed that,
at long last, the situation warranted this, so she crossed the street.
However, a girl got in ahead of her and, going up to the bench
from behind, she covered his eyes with her hands, saying, "Guess
who?" Three meters away, Rita heard the answer, and saw the man
turn around and kiss the girl. No, that one wasn't Gabriel either.
Luckily.


Now, it's time to give an account of Bundó's supernatural intervention. Parapsychology must have a name for this phenomenon,
but I don't know what it is. The fact is that on Friday morning,
thirty hours before Gabriel's appointment with suicide, he woke
up with an excruciating earache. Expanding waves of pain had fil-
tered into his sleep, swamping whatever dream he was having, and
hadn't stopped jabbing at him until he opened his eyes in a state
of anguish. Searing pain shot out from deep inside his right ear. It

gushed forth from his brain, radiating out in concentric circles to ravage all the nerve endings on that side of his skull. Pain surged through his blood with each beat of his heart. The few steps to the bathroom produced the distressing sensation of a continuous detonation of his eardrum. He realized that the ear was clogged with pus and he was totally deaf on that side. He looked in the mirror to make sure that the afflicted side of his face still existed. His right eyelid was twitching. Once Petroli had tried to describe the pain of a full-blown ear infection: "It's like toothache but with all your molars at once." He and Bundó had accused him of exaggerating, but now Gabriel conceded he was right. In such a situation he thought what all of us would have thought: "With this pain, I can't kill myself tomorrow."

If it had ever sunk in, which is doubtful, Gabriel had forgotten that he had an appointment with the insurance company's ENT man precisely that Friday. Furniture movers going around in trucks don't have leather-bound diaries for writing these things down (they might steal them at times, but then they usually give them to somebody else). The procedure tended to be more pedestrian. Obliged by Senyor Casellas, Rebeca gave them the papers in question; they immediately mislaid them; two days before the doctor's appointment, Rebeca reminded them, and they slotted it into their immediate memory. But this time, Rebeca hadn't said anything to Gabriel because he no longer worked at La Ibérica. If the list of appointments no longer had any meaning for him after the accident, it meant everything to Rita, who'd rescued it and was clinging to it as if her life depended on it.

Yet, the fact remains that Gabriel woke up that Friday morning with a dreadful earache.

Since he'd got up and dressed, his ear had started suppurating, discharging a revolting green liquid that he stanched by wadding his ear with cotton puffs. It was nine in the morning. Unable to eat anything solid because each bite would have been torture, the truck driver Gabriel decided that his only option was to present himself at the Emergency Department of the insurance company's clinic and get them to stop the pain. He arrived there an hour later, at ten o'clock, having changed buses twice to cross the city. The other passengers looked at him compassionately, and he felt that his ear was swelling with every blaze of pain. For the first time in all those months he'd wished he was in the La Ibérica van.

When Gabriel was entering the Clínica Plató, Rita was walking up Carrer Muntaner. It was still too early for the appointment noted on the piece of paper but, as on the previous Friday, she wanted to get there in good time and monitor the entrance. Gabriel looked for the receptionist and asked for the Emergency Department. They wanted to know what the problem was. When they saw his ear in such a state, so red and purulent, they sent him straight to the ear, nose, and throat specialist. Once he got there, the nurse asked him for his insurance company card and, on reading his name, told him they were expecting him. He'd come early but they'd put him through straight away so he didn't have to suffer any more. Gabriel told himself that such coincidences were pain-caused hallucinations.

Five minutes later, when the doctor called him into the consulting room, Rita was coming up the stairs on her way to the ear, nose, and throat specialist. Since it had yielded good results with the oculist, she told the new nurse the same story she'd come up with the previous week. She'd come to meet a friend who hadn't shown up yet. She had a bad earache and had lost her sense of balance. The nurse believed her, and Rita sat down to wait for her appointment—or disappointment?—with Gabriel.

Gabriel's meeting with Dr. Sadurní lasted twenty minutes. From her vantage point in the waiting room, Rita could hear the doctor talking with another man, but she couldn't make out what they were saying and didn't suspect it was Gabriel. She kept her eyes on the door, and every time someone came in her heart gave a leap.

In the consulting room, Dr. Sadurní asked Gabriel to sit on an examination bed and looked at his ear, first with the naked eye and then with an instrument that resembled a cornet. Gabriel vaguely remembered the doctor from a previous checkup, which calmed him down. He was a friendly, well-mannered man, of the old school. He was over sixty, wore suspenders and an elegant tie, addressed his patients with the respectful second-person *vós,* and shouted (maybe because most of them came to him half deaf). He poked around inside Gabriel's ear with a cotton swab. Gabriel couldn't suppress his groans of pain and the doctor tried to ease it by repeating some mysterious sounds: *"Berebé, berebé, berebé."*

After long years of experience and having tried multiple combinations, he'd reached the conclusion that by linking the vowel *e* with *b* and *r* he'd come up with the sound that most effectively soothed infected ears. He held an aluminum bowl under the ear and, with a syringe, flushed out the auditory canal with hydrogen peroxide.

"This is going to hurt for a second," he warned.

Gabriel endured the gush of hydrogen peroxide with his shoulders hunched and eyes shut tight. He was paralyzed by the shock but, indeed, only a second later the pain vanished in a stream of liquid. His ear was unblocked and the new void was occupied by an exasperating jabbering noise.

*"Berebé, berebé, berebé . . ."*

The doctor touched his back so he'd stay still. Using another cotton swab, he took a sample of the pus that was now streaming from his ear and spread it on some white paper. It was lizard green with opalescent spots. He showed it to Gabriel like someone displaying a precious stone.

"You have a fine old infection here, my friend. One of the strangest I have ever seen. Six or seven cases in all the forty years of my career . . . What more can I say? Now, let me see where this is coming from so it doesn't happen again."

The doctor disinfected the ear and, with the aid of another cotton swab, daubed the auditory canal with some ointment. Then he covered it with gauze and adhesive tape. It was a spectacular bandage, but Gabriel was grateful for it because the beast inside his ear was now assuaged.

"Keep it protected from the air for five or six days," the doctor ordered. "I'll give you a prescription for an antibiotic and this ointment. Change the dressing every morning. Sleep without it, please. You'll have a soiled pillowcase but that doesn't matter. Ears also have a right to breathe and express themselves as well as to listen."

Gabriel nodded automatically, as if waking up for the first time that morning. The doctor took the piece of paper with his sample of pus, sat down at his desk, and opened a very thick medical textbook. As he turned over the pages he kept nodding to himself. Then he took another big book and studied some photos.

"You have a very atypical acute inner-ear infection, as I told you," he finally pronounced. "Your sinuses have gradually been clogging up with a rare chemical compound. Permit me a personal question: Has there been a recent death in your family, or some personal distress?"

It didn't take Gabriel long to answer.

"Yes, a friend died. He was like a brother to me."

"I imagined so. And when did he die?"

"Eighty-two days ago, today."

"Goodness gracious. That is a long time. And, tell me, did you cry at all when he died?"

"No," he answered sadly. "To tell you the truth, I haven't been able to cry for him. There's no way I can."

"Now I understand. It may seem strange to you but, over all this time, those unwept tears have ended up bringing on an infection, my friend. That is what happens. Tears come from some little sacs called lachrymal glands. The human body is very intelligent, you know. When you need to cry, the sac fills up but, if the tears fail to come out, then you end up with a surfeit of sodium and potassium that inflames the organs and destabilizes the whole system. You must help this ear and try to cry for your friend. It would be the best cure of all. Take this infection as if he were begging you to do it from the hereafter."

After thanking Dr. Sadurní, a disoriented and serious-looking Gabriel walked out of the consulting room. You couldn't say he was completely done for, not yet, but the doctor's explanation had greatly unnerved him, and he was struggling to get his thoughts together. His inner battle gave him an erratic, distracted appearance, and, seeing him returning into the waiting room, Rita instantly recognized the Gabriel of the airport.

This broken man was screaming to be looked after.

He no longer had his arm in a cast, but the bulky dressing covering his ear made for a pathetic sight. The time had come. She clutched the folder and stood up trembling like a leaf, but Gabriel walked past her, unseeing.

That was okay. She understood. She followed him down the stairs (while in the background she could hear the doctor burbling to someone else, *"Berebé, berebé, berebé . . ."*), keeping a prudent distance. Now in the street, Gabriel trudged toward Carrer Muntaner. He couldn't get the doctor's words out of his head and was walking slower and slower. Rita had to stop so she wouldn't bump into him. Gabriel was so absorbed that he wasn't aware of anything else. Part of his being, the more rational part, refused to connect the earache with Bundó's death, but then guilt won the day, accusing him of being utterly spineless and mean. A voice inside him, as if from beyond the grave, even ticked him off for considering suicide. What a coward! He was drowning. He was suffocating. He stumbled, and Rita thought she'd have to pick him up from the ground. Gabriel took a few more steps, crossed the road, and sat down on a bench in Plaça Adrià. It wasn't the same one used by the couple eight days earlier but one more tucked away, half hidden by vegetation. Rita let him do his thing. She had to act with great care and, above all, not jeopardize anything. It looked as if Gabriel was calming down.

At that hour of the morning, Plaça Adrià was an oasis of calm.

Gradually, with his whole body juddering like the Pegaso engine when it refused to start, Gabriel started to weep. First, one big tear flooded his right eye and spilled over and then another one did the same in the left eye. The flow stopped for a few seconds and it seemed as if that would be all, but two more tears brimmed up, one in each eye, salty, lush and assertive.

If the engine continued to balk on the cold winter mornings of the North, Bundó used to yell. "Come on, get going, you bastard, don't be such a wimp!"

The rush of tears was building up, and Gabriel couldn't control the first spasms of his body. A high-pitched howl escaped him, soon to turn into a dirge.

"That's it, that's the way," Bundó would bellow, "let yourself go! Show us what you've got, Pegaso!"

Then, doing honor to its name, it did its truck's equivalent of pawing the ground, snorting, proudly huffing and puffing as Bundó laughed, joyfully thumping both hands on the steering wheel and looking at his friends to solicit their approval. Gabriel was now bellowing, bawling with his eyes and his whole body, which was convulsed with spasms.

When she judged that a judicious time had passed, Rita went to sit on the same bench, a little way away from him. He glanced at her with a woebegone expression. He didn't stop crying. Now he couldn't. His eyes were red and burning, his cheeks lustrous with all the tears rolling down them. Rita held out a handkerchief, and he took it babbling some sort of gratitude. Rather than mopping up his tears, he used it to blow his nose so he could keep crying.

Three hours went by, no exaggeration, during which Gabriel wept in all possible registers as if, that way, he could sum up his life at Bundó's side. He wailed like a baby in diapers wanting the breast. He shed the crocodile tears of the kid up to no good. He whimpered like an adolescent blubbering over the pains of love, and like the adult who swallows his tears pretending to have a cold. He cried like you cry in the cinema watching a drama in the dark, cried like you cry on the soccer field, in front of everyone, when your team loses the final. He cried with rage, sorrow, physical pain, and seeking compassion. He cried without knowing why, out of pure depression, cried like a crybaby, for pleasure too, re-creating himself in it. He yelped like a beaten dog. He got the hiccups from so much crying. He roared, he lamented, he whimpered. His chest hurt, the muscles of his face hurt, and his eyelids were burning. When he tried to catch his breath, he sniveled for a while. When it seemed he'd run out of tears, he only had to think of Bundó and the depths of his eyes rewarded him with a few more liters.

Three hours went by, I say. If he'd collected all those tears, dried them, and extracted the salt, he could have seasoned his meals to the end of his days.

Rita remained at his side. Some time earlier she'd started to cry too, letting out the tension and fears of all those months, the weariness of so many futile kilometers covered in Barcelona. That corner of Plaça Adrià was a vale of tears, a cryodrome.

All at once it started to rain, a shower of fine, gentle drops and, to both of them, this seemed the most logical corollary. Even meteorology was joining in. Finally, Rita picked up the folder and handed it to Gabriel. He opened it, recognized the papers, maps, Bundó's lists, and, therein, found yet another reason for crying. After a while, he turned to her and asked, "Why are you crying?"

"I'm crying with happiness. Because we've found each other at last. And you?"

"I'm crying for a friend who was called Bundó."

At this point, Christophers, will you permit me a devious maneuvre that sums up everything that happened next? This is it: We could take a leap ahead in time and all that weeping, all those rivers and streams of tears could be concentrated in one single outpouring, that of my bawling when I shattered the silence of my first second of life, just after the midwife smacked my little bottom. Nine months plus five or six days had gone by.

# 6

## The Fifth Mother

It's a pity that human beings aren't born well informed, with a fully stocked and operational memory from their first breath of life. Right now, for example, when we're trying to describe Gabriel's relationships with our mothers, we'd find such a gift most useful. We'd be able to recall exactly what happened on the days when he came to visit us and stayed in our homes. What confidences they shared, when they fought and why, and whether they ever felt like a proper couple. In short, whether they ever managed to make their relationship seem normal. (They didn't, of course, since Gabriel did nothing to foster the mature feelings that are necessary when two people live together.) On the other hand, since the four of us were too young to understand anything, we have to trust what Sigrun, Mireille, Sarah, and Rita have chosen to tell us. It's a telling sign that all four mothers portray Gabriel as a good man, independent, evasive, and certainly not someone to have and to hold. A sweet affliction, they say, a bitter gift.

Let's indulge in a touch of filial vanity, Mothers. If we four didn't exist, it's probable that Gabriel, progenitor of the Christophers, would be no more than a minor footnote in your stories, testament to an age of sexual joys and amorous doubts that you'd sometimes remember with pride and sometimes with contempt—like so many other things in life.

Someone looking at the story from outside will ask perhaps: Was there anyone else afterward? Yes, of course, all four of them met other men, but none of them could ever replace Gabriel, so they have no place here.

The main purpose of our meetings has been, and still is, keeping on our father's trail. Only we four are with him, about him, for him, against him (add all the prepositions you wish) and hence our mothers are not included. They, it must be said, are very happy with our decision.

As we made clear from the outset, Bundó's traumatic death put an end to our father's journeys, and he never visited us again. Maybe the fact that our mothers took it fairly well and ended up forgetting him—each in her own way—reveals the fragility of their relationships with Gabriel. At the end of the day, they never stopped being single moms and living as such.

We could say that if the accident in the Pegaso hadn't happened early that Saint Valentine's morning, everything would have turned out differently, but that won't get us very far. It's better to be pragmatic and accept that the situation would eventually have become unsustainable for Gabriel. The deceit would have eventually become rotten to the core.

"At last the secret is out!" as the poem says. *Per fi s'ha revelat el secret. Enfin le secret est percé. Das Geheimnis ist gelüftet.*

Without intending to, Gabriel had emerged again after some months of not visiting his trans-Pyrenean sons and women. On the face of it, the meeting with Rita in Barcelona and the birth of Cristòfol should have been his big chance to hang up his spurs. Just one family, just one city. However, it didn't take long for Gabriel to realize that he was no good at conventions, and he went back to his old solitary ways. Rita sums it up very well—"when the present prevailed"—but, once again, Cristòfol asks permission to fill us in on those early times.

You've got five minutes, Cristòfol, and that's it. Ready, set, go!

Thank-you for your boundless generosity, Christophers. Let me say, to begin with, that Gabriel never lived with us in Carrer del Tigre. He spent many nights and days there looking after the tiny tot that was me. Rita says he even learned to change my diapers. How about that?

"Just a moment. Excuse me. He changed my diapers, too, when he had to," Christof interrupts.

"And mine."

"And mine."

Okay, so there's nothing original about me. But let's see who can do better than this: When I was about four months old, my mom went back to work at the airport, and there were some weeks when Gabriel stayed over every day. Every single day. A whole week. Day and night. How about that? Yet, for all his perseverance, he never saw our place as his home. Just to make things clear, his name never appeared on our mailbox. This family ambiguity didn't bother Rita at first. It was in the seventies, Franco was still dying (without finishing the job properly), and Danish pediatric theory was all the rage among young mothers. Besides, as a militant orphan, Rita didn't set much store by parental authority and liked the idea that I should grow up slightly, ever so slightly neglected. I imagine that she got used to Gabriel's intermittency in those days. His comings and goings fitted into a certain lifestyle and should be seen as the counterpoint to the total, passionate surrender with which he gave himself to her when they were together.

You recognize the situation, don't you Christophers? I'm sure he acted like that with your mothers too: It was as if he was eternally grateful to them and knew that he was making up for long hours of absence and waiting with his brief presence. Although it was never made explicit, this modus operandi worked from the very beginning and he got better and better at it . . .

"Words are flowing out . . . like endless rain . . ."

"You see what happens when you start going on about yourself? You're provoking him. We agreed on five minutes, Cristòfol."

"We know the score . . ."

Okay, okay. I'll be brief. At their meeting in the vale of tears, Rita told Gabriel that she'd been looking for him ever since he'd lost a bag and tried to reclaim it at the airport. Eighty days earlier. Gabriel didn't remember her, but the girl's courage touched his heart, and he let himself be adopted. Make note of that expression because I think it's crucial, Christophers: He let himself be adopted. The long crying session had dried his mouth and he was thirsty and hungry. They had something to eat and drink in some bar or other. They talked with their mouths full. Rita was delighted to describe her nighttime vigil in Via Favència, how cold she'd been as she kept watch. There was not a trace of reproach in her words. Instead of seeing her as a lunatic or recoiling in panic, Gabriel was grateful that someone had been thinking about him during those dark days. They laughed when he recalled that he'd heard the doorbell from inside the apartment but didn't have it in him to do anything. Yes, they laughed. "It was better like that," Rita thought. "All's well that ends well, right?" The blind date orchestrated by Bundó from the great blue yonder was working fine.

That night Gabriel didn't sleep in the Via Favència apartment, and his ear suppurated on a new pillow. Rita fixed him another dressing the next day. Thanks to all the tears shed for Bundó, his ear was on the mend. On Saturday and Sunday they didn't leave the apartment. They stayed in bed and reconstructed their separate pasts, leaping from one story to another. Conrad and Leo's plane accident. The Pegaso accident. We should assume that Gabriel was more selective and chose what he could say and what he couldn't. They were thrilled to discover what they had in common when he told her about the La Ibérica pilfering racket.

"We filched a suitcase, or box, or packet from every move..." "Really? We do exactly the same at the airport! We keep lost suitcases. We're soul mates." "Yes, we are."

On Monday, Gabriel saw Rita to the bus stop and then returned to the Via Favència apartment. His first retreat to his winter quarters lasted just one day. The next day he slept at Rita's again. The second retreat lasted two more days. Rita didn't want to pressure him because she understood that he was delicate and insecure and could see that he needed to be alone. One night, Gabriel told her about his decline after Bundó's death, without sparing her the episode of his would-be suicide. They both knew that, by turning up as she did, she'd foiled his plan to throw himself off the

Columbus monument. (Some months later, by the way, with Rita now pregnant, Gabriel insisted on going up to the lookout at the top. They were going out to have a drink before lunch on a Sunday morning, and he thought it would be a good way to bury those distressing thoughts once and for all. When they were up in the cupola beneath the feet of the statue, contemplating from aloft the port, Montjuïc, and the Ramblas all decked out for Christmas, Gabriel realized that it wouldn't have been easy to throw himself off the top. The windows had been reinforced. Then he said to Rita, "You know what? If it's a boy, we should call him Cristòfol, like Columbus." Convinced she had a boy in her belly, she thought it was a great idea and they called me Cristòfol thereafter.)

Mom says there was a period after my birth in which Gabriel spent a lot of time with us. Meanwhile, he tried going back to work at La Ibérica. His savings had run out, and Senyor Casellas took him back as a driver. He asked to do short trips with the DKV van, only around Barcelona and the province, but he gave up after a few weeks. He got tired more quickly than before, his broken arm often swelled up, and the routine reminded him too much of the good old days with Bundó. Seeing him so dejected, Senyor Casellas felt guilty and suggested he could go back to doing international moves. They'd just bought a new truck, and the trips were more comfortable now. Gabriel preferred not to and six months later left La Ibérica once again, this time for good. (We'll have to assume that his return to the European motorways would have entailed too great a moral effort on his part, that of getting his other sons and women back.) He left the job without the safety net of any other employment. For a time he spent his days doing odd jobs here and there. A messenger in the neighborhood had a hernia, and Gabriel took over until he'd recovered from the operation, driving his 2CV van and delivering his packages, this time without keeping any. Just before I was born, Rita finally got the insurance money for the deaths of her parents and now had something put aside in the bank. One day she offered to buy him a vehicle so he could set up his own messenger service. He couldn't imagine being a boss, not even of himself. Rita knew that lukewarm reaction: It was the same one she'd got a couple of times when, half jokingly, she'd suggested they could get married.

By autumn 1975, Gabriel was moving away from us. Then one day he left and that was the end of it. Rita never had any illusions that he'd come and live with us, but she had managed to drag some kind of family feeling out of him for a time. We went out for walks together, he carried me on his shoulders, he sang songs to me, and he seemed happy. Then his visits were further and further apart. At first, he'd turn up unexpectedly or would phone at the last minute to say he wasn't coming. Rita had grudgingly got used to this maybe-maybe-not situation and accepted it out of love, but he must have been feeling guilty because eventually he preferred not to commit himself. No more of this on-such-and-such-a-day-we'll-do-so-and-so. No, he preferred things to be more open, freer. When Rita asked him why it was so hard for him, he replied that the Via Favència apartment was too far away. It was almost in another city, another Barcelona, he said. Sometimes I wonder about this and think he's not referring so much to space as to time. Perhaps, for him, living in Carrer del Tigre, a hundred meters from his old boarding house and almost next to the House of Charity, meant moving in the past. The set hadn't changed much but the dramatis personae were different. Or maybe when he visited us he felt as if he was traveling into a future, a future that didn't match the one he'd imagined.

Although Gabriel gave the impression of fading out slowly, we actually know the date of the last day he spent with us. It was the twentieth of November. Rita remembers it clearly because it's the day Franco died. We hadn't seen Dad for a week and that afternoon he turned up out of the blue. After dinner, when he and Rita had settled me down to sleep, they went down to the Principal, the café on the corner, to see what the atmosphere was like. The owners had put a radio on the bar. Every time the musical program was interrupted for a news bulletin, the whole place went silent and everyone listened. Some faces were tight and worried, but most of the clients and waiters punctuated the broadcaster's grave utterances with sarcastic comments. He's never going to kick the bucket, that fucking butcher. If he's suffering so much they should kill him off now. Let's hope the champagne hasn't gone flat after so much waiting. He hasn't died yet because hell doesn't want him either.

Rita was twitchy because they'd left me alone so they came back home. She turned on the TV to see if there were any new developments, but the hours dragged by hypnotically. They were just about to go to bed when they heard the pop of a champagne cork and the gleeful shouts of someone letting it all out. Infected by the neighbor's joy and eagerness to celebrate, they poured a couple of glasses of wine and drank a toast. The fun and games woke me up. I was wide awake so I got out of bed and started playing with Mom and Dad. It was early in the morning and Rita, carried away by all the euphoria, dared to propose to Gabriel that he should come and live with us for once and for all. As always, he didn't say yes and he didn't say no. Nothing could ever be definitive.

The previous day, Gabriel had arranged with the messenger that he'd do the early-morning delivery round with him. At six on the dot we heard the van's horn tooting their agreed-upon signal from the street, and Dad left. Mom picked me up and we waved good-bye from the window.

"You've got one minute left, Cristòfol. Sorry."

"*Tick tock, tick tock . . .*"

"I'm a loser, and I'm not what I appear to be . . ."

"Fuck off, Chris. Okay, that's it, I'm finishing. Let's see, short, short, like dictating a telegram. Gabriel. Distance. Silence. Days pass. Vanished. Doesn't return. Stop." Pause to breathe. "Rita. Tired. Too long. Scared. What happened to him? Desperate. Invents ridiculous political plots. But it's just coincidence. Goes to his place. Never there. Disappointment. Gone for ever. Time heals all wounds. Stop." Pause to breathe. "Me. I miss him. Mommy, where's Daddy? I forget him. I turn three. I turn four, five, six. I forget him with rage. I hate him. Stop." Pause to breathe. "One day, for the hell of it, we go to his apartment looking for him. Sold a while back, they tell us. We're forced to forget him. Want to. Twenty years pass. Even more. Stop." Another pause. "Police call. Us, the Christophers. We meet. We start looking. Now is now. Now. Present."

"Time's up!"
"Ouch! That's inhuman. How cruel."
"Thanks, Cristòfol."
"Yes, thanks."

We think we know the people around us and that we can anticipate their emotions, but that's just an illusion. The inner life of a person is the most impenetrable secret in the world, an armor-plated chamber. During all this time we've been looking for Gabriel, all the hours we've spent tracing his movements until he disappeared off the face of the earth, we Christophers have wondered more than once: Do we really know him yet? But the question's based on a fallacy. Although you can only live by moving forward, existence, any existence, only makes sense when you look back and try to understand it as a whole. We leave a biography behind, like the trail of a snake in the sand. Well, this is the comforting illusion that many people cling to. In the end, it's not unlike the risky exercise of trying to interpret a dream. We take four or five scenes that we cling to just as we're waking up, sensations we're only able to recognize blearily, like flotsam after a shipwreck, and then we cobble them together with a narrative thread, trying to make the end result comprehensible. But life's different. What matters in any life is life itself, what we construct every day without being aware of it. That's why, when we're in the thick of them, most situations have no special meaning. The illusion of sense comes later. We sit in a cafe, talking with a friend, and we rationalize the past by looking back. We tidy it up. We make a virtue out of the necessity of understanding our days. This process isn't very different, either, from scribbling a few clichés to sum up our summer vacation on a postcard and sending it last minute (so our parents and friends get it when we've already returned safe and sound). We reduce life to a few words, we simplify it, but its real meaning is complex, contradictory, and uncertain.

Sorry about all the philosophising. We Christophers have remarked more than once that, with these pages, we've saved ourselves quite a few sessions with the shrink. The whole thing becomes relevant now because yesterday, Saturday, at last—at last, indeed!—the line of the past and the line of the present came together, and all at once we realized just how brutal the experience of retracing Gabriel's footsteps had been. We thought we knew it all but that was only in retrospect. Actually, we knew nothing.

The thing is, that on Tuesday night, with barely three days to maneuvre, Cristòfol called us to a new meeting.

"I've got some interesting information," he announced to us, one by one, "but I can't tell you over the phone. It would take too long. You'll have to trust me and come to Barcelona. Maybe I'm wrong and it will turn out to be a damp squib, but I think Saturday night's going to be exciting."

Our previous meeting, it's worth recalling perhaps, had taken place only three weeks earlier and had turned up a few clues. The bartender at the Carambola confirmed that his boss, Feijoo, had been after Gabriel for months because of gambling debts. Didn't look good. Another promising clue was the neighbor on the mezzanine floor in Carrer Nàpols, Giuditta the former circus artiste. When we visited her, Christopher had found the joker with the third eye hidden in the crevices of her sofa, but there was no way of interpreting the find. What should we think of this neighbor? Was she an ally or someone we had to keep an eye on? Gabriel could have mislaid the card months ago, during a friendly visit, or he might have surreptitiously hidden it because he saw he was cornered by someone, or he could even have done it later when Feijoo, Miguélez, and their henchmen were torturing him before the pitiless gaze of that Italian woman . . .

Cristòfol's words were seductive and, needless to say, we other brothers gladly abandoned our respective solitary plans. Christof canceled a show he was doing with Cristoffini on Saturday afternoon: Some rich kid in Berlin had to go without a ventriloquist at his birthday party. Christophe had to correct some university exam papers, from second-year quantum mechanics, but it was so straightforward he could do it on the plane or when he was killing time (Christophe only sleeps four hours a night). Chris was supposed to be going to a record fair in Bristol on Sunday. He had an appointment with a client who wanted to buy the first Spanish edition of the Beatles' "Let It Be." This was something of a rarity because they'd brought it out with this title and those of other songs such as "The Long and Winding Road" translated into Spanish: "Déjalo estar," "El largo y tortuoso camino" . . . But in England there's some fair or other devoted to the Beatles every weekend, and he's pretty fed up with them so he told the client to wait however long it was going to take.

The sense of urgency that suddenly took over the quest for Gabriel predisposed us to adventure. Our planes took off from Berlin, London, and Paris, tracing elliptical red lines on the map of Europe that converged in Barcelona. We carried our hand luggage with the gravity of men on a secret mission. Yesterday, Saturday, at two in the afternoon when all four of us met as arranged in the lobby of our usual hotel, all we needed was a secret password, something cryptic and poetic like "The bees are pollinating the magnolias," or "Bertie said all the whales have syphilis."

The electric charge was with us all day and, indeed, the shock hit us some hours later. While we were having lunch in the hotel, Cristòfol brought us up to date.

"As we agreed, Christophers, I've been checking out the apartment these last few weeks. I hung around there, making sure there were no unwelcome developments, and then went back to wherever I'd come from. Tuesday night was the last time. The apartment was the same as always, with that stillness we all know but, when I left, I decided to go by the Carambola. I wasn't expecting much, to tell you the truth, but there was nothing to lose by trying. I found the talkative bartender, but this time he was mute, and he wanted me mute too because as soon as he saw me coming in he put his finger to his lips. It had just turned seven in the evening, and the boss, Feijoo, wasn't there. "He'll be back any minute," the bartender told me, as if he'd read my thoughts. "He's gone to get some whisky from a warehouse over near Santa Coloma. It's black market and cheaper for him. Go now. I'll phone you as soon as I can . . ."

"Why do you need to phone me?" I asked trustingly.

While I was waiting for his answer I checked out the clientele. A boy and a girl, half barricaded behind high-school folders and books, were holding hands at the most out-of-the-way table. A granddad nodding off in front of the TV seemed to be agreeing with everything the voluptuous presenter had to say. Two girls drinking Coca-Cola at another table were turning the pages of a wedding-dress catalog. The one facing me hadn't stopped staring at me since I walked in. Since the bartender was still dithering and taking his time about answering, she got up and came over. She was young and attractive but with a sly look she couldn't hide. I noticed her apron, which was longer than the skirt she was wearing underneath, and deduced she must be the lady of the bar, Feijoo's wife, the bartender's lover. "Hi," she said, giving me the once-over. Then she nodded and asked, "Did you tell him or not?" She had a husky, very sexy voice. It was evident that she had him wrapped around her little finger. Still unwilling to talk, he said, "You keep out of it . . ." but she cut in, "Either you tell him or I do. He has to help us, doesn't he . . ." and, sashaying back to the table, she demonstrated the art of butt wiggling in five meters. "What have you got to tell me? Why do I have to help you?" I asked. Then the bartender told me that two days earlier he'd overhead a conversation between Feijoo and Miguélez, the retired cop. They were talking about someone called Manubens, a well-heeled businessman who likes gambling. They'd organized a game for Saturday night (which is to say tonight, Christophers). The bartender said the stakes are very high. And that Miguélez, Feijoo, and another member of the gang wanted to clean him out, right down to the last cent. I asked the same thing that you would have asked, Christophers: What's that got to do with Gabriel? Then he came out with it, in these exact words: "I don't know if it's got anything to do with him or not, but the thing is, his name came up in the conversation. Miguélez, who doesn't mess around, was talking about the 'Delacruz system' for getting their hands on Manubens' brass. What he actually said was, 'Don't worry, Feijoo. If we apply the Delacruz system we'll take him to the cleaners, and then he killed himself laughing at his own wit. I tell you, it's got something to do with this Gabriel . . ."

"And did Miguélez say anything about using the pistol?" I asked, but he denied it. No, no way. Feijoo himself told him not to bring the pistol. It wasn't necessary and, anyway, Manubens would take fright."

All four of us agreed that the bartender's words were the most substantial lead we'd had in the last few months. Now, the main riddle was summed up in the words "Delacruz system" that Miguélez referred to with such conviction. Was it simply a trick of our father's that had inspired them (teachers always spawn deplorable students) or, out of some kind of unlikely sympathy, would he be playing cards there in person? We tried to figure it out, but our guesses weren't brilliant enough. Any insight we might have had about Gabriel had dried up out of pure exhaustion. The only way to know what was going on, then, was to turn up at the bar. The bartender finished by telling Cristòfol that the big game was beginning at eleven. We had to work out a strategy.

At four in the afternoon, after lunch, we got a taxi to the Arc de Triomf. Once there, since we didn't trust the Italian neighbor, we separated to take different routes and got to the building four minutes apart, one after the other. The idea was to go up to the apartment without making any noise on the stairs or landing so she wouldn't suspect we were there. Cristòfol, who had the keys, went in first and left the door ajar. Then the rest of us sneaked up just as carefully. Chris had brought a bottle of Scotch and we decided to have a tipple. We had to wait seven hours before going into action and, if we were able to make it last over the course of the afternoon, it would give us the sangfroid and daring we were going to need that night. We sat around the dining-room table and discussed what we had to do. We spoke in the hushed conspiratorial tones that plot hatching requires. Christophe, using the time to correct exam papers, came up with a conservative option: We should monitor the door of the bar, starting one hour before they were due to meet. Thus, the first thing we'd find out was whether Gabriel was one of the cardsharps or not. Chris offered to go into the lion's den—they didn't know him in the bar—and keep an eye on things from inside. Cristòfol jotted down all the suggestions, as if taking minutes, and reminded us that we had to proceed with care. We knew from the bartender that those guys could be dangerous. Christof drew a map of the zone where the bar was located so we could identify our lookout points later on. He was also very alert to noises outside the apartment. If we heard any rustling on the landing, however slight it was, he rushed on tiptoes to the door and looked through the peephole.

We were in the thick of our summit when we were alerted by a crunch of old wood, which immediately turned into scrabbling noises like an animal scratching at a door. It came from the bedroom. We were amazed. Chris got up slowly, picked up his glass of whisky and downed it in one gulp. The rest of us copied him. With extreme caution, we peered into the bedroom, but there was no one in sight. We went in. Using gestures picked up from some TV crime series, Christof pointed at the half-open window and we all nodded. The noises seemed to be coming from outside. Whoever it was, we'd catch him red-handed. We stood there in silence, peering at the raised blind and the curtains waving gently in the breeze. Then we ruled out the window as the source of the noise. The vibrations were coming from inside the walls themselves, or from beneath the floor, like a geyser about to blow. The moment we realized that the sounds were being made inside the wardrobe, they stopped.

The new silence was so premonitory, so loaded with tension, that we were frozen to the spot, and then, while we were standing there as motionless as statues waiting for years and centuries to tick by, something extraordinary happened. The wardrobe door was flung open and, as if emerging from the bowels of hell, out popped Senyora Giuditta.

Once upon a time in Paris, a girl had got into a wardrobe of Gabriel's. Now in Barcelona, another woman was coming out of another one.

She was so sure of herself and we were so quiet that she didn't see us at first. She was in her house clothes and her expression of great concentration suggested that her head was well and truly elsewhere. She looked as if she'd just been hanging out the washing or had been to ask a neighbor for a pinch of salt. It was evident that she often came in and out of the wardrobe. She exited backward and her contortions as she emerged from her lair were proof that her body was still good for the circus. Once outside—as we remained motionless and silent—she stood up straight, recovering her usual form, shut the door, and fiddled with her hair. There was a full-length mirror on the outside of the wardrobe. When Giuditta looked at herself in it, she discovered us reflected there. A sharp cry shrilled from her throat as if we were four zombies about to rip into her. We took fright at her fright and also screamed, each of us in keeping with the guttural particularities of his own language in such a way that the five of us joined in chorus to create a magical moment of universal fear. The reverberation of our respective fright gave way to mutual recognition. We four. Her.

*"Madonna! Che shock!"* she yelled at the top of her lungs in the purest tradition of Italian sopranos, with heavy panting and a hand clutching at her breast. You could never have imagined that such a little body could produce such power. "What are you doing here?"

"We might well ask you the same," we said. "What are you doing here, in our father's apartment? How come you've just emerged from his wardrobe?" Chris brought her a glass with one finger of whisky, which went straight down the hatch, as if she was taking medicine.

"I didn't hear you arrive . . ." she answered. "But what a stroke of luck that you are here! In fact, I wanted to go through your papers to find some telephone number or address where I could find you . . ." She was talking in fits and starts and paused for a moment to catch her breath. "Your father will kill me . . . He didn't want me to say a word, but they've had him kidnapped for some days and . . ."

"Kidnapped?" we interrupted in one voice. The word summarily put an end to any adventurers' joys we might have had.

"I wanted to persuade you to go there . . . tonight, without him knowing. They've abducted him to make him play. You must go and save him tonight—you're his sons."

We poured her another whisky to calm her down. Of course we'd do everything we could to help our father, but first she'd have to tell us the whole story, from beginning to end. She asked us to follow her and, as if undergoing an initiation rite, all four of us passed through the wardrobe's secret passage one by one. Christof, the most strapping (he doesn't want us to say "fat") of all of us, almost got stuck. Once in her place, we distributed ourselves around her now-familiar couch and armchairs to hear from her lips the latest—and most unknown to us—chapter in Gabriel's life.

"Where shall I start?" Giuditta asked.

The first incredible revelation, which left the four of us dumbfounded, is that Gabriel had never left that building in Carrer Nàpols. On the contrary, he'd been holed up there the whole time, with her help. We struggled with our feelings of frustration. How far off the mark we'd been when we imagined him roaming all over the place, and how close he was when we were holding our meetings in the mezzanine apartment!

Just as we'd suspected more than once, the disastrous game with Feijoo and Miguélez more than a month before had forced our father into hiding. Gabriel refused to return the money they'd loaned him as he believed it was his. If he'd played without their pressure, he said, with his faculties in top form, he would certainly have won. Moreover, it was a matter of pride. He'd wanted to teach that gang of crooks a lesson . . .

"At that time," Giuditta informed us, "he'd been playing cards (with sleight of hand when required) as his only profession for about two years. When I asked him if at least he found it diverting he said not really, or only sometimes when he detected that someone was trying unsuccessfully to cheat. He knew of about three or four big-time card games in the city. They were always on Friday and Saturday in simple, working-class bars, nothing flashy, places notable for easy-money exhibitionists and even easier inebriation. Gabriel went from one game to another so nobody would suspect that he lived off them: He never played with the same group two weeks in a row . . ."

As the bartender had guessed, after that last night in the Car-

ambola Miguélez had gone to the police station and found out
Gabriel's address. On Tuesday evening he and Feijoo turned up
at the apartment. The two men, full of cognac and rage, battered
at Gabriel's door, threatening to kill him if he didn't return the
money. Perhaps he'd forgotten, but they had a pistol. Despite the
racket, Gabriel gave no sign of life, and after an hour they got fed
up and left . . .

"But the next day they were back. And the next. And the
next . . ." Giuditta told us. " 'We know you're in there, you son of
a bitch, and we won't stop till you come out,' they bellowed in
turn. They had no special timetable. One day they'd come in the
morning and the next in the evening. Sometimes, when I got home
from work, or went out shopping, I saw one of their thugs hanging
around in the street a couple of buildings down from us. It was
obvious he was watching our doorway. One Friday, I think it was,
they turned up again and Miguélez added a new line to his spiel.
'It's in your interests to come out, Delacruz,' he announced. He
was full of himself, very arrogant. It gave me the shivers. Gabriel
said it was Franco's cop coming out.

"It's not about the money now, you bastard. It's a question
of honor, a personal matter, and, I swear by my holy mother, we
won't stop till we flay you alive. I've got good friends in the police
force, you know that? And, if necessary, I'll slap a search warrant
on you and we'll break your door down.' He drew out the words
("o-u-u-ut," "mo-o-o-ney," "b-a-a-astard," "hono-o-o-or," "frie-e-e-
e-nds") and, I don't know how to put it, but you could hear the
paranoia in those stretched-out vowels. He sounded like someone who was used to dealing out threats and torture . . ."

When Miguélez's obsession over his lost honor, sainted mother,
or whatever, led him and Feijoo to intensify their siege, Gabriel
had already been holed up for a week without going out. Years
earlier, just after Giuditta moved into the next-door apartment,
she and our father had embarked on an—let's say—unlikely amorous relationship. And here we have the second bombshell. The
Christophers have a new stepmother, if that's what we want to
call her (not that it makes any difference now), the fifth mother,

the Italian one, though she wasn't of an age to bear another Christopher. From the outset, Giuditta and our father had agreed that they'd each live in their own apartments and preserve a certain degree of independence. They'd be together when they needed one another . . . the same old story that all of us had heard from our mothers.

"There were weeks when we only saw each other on Sundays, but that was no problem," Giuditta said. "The celebration more than made up for it. In addition, the neighbors didn't suspect a thing and the clandestine atmosphere was exciting. Gabriel, as you've seen, lived like a refugee, a fugitive with just a few belongings, as if he was waiting for the signal to flee the country pronto. I knew all about this temporary feeling when I was in the circus. One day, for example, he rang at my door, standing there with a travel bag in his hand and beaming from ear to ear. 'Are you going somewhere?' I asked him, pointing at the bag. 'No,' he said, surprised. 'I've come to spend a couple of days with you. Well, that's if you want . . .' That night, before we went to bed, he realized he'd left his toothbrush at his place. 'Why don't you go and get it?' I asked, but he didn't want to. 'Too far,' he said. I thought he was joking but then I saw the unbridgeable distance in his eyes . . ."

Yes, the fondness with which Giuditta spoke of Gabriel made us think of our mothers: All of them had wisely opted for the same stoicism in their love for him. However, she did confess that the amorous association worked more in our father's favor. At first she'd hinted a couple of times that they might live together some day—"even more together," she'd said—but he said he wasn't made for conjugal life. Then, like someone displaying the scars of an old wound in order to condemn war, he'd told her that he had four sons scattered around Europe with four different mothers. Once she'd taken in that news—subsequently backed up with photos—she had a better understanding of the man's social limitations . . .

"Ironies of destiny," Giuditta resumed. "Feijoo and Miguélez's harassment pushed us into marital life. Early on Monday morning, three days after the previous visit, Miguélez turned up in the company of another cop from the Policia National. Luckily we'd slept together that night, and Gabriel was still here at my place. All of a sudden we heard a din of footsteps stomping up the stairs. The cop knocked at the door demanding that whoever was inside should open up in the name of the law. He had a search warrant! Obstruction of the law would be punished with heaven knows what! That was the first time we were really scared. Since the situation was getting hairier by the minute, Gabriel made a decision. He gave me the key to his apartment and asked me to go out onto the landing. Meanwhile, he hid in the wardrobe. I opened the door and told the policeman that Senyor Delacruz had gone away for a while. A very long while, to be precise. He'd left me the key in case of emergency. Miguélez (now I could see the face of this monster in all its vileness) interrupted me to ask where Gabriel had gone. I acted all innocent and said I had no idea. He'd just said he was leaving the country and going far away. 'What did this man do wrong?' I asked. 'He seemed so reserved...' The policeman dodged the question. 'Sometimes,' he said, 'there are apartments like this one, that are officially empty but they're sublet and used as fronts for prostitution or gambling rings.'" Giuditta smiled. "'Or dens where they pack in illegal immigrants.' Then they asked me for the key. All three of us went into Gabriel's apartment (I didn't want to leave them alone in there), and the policeman searched it, but very superficially. He went into the bathroom, pulled back the shower curtain, opened the cupboards, and that was that. He did it roughly, just getting the job done. It was all Miguélez could do not to join in. He would have loved to open drawers and snoop along the shelves. It was clear that the cop was uncomfortable. He was doing a favor for a friend, or returning one maybe, but didn't want to get tangled up in anything. There was a pack of cards on the dining-room table. Sometimes Gabriel killed time playing solitaire. Miguélez picked it up and examined the cards one at a time, looking for some sign of cheating. 'This is confiscated,' said the cop and he took the pack. His show of authority satisfied them both and they went off. 'Ah, and if Senyor Delacruz turns up again,' the cop warned me, 'tell him we're looking for him.' Miguélez chipped in, 'And sooner or later we're going to catch up with him.'"

They were still suspicious because Feijoo and Miguélez repeated their visits over the next couple of days. Without the cop's presence they were less about psychological torment and more about action, violent and brutal. They seemed to be enjoying themselves. They started to knock at Giuditta's door to ask for the key, but she wouldn't open it. From her side of the door she got rid of them by asking if they had another search warrant. Out of an elementary sense of precaution, then, Gabriel stayed in Giuditta's apartment day and night. If he needed anything, they waited until it was good and late, in the early hours of the morning, and she discretely slipped into his place and brought him whatever it was. The honeymoon—to use Giuditta's expression—lasted three months . . .

"To sum up, I don't believe that Gabriel ever came to think of my place as his place. He liked to say he was spending a while in Italy. That was something he'd always wanted to do. When he was a truck driver he traveled around half of Europe but had never been in my country. He asked me to teach him a few words in Italian and then he mixed them up with words from other languages he'd picked up. As a result, we had the craziest conversations. When we were at home together we talked about our travels as a way of escaping. He reminisced about his adventures in the truck and I relived the endless wandering that was part and parcel of working in a circus. We toyed with the idea, and it wasn't totally off the wall, that the La Ibérica truck might have stopped, years ago, in some town where we were camped." Giuditta was struggling not to lose herself in these sweet memories and to stay with the present. "Gabriel's roving, weightless existence, which I compared with the gravity-defying hours I spent on the trapeze, finally came to an end . . ."

Another highly significant part of the story dates from about this period: the destruction of Gabriel's apartment. Perhaps that's exaggerating a bit; let's say its overall neglect. One morning a worker from the electricity company turned up to do some repairs in the building. He was in uniform and carried a tool box. Giuditta opened her door to him and he showed her his company ID, after which he fiddled with her electricity meter for a while. Gabriel had hidden in the bedroom while she kept an eye on the worker, who was connecting wires and offering all kinds of incomprehensible explanations for the repair job. When he finished, the electrician asked if she knew the next-door neighbor. He'd rung the bell but nobody answered. She very straightforwardly offered to open up the apartment for him. The worker gave nothing away. If anything, he seemed grateful for her help. He went inside and, there too, fiddled with a few wires in the meter, under Giuditta's constant vigilance. When he finished, he thanked her and disappeared without going up to the other apartments. They thought that this was odd but at no point had any misgivings about the man. That night, however, Giuditta went to Gabriel's place to get something for him and found that the lights weren't working. She lit a candle, inspected the meter and thought it looked as if it had been disconnected. She decided she'd phone the electricity company the next day to complain. She wasn't quick enough. The doorbell woke them very early in the morning. Giuditta got out of bed and took the precaution of looking through the peephole. It was Miguélez. He'd come back. This time he wasn't shouting. In a slimy, snaky voice he hissed, "I know you won't open up for me, but that doesn't matter. When your neighbor comes home, ask him how he's going to manage without electricity. We've got him surrounded. We're looking for him twenty-four hours a day."

Gabriel took this predicament as a personal defeat, a battle lost. He'd underestimated Feijoo and Miguélez. They were craftier than he'd given them credit for, and there was no doubt that the siege would continue. These people never give up. Again, reporting them to the police would be useless. It might look like a cowardly decision but, right now, his only solution was to make them believe that he really had left the country. Desperate measures were needed. The first step would be to stop paying his rent, water, and electricity bills. He'd won a lot of money playing cards and could keep going without joining other games for a good long while. Anyway, he said, he'd already been a recluse once in his life, and going into seclusion again didn't bother him in the least. Giuditta wasn't impressed by this display of stoicism and asked how much he owed them. She could just give it to them and that would be the end of it. Gabriel firmly rejected her offer.

"These people never have enough. Anyway, I'm sure that it's not because of the money that I owe them that they're so angry," he admitted. "It's because of the money I've been taking off them over time." He got a piece of paper and a pen and did a few sums, adding and multiplying. The figure was impressive. "You could say that they and they alone have been maintaining me for a year and a half." Giuditta whistled in admiration. "But now, for some reason, the penny's suddenly dropped that I won by cheating..." Gabriel mused.

While he was formulating his hypothesis he had a hunch. He went to get the jacket he'd been wearing the night of the last game, sat down on the couch and felt around in the sleeves. He pulled out two cards, one from each sleeve, and carefully examined them. One was a joker, and he soon found Feijoo's mark, the third-eye spot. "I'm done for," he said, tossing away the card in a gesture of despair.

"That afternoon, Gabriel started to measure up the bedroom wall," Giuditta went on. "When I wanted to know why he was doing that he just asked me to go to the hardware shop and buy him a chisel and a mallet. He was patient and resigned, with the conviction of someone with a plan to carry out. 'If I have to stay shut up here for a time,' he explained, 'at least we'll be able to cross the border between Italy and Spain whenever we feel the urge.'

"The following morning he tuned into a music program on the radio and turned it up full blast to cover up the mallet blows. He emptied the wardrobe, traced a window with a pencil and set about breaking through the wall. Crouching there inside with dust all over his face and surrounded by rubble, he looked like Steve McQueen in *The Great Escape*. Three hours later, he'd opened up a hole that was eighty centimeters high and almost the same width, large enough for us to cross to the other side, which is to say into the wardrobe in his bedroom. In the afternoon he made it easier to move through. He smoothed off the edges of the bricks and then covered up the hole with some wooden panels and a few empty shoeboxes. That night we crawled across the border and, for the first and only time since we'd met, he insisted that we should sleep together in his place. Maybe it's stupid, but that made me very happy . . ."

We Christophers listened to Giuditta in utter amazement. What she was recalling for us was well beyond what we'd ever imagined. We're used to our father's existential tangles. We've grown up with them, but this last episode was too much. The physical proximity of the events only exacerbated matters. We were sitting on Giuditta's couch after crossing through the hole made by Gabriel. Even the mezzanine apartment, which we'd turned into a sort of pretentious Christophers Club, took on a mythical aura as if we'd been living in two parallel dimensions, his and ours. Now, having passed through the wardrobe, the Christophers had gained access to the other dimension.

The afternoon was waning and it would soon be dark outside, but we still had more than three hours to kill before the card game began. Giuditta continued with her story and we started to feel slightly self-conscious: The Christophers were about to take center stage. The plot was thickening.

"At first I had the idea that we were making one home out of two and that would bring us closer but I must confess that I ended up hating the secret passage. Gabriel slowly went back to his old ways. Instead of going out on to the landing and entering his apartment through the door, he used the tunnel. We were sleeping together at my place but, when I went to work or out to have dinner with a girlfriend (luckily I hadn't totally neglected my social life), he went to his place. When he heard me arriving he came back. For me, this waiting, hanging around hour after hour, would have been unbearable, but I fear he didn't see it as a transition, rather as a permanent state. I brought him the newspaper, and he did read that, but I can't give you any real idea of how he amused himself. He never watched TV because he said he'd got a gutful of it years before. I also know that he did some exercise in the morning to keep fit . . . In any case, his strategy started to bear fruit after a couple of weeks and Miguélez and Feijoo stopped harassing us. They ignored us. It was hard to believe. In the beginning I tended to be very watchful when I went out in case someone was following me or spying on me. The road was always clear. We relaxed. Meanwhile the gas and water had been cut off too, so Gabriel's apartment became the bunker that you inherited. Everything was topsy-turvy because, at the end of the day, the hole he'd excavated inside the wardrobe led into a prison. Yet the state of his place didn't worry Gabriel at all. To my surprise, he assured me he'd lived in worse places. One bright sunny Sunday in spring, I suggested that he should start going out again. It was almost a year, I calculated, since that god-awful game of cards, and he hadn't set foot on the street. Now we didn't have to worry any more, and it would be good for him to have a stroll in Ciutadella Park. He could fill his lungs with fresh air. He refused, saying it was too soon and we should wait a couple of weeks more. Then I realized what was happening: Your father had turned into an invalid who didn't want to get better. For him, coming to my place, passing through the secret hole, was the same thing as going into the outside world. He was going to Italy and I was cooking him pasta, and there you have it. The situation, as you can imagine, was trying, boring, uncomfortable, and it was killing our relationship. We'd never argued before and now we were at each other's throats over the stupidest things. If we got annoyed with one another, he went back to his place in a huff. One night when we'd been fighting I was lying in my bed unable to sleep and he was in his. The wardrobe door was half open and that tunnel thing was connecting us. If I listened carefully, I could hear him tossing and turning, a martyr to insomnia, and I wanted to help him, wished we could comfort each other. It was then that I decided to act . . ."

Giuditta's boldness ended the stalemate, but then they had to face new unknowns. When Feijoo and Miguélez's siege was at its peak, she'd suggested to Gabriel that he should try to get into contact with us. We were his sons, weren't we? She was sure we'd help him. He categorically refused. He hadn't seen us for years, many years, he said, and he didn't know where to find us (false). Furthermore, he explained, we Christophers didn't know each other. It would be a shock (it was) and a trauma (it wasn't). In a moment of weakness, he'd confessed to her that we were the great frustration of his life, proof of his inability to lead an orderly existence. He'd abandoned us, and now he had no right to expect anything of us. "Maybe they're not like you," Giuditta had retorted, which made all four of us blush and feel uncomfortable. In any case, the morning after that double sleepless night, Giuditta betrayed our father. For a good cause. What did her betrayal consist of? After talking with the other residents of the house and the owner of Gabriel's apartment, she went to the police station to report him missing. Her neighbor, she explained, had given no sign of life in six months. Carried away with her story-telling, she even added that there was a smell of something dead in the stairway, a highly suggestive touch as far as the neighbors were concerned. As it turned out, her strategy was spot on. They would start the legal search, as is required in such cases.

From that point on, we Christophers had a pretty good idea of the facts leading up to our meeting. Even so, Giuditta presented them from another angle: hers. Shortly after she reported him missing, the police turned up at the apartment with the owner and certified yet again—but this time officially—that Gabriel had disappeared. It was necessary to go ahead with the appropriate procedures. This was first thing in the morning. That night, our father had slept in Italy, so to speak. In the wee hours, before he woke up, Giuditta had stealthily crossed the border to leave a piece of paper on the bedside table of the other bedroom. Our four names were written on it. In the hands of the police the list was further proof, so they began the search as she'd envisaged: the first thing they did was to locate Cristòfol. If that boy has the tiniest shred of curiosity, she reasoned, he'll try to find out what the other names mean, or go looking for his father . . .

"I've thought so often about the first time you came, Cristòfol," Giuditta resumed. "It was a miracle you didn't bump into Gabriel! A few seconds before you opened the wardrobe door, he'd slipped away to my place, making sure that the entrance to the passage was well disguised. What would have happened if, besides the cards hidden in his sleeves, you'd found the tunnel? I've wondered that so many times . . . You probably would have been terrified and run away, and we wouldn't be here now. Never mind. It's better not to think about that. The important thing is that while you were walking around the apartment getting used to your father's absence, he, on the other side of the wall, was more worked up than I'd ever seen him. He deserved it because of his stubbornness. How many hours were you there? Six? Seven? Gabriel had his ear glued to the wall listening to your footsteps. 'Who could it be?' he kept asking me every five minutes. 'Do you think Feijoo and Miguélez have come back? Did the police give them a key?' I spared him any more suffering. 'It's okay,' I told him. 'I didn't want to tell you so as not to worry you, but the neighbors and the owner of the apartment have reported you missing. When someone disappears, the police usually go looking for the next of kin. It must be your Barcelona wife, Gabriel, or, more likely, your son.' I spelt out the details of my hypothesis with all the care in the world because I was afraid he'd get really upset, but he reacted very well. Suddenly, the idea of seeing you again didn't distress him. I saw this as the first victory. 'How old would Cristòfol be now?' he wondered, and then he got lost in his calculations . . ."

From here onward, the Christophers' story runs in parallel with our father's wishes. He was overwhelmed by the idea of meeting up with us again, but Giuditta told us he was also following our moves with enormous expectation. The first day the four of us visited the apartment together, Gabriel was on cloud nine. We like to put it like this: Now that the widely scattered elements of his lost past unexpectedly came together, they assumed new meaning. On weekdays, when there was no danger that we were going to turn up, Gabriel went to the apartment and reviewed our findings. Then he tidied up his belongings to make our task easier and went over the notes we jotted down about our investigations. He read Carolina's letters, listened to our interview with Petroli, and spent hours gazing with an archivist's devotion at all the photographs we'd brought. Although meeting up with us again would have been mortifying for him, he somehow liked the feeling that we were nearby, so close, in fact, that one Saturday when he'd gone to sleep at siesta time we came into the apartment and were on the point of nabbing him. According to Giuditta, there were days when it seemed that he wanted just that. It was as if, with our decision to keep paying the rent and getting the light, water, and gas put on again, we were giving him oxygen. All his life he'd been uprooted and, now at last, at the age of sixty and for the very first time, he felt some kind of bond with this earth.

"I thought that he was very ripe, very ready," Giuditta recalled. "I mean regarding you. I was convinced he wouldn't be long in letting himself get caught. One important sign was that he'd given up his seclusion and started going out. He put on some sunglasses and a hat I bought him and went for walks in Ciutadella Park at times when there weren't many people. Maybe it wasn't such a big deal, but, for me, this was a major change. His willingness to meet up with you again was growing by the day, thanks to all the things you were leaving in his place . . . Then, three weeks ago, your investigations hit the bull's-eye and everything changed again . . ." At this point, Giuditta was getting emotional. We poured her the last dram of whisky left in the bottle. Then she pulled herself together and continued, "Unfortunately, Cristòfol, the beast was aroused again the day you went into the Carambola asking about Gabriel. It's as if Feijoo had an attack of jealousy because another hunter was on the track of his prey. Besides, if some stranger was looking for him in these parts it meant that he wasn't too far away. This time Miguélez and Feijoo were more patient, more subtle. Instead of immediately turning up, bellowing and beating at the door of his apartment, claiming their money and hassling us with their threats, we think they must have been studying our movements for several days. I can just imagine their stupefied expressions when Gabriel began walking around the streets like a man without a care in the world. We'd relaxed, as I told you. Then, last Monday, all hell broke loose. Gabriel went for a walk in the morning and didn't come back for lunch. At first, I took this as a good sign and imagined all sorts of reasons. Maybe he felt more confident and had ventured further, or he'd had lunch in some restaurant, or he might have visited his old workmates at La Ibérica. By midafternoon, I was worried because something wasn't right. Now that he'd got his freedom back, would he have left without a word, like the man who goes out to buy a packet of cigarettes and never comes home? I remembered what he'd done to your mothers and my stomach knotted. To calm down, I told myself that now we were fine, the two of us, and there was no call for alarm, but then my fears spiralled off into possibilities that were even more upsetting because they were beyond my control. What if Feijoo and Miguélez were back on the job? At midnight, thank God, I heard his door open and breathed more easily but I was still a nervous wreck when I hurried through the secret passage. On the other side, as if that wardrobe was a time machine, I found a Gabriel who'd aged ten years, haggard, trembling..."

They'd abducted him, our father told Giuditta. Feijoo and Miguélez had done it. The usual suspects, of course. That night they'd forced him to play a game of cards at the Carambola. It was a trial run, a warm-up exercise. They didn't ask him for the money. They wanted him to play for them. More precisely, to win for them. From them on, he was their worker. Or, if he preferred, they said, pointing the pistol at him, their slave. They were going to make him play at least twenty games, and he'd have to win them all, of course. That was the only way he could repay his debts. They'd have a great time, he'd see. They'd reel in the victims, big fish primed to leave a nice pile behind them after a long night. Ah, and he'd better not think about escaping or going to the police. They'd take turns watching him if needed. Now he couldn't escape. That went for the Italian neighbor too. Not a word to anyone. He had to take it calmly. It was very simple and profitable for everyone. Two months of raking in money for them, and then it would all be over...

"Lying on his bed in the semidarkness," Giuditta went on, "Gabriel reeled off their conditions. I had a flashlight with me, and every time I shone it on him I saw a resigned, scared, crushed man. It was a farcical scene and it only emphasized the level of insanity we'd reached. 'I haven't played for a long time,' he said, 'and I don't know if my fingers are up to it. When you cheat at poker it's like what happens with pianists. It's all about fingers, always fingers. And I'm not as fast as I used to be, my brain's not as sharp . . .' I tried to cheer him up by telling him that there were other ways around this. I let slip your names, but he wasn't listening to me. He was too obsessed about the games he had to play. The next day, which was Tuesday, he spent the whole morning practising with his cards. He sat at this table here, with his jacket on and smoking one cigarette after another. He pulled the cards out of his sleeves and tucked them away again so fast that the human eye could barely see it. Sometimes the movement wasn't precise enough, and the card jumped into the air. It was a comical effect but he wasn't amused. At eight o'clock they came to get him. They were playing the first proper game that night. They knocked very politely at his door, and he followed like a lamb to the slaughterhouse. The same thing happened on Thursday and last night, Friday, at the same time. I could see that he was coming back more dejected, more broken each time, and it was clear that the tension had really got to him. He's destroyed. 'There's a big difference between winning for yourself and having to win for other people,' he says. During the day he hangs around at home, like a man on death row, waiting, waiting, waiting. If he goes on like this he won't last long, and that's why, when I saw him leave with all that dread weighing on him today, I decided to ask for your help. I only needed a telephone or an address to find you, but providence stepped in and eased the way. All of a sudden the four of you materialized. It's a miracle wrought by the wardrobe." She stopped and looked at her watch. "I think it's getting late . . ."

Yes, it was getting late. We were so enthralled by the story that the hours had flown by.

"Isn't the game at eleven?" Christophe asked. Giuditta nodded. The four of us racked our brains about how to save our father. "We've got an hour to get the whole thing ready."

"How long ago did they take Gabriel away?" Chris asked.

"After lunch. It must have been about four . . . Lord knows where they hide him until it's time to play."

"Have you got a car, Giuditta?" Christof asked. "Can we use it?"

"An Opel Corsa. Why do you want it?"

"If we're going to rescue Gabriel," Cristòfol chipped in, em-boldened by the turn of events, "we need a getaway car. A black luxury car with smoked windows would be perfect; I suppose a Corsa would do..."

It was time for action.


## THE RESCUE

The Carambola was in Carrer Sicília, on the left-hand side going up, between Gran Via and Carrer Diputació, on rather a dark cor-ner. The streetlights in that part of town leaked an orangey glow, and dense shadows cast by the leafy old plane trees swallowed up most of the light they gave. There was no other bar or business in the vicinity, and the Passatge de Pagès, the ghostly alley running off Carrer Sicília, only added to the impression that the whole area was under an evil spell. This setting worked in our favor. We'd come up with a plan that at first seemed like lunacy, but we had blind faith in it. Probably because we had no alternative. We Christophers had all tried to remedy our childhood loneliness by reading superhero comics. Adults had always told us that real life was rather different, but here we were out to contradict them. We were having fun, like a bunch of kids.

At eleven on the dot, when we double-parked the Opel Corsa not far from the bar, the street was dead quiet. We'd managed to persuade Giuditta to stay at home, and, while we other Christo-phers waited in the car, Cristòfol went to check out the situation. The blind was halfway down. You could make out a thin light at the back of the bar. Five minutes later, our bartender accomplice said good-bye to someone and left the bar, crouching to pull the blind right down. As he did, Cristòfol walked past him, not stop-ping, not breaking his step, and murmured, 'Don't lock it, please.' The young man was startled but soon recognized the figure and the voice and nodded, right, okay.

Cristòfol came back to the car, and we waited another half an hour. It was better for us to make our triumphal entry when the players were well into the game. Meanwhile, we calmed down by passing around another bottle of whisky that Giuditta had presented us with just before we left. As we drank, we laughed at the way we were dressed. We weren't wearing masks, or multicolored capes, or balaclavas, but we'd foraged around in Gabriel's and Giuditta's old clothes and dressed up to get into the mood. We made a dramatic foursome and were counting on this theatrical show working in our favor. Christof, wearing a polo-neck sweater, in existential black from head to foot, might have passed as a Cold War spy. Chris, the tallest and thinnest brother, was decked out in a very distinguished striped diplomat's suit (nicked by our dad thirty years earlier, on Trip 123 to London) and had combined this with an eccentric cravat that transformed him into a David Niven–look-alike gentleman thief. Christophe, the shortest brother, had gone for the harlequin-style flourish of one of Giuditta's circus costumes and stood out like a madman, a seriously deranged psychopath, first cousin to Batman's nemesis, the Joker. Cristòfol, wanting to pay homage, finally chose a simple shirt and trousers. They were elegant but old fashioned, representing a style in danger of extinction, part of the last lot of booty that Bundó didn't get to enjoy, Number 200. This gave him a slightly shabby air, as though he were Jekyll caught midway in his transformation into Hyde, and he reeked so badly of mothballs that we had to open the car windows.

Christopher got hold of the bottle of whisky and took a long swig.

"Where would Porras, Leiva, and Sayago be now?" he wondered. His question was so unexpected that it cracked open like a piñata filled with nostalgia.

"They must be here in Barcelona," Cristòfol ventured. "Like Senyora Natàlia Rifà, if she's still alive. Her boarding house isn't there any more, but maybe we should try to find her and go and visit her one day."

"Yes, whatever happens with our father, Christophers, we have to round off our research," Christophe interrupted. "Footnotes. They're necessary. There's nothing sadder than those half-empty municipal museums..."

"Petroli, El Tembleque, Senyor Casellas (he must be dead by now), Carolina... our mothers, Christophers, our mothers! It's so strange thinking about them all, here and now," Christof muttered.

He was right. We were five minutes away from finding our father again, and the whole gallery of characters who'd led us to him, his escorts in memory, suddenly rose up one by one, like links in a chain, to join us with their mythical presence.

We toasted everyone who'd helped us get to this point and then, united in brotherhood by blood and full of unaccustomed courage, we got out of the car.

Since the game was being played at the back of the bar, you couldn't hear so much as a fly buzzing on the other side of the blind. Our plan was to raise it slowly—as many centimeters as required—and sneak in, creeping along in the shadows. Once all four of us were inside, we were going to swoop on them, roaring at the tops of our voices (which we hadn't rehearsed) and take them completely by surprise. Christophe was in charge of the blanket, and Chris had the ropes and hooks. Christof was going to drive the car. Cristòfol would be spokesman and translator.

The first attempt to raise the blind derailed our plan because, in those few centimeters, it let out a short, very shrill screech of the kind that makes your skin crawl and sets your teeth on edge.

"It's worse than chalk squealing on the blackboard," Christophe muttered.

We looked at each other, listening hard, trying not to get the giggles, and waited twenty seconds. Nothing. They hadn't noticed. Taking them by stealth would be impossible. By means of gestures we agreed that the only alternative would be to burst in and take over the show. Christof and Christopher grabbed the blind. They counted to three—one...two...three—and heaved it up together. Up! The deafening noise worked in our favor. We flew into the bar and ran to the spotlit table.

"*Sitzen bleiben!*" Christof yelled with all his lungs.

The five players saw him fly out of the shadows like an exterminating angel. The Nazi associations were inevitable, horrifying and extremely useful. They threw our victims into a state of terror.

"Don't move. Stay exactly as you are!" Cristòfol translated, trying to sound guttural. The situation was so fictitious, so unnatural that the words came out in Spanish, just as they had when he was a small boy playing cowboys and Indians.

The whole operation lasted five minutes, as we'd calculated—in and out—but now that we're replaying it, it seems to have taken much longer. Throughout the mayhem the players remained rooted to the spot. Dazzled by their bright pool of light, they tried to make out who we were in the shadows. The green baize cloth on the table was covered in banknotes. The four of us were hoping to catch Gabriel's eye, but he was sitting with his back to us, and we could only see the nape of his neck, his rigid back. In spite of the general alarm, he sat there immobile, still holding his cards. He must have had a good hand. Then we checked out the others. On Gabriel's right was an absolutely petrified gentleman of about fifty. He dropped his cards face up on the table and raised his hands, timorously, as if he thought this was a holdup. His tanned face—hours in the solarium—was getting paler by the minute. The smoke from a Havana wafted up from his lips, stinging his eyes, but he didn't dare take it out of his mouth. He looked exactly like someone called Manubens, the rich twit whose turn it was to be fleeced that night. The man next to him was pouring sweat, greasy sweat. His look of an itinerant fritter vendor marked him as one of Feijoo's gang. He was blinking nonstop and didn't dare look us in the eye. Glinting on the little finger of his right hand was a ruby ring. Without a word from us he took it off and put it on the table. Beside him was Feijoo, the host. He seemed calm, attentive, on the alert, but glanced sideways at Miguélez and kept gnawing on a toothpick. Last, on Gabriel's left, was the famous Miguélez. We checked out his lardy, flaccid face (of great advantage when it came to bluffing), the ragged moustache, the toadlike body that had so often attacked the door of Gabriel's mezzanine apartment.

He'd adopted an insolent air. His mouth was twisted into the sinister smirk of a wolf on the scent of blood. He, needless to say, was the one who broke the silence.

"Let's see-e-e, boys, now te-e-ell me where it hu-u-u-urts..." He drew out the vowels to convince himself and convince us that he had the situation under control.

Christof, as a man of the theatre, was really getting into his role. In two quick strides he went over and dealt him a resounding openhanded slap, a circus clown's wallop.

*"Sitzen bleiben, habe ich gesagt!"* he screamed.

"Sit down, motherfucker!" This time, imitating Miguélez, Cristòfol adopted the tone of a member of the Guardia Civil in the midst of an attempted coup.

The authority achieved by something as simple as a good hard smack is an amazing thing. Gabriel was unperturbed, but the gentleman with the ring joined his hands in prayer, and Manubens whimpered (sprinkling the lapels of his jacket with ash from his cigar), while Feijoo tensed his body and spat the toothpick on to the floor. Miguélez had too much military pride to be cowed. In an instinctive gesture, he touched his burning cheek and made to get up again as if warding off a blow, at which point Christopher burst out of the shadows and—*click!*—got between him and Christof. Light flashed off the blade that he'd just released. The astounded Miguélez immediately reconsidered and sank into his chair again.

"She's thirsty," Chris informed him in English, glaring at him and raising his arm, making sure they all took note of the stiletto elegance of the switchblade our father kept in his apartment, timid and withdrawn like himself because it was always in hiding. "My lovely dagger is thirsty..."

*"La navaja tiene sed..."* Cristòfol offered something resembling a translation.

Then Chris snapped his fingers like a man used to giving orders and, in the midst of the general commotion, Christophe went over to Gabriel to carry out the next stage of our plan. With a grand gesture, mentally rehearsed a hundred times that evening, he shook out the blanket as if it were his cape and dropped it over our father.

Christof immediately came to his aid, pinioning Gabriel. With a few deft movements they soon had him trussed up and secured with ropes and hooks. Then, in order to discourage any resistance from their captive, Cristòfol shouted in his ear, "Easy now, Delacruz. Our mission is to hand you over alive to Mister Bundó."

Hearing that name, the magic word that sealed out brotherhood, the bundle relaxed and let out a laugh. He got it. Without wasting another moment, Christophe and Christof made their way to the car, opened up the trunk, and got Gabriel settled inside.

"Can you breathe okay?"

The bundle obediently indicated it could. Before closing the trunk, they told him they were putting him in there because it had to look like abduction, but that was the last spot of bother he was going to have from them. They got the engine started and tooted the horn as agreed. Chris, meanwhile, was still threatening the gamblers with the knife. He snapped his fingers again to get Manubens' attention and ordered him to pile up the money on the table. Then he took it and stuffed it in his pocket.

"Keep playing now," he ordered, pointing the knife at them. He was starting to enjoy himself. "And don't move till you have finished the game. Understood?"

"*A seguir jugando,*" Cristòfol translated, "*y que nadie se mueva hasta que haya terminado la partida. ¿Queda entendido?*"

"So who the hell is this Bundó?" Miguélez dared to ask when they were on their way out.

"You wouldn't really want to know, Miguélez," Cristòfol replied, still in Spanish. "Or you, Feijoo. Or you, Manubens. You wouldn't want to know, would you, Manubens?" The businessman let out a lily-livered "no," beside himself because these strangers knew his name. "Naturally we know who you are, the lot of you. However, we are gentlemen, and, since you asked, I shall answer. Bundó is a code name. It's the cover for an international cartel that operates in the world's best casinos. In case you yokels hadn't noticed, this Delacruz is the crème de la crème. We've had our eye on him for a long time now, but you cretins had to go and muck things up. What a bunch of idiots! From now on, he'll be facing more spectacular challenges. Monaco, Nice, Saint Petersburg, and maybe Las Vegas if he improves a bit . . ."

Feijoo and Miguélez's faces were pure poetry. The horn of the Opel sounded again with our signal. Chris snapped his fingers once more.

"Come on, let's go. Let's go!"

*"Venga, vamos, vamos,"* Cristòfol was still translating, and, at the last moment, just as we were leaving the bar, he turned back and gave them one last blast, still in Spanish. "Ah, and for your own good, Feijoo and Miguélez, we don't want to hear any more stories about you harassing and bothering Delacruz. Or the Italian lady next door. He's ours now, and you've seen for yourselves that the German gentleman is itching for some action."


We were over the moon on the short trip to Giuditta's apartment. We were shouting and clapping our hands in the car, pumped up with adrenaline, and guffawing to recall the whack Miguélez had taken. Despite all the excitement, Christof drove smoothly, trying to avoid any bumps. Now that we'd finally recovered Gabriel, we had to get him home safe and sound. We left the car in Giuditta's parking spot and opened up the trunk. Now we had him. Our father. Outlined in the blanket was a still but alert figure, a Houdini about to make his getaway.

"Don't worry, we're the good guys," Cristòfol said, patting him. Since the bundle didn't move, he touched it again and asked, "Hey, can you breathe?"

The bundle could. We picked him up and all four of us carried him upstairs to the mezzanine still wrapped in the blanket. We were tickling him, and he was laughing. It may seem that this extra delay was an act of cruelty that a father doesn't deserve, but we Christophers believed it was essential. We'd agreed that we wanted to be reunited with Gabriel all together, at the same instant, and that he should experience it in the same way as we did.

Giuditta opened the door giving thanks to all the saints in heaven and all the Madonnas in the Italian calendar of saints' days. We deposited our father in a sitting position on the couch, undid the ropes and sat in a semicircle before him.

The hulk shed the blanket and ropes with a few thrusts of its arms and then, from underneath, emerged Gabriel, our father. Sweaty and dishevelled, he reminded us of an actor who's just walked offstage and flops on to the couch in his dressing room to listen to the applause still echoing from the stalls.

"Thank-you," he said at last, gazing at us one by one. "Thank-you very much."

We won't be so crass now as to throw away in a few phrases what each of us experienced right then. Neither will we get carried away by our emotions. We Christophers deplore sentimentality—the legacy of an imperfect orphanhood, no doubt—and Gabriel . . . well, Gabriel had become immune many years earlier when he finally wept over Bundó's death, and his tear ducts had dried up forever.

Moreover, as we saw it, this had to be a beginning, not an ending.

But.

But, one day, during one of our first get-togethers, we Christophers had amused ourselves with quite a dicey game. Each of us had to describe, using a metaphor, the mixture of feelings he had regarding Gabriel. Someone, and it doesn't matter who, came up with an image that we all thought fitted the bill.

"Imagine that one day, because of something that life's served up, you're so desperate that you end up playing Russian roulette," this Christopher said. "It's your turn. You're holding the revolver in your hands, you put one bullet in the cylinder (the one that might kill you), and you spin it. You place the muzzle against your temple and pull the trigger. You try to concentrate on that extremely brief shiver between yes and no. For me, Dad's absence is like the empty chamber of that revolver.

*Click!*

*Click!*

*Click!*

*Click!*

# 7

## We Have the Same Memory

Now here's a nice thing: All four Christophers have the same memory of that moment, of the glorious day when the lines of past and present came together at last. Right now we are a memory for the future. The years will go by and we'll see each other perhaps more often or perhaps less often. Who knows? Each of us will construct his own narrative around this memory and inform it with whatever meaning suits him best, but what makes us proud, what makes true brothers of us, is that the origin of it will be the same for all of us. Yes, that's right: it's the present—Sunday morning.

The sun's just risen. The city's awake, and we haven't slept yet. We're exhausted, but struggling to prolong the excitement that has kept us going all night with clear heads and open eyes. At six this morning we took the decision to go out and get a bit of air, so we wandered down to Pla de Palau. Gabriel knows a bar there that serves breakfast at this early hour. All this palaver's made us hungry. Two young guys in tracksuits were running in Ciutadella Park, and a drunk was trying to arrange himself in the best position for sleeping off his hangover on a bench. In the distance we could hear the calls of the birds in the zoo as they were waking up with the first glimmers of light. As we passed El Born market we stopped for a moment and contemplated the silent structure. A dribble of light outlined the empty space giving it an air of transcendence. Cristòfol went over to the entrance and broke the silence with his imitation of the wails of a newborn baby, which

echoed like those of our father sixty years earlier. A startled pigeon
flew out.

"Yes, yes, you're right," Gabriel said by way of response. "You
might say I was born here. It was my first cradle. But it's changed
a lot over the years. You couldn't begin to imagine how."

"And the salt cod seller?" we asked. "Did you ever see her
again?"

"No, not that I know of. I lost track of her a long time ago but
I've never stopped thinking about her. It's curious. If anyone asks
me what my mother was like, I always describe that lady."

Gabriel speaks confidently, without any attempt at evasion,
looking us straight in the eye. There are some moments when we
could say that his words are just seeking to comfort us, or pass a
test. It's as if, shut away in the mezzanine apartment, he's been
studying the clues and notes we left behind and is now trying to
play the part of the character we gave him. Maybe he does it because he doesn't want to let us down any more, and we're grateful
for that. Or perhaps it's just a product of our imagination, a residue of reluctance and disillusion that won't disappear overnight.
Whatever the reason, we've been together more than seven hours,
and we can now say that his rough edges have vanished.

As soon as we got to the apartment last night, Giuditta opened
a bottle of champagne and we toasted our successful rescue. Then
our exhilaration subsided, and we all went quiet. Where should
we start? Who should speak? The silence threatened to asphyxiate
us. Giuditta realized that she was in the way and went back to her
place under some pretext. Then our father broke the ice.

"Look, boys, I'm not going to apologize. Too much time has
gone by. I've often regretted what I did or, rather, what I wasn't able
to do . . ." He stopped to see how we were reacting. He looked despondent, and the words came out faint and tired, as if they'd spent
too many years aging in his craw. "Of course I'm happy to have you
back again, but I'm also quite embarrassed that it had to happen
like this. Things can't be changed now. If only they could . . . You
can reproach me all you like, and you'd certainly be right to do so.
But I won't ask for your forgiveness. It's been too long."

"You're talking as if you've committed some sort of crime," we said.

"And isn't it a crime? Abandoning your sons?"

"It depends how you look at it. Maybe, more than a crime, it's a sentence you've imposed on yourself."

"Yes, but . . ."

It's impossible to reproduce the ensuing five-way conversation with all its ins and outs. Conventions failed us, and we felt awkward, unable to find the appropriate middle ground between intimacy and distance. Did we have to act like strangers or did the blood bond remove all barriers? We tested the waters. The most valuable and upsetting revelations alternated with conversation that was about as inane as any you'd come across in an elevator. We couldn't find the proper balance and teetered from the aggression of police-style interrogation to the distancing of diplomatic *froideur*. We tried to cover up uncomfortable silences with over-familiar remarks. Fortunately, as we kept talking the roller-coaster highs and lows started to level out. Then again, our jitteriness set off a babble of different languages that we vainly tried to harmonize. Our father answered us with his do-it-yourself linguistic skills, and at last we could hear, still intact, that cadence of his that had bewitched our mothers. Gabriel took it all more coolly than we did, without any dramatics, and resorted to his memories of us when we were small. Then, if one of his anecdotes made us laugh or got us feeling nostalgic, we responded at once by ticking him off. He counterattacked by asking about Sigrun, Sarah, Mireille, and Rita—if we'd told them anything, if they'd taken it well, if they hated him, or if we had some recent photo of them—and we gave in once again. It also happened that we four brothers were not always in agreement, and one would sometimes act offended and the other three would make fun of him. Or the opposite happened: A solitary laugh mocked three gawking faces. As the night progressed we confirmed that all alliances were possible. At one stage, one of the Christophers joined forces with Gabriel to keep his brothers in check.

"I must confess," our father said in a moment of weakness,

"that I was more afraid of this meeting than happy about it. All my life I've imagined you cursing me to hell and back, wherever you were. I thought you wouldn't want to know any more about me."

"You weren't far off," we said. "Every one of us, before we knew each other, would have paid you back in contempt for all those years of silence. Even if it was just to avenge our mothers' suffering. But we were lucky enough to get together to look for you. Curiosity got the better of us and with each new discovery we were more and more susceptible to what we call the South Pacific syndrome."

"What's that? I only know about the Stockholm syndrome."

"Well, it's the opposite thing. We invented it ourselves. We call it the South Pacific syndrome because the Pacific Ocean is the antipodes of Stockholm. Stockholm syndrome is when the kidnapped person gets fond of the kidnapper, right? In our case you did the opposite of kidnapping us. You abandoned us. But while we were looking for you we grew fond of you, and now we want to know all about you."

"All! You're not asking much . . ." Gabriel countered, playing for time. Suddenly he looked irresolute and scared. "But the thing is, I'm reserved by nature, and it's hard for me to talk for talking's sake. I'm not used to it. It would be better if you asked me what you want to know. That would be easier."

We didn't need to think too long. We could have asked him "Why?"—short and to the point—and then let Gabriel head off wherever he wanted, but there was one question that preceded us. It was a question that defined our lives to the extent that we had the feeling it had been planned.

"Why are all four of us called the same?" Then we rattled off our names as if ticking off a list: Christof, Christophe, Christopher, Cristòfol.

"I thought you'd ask that," he answered. He seemed relieved. "Let's see. I don't know if I can give you an exact response, but I'll tell you about something that happened to me when I was a little boy. Yes, it's high time I told the story. Apart from Bundó, who had first-hand experience of this, nobody else knows, not even your mothers. And if anyone deserves to know, it's you four." He paused, taking a deep breath or plucking up courage. "I guess your mothers . . ."

"Just a moment, please," Christof interrupted. "Let's give it a title."

"A title?"

"Yes, sorry, but the Christophers have got into the habit of giving everything a title."

"The Christophers, you say? Very well. Then it could be called 'The First Christopher.'"

"Go ahead."

## THE FIRST CHRISTOPHER

Your mothers, then, have told you that I grew up in an orphanage, the House of Charity. Well, the nuns who ran the place bent over backward to give us a strict Roman Catholic education. Although kids from poor families were sent there too, because their parents couldn't afford to raise them, most of us were orphans or foundlings, and the nuns were convinced that if they didn't make upright citizens of us we'd end up being a blight on society. So we went to class, learned the catechism by heart, and observed every holy day in the calendar. That was where I met Bundó, who was an orphan like me. We were about four or five years old and made friends immediately. We protected one another when the older kids hit us, or teased us, or tried to get us into trouble with the nuns. Well, you already know all that, and it's not so important any more . . . I'm just telling you to set the scene.

One Saturday afternoon—we were seven by then—Bundó and I were playing ball with some other kids from the house. I liked being goalie because then I didn't have to run after the ball. All of a sudden, Sister Rosario came out into the playground and called my name. I had to go with her to see the Mother Superior, Sister Elvira. These summons that came out of the blue terrified us because they could only mean two things: Either she was going to haul you over the coals for something you hadn't done, which is what happened ninety-nine per cent of the time, or they'd found a family to adopt you.

In 1947, eight years after the end of the Civil War, only a few orphans were being adopted. A few years later it got to be fashionable, especially with the well-to-do couples that couldn't have children, but in the period I'm talking about it was a risky decision and, to some extent, desperate. That Saturday, at about midday, the nun brushed the dirt off my pants, made me wash my hands, and combed my hair, after baptizing me with a good splash of cologne. Like that, she said, I smelt like a good boy. Outside the office she knelt down and kissed me on the forehead, which was unheard of, and told me to be on my best behavior. I'd have to be grown up now. Then she made me go into the office all by myself. When I opened the door, the Mother Superior was in there talking with a lady and gentleman, both very smartly dressed. The three of them turned around and gazed at me in a gush of admiration. I felt embarrassed.

"Come here, Gabriel," the nun said. "Say hello to the lady and gentleman. Shake hands."

"Hello . . ." I mumbled and held out my hand.

The man squeezed it with his left hand, which surprised me a lot. Then I noticed that the right one hung limply at his side. The lady knelt down, exactly as the nun had done a minute earlier, and did something that was meant to be affectionate but it turned my stomach, precisely because she wasn't a nun: She licked her finger and rubbed my cheek to remove a smudge of grimy sweat.

That was more than fifty years ago, and I've never forgotten the impression the whole thing made on me. I'm sure that my child's eyes made them look older but, in reality, they were a couple of twenty-seven (her) and thirty (him) years old. She was called María Isabel, but they called her Maribel, and I thought she was very beautiful. She was tall with a full, voluptuous figure, red hair, green eyes, a princess's tip-tilted nose—I say princess because a few years later, when those Empress Sissi films came out, they reminded me of her—and what you'd call a small rosebud mouth.

Despite her good looks, she seemed fragile. It didn't take me long to find out that Maribel was lifeless. She had no will of her own. Even to a kid like me, it was obvious she was unhappy and, in the days that followed, I resorted more than once to all sorts of clownish antics trying to make her laugh. He, in contrast, seemed to be quite a character, with a friendliness bordering on the ridiculous because it was so fake and so extreme. He was called Fernando—yes, like the Catholic King Fernando, the one married to Queen Isabel—and was wearing a very elegant suit, with a tie and cufflinks. You could see he didn't know how to handle the situation because he kept repeating the same silly words and noises, over and over again. Hey, eh, good, ooh, mmm, lovely, oho, you see, aha.

"Hey, aha, come on, that's good, that's good!" he said when Maribel took a present out of her crocodile-skin handbag and handed it to me. I opened it, and it was a toy car, an olive-green Bugatti.

"What do you say, Gabriel?"

"Aha . . ."

"Thank you."

"That's it, that's it . . ."

"Thank you *very much*. You'll get to know him," the nun went on. "Gabriel is a very well-mannered boy and a very nice boy, isn't that right, Gabriel? He's a little shy now, but that's because all this is new to him."

"That's understandable."

"Of course . . ."

Fernando Soldevila and Maribel Rogent had spoken Catalan when they met, but their families were on the winning side of the war so the whole lot of them had switched to Spanish.

"Well, Gabriel, what do you think of Maribel and Fernando?" the Mother Superior asked me. "You like them, don't you? From now on they're going to be your mommy and daddy. What a lucky boy you are! You'll see what fun you're going to have with them. And soon you'll be going to a real school, not like the one here. A school where you can work toward a wonderful future."

The other nun came to get me. While Fernando was sorting out a few papers with the director of the House of Charity, the

other nun and my new mother took me to the dormitory where
they put my clothes and a few books in a bag. Maribel kept saying
they didn't need the clothes because they had new ones at home.
I must have looked scared stiff because the whole time the nun
tried to convince me that I'd been very lucky, that I shouldn't worry
and that I could always come and visit my friends. Then she took
me to the playground where the other kids were running around
and called them over. When they were all clustered around us in a
group, she told them that a family had adopted me and now they
had to say good-bye. Most of them, the older ones, shouted "Bye-
bye," and went back to play as if nothing had happened. Bundó
just stood there without saying a word. Then he came over and
whispered in my ear, very softly so I was the only one who could
hear him.

He said, "Good luck, Gabriel. Come and rescue me as soon as
you can."

Then we went home in a taxi. It was the first time I'd ever
been in one, but even the novelty of that didn't help, and I whimpered all the way up to the posh part of town where I was going
to live. I was sitting between my new mother and father and he,
Fernando, was trying to console me with his oohs and ahs. Meanwhile, Maribel was squeezing my hand, almost hurting me, and
was staring out the window, anxious to arrive.

They lived in the second-floor apartment of a mansion in Passeig de la Bonanova. You went up a marble staircase with wide
steps and a red carpet. Surrounding the house there was a garden,
with pond and toad included, and it was for the exclusive use of
the three families living in the building. When we got to the apartment, Maribel took hold of my hand again and wanted to show
me my room before anything else. I remember the endless tortu-
ous journey through all those barely lit or unlit rooms. Growing
up in the House of Charity, we kids were used to darkness so I
thought when they weren't looking I could disappear into one of
those corners and they'd never find me again. As we walked along
the passageway, a door opened slightly and two inquisitive girls in
uniform peered out.

Finally, we stopped before some double doors, which Maribel flung open, exaggerating the majestic gesture, I'd say. It was like discovering a new world. All my woes melted away. My room was literally bigger than the House of Charity dormitory into which they squeezed all the kids aged between six and ten. They'd planned this space for a child, and put a lot of thought into it. It was a room with two parts and the walls were decorated with scenes from fairytales. I didn't know where to start. Hansel and Gretel were there, wandering lost in the forest. Little Red Riding Hood was there too, going to her grandmother's house, and you could spot the wolf's muzzle behind the curtains in the window. In one corner of the room, my bed was made out of wood, in the form of a pirate ship, with a mermaid for its figurehead. The dark blue sheets imitated the waves and, on one part of the wall, there were some drawings of Peter Pan and Tinkerbell—not the Walt Disney ones; these were more classical, probably the original illustrations—to make sure I'd sleep well and not have nightmares. A gigantic fireplace, the biggest I've ever seen, as deep as a cave, took pride of place in the playroom. It was sculpted in the form of the mouth of a mysterious dragon. On either side of it the fangs were made into small cushioned chairs so my friends and I—Maribel told me—could sit by the fire and listen to stories when winter came. It didn't take much for me to imagine that Bundó would soon come to live there too. There was plenty of space to put in another bed. Or, if necessary, he could also hide in the Indian tepee that had been put up at one end of the room.

At Maribel's suggestion, I started opening up cupboards and checking out the shelves. They were full of puppets, puzzles, stories, toys, and drawing books. I went greedily from one thing to the other, unable to take it all in. It was as if all my Christmases had come at once or like opening everyone's presents at the orphanage, the whole lot and then more, but all of them for me. Sometimes the nun's words came back to me, and then I looked up and said thank-you, thank-you very much. Maribel and Fernando stared at me from the doorway, not daring to interrupt me. They seemed fascinated, and she was wiping away tears of happiness with her handkerchief. After a while, I remembered to say thank-you again, but they'd left me alone, and I was happy about that.

At dinnertime Mother came to get me. She came with a maid called Otilia, and she and Tomasa, the other maid I'd seen, were going to make sure that I didn't lack for anything (don't ask me why, but all the maids in those days had names like that). I only had to behave myself and obey them. I ate everything they put before me like a good boy, and then they let me play a little bit longer. That first night, Mother got me into my pajamas and put me to bed. Then, just before she turned out the light, Fernando—I just can't use the word "father"—came in too, to say goodnight. They tucked me up in the pirate ship, kissed me, and then Mother said, "Daddy and Mommy are very happy that this is going to be your new home. You're happy too, aren't you?"

"Aren't you?" Fernando echoed.

My answer was a wholehearted "Yes!" No other answer could possibly have occurred to me.

"We only want to ask you one thing, darling. From tomorrow onward, we're going to call you Cristóbal, starting from when you get up in the morning. We like this name better. Do you agree? You'll just have to think that Gabriel has been left behind in the orphanage and that you've come here as Cristóbal. You'll see how quickly you get used to it."

"Cristóbal! Lovely, ooh that's lovely!" Fernando said.

I was dog tired and my eyes were closing while I was forcing myself to say yes. If that was the price I had to pay... I liked Cristóbal too. There was no other kid at the orphanage with that name. In addition, I told myself, if I did them this favor now then maybe they'd soon agree to Bundó's coming to live with us.

The next morning, Mother woke me up by drawing back the curtains. The sun dazzled me with its brightness and warmth like a blessing from heaven.

"Good morning, Cristóbal darling!"

I nearly told her that my name was Gabriel, Gabriel Delacruz, but the surprise of waking up in that bed, in that bedroom, made me remember the conversation of the previous night. One thing led to another. Now, in that marvellous place, I was called Cristóbal. Otilia gave me breakfast in the kitchen, and then Mother dressed me. She opened up drawers full of shirts, T-shirts, and trousers, all nicely ironed and very neat, and started choosing what she was going to put on me. (Needless to say, I never again wore the clothes that had come with me from the orphanage.) She gave me some long trousers. I'd never seen any kid in long trousers, and I must have pulled a face because she told me that it was Sunday, and on Sundays you had to get dressed up for eleven o'clock Mass.

Fernando was waiting for us in the street, smoking a cigarette, and the three of us walked to the church in Bonanova. We strolled along slowly, and Maribel looked very proud, as if she was parading me before the whole neighborhood. She was holding my hand. I was between the two of them, with Fernando on my right so he could give me his good hand. It was a cold day, and the leaves were starting to fly from the trees, but the sun was gamely shining and he kept repeating, "What a lovely day. What a beautiful day."

When we came out of Mass, I realized that a lot of people were looking at us and greeting us from a distance with a nod of the head. Mother told me that next year, God willing, I'd be making my first communion in this parish. I'd have to go to catechism classes. An old couple came over and stood in silence in front of me. They didn't know what to say.

"Look, Cristóbal," Mother said, "these are your grandparents from Barcelona. Give them a kiss."

They were Fernando's parents. I've forgotten their names. I do remember that when the lady bent down to give me a kiss I was scared because she was wearing very big earrings, like two gold pumpkins, and her face was masked with powder to cover up her wrinkles. I started to whimper again. The grandfather, in contrast, held out his hand as if I were a gentleman, and kept his distance.

"Next Sunday, God willing, Cristóbal, you'll meet your other grandparents, the ones who live in Matadepera," Mother added, trying to calm me.

I could go on remembering similar scenes. Relatives and more relatives, friends and neighbors. All my life, as I've moved around the world, I've come across the same sideways looks, the sly smiles and the hypocritical ones, the blunders and the misunderstandings. Now I understand better what was going on around me at the time. I could also give you a blow-by-blow description of the dizzy feelings of a little boy who is installed without any warning in a foreign land that he has to conquer at any price. But it's not worth it. What counts is how easy it is to get used to luxury when you're a kid, but also how it all turns out to be superfluous if you haven't felt loved, not even for five minutes.

El Tembleque, one of the truck drivers I worked with, used to say, "It's the working days that count. Weekends are a tip to squander." After all the excitement of that Sunday, Monday showed me the other side of my new life. Now I think the three of us should have gone off for a week's vacation, escaped to some place where we could get used to being together, but Maribel and Fernando were in a hurry to get back to normal. In a well-off Bonanova family that meant I was soon spending more time with the maids than with my parents. Fernando worked all day, till late, and often came home after I'd gone to sleep. She, Mother, disappeared for hours on end into some room or other of the house to do what she called her "needlework." For some mysterious reason I wasn't going to school yet so it was like a permanent holiday. Otilia looked after me, and I had so many toys I never got bored or fed up with being alone.

One afternoon, three or four days after I arrived, the two of us went down to the garden they had at the back of the house. I'd seen a swing from my bedroom window and was dying to try it. When we finished afternoon tea I made a scene and convinced Otilia to come down with me.

"Go and ask your mommy," she said. "If she gives you her permission . . ."

No sooner had she said this than I ran all around the apartment looking for Mother. I called her, opened doors, and went into rooms I'd never seen before. The library, the drawing room, the guest room. I couldn't find her anywhere. Otilia ran after me but didn't manage to catch me. When I realized this, it turned into a game. Hide-and-seek. The corners and tucked-away spots of the House of Charity had taught me all the tricks in the book. I gave her the slip and ran in the opposite direction. Then I opened a door into a narrow room, a sort of sewing room, and hurtled inside, crashing into Mother's skirt. I jumped back. She looked at me as if I were a thief, a wild beast, a ghost, and let out a cry of panic. I burst out laughing because I'd given her a fright, a kid's victory— Ha ha! Ha ha!—but the expression on her face got even darker. Luckily Otilia turned up just then.

"Cristóbal, Cristóbal, come here!" she shouted. "I'm sorry, madam."

"Cristóbal? What Cristóbal?" she said, staring at me with an expression of shock. "It can't be . . ."

Otilia removed me immediately and, without asking permission or anything, took me down to the garden. It was starting to get dark, there was a cold wind and she put an overcoat on me. I swung up and down till my arm muscles started to ache. Otilia pushed me higher and higher and, as I flew up and down on the swing, something, I don't know exactly what, lifted from my shoulders. It was a kind of guilt that I'd made Mother tremble with fear.

Back in the apartment again, I took the coat off. When I tugged at one of its thick sleeves, I realized there was a rip in the elbow. I hadn't done it. No way. My first reaction was to cover it up with my hand because, if we made a hole or ripped our clothes when we were rolling around on the ground at the orphanage, the nuns pulled our ears and told us we'd have to darn them ourselves, like girls. Pretty quickly, though, I remembered that I didn't have to worry about that any more so I showed it to Otilia, sticking my finger in it.

"It wasn't me," I said.

"I know, dear, don't you worry about it," she answered. "It was probably already there. We'll sew it up and that will be that."

"But who did it?" I asked.

"Nobody, love," she replied after hesitating a moment. "It happened all by itself."

Tomasa, the other maid, who was also the cook, told us that

my dinner was ready. Otilia took me to the bathroom to wash my hands with soap. She wanted to come in with me, but I wouldn't let her because I was a big boy now—in four days I'd learned to give orders like a pint-sized tyrant—and knew how to do it by myself. I washed them, then, and went to the kitchen where Otilia was waiting. The door was ajar, and I crept up to it without making a sound. I wanted to give the two maids a fright, like I'd done before with Mother. I was about to open the door when I realized they were talking in low voices, as if they were telling secrets. Of course I tried to eavesdrop.

"... So what did she do?"

"Nothing. She was really shocked. She nearly fainted. I think she thought it was the other one."

"Oh, my God. Poor little boy."

"That's because she pays too much attention to her husband. I tell you they've brought him too soon."

"We can't get involved, Otilia. We're just here to be bossed around."

"No, I'm not getting involved. But the little boy . . . Cristóbal!" she shouted then, "Dinner's ready!"

Just then I pushed the door open with a good loud yell, hoping to give them a fright. They both pretended to be scared out of their wits, trembling and rolling their eyes back, to make me happy.

That night it was Fernando who put me to bed and read me a story. Even though he was really into it, I recall that he didn't know how to read stories. He shouted too much and didn't like being interrupted with questions. So, instead of making you sleepy it left you more awake. I closed my eyes so he'd leave me alone. He turned out the light and left. In the darkness, as I was dropping off, I had a thought that crept into my dreams: "I'm not the first Cristóbal."

The next morning, the idea came back more clearly and I told myself it wasn't a dream. The revelation was too much for a boy of seven, and I began to invent a story to explain it. I wasn't the first boy adopted by Fernando and Maribel. There was one before me, another Cristóbal, but he didn't love them enough so they sent

him back to the orphanage. Who could it have been? If I wanted
to stay in that house, if I wanted Bundó to come too one day, I had
to behave like a good son. I had to make them love me, just like
the nuns had told me. In the grip of that desire, I was overcome
by my strange sense of guilt about Mother for the next few days,
but I didn't know why I felt guilty. Her very presence was enough
to make me believe that I didn't deserve her. Whenever I managed
to catch her in the apartment, always alone, silent, downcast, I did
my best to make her happy. I sang her songs we'd learned at the
orphanage, invited her to play with me, or asked her questions to
make her speak. Sometimes I was able to get her to sing and even
to coax an uninhibited little laugh out of her, and then that invisible weight was lifted from her shoulders, and I felt welcome and
protected by the most beautiful woman I'd ever seen.

"What's wrong, Mommy?" I asked in Catalan, as I ran my hand
through her red hair, as if hoping some of the color would rub off.

"Nothing," she answered in Catalan without realizing. "It will
be all right, really it will."

From then on, every new clue led to my discovery of the existence of the first Cristóbal. I did handwriting practice with Otilia
and learned to write and read my new name. One morning when
I was getting dressed I saw that, stitched into the neck of all my
clothes, there was a name tag with words embroidered in colored
letters. I slowly read them: Cristóbal Soldevila. In the orphanage
we always inherited the well-worn, scruffy clothes of the bigger
kids, and now all this was mine. I asked Otilia why they had my
name on them, and she said it was for when I went to school,
which would be soon, so the other kids didn't mistake my things
for theirs. Later, I discovered that instead of patching up the overcoat—which the first Cristóbal must have ripped—they'd bought
me a new one and sewn my name-tag into the neck.

Another afternoon, nearly two weeks after my arrival in the
Soldevila mansion, I was rummaging around in a cupboard I
hadn't checked out before and found a box full of musical instruments. Most of them were plastic, cheap imitations so kids could

discover whether they had musical leanings or not and parents could curse them as they covered their ears. I was so happy that I wanted to try them all, one by one. I played them for about half a minute to hear what they sounded like and laid them out on the ground as if they were an orchestra. I played some maracas, a flamenco guitar, a drum, and a xylophone. I took a canary-yellow trumpet from the bottom of the box and blew hard, but a muffled note came out of it. I tried again, with my eyes closed and cheeks puffed out but only succeeded in making my head spin. Then I had a look inside the trumpet, which was long and narrow, and my fingers felt something inside. I tugged at it and a rolled-up bit of paper came out. I forgot about the trumpet and smoothed out the paper, but it sprang back into a roll. When I managed to open it again, pinning it down with both hands, I was alarmed to see that it was a kid's drawing.

Give a box of colored pencils to any seven-year-old kid and tell him to draw his family. The result will be very like the drawing I found. The mother had flaming-orange hair, bright like the sun, and the father was waving hello with a big hand, while his other hand was little and glued to his body. The boy—the first Cristóbal—had drawn himself smaller, between the two of them. In the background was a house with a tree and a swing. A cloud of white smoke rose from the chimney.

When I understood that this was my predecessor's drawing, I quickly rolled it up again and tucked it back in the same hiding place in the trumpet. I realized that I had to do a better drawing and show it to Mother and Father. I called Otilia and asked where the box of colored pencils was, I wanted to do a picture of Fernando and Maribel.

I'm no good at drawing, never have been, and that was clear at the age of seven. I've got no patience for detail. Not that you could say that they taught us much at the House of Charity. When I finished the portrait of my new parents, I compared my drawing with that of the first Cristóbal. Mine—and there was no doubt about it—was not nearly as good as his. It was a very bad copy, really horrible. I tore it out of the book, screwed it up into a ball and started a new one. After five minutes, Otilia called me to come for dinner, and I had to leave it.

While I was eating in the kitchen, Fernando arrived from the office and came to give me a kiss. On the days when he got home earlier, Mother liked me to sit with them at the table or play in the dining room. She wanted to have me near her, and I was pleased because it was a chance to make her happy. It also amused me to watch Fernando eating with only one hand. He was probably born disabled—but I'm not sure about that—and he managed the cutlery very well. He didn't like being helped. I'd realized this. When they had meat, always well cooked so it would be very tender, he cut it up first, using some scissors—very sharp scissors—and then he stuck his fork into it, like anybody else. That day, while I was with them, Fernando asked me how I'd been amusing myself during the day. I didn't know what to tell him. I'd done so many things they were all mixed up in my mind. Otilia, who was collecting the plates, answered for me, "What have you been doing, Cristóbal? Don't you remember? Well, he's been drawing, sir. He drew his mommy and daddy."

"Aha! Hmmm," Fernando said. "Mommy and Daddy! Let's see, let's see . . . Why don't you show us?"

I was only too keen to please them and make them happy. I ran to my room without a moment's hesitation and brought them the drawing done by the first Cristóbal, which was better than mine.

Mother had hardly said a word throughout dinner. I'd been watching her out of the corner of my eye because I was aware of her reserve. Her way of withdrawing from the world made me anxious. It was my fault. Ever since we'd arrived that first Saturday, her face had become more and more pinched. It was as if I could see it—as if it was my obligation to capture it—and Fernando couldn't. That night, the paleness of her skin contrasted even more than usual with the redness of her hair. I remember it very well because that was the last time I saw her. I went over and handed her the drawing.

"That's lovely . . ." she said as she unfolded it on the table, but it didn't take her a second to see that it was the other Cristóbal's drawing. Mothers know, they know these things. She pushed it away in horror and tipped over her glass of wine. She closed her eyes and seemed to have stopped breathing. Then she said in an anguished, feeble voice, "I can't take any more, Fernando. Really. I can't pretend..."

Even a boy of seven could grasp the despair behind those words. I gulped a bit and, admitting defeat and feeling very miserable, said, "I know the other Cristóbal drew better, Mommy, but I promise I'll learn soon."

She let out a long wail. She seemed to be gasping for air, and then she started to cry with her whole body, as if she was never going to stop. Her weeping affected me too, and I went sort of crazy. I didn't know whether to touch her or throw myself on the floor.

"Get to your room at once!" Fernando yelled at me, pointing at the door with his good hand. "Look what you've done to your mother..."

Otilia, who'd been secretly listening to the whole thing, came to me in the passageway and took me to my room. That night she undressed me and helped me to go to sleep. She hugged me tight and stroked my hair, telling me it was all right, that I was innocent, innocent, innocent.

The next morning they told me that Mother was ill and had to spend the day in bed. A doctor came to visit her, but they wouldn't let me see her. Halfway through the afternoon, Fernando came for me and took me back to the House of Charity. Otilia had already packed a bag with all the fine clothes. I got the new coat too. I don't recall whether I cried at any point during the taxi ride, which you might describe as my social descent down the steep slope of Career Muntaner. I don't remember, either, whether Fernando said anything to me, good or bad. He must have been too ashamed. So, like a defective piece of furniture being sent back, I was abandoned for the second time. The first time I'd been left naked with a bit of paper saying "Gabriel" stuck to my stomach and now, at least, they were giving me a collection of clothes, plus another label that said "Cristóbal Soldevila."

The nuns were waiting for me. At first they gave me special treatment. They kept an eye on me and fussed over me too much, and the other boys got jealous. I hated that kind of popularity. The good thing was that I went back to being called Gabriel. They unstitched the labels from my clothes, but I kept wearing those trousers and pullovers until I grew out of them. When they were too small for me, some other kids in the orphanage must have inherited them.

Bundó was very happy that I was back in the House of Charity. For some weeks I missed all the toys and Otilia's attentions. I had trouble going to sleep without Peter Pan watching over me, and I had nightmares that always featured a one-handed man who was kidnapping me. Those two privileged yet traumatic weeks slowly faded away. Yes, in the end, it's the working days that count and the rest is a tip to squander.

Maybe you're wondering why there are such cruel people in the world. I'm not accusing them. We're talking about a time in which people with money and on the winning side of the war had it all sewn up. Was that their plan? Reality can be altered just like that? Well, it can. At least the political reality.

Whatever the case, this story has a second and a third part. Ten years later, when Bundó and I went to live in the boarding house, the Mother Superior apologized in the name of the orphanage. I was grown up, she said, and could now understand what had happened. She told me that my adoption had been the idea of that man, Fernando. They'd lost a son called Cristóbal three months earlier, and the only thing he could come up with was to look for another one to replace him. The mother, Maribel, couldn't handle it. As I say, I don't blame them, and I even feel sorry for her (in such a short time I came to love her a lot). As for the first Cristóbal, I don't know what he died of. Rich kids tend to die of sudden illnesses or terrible accidents. Decapitated in some stupid game, shot by a hunting gun, crushed by a horse running amok (and the horse is always slaughtered afterward in the stable).

Part three happened some ten years after that. One day, when we were doing a move in Barcelona, we landed at the mansion in

Passeig de la Bonanova. A family from Matadepera was moving in there, and La Ibérica was bringing the furniture. As soon as I recognized the marble staircase in the entrance, the majestic steps and the red carpet, those two privileged weeks of my childhood came back to me. And I have to say it wasn't a bad memory. You might say I'm kidding myself, but I also came to the conclusion that if I'd stayed with that family I might not have lived as much as I have. The fox says the grapes are green when he can't reach them, right?

In any case, while we were leaving the furniture there, I walked around rediscovering each of the rooms. The house no longer seemed as big as it had before.

"Excuse me," I asked the boy who came with us to open up the house, "do you know anything about the family that used to live here?"

"Not much," he said. "They were relatives of my mother's, and now she's inherited the place. In any case, it's more than fifteen years since anyone's lived here, and it's been closed up all that time. Apparently something awful happened. One of those family episodes that no one wants to talk about... Luckily, the apartment is very well preserved. Good materials."

Just then Bundó, who was doing the move with Petroli and me, whistled in admiration as he was coming back from one of the bedrooms.

"They lived here like princes at the very least," he commented. "Have you seen the kids' room?"

I didn't want to say that this was the house I'd been adopted into twenty years earlier. Jokingly, in his way, he would have reproached me for being unable to seduce that family, for failing to convince them to adopt him as well. I took advantage of a pause in the move to light a cigarette and go back to my old stamping ground. It was just the same but without the furniture, as if no time had passed. The drawings on the wall of Hansel and Gretel, Peter Pan and Tinkerbell, the fireplace in the form of a dragon... This vision stirred up one of my old memories. The morning after that terrible night, before Fernando came to take me back to the House of Charity, I'd spent some time alone in my room. I took the drawing I'd done,

all crumpled up as it was, and looked for a hiding place for it. As I
imagined the first Cristóbal had done, I decided to leave a clue for
the adopted boy who was going to take my place. I went to hide
it in the guitar, as my precursor had done with the trumpet, but
then I thought that would be the first place Fernando and Maribel would look, so I climbed up on one of those dragon fangs and
found a kind of niche inside the fireplace, a cavity in its mouth.
That day of the move, I got inside the fireplace—I'm sure it had
never been lit—and looked for it. And it was still there, dusty and
discolored. I took it out, signed it with a pen—Cristóbal—and put
it back so that the kids occupying that room would find it one day.

Then I went on lugging furniture like an idiot, up and down
those stairs all day long, because that was what I knew how to do.

In some cemetery of Barcelona, there's bound to be a marble
pantheon, one of the ones that are still standing, and there must
be a stone that says:

CRISTÓBAL SOLDEVILA ROGENT
(1940–1947)

For two weeks I did what I could to prolong the life of that boy.
I tried but wasn't able to do it. For me, ever since then, Cristóbal—
or Cristòfol, or Christof, or Christophe, or Christopher, whatever
variations you want—has meant happiness. Or, rather, a chance
to be happy in life. That's how you got your names, Christophers.


Our father's gone quiet. Since we didn't react, he clapped his
hands, just once, hard, and the four of us all blinked together.

"What an earful I've given you," he said. "And you haven't slept
for ages."

It wasn't that. On the contrary. His confidences had churned
us up, and we were overwhelmed, mesmerized. We hadn't asked
that much of him. Still feeling awkward after the revelation, we
thanked him a thousand times. He saw that we were somewhat
out of our depth and changed the subject to make things easier.

"How about some breakfast? What do you think? My mouth's dry and my stomach's rumbling. That's enough questions. Now you know the whole story, I hope."

We don't know anything. Before we didn't know anything either. That's the truth of the matter. The story of the first Christopher has filled the veins of our story. The little boy who was sent back to the orphanage has pumped the blood necessary for us to live. This is the paradox: It's only now that we've found our father again that we Christophers have truly managed to capture his past.

And here we are on Sunday morning. We experience every hour that goes by as if trapped in a strange sensation—that of not knowing whether we're saying good-bye to Gabriel or whether we've just arrived. That's how it will always be. We finally understand what our mothers have said a thousand times. When he arrives he's on his way out. When he leaves, he stays behind.

The five of us are having breakfast, enjoying our bond of friendship. We feel restored to life, oblivious to the years we've missed. The bar's been filling up with people while we've been eating. The atmosphere is warm and unpretentious. Four old men are playing cards, and occasionally a raised voice is heard celebrating some trump or other.

"Now we're done with all the hard-luck stories, how about asking for coffee and having a game," Gabriel says, pointing at the other table. "Do you like poker?"

The Christophers eagerly accept the invitation. It will be fun to see him playing after hearing so many stories about it. Our father asks a waiter to clear away the plates and to bring us some coffee and a pack of cards.

"What if we play with cash?" he asks. "Nothing much. Minimum bet of a euro. Otherwise, there's no fun in it."

We empty our pockets and spill the change on the table.

"Hang on," Christopher says. He opens up his wallet and pulls out the wad of banknotes that he swiped yesterday from the table in the Carambola. It's gambling money, predestined, and we'll share it out like good brothers.

Gabriel shuffles the cards with the elegance of a croupier and deals. He could get a job in a casino, we think, but that could be too much of a temptation for a professional cardsharp. Each one of us looks at his hand and the betting begins. At last we're observing the famous poker face. The cards fly on and off the table. We're keeping an eye on his hands in case he slips something up his sleeve, but at no point do we see anything strange. Then he starts to win and doesn't stop until he's pocketed the last cent.

# ACKNOWLEDGMENTS

I'd like to thank Stefanie Kremser, Jordi Cornudella, Enric Gomà, Ignacio Martínez de Pisón, Mònica Martín, Toni Munné, and Eugènia Broggi. They have all read the novel at different stages and have been most helpful with their comments, doubts, questions, and suggestions.

Xavier Folch and Bernat Puigtobella were the first to listen to the story of the three truck drivers who traveled around Europe. This was in 2003, and, instead of telling me to forget about it, they encouraged me to present it for the Octavi Pellissa Prize. Thankyou, too, to the jury for supporting the project.

Rita da Costa has translated the novel into Spanish. Her attentive reading spared me several headaches and helped me to polish the original text in Catalan. My thanks also go to Sigrid Kraus, my publisher in Spanish, for her confidence in me in all these years.

Mercè Gil told me her childhood memories of the House of Charity in the 1950s. Albert Romero supplied me with memoirs by, photos of, and readings about the situationists and May '68.

At several points, writing this book has obliged me to leave home. I wish to thank Miranda Lee and Terry N. Hill, Lise Schubart, and Jan Streyffert, and Montse Ingla, and the publishing company Arcàdia for their hospitality.

In the spring of 2009 I wrote the last part of the novel at the Santa Maddalena Foundation, which has been founded in Tuscany (Italy) in memory of Gregor von Rezzori. Hence I should like to say how grateful I am to Beatrice Monti della Corte for her invitation. I also wish to express my thanks to Bill Swanson and Nayla el Amin for their support. In Santa Maddalena I met the writers Sheila Heti, Tristan Hughes, and Adam Foulds, and I'd like to thank them for their friendly company and fine conversation.

There were four specific sources of inspiration as I was writing the novel, for which I should also like to express my gratitude. The book of photographs that the Christophers buy at the Sant Antoni market—Chapter 5, Part I—is *Barcelona blanc i negre* (*Black and White Barcelona*), by Xavier Miserachs (1964). In my references to the Camp de la Bota—appearing at the end of this same chapter of Part I—I am indebted to Francesc Abad's artistic project of the same name, which he embarked upon in 2004 and which he is still continuing on the Internet. Gabriel's ear infection and his subsequent visit to the otolaryngologist—in Chapter 5, Part II—were suggested to me when I read *The Year of Magical Thinking*, the essay on mourning written by Joan Didion. The image of Russian roulette that closes Chapter 6, Part II, comes from a musical number performed on *Saturday Night Live* by the actor Hugh Laurie on November 25, 2006.

I finally wish to express my gratitude for the digital files of the newspaper archive of *La Vanguardia* and the magazine *Triunfo*. They cleared up many of my doubts and frequently acted as a time machine taking me back into the past.